ABYSSAL ARCANIST

ASTRA ACADEMY BOOK III

SHAMI STOVALL

Published by
CS BOOKS, LLC

Cover Design: Darko Paganus

Editors: Nia Quinn, Celestian Rince

IF YOU WANT TO BE NOTIFIED WHEN SHAMI STOVALL'S NEXT BOOK RELEASES, PLEASE VISIT HER WEBSITE OR CONTACT HER DIRECTLY AT

s.adelle.s@gmail.com

Contents

To John, my soulmate.
To Justin Barnett, who is way too good to me and helped so much.
To Gail and Big John, my surrogate parents.
To Drew, my agent.
To Henry Copeland, for the beautiful leather map and book covers.
To Mary, Emily, Scott, James, Ryan & Dana, for all the jokes and input.
To my patrons over on Patreon, for naming the Academy.
To my Facebook group, for all the memes.
And finally, to everyone unnamed, thank you for everything.

A Recap of Events

L ast time in the Astra Academy series, Gray Lexly had discovered something terrible. The broken Gate of Crossing, which led to the abyssal hells, was still active, and the gate fragments had scattered in all directions.

While on a camping trip with his fellow classmates and twin brother, Gray stumbled across these "gate fragments" and realized his mere presence activated their teleporting function. Strange corpse-like monsters from the abyssal hells attacked, and the camping trip ended early.

Once back at Astra Academy, Ashlyn Kross, the typhoon dragon arcanist, announced she would be having a cotillion—a celebration of her coming of age, and becoming an arcanist. Gray, desperate to attend, despite the fact he isn't a noble arcanist, convinced his new professor, Roark Ren, to give him an invite.

While studying magic at the Academy, Gray learned of the five layers of the abyssal hells, the existence of magical plants and animals, the ability to enchant yourself with runes, and that Headmaster Venrover had collected several gate fragments himself and was keeping them inside the Academy. Not only that, but the headmaster also had Death Lord Deimos's personal weapon—a trident made of abyssal coral.

Determined to live a normal life, and forget about the frightening encounter with the Death Lord, Gray went to Ashlyn's cotillion on a tropical beach far from Astra Academy. However, a few hours into the celebration, it was attacked by a mystical creature from the deepest depths of the ocean... A midnight depths kraken.

While fighting to save individuals from the devastation, Gray was attacked by Deimos's followers, who had hidden themselves in the celebration. One follower threw a gate fragment into Gray, which allowed Death Lord Deimos to astrally project a portion of his soul into Gray.

Deimos, struggling to control Gray, traveled to Astra Academy to gather the other gate fragments, and his trident, Vivigöl, Silencer of the Damned.

With his weapon in hand, Deimos defeated Professor Ren, and then turned his sights on Professor Helmith. However, Helmith pulled Deimos into the dreamscape, and with the help of Gray, managed to lock him away in a permanent cage within the dreams, forever trapping a fragment of Deimos's soul in Gray.

Fortunately, that meant Gray was free of the Death Lord's control—while still retaining access to his magic. And his weapon. Vivigöl, Silencer of the Damned, answered to Gray's commands.

But after all the excitement, Gray once again looked forward to having a normal school life at the Academy.

And now it's time to continue the story in *Abyssal Arcanist*.

CHAPTER 1

PEOPLE IN MY DREAMS

I rested in the boys' dorm at Astra Academy, lying in my bed, staring at the ceiling. The full moon hung in the sky beyond the window, the soft, white light streaming into the gigantic room. My twin brother, Sorin, slept in the bed next to mine, his breathing heavy and slow.

My time at Astra Academy had been life changing so far, and not in the way the headmaster probably intended. A maniacal professor had attempted to kill me and open a gate to the abyssal hells—a place where the souls of the dead went to either be destroyed or reincarnated.

And if that had been the *only* thing to happen, my time here would've just been shocking, not life changing. No. Things had escalated to a whole new level when the gate to the abyssal hells had exploded into a million fragments and started messing with the living world. Creatures from the abyssal hells—including a Death Lord himself—had managed to influence my life.

Death Lord Deimos...

Raaza slept on the other side of the room, and occasionally, I heard his snores over the dulcet whistle of the wind outside.

The rest of the dorm was empty. Seven other beds, positioned against two walls, were all neatly made up, but no one had been in them for a few days. Knovak typically slept in our dorm, but he had been staying in the infirmary recently.

He had fought with Death Lord Deimos and lost.

Whenever I thought about the Death Lord, ice ran through my veins. It was difficult to sleep, despite the fact I was exhausted.

I had just gotten back from the infirmary. Tomorrow, I would resume my classes. It felt like an eternity since I had enrolled at Astra Academy, but in reality, I had only been here for a few months.

At the end of my first year, I was supposed to pick my specialty and then go into advanced training, but sometimes it felt like I would never get there. I had almost died twice now, and I hadn't even been looking for trouble.

"Gray?"

I flinched. The quiet voice belonged to my eldrin, Twain. He emerged from the depths of my white blankets, his orange fur practically shining in the moonlight. And it was everywhere. The sheets, my pillow. He shed whenever he moved. But I never mentioned it. Twain's eyes, one gray, one pink, stared into mine.

"Are you okay?" he whispered.

Twain was a little house cat kitten, but his ears reminded me of a lynx's. They were large, and puffy at the tips. He also didn't have much of a tail—just a little nub.

"I'm fine," I replied in a quiet voice. "My mind is wandering."

"You need to stop that. One day, it isn't going to come back."

He wasn't really a kitten, but a mimic. He called himself a *copycat*, and I understood why. His shapeshifting abilities were quite powerful.

With a gentle touch, I patted his head.

"Maybe if you stopped talking to me, I could finally get some rest," I said.

My little mimic huffed a grunt and then turned away from me. Twain curled into a tight circle and snuggled into my fur-speckled sheets. That got me chuckling. He was so cute when he was angry.

I tucked the blankets around both our bodies, content with his company. Then I stared at the ceiling again, my gaze unfocused.

The dark stone bricks of the Academy gave the room a gloomy appearance, even when the moon was so bright and wondrous. I closed my eyes and tried to think of anything other than the darkness, the abyssal hells, or having my body controlled by a vengeful Death Lord.

It should've been easy...

Fortunately, sleep took me before my mind could wander back into dangerous territory.

Dreams were significant for me.

I had first met Professor Helmith in a dream, after all.

But they were also the source of some of my greatest fears. From the freakish *soul catcher* creatures trying to kill me while I slept to fighting Death Lord Deimos in an ever-shifting dreamscape, it seemed my slumber was no longer safe.

So, when I opened my eyes and realized I was in a dream, my heart hammered. I wasn't like a normal person who slept and lived through dreams as though they were reality. I knew when I was dreaming—always. Perhaps my mind had latched on to my dread and painstakingly paid attention to all the details to the point I could no longer experience a dream like a normal person. Or perhaps it was Professor Helmith's lingering magic. Her dreamweaving abilities had been with me for years.

Either way, I was aware of my dream location, even before I glanced around.

This dream was odd.

I stood in a grand dining hall—something straight out of a history book. It was a castle, or a palace, and the room was so vast, pillars were positioned every twenty feet to keep the roof from collapsing. Those pillars betrayed the age of the building. Who used pillars anymore? Most modern construction used archways and other tricks to support the roof. It made rooms more open and spacious.

This place felt like a luxurious prison.

People were gathered in large groups, but the dream was vague—I couldn't make out their faces. Large, mystical creatures hung around in the far corners, their shapes and colors also obscured. Classic dream logic: I knew they were there, but I couldn't really see them.

In the middle of this glorious dining hall was a bronze statue of a dragon. The statue, bizarrely, had a hatch on top, and the statue itself seemed hollow.

I walked through the crowds, my legs shaky. The air smelled of smoke and bloodlust.

And while I considered myself tall—almost six feet, though I never measured—the people around me were giant. Not only were they taller, but they were thicker with muscle and clad in armor that shone.

Candles lit the dining room.

They were made of tallow—a type of animal fat. It was a bizarre fact to notice, but my father was my home island's only candlemaker. He made candles with all sorts of ingredients, but animal fat was the cheapest and easiest. I would recognize it anywhere.

But tallow candles were old-fashioned and cheap. No palace or castle would use them, not when they could use the most expensive beeswax candles. Tallow candles let off a weird odor, and they sometimes smoked or caught fire. Beeswax always burned cleanly. It was preferred, so long as you had an apiarist to harvest it for you.

How old-fashioned was this place?

As I wondered where I was, something strange happened. The people in the room clustered around the hollow dragon statue. They smiled and laughed, though I still couldn't make out their faces or identities.

A couple of them dragged a man to the statue. The man was bound at the ankles and wrists with chains, but he still tried to escape. He couldn't, no matter how hard he struggled.

Then he was placed inside the statue, and the bronze hatch was closed and locked.

When the man screamed, his voice echoed through the throat of the dragon and exited through the mouth. Again, because this was a dream that operated on surreal logic, I somehow knew the throat of the statue had been designed with a system of tubes and stops so the man's screams were converted into sounds that resembled the roar of a dragon.

Then the crowd of people built a fire under the statue.

The flames heated the metal.

I stumbled backward, away from the crowd, and away from the statue. Were they roasting a man alive inside of it? What kind of nightmare was this?

I turned, my breath shallow, and then I stopped dead in my tracks. There was a cage made of rock at the far side of the room. A prison cell. The rocks had jutted up out of the ground and crossed to form an *X* shape. Most of the rocks were so close, they formed a wall, but on one side, there were bars, allowing anyone to peer inside.

The bars were so thick, and so close together, that I wouldn't be able to fit my hand between them, yet I could see.

The prison cell...

Professor Helmith had made that. Gossamer threads of magic held the whole cell together, the power of the structure so vast, I felt it from twenty feet away. It felt like the heat from a bonfire.

And inside...

The dragon roared. I jumped and spun on my heel. The eerie thunder of the statue filled the room with a noise that caused my blood to curdle.

"Mimic arcanist," someone said from within the cell. Their voice was rough and gravelly, with a slow and deliberate cadence. "Release me." The icy command sent a chill down my spine.

The crowd in the room laughed and cheered as the dragon's roars grew louder and more frequent.

"Release me or suffer the consequences."

That voice—it belonged to Death Lord Deimos.

A fragment of his soul was trapped within me, locked away by Professor Helmith's true form magic. But despite his confinement, he still spoke.

It was almost too difficult to hear him, though. The roaring of the dragon... It hurt my ears.

"Gray? Wake up."

That wasn't Deimos. Who was it?

Someone wrapped their arms around me.

"Wake up."

I recognized the voice. It was Sorin. In my dream, I reached for him, and then I woke up, my body drenched in sweat, my heart pounding. As soon as my eyes focused, I realized I was back in the dorm, the moonlight illuminating the room with a gentle glow.

Sorin knelt next to my bed. He had his arms around my chest. He kept me close, even while I gulped down air and calmed myself.

"I'm here," Sorin whispered. "Everything is okay."

I nodded once and then pushed him away. "I'm fine," I said, curt. "I'm fine," I repeated, softer and slower.

I wore a sleeping tunic and a pair of soft trousers, but under my clothes was a gold piece of jewelry that wrapped around my neck, my shoulders, and upper arms. It was actually a weapon from the abyssal hells —and anyone but me who touched it would be hurt.

Not only that, but bandages covered my forearms and legs. I had been burned, and while arcanists naturally healed faster than mortals, I still needed time to recover. It hurt whenever someone applied too much force to my injuries.

So I couldn't allow Sorin to hug me for too long. I had to keep him at arm's length.

Sorin stared at me. He had the same blue-gray eyes and black hair I did. But he was larger than I was. He reminded me of the people in my dreams. Muscular. Imposing. Where did he get all his bulk? Sorin didn't eat more than I did, and he didn't exercise to excess. It was like he supped from the universe, gaining nutrients from nothing.

I ran a hand down my face and cleared away the sweat.

Twain stretched and blinked his eyes. "What's going on?"

"Thurin heard Gray moving around," my brother said. "So he woke me."

Sorin rubbed the arcanist mark on his forehead. It was a seven-pointed star with a cape and a shield. He was a knightmare arcanist, and Sorin's eldrin roamed the darkness like a fish roamed the water. Knightmares were hollow suits of armor that didn't need to eat or sleep. No wonder Thurin was watching me—what else was there to do in the still of night?

"Were monsters attacking you?" Sorin asked.

I shook my head. "No. It was just... a normal nightmare."

Twain yawned. Then he tilted his kitten head. "Maybe every night I should transform into an ethereal whelk, and I'll create nice dreams for you."

I patted his head. "Nah. It's fine. I'm fine. Everything's fine." I rested back on my bed. "No one needs to worry about me, okay? You're all too paranoid."

Sorin didn't say anything for a long moment. Then he muttered, "It seems like you've gone through a lot of traumatic events in a short period of time."

"Hm."

"I'm here for you."

"Thank you," I whispered.

Sorin stood and loomed over me. In the dim moonlight, he almost looked like a shadow warrior. With an oddly dramatic poetic rhythm, he said, "*Loyalty is a promise kept, a commitment that's met.* I'll be there for you, Gray. You don't have to worry. We'll make sure the nightmares leave you for good."

I nodded once. "All right. But first, we should get some sleep. I want to at least *pretend* like I'm a normal student at Astra Academy."

After a short chuckle, Sorin took a seat on his bed. It groaned under his weight, practically begging to be put out of its misery. I imagined the bed frame would shatter at some point before the year was over.

"All right," Sorin said. "Good night, Gray. See you in the morning."

As long as I kept Death Lord Deimos out of my nightmares, I was sure I would see my brother again at dawn.

That wouldn't be too difficult. I hoped.

CHAPTER 2

DEFIANT DRAGON

My class for the day was *History and Imbuing* with Professor Jenkins, though everyone just called her *Piper*.

Since I hadn't slept well, a fog lingered over my thoughts. Our classroom was relatively large, with five long tables and a giant window at the back that was kept open to allow for bigger eldrin to enter without damaging the doors within the Academy. Not everyone's eldrin was as cute and small as Twain. Some people had dragons or yetis or leviathans, and those mystical creatures were way too big for even a hallway.

A gigantic treehouse, whose branches grew along the outside of Astra Academy and wrapped around the dark bricks of the Academy's walls, acted as a pathway for mystical creatures. They traversed the branches and lived in rooms within the trunk of the massive redwood tree.

The open window allowed the autumn breeze to waft into the classroom, and I enjoyed the smell of crisp leaves.

I wondered what it would be like to sleep in that tree. That sounded amazing.

"And that's why most guilds closed down operations," Piper said. She tapped the chalkboard. "You see, the construction of several arcanist academies allowed for new arcanists to gain a *broad education* before picking their vocations."

Our classroom was quieter today, but that was because several students were absent. I sat at my usual table and stared at the chalkboard without seeing.

Sorin sat next to me.

A little *too* close.

He scooted his chair over so we stayed within inches of each other. I would've rolled my eyes, but I was too tired for any of that. Instead, I allowed my brother to hover over me like a fussy hen over her chicks.

He wore his robes over a simple white shirt and black pants. The symbol for Astra Academy consisted of four images within a square. A seven-pointed star, a globe, a sundial, and a set of upside-down gates. *In life, through time, with magic, till death*—Astra Academy's motto—rang in my ears as I stared at the symbol for longer than any sane person should have.

It would be ironic if I died at the Academy.

I would probably be the first one.

Sorin elbowed me. I glanced over at him. He silently motioned to the chalkboard with a tilt of his head.

I returned my attention to the front of the room.

"Some guilds are still operating." Piper half-shrugged. "But they're the oldest of the guilds, and they're typically funded by a specific nation. Newer arcanists consider joining a guild at fifteen to be an antiquated custom."

Piper walked to the side of her desk, and it only occurred to me then that she wasn't wearing her robes. She wore a white dress made of flowing fabric that moved with the wind. A simple silver rope kept her slender waist apparent, but everything else was ethereal as it fluttered with a feather-like consistency.

It drew my attention.

Everyone's attention, really.

When I glanced around, I realized the other students were staring at her with wide eyes—some of them a little *too* intently.

"Is everyone taking notes?" Piper asked. Her long, black hair, silky in appearance, was neatly tied up in an elegant bun.

Which was unusual. Normally, she showed up to class late, her hair a mess, her eyes dragged down by black bags. Today was the exact opposite. Her tanned skin practically glowed with health, and she looked more put together than a dolled-up debutante.

The arcanist mark on Piper's forehead was a seven-pointed star with a rizzel wrapped around the points. The ferret-like rizzels were masters of teleportation, and her eldrin popped into the classroom with a puff of glitter. He landed on the front desk, his white fur—striped with silver—glittering in the morning light.

"Reevy?" Piper asked.

The little rizzel twitched his nose. "Nothing to report yet."

Reevy was about the size of my arm, perhaps a little smaller. His dark eyes shone with intelligence as he scanned the room.

"Then what're you doing here?" Piper whispered. She waved her rizzel away. "I need you to keep watch. This is important."

Reevy replied with a sarcastic salute before disappearing in another puff of glitter and a pop of air.

After a deep breath, Piper straightened her dress, glanced at the door, and then returned her attention to the class. "Okay. Where was I? The guilds..."

A collective yawn echoed throughout the room. There were normally nine arcanists in class, but today, there were only five, and that included me.

Nini Wanderlin sat on the other side of my brother. She had to lean onto the table in order to get a better look at the chalkboard. Her glasses slid down her little button nose, and she pushed them up to keep them from falling off.

Her blood-red hair...

It matched the cape of her reaper eldrin.

Nasbit Dodger and Raaza Luin sat at different tables, which they all to themselves. The two of them were easy to spot, even in a large crowd, but especially in a half-empty classroom. Nasbit was, after all, the heaviest-set man I had seen in the Academy. Perhaps calling him *portly* was a better term... He wore his robes well, and he kept his brown hair slicked back.

Nasbit's eldrin, a massive stone golem, lumbered around the back of the classroom. The beast had no eyes or mouth—it was just a collection of boulders held together by invisible magic. Whenever it stepped, the stone of its "foot" slammed hard against the stone of the floor.

Raaza was the exact opposite of Nasbit in all ways. Raaza's eldrin was even tiny and silent. He had bonded with a kitsune, a trickster fox with fake flames that sparked from her paws.

And Raaza was lean with muscle. Not only that, but he carried himself like he would mug people in a back alley if they weren't careful. The scars on his face didn't help. They were small but numerous, across one side like a monster had gone for his eye and just barely missed. Unlike Nasbit, Raaza didn't do anything with his dark hair. It was windswept, and some of it hung over his face.

Everyone in the room took notes about old guilds with the enthusiasm of a corpse.

"Gray?"

I straightened my posture.

Piper glowered at me, her red lips turned down in a frown. "Are you paying attention?"

I wasn't, so in order to quickly change the subject, I hardened my expression and asked, "Professor? You know a lot about history, right? Do you... happen to know about ancient torture methods?"

My question must have caught the entire class by surprise, because even my brother stared at me with wide eyes. They were probably wondering why I would ever ask something so morbid.

Piper fluffed her bun. "Uh, *yes*. I do know a thing or two about torture methods." She narrowed her eyes. "Why?"

And just like that, she had forgotten I hadn't been paying attention.

My brother waited with bated breath. He clearly wanted to know.

"I was wondering if you've ever heard about a bronze statue shaped like a dragon," I said. "The statue is hollow, and someone is placed inside." I tried to gesture with my hands to better describe the shape. "There's a hatch on top so you can lock the person within. And then you start a fire under the statue..."

Nini gasped. She pulled both hands up to her mouth.

Unlike the other students, Nini wore enough clothing for three people. Her long sleeves provided her plenty of cloth with which to hide most of her face.

"Is there a *reason* you read up about old-world torture devices?" Piper asked. "Because I'm beginning to worry about your mental health."

With a chuckle, I replied, "Well, after all the nightmares I've had, I figured I should give my subconscious more fuel to work with. The same old *I'm going to die at any second at the hands of a weird puppet* is getting boring."

I had meant it as a joke, but absolutely no one laughed.

Twain even lifted his head and stared at me with big, glassy eyes.

"That was said in jest," I said, loud enough to make sure everyone heard. "We should all be chuckling."

Piper forced an awkward laugh. "Yes, well, the torture device you described is known as a *defiant dragon*. It's a special type of statue meant to kill someone in a slow and painful manner. Mostly enemy generals who were captured during a battle."

"They don't use them anymore, right?" I asked.

For some reason, the whole room was silent again.

"Are you okay?" Sorin whispered.

I shrugged and shook my head. "Yes. Definitely. I'm just... curious. That's all."

"Defiant dragons are considered inhumane," Piper stated. "They haven't been seen in hundreds of years. Maybe even longer." She waved away my question. "You really shouldn't be focusing any of your time or attention on learning about them."

Raaza raised his hand.

With an arched eyebrow, Piper motioned to him.

"I've seen defiant dragons." Raaza rubbed some of the shallow scars on his face. "There're at least two in Lord Oto's compound. He keeps them in his garden."

Nasbit fully turned around in his seat to frown at Raaza. The look of utter disgust was hard to ignore. "*Lord* Oto? Really? My uncles say he's a lowborn thug who just started claiming he was a lord despite having no authority to do so."

"Well, when everyone is too afraid to tell him he's *not* a lord, I guess he just gets to be one by default, huh?" Raaza huffed and rolled his eyes, leaning his elbow onto the table and poking his notebook with his charcoal pencil. "Whatever. It doesn't matter. All I wanted to say was that defiant dragons aren't as *archaic* as the professor seems to think they are."

I almost asked him if this *Lord Oto* person had used his dragons recently, but I kept that question to myself. Apparently, I was starting to worry everyone. Even Nini glanced in my direction several times, her eyebrows knitted.

But I wasn't depressed—just concerned.

Had my dream been something related to Death Lord Deimos? A memory or a thought? Or was it something else? I didn't have any magical abilities related to dreams, so perhaps something else was going on.

I rubbed my chin.

Professor Helmith was still recovering, just like Knovak. I couldn't ask her opinion on the matter, at least not yet. So I would wait. I could focus on classes until then.

Or perhaps even find a way to contact Ashlyn.

CHAPTER 3

MOVING DORMS

The lecture continued, but I heard little of it. I was only jolted from my daydreams when Piper walked around her desk and loudly proclaimed, "Oh, look at the time. We should have a break." She clapped her hands and motioned to the door. "I'll be right back."

Piper exited the classroom before anyone could get a word out. And she left with a smile, which was more odd behavior from her. Or perhaps I was reading too much into the situation.

Then a odd thing happened.

Both Raaza and Nasbit stood from their tables and walked over to mine. The tables in the room had both benches and chairs, but none of the tables were really designed for the whole class to sit at one. Raaza dragged over a bench from the nearest table, the wooden legs scraping against the stone floor until it was in place on the opposite side.

Nasbit and Raaza took a seat facing me, Sorin, and Nini. Raaza's kitsune, Miko, leapt up onto the table, her flame feet flaring once she landed. Nothing burned, but it was startling. She pranced over to Twain and lay down next to him, her fluffy fox tail wrapping around her little kit body.

I lifted an eyebrow.

"Is everything okay?" my brother asked.

Brak, Nasbit's golem, lumbered over. The golem halted at the end of the table, casting a shadow over us. It wasn't intimidating, though. Brak took a seat, practically slamming onto the floor in the process. Then it folded its legs, resembling a child listening to a bedtime story.

"Don't play dumb," Raaza whispered in a harsh tone. He glared at my brother, and then at me. "What's going on with you? *Twice* you're involved in strange circumstances related to the abyssal hells. Twice."

"It was more like one really long event," I said. "The Gate of Crossing that Professor Zahn created, and the aftermath of the explosion. That's it. And everything's fine now. No need to worry."

My statements fell on deaf ears. Everyone stared at me with frowns or hardened expressions of utter disbelief. I didn't blame them. Somehow, I kept running into major problems. I wasn't even aiming for them, which was the troubling truth. They just found me.

Nasbit shook his head. "Gray, I saw what happened to you. I saw... how you were *possessed*." His frown deepened as he added, "I apologize for not helping you more than I did, but... Well, I wasn't certain what to do. But now I think I figured out how to help you, moving forward."

He stood from the table, walked back to his, and grabbed his notebook. Then he returned to his seat across from me.

"Let's document every strange thing that happens to you." Nasbit flipped open his notebook and held his pencil poised over a blank page. "Why don't you explain why you lied to the professor about the defiant dragon?" He waited, his eyes wide.

"Who says I lied?" I asked.

Raaza scoffed.

My brother furrowed his brow.

"You obviously didn't research that torture device," Nasbit said, his tone sardonic.

Nini nodded along with the statement. "Yeah. I mean, normally you're pretty good at, uh, telling little white lies, but that was so obvious." She tapped her fingertips together. "Sorry."

"What?" I waved away their comments. "Piper believed me. And how could you all tell I was lying?"

"If you had read a book about the defiant dragon, you would've known its name," Nasbit said matter-of-factly. "You only *described it*, like it was something you had seen and not really researched at all."

Huh.

Couldn't argue with that logic.

"I'm tired," I said with a sigh. "I'll come up with a better explanation next time."

"What really happened?" Nasbit asked.

"I had a dream about the statue."

Again, everyone went quiet. Sorin placed a hand on my shoulder, and I shoved it away.

That seemed to concern everyone as well. Nini stood, and her reaper, Waste, floated closer to the table. Her freakish eldrin was nothing more than an empty cloak seemingly hanging on an invisible person. He had a chain of names, and a rusty scythe, but that was it. No face, no body—he was a phantom made of magic.

"You shouldn't push us away," Nini whispered. "Sorin just wants to help you."

"Look, everyone needs to calm down." I smiled as I tugged at the collar of my robes. "I'm wearing something that no one should touch. That's why Sorin needs to keep his distance."

The moment the gold "necklace" was visible, everyone caught their breath. With a dramatic twirl of my wrist, I showed off the sinister accessory and then folded my robes over everything so it was once again out of sight.

"What is that?" Raaza asked.

"It's a weapon from the abyssal hells." I nervously chuckled because I knew they weren't going to like this, and I added, "It's, uh, called *Vivigöl, Silencer of the Damned*."

"The necklace is a weapon?"

"It can change shape," I muttered. "This just makes it easy to wear."

Technically, I had already told Sorin this. I had told him the moment I had returned to the dorms. But he hadn't seemed to care, or perhaps he just hadn't listened. He had refused to stop showing his affection through touch. He had embraced me, held my shoulder, or otherwise kept close no matter what.

"Do you all hear this?" Raaza asked, his words steeped in disbelief.

"Gray is having dreams about torture devices, *and* he's *wearing* a weapon from the abyssal hells? He's clearly under some dark influence. Am I the only sane one here?"

Nasbit furiously took notes, his pencil moving so fast, I was surprised his paper didn't catch fire.

"Maybe you're having these new dreams because of the weapon," Sorin said. "You should take it off."

"I can't." I rubbed the cold metal that touched my skin. "I mean, I *can*, I just can't risk it sitting somewhere. If anyone else touches it, they'll get hurt." I wasn't entirely sure to what extent they would be damaged, but I didn't even want to risk it.

Sorin folded his arms over his barrel chest. "Seems like a bad omen, though."

My father always spoke about bad omens. He would tell us all the time that sometimes it was best to listen to signs whenever they appeared. Was this weapon an omen or was it the consequence of not listening to omens?

"It's *obviously* a bad omen," Raaza stated. He dramatically held up two fingers for all to see. "*Twice* you've come into contact with things from the abyssal hells. You're cursed. And it's only getting worse. And the fact we're all just sitting here, pretending you're not about to slide deeper into the hells, is a farce."

I held up a hand. "Whoa, whoa. Settle down. The gate fragments were the cause of all the recent trouble, and the headmaster is taking care of everything. He's locating the fragments, and Dr. Doon, the new relickeeper arcanist on campus, is using his magic to hold them in stasis, so they can't, ya know, wreak havoc."

The shattered bits of the Gates of Crossing that led to the abyssal hells had frightened me before, but Headmaster Venrover had discovered a solution and seemed to be implementing it as fast as possible. And as long as I stayed inside Astra Academy, away from the fragments he hadn't found yet, there was little chance of running into any more trouble.

I hoped.

Nasbit kept writing with all the haste of someone swimming to the ocean's surface for fresh air. Was he writing about my dreams? Or about the headmaster's actions?

"The headmaster actually wants you to stay?" Raaza shook his head.

"He's not trying to expel you? Heh. That's bizarre. Not what I would've done."

I shrugged. "Would you rather I wander away and inevitably aid in the opening of the abyssal hells? Because I think that option is still on the table."

"No, it's not," Twain said. He lifted his head high and his ears higher. "My arcanist isn't about to be a key with which weirdos can unlock the gates to the afterlife. Not while *I'm* around."

Sorin grabbed my upper arm and held on. "No one is getting Gray without a fight."

And while I didn't want him touching me, his hand was on the fabric of my robes. Perhaps that would be fine, but I worried.

"I'll fight, too," Nini stated. She held on to Sorin's shoulder, and my brother gave her an appreciative glance. The two stared at each other like only sweethearts did. Then Nini quickly returned her attention to me, her face red. "Uh, anyone who is important to Sorin is important to me."

Her reaper hovered close to the table. "We'll cut down the corpses of the abyssal hells and grow stronger at the same time," Waste said.

Raaza's kitsune perked her ears. "I do like the sound of gaining strength and practicing magical abilities on corpses." Miko turned her gaze to her arcanist. "You like that, don't you, my arcanist? Hm? Hmmm?" She wagged the tip of her tail.

Was she on my side?

Raaza eventually rolled his eyes. He leaned onto the table and patted his kitsune. "No one is going to listen to me, anyway. I might as well kill the corpses that rise from the crypt."

Miko smiled. "Oh, yes. I like this."

"But if *you* turn into a monster," Raaza said, glaring in my direction, "I'll cut you down, too."

What a hero. I almost made a quip, but I kept it to myself.

"Hm." Nasbit finished writing a sentence and then glanced at the door. "Professor Jenkins isn't back yet."

"Piper," Sorin corrected. "Just call her *Piper*."

"The professor," Nasbit said, clearly trying to avoid her first name at all costs, "should be back by now. But she isn't here." He closed his notebook. "I was thinking... Perhaps we can take a few minutes—before the professor returns—to move some of my things?"

"Move things?" I asked. "What do you mean by that?"

Nasbit stood and gathered his belongings into his arms. His stone golem also stood, the boulders scraping along the floor and creating a brief ruckus. Once the golem was on its feet, Nasbit smiled.

"Hm," he said. "I figured, if I want to help you and perhaps learn more about the abyssal hells, I should switch dorms. I'm not really getting along well with my current dormmates anyway, as all the men belong to a different class."

Raaza shot him a sidelong glare. "Oh? Your highborn peers didn't work out, so now you want to slum it up with all us lowborns? What will your family think of *such a disgrace*?" He spoke the last few words with faux distress.

"*Hey*," Sorin growled.

"What? That is what's happening. Nasbit could've stayed in our dorm when we first enrolled in the Academy—the dorm the rest of his classmates were in—but instead, he chose the dorm of the aristocracy." Raaza motioned to Nasbit. "Admit it."

Sorin stood, and I almost wished I weren't so tired. Why was my brother getting so agitated? What was he thinking?

"Nasbit's trying to help." Sorin gritted his teeth for a moment. After he was a little calmer, he added, "It doesn't help anybody to start a fight like that. We *are* in the same class. Nasbit *did* help Gray by informing the professor when he saw Gray possessed. I think it's fine if he joins our dorm."

Ah, Sorin. Always advocating for peaceful camaraderie. He was *too* nice, but I'd never be able to convince him to be otherwise.

Nasbit hadn't said anything during the exchange. If anything, he had just stared at the table, his expression twisted, almost as if he were ashamed, but I was guessing. I didn't know Nasbit that well.

"I think it's better if we're all in the same dorm," I said, trying to keep my tone casual. Fighting about bed arrangements seemed petty. "Besides, we need someone to even out Knovak. That man fancies himself the most noble of nobles, and if Nasbit is around, he won't bother all of us about which shirts match his belt buckles."

Again, Raaza scoffed. Then he threw his hands up in the air. "Fine. I suppose we weren't using half the beds anyway."

"I wish I could join you all," Nini whispered.

Sorin turned to face her. "W-Well, I mean, we would all be respectful, but we do use the dorm to change. And other things."

Nini's eyes widened. She straightened her glasses as her cheeks grew red. "Oh, um, actually. Forget I said anything. I didn't think that through." She glanced away, and even tugged at her some of her shoulder-length hair, as though using it to cover her face.

Her reaper floated close and made a sound akin to a growl.

I glanced over at the door, ignoring the odd conversation.

Piper still hadn't returned to the classroom.

"If I am welcome in your dorm, we should move my things now," Nasbit muttered.

"Why?" I narrowed my eyes. "We should probably just wait until after class. We'll have more free time then."

"Well, I would prefer not to explain to the others in my dorm what I'm doing." Nasbit slowly rubbed his gut. "They mock me a lot, and I suspect if they were there while I was packing my trunk to move to your dorm, I would forever be haunted by their howling laughter."

It was just that pathetic to be in a lowborn dorm? People were cruel sometimes. I had barely ever experienced this before enrolling at Astra Academy—our small home island didn't have any noble families. We had a single arcanist and a herd of hippogriffs that cared for us as much as we did for them. That was it.

My father made candles, and—somehow—he was a prominent figure in the community. We weren't really swimming in dukes and duchesses.

"All right," I said. "Let's go now."

"Wait, Gray—what if we're late returning to class?" Sorin asked.

I motioned to the front desk. "I think we can just point out we weren't the first to be late, and Piper will understand."

CHAPTER 4

STRANGERS ON CAMPUS

We left our classroom and walked the halls of the Academy. No one else was around—probably because they were in their own classes.

When I wandered by one of the large windows, I noticed a class of arcanists training out on the gigantic field. They were swinging wooden weapons in a semi-coordinated fashion. Were they learning how to fight?

Clouds lingered around the edge of the field, obscuring the dirt track and the weapon racks. I wondered why that was the case. Astra Academy was built on the tops of several mountain peaks, but the weather and the clouds were kept perfectly controlled. If clouds were around the field, it was because they had been placed there.

Who had done that?

I held Twain close to my chest, gently stroking his head and scratching behind his large ears. All our eldrin were with us except for Brak, who was much too loud to stomp around the halls of the Academy. The stone golem waited in class for us to return, but since it didn't speak, it wasn't like the golem could explain where we had gone. Instead, Nasbit had left a note.

"We should do this quickly," Nasbit said in a higher-pitched tone, concern evident in his voice.

"*Oh, the late nights we'll spend studying.*" Sorin placed a hand on his chest. "*Laughter will ring out. Our bonds will grow stronger, that is without a doubt.*" He elbowed me. "*Sharing our stories, hopes, and dreams—fabric held together with thick seams.*"

Miko hopped around our feet, her fox fire flaring around her little paws. "Shh! Shh! Don't you know anything about stealth?" She narrowed her eyes and laid back her ears. "We're supposed to be inconspicuous. We don't want to be caught out in the hallway during class, do we?"

"Is it really against the rules?" Sorin asked, his eyebrows knitted.

Raaza shot him a sidelong glance. "Ditching class is definitely against the rules. And that's what we're doing."

I held up a finger. "Is it really *class* if there was no professor? Because I don't think it is, so we aren't technically ditching anything. I like to think we're seeking out our lessons. Life lessons." I tried to keep my sarcasm in check, but it was difficult.

Raaza hesitated for a long moment. Then he finally said, "Well, the rules in the library didn't mention this scenario."

"There are rules in the library?" Sorin turned to Nini. "Did you know that?"

She shook her head. Then she grabbed the red cloak of her reaper. "Did you know that, Waste?"

"I did," Waste stated, his voice icy. "I've been in this Academy for years, and during the solstice festivals, I would spend time in the library. The rules of the Academy, as well as the Academy's goals, motto, and architects, are all etched into the wall."

"And you didn't say anything?" Nini pushed her glasses up her small nose.

"I apologize, my arcanist. Next time, I'll be more vocal."

I held Twain in front of me. His cute, little kitten face stared back. "Did *you* know the rules?" I asked.

Twain snorted. "I stayed in the Menagerie as much as possible. Me and cloak-face didn't spend time together during holidays."

The reaper hovered close, a deep growl echoing throughout his hollow body. It was rather creepy, and I kept my distance—and kept Twain close —but I didn't say anything. Most people in the Academy already didn't like Waste, considering that only murderers bonded with reapers. Well, perhaps *murderer* was too strong a word. The reaper's Trial of Worth required that someone kill a blood relative, but it didn't matter when or how. Sorin had technically been able to bond with a reaper because our mother had died giving birth to him.

Just thinking that caused me to tense.

Our mother...

I hadn't even realized we had reached the first-year dorms. I glanced up and found myself standing before the door with the others close by. Nasbit went for the handle. He turned to us with a frown.

"Please try not to touch anyone else's things." He sighed. "The others get fussy if their possessions are disturbed in any way."

Possessions? What possessions? When I had arrived at Astra Academy, I had barely had a bag of clothing. We didn't have anything else. Our dorm was a series of beds pushed up against the wall.

Nasbit opened the door and ushered us all inside. Sorin, Raaza, and I entered, but Nini stayed out, shifting her weight from one foot to the other.

"I'll keep watch," she whispered.

However, I barely heard her. My sense of sight was bombarded by so many gaudy displays of wealth that it impaired all my other senses.

Several tapestries hung on the walls.

Multiple colorful rugs covered the floors.

Each bed—there were ten in total—had its own theme. One was a deep green with forests stitched into the hem of the comforter. Another bed had sun patterns across the many pillows. A bed at the far end of the room had a privacy canopy hanging from posts on each of the bed's corners.

I didn't even know why, but someone in the room had taken the effort to bring a small aquarium to the Academy. A tiny school of silver fish swam around the glass enclosure, flitting about with gusto.

I could've taken a bath in the aquarium, that was how large it was.

"Is that a painting?" Sorin asked, pointing to the wall next to the door.

A portrait of one of the students hung there. It was a giant portrait, too—and the person in question was a griffin arcanist. The man's face was painted in a stern expression, his griffin in the background. His hair was slicked back, and so was the mane of the griffin, like they were attempting to match.

"Oh, that's just *Rutledge*," Nasbit said with a wave of his hand. "He fancies himself the handsomest bachelor in all of Astra Academy."

I glanced back at the painting. His eldrin was more handsome than he was, but I wasn't about to comment.

Sorin examined the artwork and frowned. "He brought this to the Academy?"

"Oh, yes." Nasbit hurried to the end of the dorm room. "This way, gentlemen. My belongings are over here."

"Why do you have so many things?" Raaza asked, breathless.

"It's very common for new arcanists to bring pieces of home with them to Astra Academy."

"Maybe for nobles..."

Nasbit rubbed his chin. "Well, *yes*. I only know what's common for noble-born arcanists. I assume it's different for all of you?"

Raaza didn't reply. Neither did Sorin or I.

With his kitsune in tow, Raaza ambled after Nasbit.

Sorin and I stayed next to the painting. I rubbed my sides, itching at some of the bandages around my rib cage. When I had been possessed by Death Lord Deimos, he had used my body to fight some of the professors, and the burns from the conflict still bothered me.

Arcanists had a naturally fast healing rate, but burns always seemed to take the longest to mend themselves.

"Are you okay?" Sorin whispered.

When I turned to him, he stared at me with genuine concern. I shook my head. "I'm fine."

"You've been through a lot. You should've taken the headmaster's suggestion to just rest."

"I didn't want to be alone," I said, my voice almost inaudible. "Besides, I'm well enough to walk. You don't have to fuss."

Sorin didn't like that. He clenched his jaw and stared at the painting, his eyes unfocused.

"Lexly twins?" Nasbit called out. "Are you coming? I'm afraid I need your assistance."

Sorin and I strode through the luxurious dorm and stopped at the last bed. Nasbit's blankets were the same sandstone coloration as his golem, with gold threads sewn throughout, to give the sheets a shimmering appearance whenever they moved. He carefully folded them up and then stuffed them into a solid oak trunk.

Nasbit motioned to a second trunk by the head of his bed. "These are both mine." He gathered his personal belongings—books, notebooks, pencils, and clothing he kept in his personal wardrobe—and then locked both trunks.

"We need to take these to my new dorm," he said, wiping sweat from his brow.

Nasbit had barely done anything, but he already seemed out of breath.

Sorin knelt, picked up an oak trunk with both arms, and then stood, lifting the weight with his back. He grunted as he did so, and his arms shook. "I, uh..."

The shadows around his feet shifted and fluttered at the edges. Sorin's eldrin lifted from the darkness underneath him. Shadowy tendrils wrapped themselves around my brother's body as he was quickly encased in a suit of midnight-black armor. It wasn't a complete set of armor— pieces were missing, like one of the gauntlets—but it mostly covered him, especially his vital organs.

It was like Sorin had half a set of full plate, and each bit was made of the purest darkness.

Thurin, Sorin's knightmare, had merged with him. They would live and die as a single creature so long as they remained merged, but as a benefit, their strength was increased.

Sorin hefted the oak trunk higher onto his chest. "Excellent," Sorin and Thurin said as one, their voices intertwined. "Thank you, Thurin. Together, we can handle this."

Raaza slowly turned to me. He frowned and then glanced over at the second trunk. "You think both of us can handle this one?" He gestured to my arms. "Unlike Sorin, you *look* like a candlemaker's son, if you get my drift. Can you handle something like this?"

I huffed a laugh as I tapped the side of my head. "Work smarter, not harder, my friend." Then I offered Twain a smile. I set him near my feet and pointed to the second oak trunk. "You got this, Twain."

My eldrin narrowed his eyes and puffed his orange fur.

Before he could protest, I knelt next to him and petted him from his head to the nub of his tiny bobtail. "Ah, c'mon. You know I'm just teasing you." I scratched behind his ears. "You're the best eldrin here. Will you please help us?"

Twain straightened his posture and held his head higher than before. "Oh, well, when you put it *that* way, of course I'll help." He hopped over to the trunk in his little kitten form.

Then I closed my eyes.

As a mimic arcanist, I had the ability to *feel* magic. The sensation was like fiddling with threads—or strings—and like a kite, the threads led to something wonderful. There was a thread for Thurin, my brother's knightmare, and another thread for Miko, the kitsune.

Twain didn't have a thread.

Or, if he did, I couldn't sense it.

But I could sense Brak, Nasbit's golem. And that boulder beast was plenty strong.

Lastly... there was a thread in *me*. A sliver of magic that led straight back to the fragment of Death Lord Deimos's soul locked away deep within my body. He was an abyssal dragon arcanist, and his magic was powerful...

I tried to ignore the thread. A dragon wasn't needed in this situation.

I tugged the thread of the stone golem, and it tightened to something taut. Twain bubbled and morphed straight into a sandstone golem, his fur disappearing as it hardened into stone. The transformation happened within a few short seconds, and my forehead burned throughout the process.

All arcanists had a mark—and mine was normally an empty star. But whenever Twain transformed, my star reflected the new kind of creature he had become. Now my seven-pointed star was laced with the formidable form of a golem.

Twain, with all his new might, effortlessly lifted the oak trunk.

"Ta-da," I said with sarcastic showmanship, waving my hands around Twain.

Raaza crossed his arms and frowned. "Heh. What? You want an award for using your magic like any normal mimic arcanist? It wasn't *that* impressive."

This guy.

Nothing impressed him, apparently.

I shrugged. "Well, let's head back to our dorm, shall we?"

Sorin, merged with Thurin, walked out of the dorm with the trunk in their arms. The clink of Sorin's shadowy armor was a harsh reminder of his powerful magic. His knightmare was still young, and Sorin still needed to refill his magic, but I could tell. If Sorin didn't one day become a famous knight, I would eat my words.

Twain, as a golem, lumbered out of the dorm. He slammed one of his boulder legs into the side of a bed, probably by accident, but Nasbit barked out a concerned shout.

"D-Don't!"

He flew over to the bedpost and examined everything. Then he carefully nudged it back in place.

"Please be gentle," he whispered. "The others won't be so understanding if any of their things are damaged."

Twain carefully made his way to the door. Then he turned his whole body sideways and shuffled out. He had to awkwardly maneuver himself to get the trunk out without damaging anything.

All the first-year dorms were in the same area with a common lounge area between them. There were four dorms in total—two for the boys, two for the girls—and each had ten beds. There weren't that many first-years at Astra Academy this time around, which was why there were so many empty beds.

Nini joined us as we traveled across the lounging area. She opened the door and ushered us in without following.

Our dorm wasn't nearly as fancy as the other. Except for Knovak, who had coin to spare, the rest of us had arrived at the Academy with next to nothing, so our beds were covered in simple white sheets and nothing more. There were several rugs—all Academy colors, including blue and white—and a wardrobe next to each bed for us to use.

Not much else.

But when I walked into the dorm, I caught my breath.

Two people were here, and neither of them were Astra Academy students, that was for sure.

CHAPTER 5

BEDSIDE MANNER

T he two strangers in our dorm turned to face us.

The first was a man as tall and as thin as a birch tree. He had a sharp nose and blue eyes that practically blended into the white around them. His black hair, slicked back into a tight ponytail, revealed his arcanist mark—a glowing, seven-pointed star a squirrel tangled between the points.

A glowing arcanist mark...

It meant his eldrin had achieved its true form.

The man wore a tailored suit of fine, black cloth, and a silver pin in the shape of a hammer adorned his lapel. Everything about him screamed *prim and proper,* but his icy-blue eyes were wide in seemingly worry and surprise.

The woman next to him was *much* shorter, probably just five feet exactly, but there was a strength in her gaze that belied her size. Her dark hair fell loosely around her round face, and she wore thick leather gloves, rough trousers, and a sturdy apron filled with measuring tools. The arcanist mark on her head was a normal seven-pointed star with a gargoyle clinging to the center.

She, too, wore a silver pin of a hammer, only hers was attached to the strap of her apron.

"Who are you two?" Raaza barked out. His kitsune stood between his legs, her fox face narrowed with a suspicious glare.

"You're not supposed to be here," Miko said with a cute growl in her words. "This is a private area!"

"Oh, pardon us." The man smoothed his vest. "We were told the students would all be in class. I'm Architect Slater, and this is my associate, Architect Joyce. We're here to help Headmaster Venrover improve the Academy."

"Improve its *defenses*," Joyce added in a low and smooth voice. "Not the aesthetics."

"Yes." Slater cleared his throat. "Well, to be frank, we could improve some more things while we're here." He motioned to the dorm room around us. "This entire space lacks symmetry. It throws off the balance of the room, and I just don't like it."

"We should focus on the treehouse and the entrances to the Academy," Joyce said, her voice as calm, even if it was a bit critical. "That's what the headmaster wanted."

"Hm. What's the point of doing a job if we're not going to be thorough? The tree is wonderful. I know, *I'm* the one who grew it." Slater stomped closer to the window. "Look at how marvelous that is. There's nothing in the world like it, and that only came from complete dedication to the job."

While the two architects bickered over the construction of the Academy, Twain the golem carried Nasbit's trunk into the room. Sorin, Raaza, Nasbit, and I entered afterward, though the three of us came to a halt and stared at Nasbit. Which bed did he want? Six of them were completely unclaimed, and all identical. The only bed that had any pomp or frill was Knovak's. He was the wealthiest of us lowborns, a fact he somehow managed to slip into several conversations.

"That one," Nasbit said, pointing to the bed directly next to Knovak's. "I like being close to the door."

Twain set the trunk down with a loud *thump*. It drew the attention of both Slater and Joyce. They glanced over.

"Careful there," Joyce said. "If you chip the stone floor, I'll have to smooth it all out with my magic."

Sorin lifted both eyebrows and shot me a smile. "Gargoyles can manipulate stone."

"I know," I muttered. "Professor Helmith told me all about it." And I was fairly certain I was the one who had told Sorin.

Raaza lightly smacked my shoulder. Then he whispered, "What kind of arcanist is the man?"

Before I could answer, a mystical creature hopped along the treehouse walkway and came to a stop at our windowsill. The branch paths that led from the Academy to the massive tree trunk were impressive, but they paled in comparison to the bizarre and highly magical creature that was now in our midst.

It was a squirrel the size of a large house cat.

And not just any squirrel—it was made of crystal, and sparkled with an inner magic. The two stripes on its back glowed a vibrant, emerald green, and its eyes were a shining ocean blue. Its crimson fur gave it a look of *elements*, as though it were a mix of fire, earth, and water. It also had a tiny horn in the middle of its head, similar to a unicorn.

"That's a *ratatoskr*," I whispered.

The ratatoskr leapt into the dorm and then scampered over to Slater. Its squirrel body matched the shape on Slater's glowing arcanist mark.

"I inspected everything," the ratatoskr said. He gave his arcanist a little salute. "The treehouse is in tip-top shape, but it, too, lacks major defenses. I recommend overhauling the main rooms in the trunk. Perhaps some atlas tortoise magic to create barriers, or even nullstone to keep tricksters from infiltrating the ranks."

Slater smiled, his lips thin and practically a crude line. "Thank you, Rollo. We should write up our suggestions and assessments, since they're becoming too numerous. The headmaster will want to hear all this."

Rollo, the little ratatoskr squirrel, saluted a second time. Then he tapped his back paws together, spun around, and leapt onto the windowsill. "I shall investigate further, my arcanist. Perhaps there are weak points around the perimeter."

"Don't worry about that." Joyce pointed to the far edge of the Academy. "My eldrin is checking the mountain peaks as we speak. You should focus on the building and foundation, especially the rooms that were apparently... uh..." She reached into her apron pocket and withdrew a piece of parchment. Then she frowned as she said, "The rooms that were *exploded*."

Sorin cringed at the word. He turned to me and shook his head.

Fortunately, he said nothing on the matter. I really didn't want to tell the two architects that the Academy was having structural issues because of an incident that had involved me.

Nasbit unpacked some of his belongings from the trunks. While he worked, Twain bubbled and shrank. With a slight uttering of a warble, his stone body shifted back into an orange kitten.

"Is it true that you're the man who made the treehouse?" Nasbit asked as he placed a small stack of clothing on his bed. "I've always wondered who did it."

Slater turned on his heel—much like how his eldrin had—and nodded once. "That's correct. We ratatoskr arcanists are capable of growing gigantic trees. Our magical auras are specifically tailored for that purpose." He stood a little taller. "I daresay this is the largest, and most beautiful, tree a ratatoskr arcanist has ever made. I'm surprised they haven't mentioned my name in a few of your classes."

What a humble man.

The expression on Joyce's face—her lips turned down at the corners— told me I was probably correct about my sarcastic observation. "Look," she muttered. "We should focus on the task at hand. The headmaster specifically wanted an estimate to make all the repairs and changes, and he wanted it by this evening... We're not going to get that if you keep talking to people. Or getting upset by the symmetry of the rooms."

Slater waved away her concerns. Then he stomped to the windowsill and stepped up to the branch pathway. "Come, come, then. We should examine the Academy from the outside and see what we can glean."

The woman's height became noticeable again when she hurried to the sill. It took a moment to get her leg up, and then her whole body onto the walkway. She followed after the other architect, not even bothering to glance over her shoulder as she went.

The wide branch of the treehouse made for an excellent walkway, but there were no railings. The two architects pointed to the side and made notes before continuing their trek to the trunk.

"I thought they had already repaired the Academy," Raaza muttered.

Nasbit closed the lid of his trunk. "I'm sure it was a quick repair. If the headmaster is hiring architects to improve defenses and strengthen foundations, he's probably worried about additional damage in the future."

Everyone awkwardly turned to face me.

I crossed my arms over my chest and lifted an eyebrow. "What? I'm not going to destroy any more of the Academy, if that's what you're all thinking."

Twain bounded over to me. Then he got up on his back paws and reached high up to my knee. I bent over and scooped him up. "We need more defenses," he said with a purr. "What if more people come for you? We should be prepared."

"Hm."

"Okay, I can set up my belongings later." Nasbit went to the door. "We should get back to class. What if the professor returned to find the room empty?"

Sorin opened the door for everyone, practically startling Nasbit with the burst of movement. "Definitely. We need to get back."

Nini, who had been standing just outside, leapt backward into her reaper eldrin. The empty cloak was practically a curtain as she stumbled through him. Waste mumbled something under his breath as his arcanist untangled herself from the red fabric.

"S-Sorry," she said. "I heard talking, so I thought I would listen in."

We all exited the dorm, and I motioned to the hallway, trying to steer us all in the correct direction. "There were a bunch of architects in the dorm. Nothing to worry about."

"They're going to make the Academy safer." Sorin walked closer to Nini and smiled down at her. "I think these are good signs."

Nini smoothed her crimson hair. "I hope so."

No one else said anything as we traveled to our classroom. When we arrived, I was shocked by how quiet and empty it was. Had Piper really not returned yet? Where was she? While she wasn't the most reliable professor, she wasn't usually absent, not in the middle of class.

Everyone took their seats. Raaza leaned onto his table, his chin in his hand. "You think she was attacked by an abyssal monster or something?"

Nasbit held the collar of his robes. "Don't say things like that."

"What? It isn't outside the realm of possibility. Maybe we shouldn't sit around like chumps. Maybe we should do something."

Before we could get into an argument about the best course of action, the door opened to reveal Piper. She hurried into the room, her black hair tangled, her rizzel bounding along the floor like only a hyper ferret could. Then her eldrin disappeared with a pop of silvery glitter. He reappeared on her desk in a flash.

"We're here," the rizzel said.

Piper chuckled as she hustled her way around the desk. "Yes. Thank you, Reevy. We're here. Everyone is here. We've always been here." She still wasn't wearing her robes, and her dress was now visibly wrinkled. "It's time to continue the lecture."

I exchanged a questioning glance with Sorin and Nini. The two of them half-shrugged.

"Where were we?" Piper stepped closer to the chalkboard. She read her own notes and then nodded. "Right. We were discussing the evolution of arcanist guilds and the importance of picking a role that best suits your magics..." She faced everyone with a forced smile. "Take notes. I'll be giving you another quiz when we meet again."

After class, and after dinner, I separated from the others. I told Sorin and Nini I wanted to take a shower, but that wasn't true. I held Twain tight in my arms as I walked the halls of the Academy, heading beyond the infirmary to Doc Tomas's office.

Doc Tomas, a golden stag arcanist, was Astra Academy's medical expert. He seemed rather skilled, even if he appeared elderly. Arcanists didn't really age, but apparently, golden stags only bonded with people who were older. It was an odd Trial of Worth, but who was I to criticize it? If I were an old geezer, I'd bond with a golden stag in a heartbeat.

Doc Tomas's office was just down the hall from the infirmary. I stopped at the door, set Twain by my feet, and then knocked.

When the door opened, a tranquil feeling came over me. The soft sounds of a babbling brook also rang in my ears, though I saw no water.

Doc Tomas met my gaze. His eyes were paler than most but still bright with intelligence.

"Yes?" he asked, his voice rusty.

He wore a long, brown robe, but that didn't hide his hunched back or lopsided stance. His rat nest of a beard had been trimmed down, though despite that, it still seemed out of control. It was as gray and wispy as the hair on his head, and his ashen skin appeared purple in some spots.

"I wanted to know if Professor Helmith and Knovak were doing any better?" I glanced over his shoulder.

His office contained hundreds of books, a desk, a wide couch, and a cabinet filled with medical tools—including jars of medicine. His golden stag rested on the cushions of the couch, the stag's thin frame light enough not to break the furniture.

Petrichor—that was the stag's name. And he was beautiful. His horns were made of the purest metallic gold, and his hooves were a mix of brass and copper. I figured he was heavy, but his slender legs were tucked under his body, and his ears twitched more and more in my direction the longer I stared.

"Not to fear, my boy." Doc Tomas chuckled. "Your classmate is perfectly fine now. I sent him back to his dorm. He was feeling a little under the weather, both with his health and his magic, but after some time, it faded. Nothing to worry about."

That was good to hear, considering when I had seen him last, *I* had been the one to attack him. Well, not me. Death Lord Deimos had attacked Knovak with my body, but still. I had seen it all, and I had failed to prevent it. I wanted to apologize.

"What about Professor Helmith?" I asked.

"Ah. Rylee is a slightly different story, I'm afraid." Doc Tomas held both his hands behind his back. When he smiled, the lines on his face betrayed the fact that he was a naturally happy individual. "She'll need more rest, but I suspect she, too, will recover."

"Can I see her?"

"Normally, I tell my patients not to have too many visitors, but Rylee said if you came asking, I was to permit you."

That was a relief. I had worried she blamed me for the attack. Was it my fault she was injured? It felt like it, and that feeling was like a poison burning my veins whenever I thought about it.

"Where is she?" I whispered.

"Just down the hall. Second door on the left. I keep longer-term patients close, just in case."

"Thank you."

I turned away from the door, and Doc Tomas closed it with a gentle click. As I walked, Twain kept pace. He rubbed his orange fur on the side of my leg whenever he could.

"I'm sure she's okay," he said.

I nodded once. "Yeah."

"You shouldn't look so worried when you see her. She's trying to recover. If you're gloomy, it won't help."

After a long exhale, I stopped in front of the door. Twain had a good point. I shouldn't be *sad* when I saw her. That wouldn't help. I took a moment to gather all of my cheer before gently tapping my knuckles on the door. It was made of thick oak with solid black iron for the hinges. Would she even hear me knocking?

"Come in," came a melodious voice from the other side.

Helmith...

I pushed the door inward and tiptoed inside.

The room was illuminated with the soft glow of candles. A single lantern—one with stained glass around the sides—sat in the corner, the many colors of the glass cascading onto the wall like a watercolor painting. It was beautiful, and it reminded me of dreams.

Professor Helmith rested back on her bed at the far end of the room. Blankets were pulled up to her armpits, and her head was cradled by three fluffy pillows.

But...

Her once-vibrant and tanned complexion was now pale, her skin gaunt. Her hair, normally silky and flowing like inky waterfalls, was tangled and unkempt. My heart practically clenched in my chest at the sight of her.

"Kristof?" she whispered as she turned her head. "I told you, there's no need to knock." But then her violet eyes landed on me. "Oh, *Gray*. I was wondering when I would see you."

Professor Helmith's body was racked with shivers as she struggled to sit up.

I leapt to the side of her bed and motioned for her to just rest. "Don't get up because of me," I said, trying my damnedest to smile. "There's no need. Really. I just came here to visit and see if there's anything you need."

Helmith stared up at me. And unlike my own pretend mirth, her smile seemed genuine. "I'm so glad to see you're okay," she whispered.

Her arcanist mark glowed with a bright, intense white. A spiral shell was between the points. She was a true form ethereal whelk arcanist.

Twain leapt onto the foot of her bed. He slowly made his way to her side, careful to never step on her body. Professor Helmith raised one of her hands to his head and gently patted him.

"I'll be better than the good winds before long," Helmith said.

I didn't know what to say. I wanted to apologize, but how? "Uh..."

"Hm?"

"The h-headmaster is improving the Academy's defenses. Isn't that interesting?"

Helmith's vibrant, purple eyes practically lit up. "Oh, yes. It's about time. I believe he's going to call an assembly to announce some of the changes tomorrow."

I hadn't heard about that, but it fascinated me. What kind of changes?

But now wasn't the time to talk about that.

As I stared down at Helmith, I realized it was a struggle for her to take deep breaths. A surge of emotion hit me—a sense of protectiveness—as I watched her fight for precious air. And although I had never really felt a powerful urge to *hurt* or *destroy*, my thoughts went straight to dark places.

Like maybe I should hunt down anyone who had ever harmed her.

And make them pay.

The thought process startled me enough to rock me out of the sensation. I rubbed my temple, and Twain glanced over, his ears laid back, his eyes narrowed.

"You okay?" Twain whispered.

I nodded. Then I forced another smile for Professor Helmith. "Um, why do you think... your recovery is so difficult?" I hadn't wanted to talk about it, but my curiosity was killing me. Why was everyone else recovering so much faster than she was?

Professor Helmith ran a hand down the blankets. She had been stabbed by Death Lord Deimos across her gut. "I suspect it's because Death Lords—all abyssal dragon arcanists—have some ability to harm souls. And when Deimos holds his weapon, his magic is more potent. He was... holding it when he struck me."

I gritted my teeth and said nothing.

My heart hurt.

With raw emotion in my voice, I said, "I'm sorry. This is... all my fault."

Professor Helmith reached her hand to mine. When she grabbed my knuckles, I realized how cold she was. "It wasn't your fault, Gray. Never assume the blame for the wicked actions of others. I would change none of my actions, and I *will* soon recover. You have nothing to apologize for."

She said everything so confidently. Even her voice, which had been softer before, was louder and firm. But her icy touch, and her inability to sit up straight, betrayed the truth.

Another feeling flooded me—one I wasn't entirely familiar with. It was a desire to be stronger. I didn't want anyone to be bedridden because they had been harmed protecting me.

I wanted to protect *her* from danger. I tightened my grip on her fingers, hoping my hand would warm hers.

"If there's anything I can do for you..." I smiled. "I'll happily do it."

"Kristof is here to care for me," Helmith said.

Then the door squeaked open. Twain's eyes went large.

"There he is," Professor Helmith said with a smile. "Gray, you should meet my husband, Kristof."

CHAPTER 6

PICKING A PATH

K ristof stepped into the small room, and I immediately straightened my posture.

He was an impressive man, even upon first glance, from his height to his bulky physique. He wore a coat of dark, heavy wool, tailored to fit snugly against his broad shoulders. Its length reached past his knees, the hem frayed from what I expected was a multitude of adventures. The lapels were lined with thick fur, serving both to keep out the chill and to add a touch of savage elegance.

"Hello," I said, my voice quieter than I wanted it to be. I silently cursed at myself, if only because I didn't want to sound weak in front of the man.

Kristof's dark gaze went to me, but then slid over to Professor Helmith, as though my presence weren't worth concerning himself with. He held a lidded tray in both hands, and he strode over to the other side of Helmith's bed without saying a word.

His chestnut hair was cut short on the sides of his head, and his face was covered in slight stubble, as though he hadn't shaved in a few days. His skin was a mix of dark and fair—somewhere in the middle.

Beneath the coat, Kristof wore a burgundy waistcoat embroidered with intricate patterns of gold and silver thread. His shirt was of a fine linen, its sleeves rolled up to the elbows to reveal the muscles of his forearms.

I rubbed my own arms, suddenly more aware of my deficiencies than I had been a moment earlier.

Kristof's arcanist mark...

It didn't glow like Helmith's, but it was impressive.

A dragon was wrapped around the seven-pointed star, the reptile's form elegant and graceful. It was a *celestial dragon*, one of the rarest dragons in the world.

"How're you feeling?" Kristof asked, his voice gentler than I had imagined. "I managed to convince one of the chefs to make you raspberry tarts." He set the lidded tray on the nightstand next to the bed. When he lifted the lid, he revealed a glass of water, a glass of juice, a bowl of oatmeal, a bowl of soup, and two tarts.

"You didn't need to get me all that," Professor Helmith whispered with a smile. She placed a hand on her husband's arm. "You know I can't eat it all."

When Kristof stared down at his wife, he seemed much less intimidating. Maybe even gentle and approachable. He touched the side of Helmith's face with his knuckles. "I wanted to make sure you had all your favorites, just in case you wanted even a nibble. I'll eat the rest."

"Thank you." But then Helmith turned to me. "This is the student I was telling you about, Kristof. This is Gray Lexly."

Kristof glanced up and met my eyes. I held my breath for a moment. Gone was all the love and gentleness—if he could kill me with his glower, I had no doubt he would.

"Good evening, Gray," he said, his voice strained. "Is there a reason you're not settling in your dorm for the night?"

"I came to see the professor."

Twain perked up, his ears pointed high. "It isn't curfew yet. We can go where we please, thank you very much."

I placed a hand on his head and then dragged him closer to me, trying to indicate he shouldn't speak. He mumbled some sort of disagreement, but not too loudly. Once he was pressed up against my side, Twain narrowed his eyes and remained still.

Kristof didn't respond.

Silence stretched between us.

"Can I have some of the tart?" Professor Helmith eventually asked, ending the awkward quiet in the room.

Kristof's gentleness returned as he carefully cut a piece off the pastry and handed it to his wife. Helmith nibbled on the tart, consuming it with the delicate mannerisms of a squirrel.

"*Gray,*" Kristof muttered. "Is that your full name? Surely, it's short for something."

I shook my head. "That's it. That's my whole name."

"Hm."

That was it. No more commentary. Kristof returned his attention to Professor Helmith and even cut her another piece of tart. I was about to mention the ratatoskr arcanist to tell Helmith all about this eldrin, when Kristof stood straight.

"Well, it's late," he said. "How you retire for the evening, my love? I'll show Gray to the door."

Professor Helmith's eyelids were drooping slightly as she nodded. "All right. But perhaps Gray can come visit again."

"Oh, I'm sure he will." Kristof spoke each word like they hurt his mouth coming out.

He walked around Helmith's bed, and with a half-sarcastic sweep of his arm, ushered me to the door. I scooped up Twain, who glared at Kristof the whole time, and then I hesitated.

"Good night," I said to Helmith.

Her violet eyes practically sparkled as she responded, "Sleep well, Gray."

I went for the door, walking past Kristof, and exited into the dimly lit hall. It was quiet. Most of the Academy had already retired for the evening. And for some reason, it felt colder than normal.

The door shut behind me. At first, I thought Kristof had shut it and stayed in the room, but when I glanced over my shoulder, I nearly jumped.

He was out in the hall with me, his dark gaze serious.

"Can we help you?" Twain asked, a cute little growl in his voice.

I rubbed his head. "Heh. What my eldrin means to say is... What's wrong? Do you need something from us?"

Kristof glanced at the thick, wooden door and then back to me. "Rylee has told me all about you, *Gray*."

There was a long pause. I didn't know how to respond.

"She's protected me in my dreams for years," I finally replied. "I've known her for a long time." But after that, I held my breath. I was about to say, *she never mentioned you*, but I doubted Kristof wanted to hear that.

"It seems you're caught up in the middle of something." Kristof stayed close to the door, his hand clenched around the handle. "You're being targeted by abyssal hell cultists, or some such nonsense."

I had nothing to say to that, either.

Kristof waited for my reply, but when it didn't come, he narrowed his eyes. "Rylee told me about how she dealt with the fragment of a Death Lord's soul. How it came *for you*."

Twain's fur stood on end. His claws practically dug into my arm.

"Now that I'm back at Astra Academy, *I'll* be the one handling things. Rylee's class, these bizarre incidents that involve you—and I'm not going to tolerate anything getting worse. Do I make myself clear?"

The harshness in his voice bordered on a threat.

Twain clearly didn't like this man. His body felt tense and coiled, like he was ready to leap from my arms and scratch Kristof's perfect face off.

"I understand," I forced myself to say.

Kristof tightened his grip on the door handle. "And you should know, if there *ever* comes another moment where Rylee's life is in danger because you live, I'm not going to hesitate to kill you."

His words had long left the realm of threat and become an icy promise.

And while my eldrin didn't like that, I couldn't even bring myself to look Kristof in the eyes.

"If that moment does come," I said, my voice low, my attention on the floor, "you have my blessing."

Twain jerked his head around to glance up at me with wide eyes. I patted his head, hoping he would understand. Professor Helmith *had* been there for me. For years. And she *had* saved me from Death Lord Deimos at a cost to herself. I couldn't take any more from her. Either I had to step up to the challenge and start handling this myself, or else...

Kristof was going to end me.

After a long exhale, Kristof's voice softened. "I understand you're important to Rylee, so I will also try to handle whatever problems arise." His tone seemed strained, like he almost regretted what he had said before. "Just get to bed. And stay out of trouble. For Rylee's sake."

"Right," I murmured.

Kristof disappeared back into the room. I held Twain close to my chest as I ambled down the hallway. My thoughts were everywhere but in the Academy. I knew—in my gut—this situation wasn't over. Deimos's brother, Zahn, was still out there, and if people at Ashlyn's cotillion had secretly been worshippers of the Death Lords, I was certain there were more.

The walk back to the dorms was a long one.

"Gray," Twain whispered. "I don't want you to die."

"That makes two of us," I sardonically quipped.

"You shouldn't talk like you will."

"I don't plan to." After a sigh, I added, "I just really don't want Professor Helmith to get hurt any more."

"We'll figure out a way to deal with whatever comes our way. Together." He purred after that, and some tension twisting in my chest lessened.

I patted his head again and smiled. "Thank you, Twain."

It didn't take much longer to reach the first-year dorms. The doors were closed, and the fire in the lounge area was snuffed. Everything had a tranquil quality.

But when I lifted my head, I spotted Sorin by our dorm door. He leaned against the wall, his considerable frame larger than most—even larger than some of the decorative suits of armor that stood the corners of rooms. The shadows around his feet fluttered and moved with a life of their own. Sorin's knightmare was restless.

I walked over, and Sorin snapped his attention to me.

"Gray?" he asked.

I nodded. "Sorin? What're you doing out here?"

"Waiting for you." He pushed away from the wall and stepped close. The shadows grew darker around us. "You didn't go to the showers," he said, his tone accusing in nature.

"No." I set Twain down.

In the dim light of the quiet lounge, Sorin's face reminded me of our father's. He had these lines of disappointment in his expression. And when he stared at me—with the same gray-blue eyes I had—the situation seemed dire.

"What is it?" I whispered.

"Listen, Gray. I don't like that you've been lying to me."

"Sorin, I—"

"No, I don't want to hear it, Gray. You've been doing it more and more lately, over even the slightest things." When he furrowed his brow, it was like a punch to the gut. "You can lie to everyone else, I don't care. But don't lie to *me*."

Did I really need this, too? I already felt an overwhelming amount of guilt about Professor Helmith, but now I had to deal with the fact I had hurt my own twin brother. What was wrong with me?

"I'm sorry," I said, my voice flat.

Sorin shook his head. After a moment, he replied, "Forget it. Just don't do it anymore, all right? We're closer than that."

"I went to see Helmith."

"I know."

I met his gaze. "She's not doing well."

Sorin crossed his arms and frowned. "Do you want to talk about it?"

"No. I just want... to be better." I ran a hand through my hair. "Why do I keep getting her in trouble? I need to be stronger, Sorin. *Powerful*. Just being an arcanist isn't enough. I need to be a skilled arcanist. Someone who can handle himself."

"You know, at the end of our first year, we're supposed to pick a specialty." Sorin rubbed his chin for a moment. "Knights, artificers, mystic guardians, cultivators, viziers... The different education specialties, remember? Knights and mystic guardians both study a lot of combat arts. They're powerful."

"Then that's what I'll do," I said. "Whatever it takes." I had liked the sound of the artificers when I had first heard our choices, but now I wanted something that would make me more physically capable. While we hadn't done much combat training so far in the Academy, I needed to learn more.

"I'll be with you," Sorin said.

I shook my head. "We don't have to pick the same path."

"I know. But I want to."

Again, I stared into his eyes—the same as mine—and I found myself wondering. "Don't think you need to. If something else sounds better, you should go for it."

Sorin shrugged his broad shoulders. "There's nothing I want to do more than study the same things with you, Gray. We've basically done everything together. Why would I want to change that now?"

"I approve," Twain said, jarring me from my thoughts. When I glanced down at him, he smiled. "Plus, I like Thurin."

The shadows around us grumbled something I couldn't understand. Then Thurin spoke from the darkness. "Yes, well, I find that camaraderie is a sacred treasure. I spent hundreds of years alone. It was a torture no one should endure. You two brothers should never let go of your bond."

"All right, all right," I said, holding my hands up. "Enough of this. I get it." Everyone's insistence on sticking together was causing my throat to tighten with emotion. I didn't want them to know that, though. Why was everyone being so... supportive?

I supposed I was just lucky.

Sorin half-smiled as he grabbed my upper arm. "Well, that's all I had to say. Now you need to come look at the dorm. We changed it around for you."

"For me?" I asked as he yanked me toward the door.

"That's right. I think you're going to like it, Gray."

CHAPTER 7

MAN CAVE

Sorin pulled me into the dorm. "Ta-da!" He held out his arms and shook his hands around with showmanship flair.

Nasbit and Raaza also held out their arms, though with much less enthusiasm.

Knovak, who stood by the door, gave me an awkward nod, but said nothing.

Before, the beds had been positioned with their headboards against the walls, five on one side, five on the other. Now the beds were crammed together in a semicircle around one singular bed, like a moat of mattresses and bedding. The lanterns had been brought over to illuminate the space, and the trunks and nightstands were placed next to each other between beds, creating makeshift tables. It was both cluttered and cozy, an interesting combination.

"Are we allowed to do this?" I asked.

Nasbit walked over to his bed. And it was obviously his bed, what with its sandstone-gold sheets and plush pillows. "According to Astra Academy rules, we're allowed to change our sleeping spaces. So, I believe this is acceptable."

Raaza grabbed some of the blankets from one of the unused beds. He attached the end of one sheet to a lantern mounted to the wall and then strung the bedding overhead, creating a canopy when he attached it to a lantern on the other side of the room. Once finished, he stepped back and admired his work.

"I like that," Sorin said. He gestured to the other beds. "We should hang them everywhere."

"It looks like we're in a bazaar," Knovak muttered.

"I still like it."

Knovak crossed his arms. He wore a white, silk shirt and fine black trousers. While they were high quality, they were plain. It was hard to understate how *average* Knovak was in appearance when he wasn't wearing his flashy outfits. He had brownish, sandy-blond hair. His skin was tanned, but with no real markings. No blemishes, no freckles—just plain.

His arcanist mark was a seven-pointed star with a unicorn intertwined with the points. Even that, somehow, seemed unremarkable.

Twain leapt from the floor up to the one bed that was surrounded by the others. "This is Gray's?" He kneaded the pillow. "Oh, yes. It smells like Gray." Then he perked his lynx-like ears straight up. "Did you move all the beds around so that you're protecting him?"

Sorin nodded as he threw himself onto his own bed. The frame groaned as my brother's solid body crashed onto the mattress. "That's right! If anything happens in the middle of the night, we'll all be close by to do something. Plus, if anyone comes trying to get Gray, they'll have to climb over us first."

"If they're not going to expel you, we should at least take some responsibility and make sure nothing happens." Raaza threw another blanket across the room, creating a larger canopy. "And while the nobles have more *things* for their dorm, that doesn't mean we can't make ours unique, too." He slapped his palms together and then admired his own work.

His kitsune, Miko, crawled out from under the blankets of Raaza's bed. Her red fur was puffed to one side. "My arcanist? Why hang all these sheets?"

"We can make a cave."

"Oh!" She snickered with the squeak of a baby fox. "So mysterious. *I love it.*"

"I still think it looks like a market stall," Knovak murmured.

I glanced over and offered him a smile. "We sell dreams and rest here." Then I went to pat him on the shoulder, but Knovak flinched away before I could touch him. He moved so far—and so quickly—he almost slammed into the wall.

That... wasn't the response I had been expecting.

Everyone stopped what they were doing and stared.

With my hand still midair, I lifted both eyebrows. "Are you okay?"

Knovak slowly moved to the moat of beds. "Uh, yes. I apologize. I just... don't want you too close. You understand." He rolled over an unused bed and then made his way to his own sleeping space on the other side of the semi-circle. "I don't think you *meant* to harm me, but given that you're plagued by terrible magics, omens, and circumstances, I'd prefer if you... kept your distance."

Last time I had seen Knovak, it had been when Death Lord Deimos had been manipulating my body. The Death Lord had harmed Knovak. I wasn't sure the extent of the injuries, but it had to have been bad. Knovak rubbed his arm and avoided making eye contact with me.

"Sorry about that," I said. "I don't think it'll happen again."

Knovak said nothing.

"Everyone should keep their distance." Raaza grabbed the last of the unused bedding and started hanging it as well. The man cave was almost complete. "Aren't you wearing a deadly weapon like an old woman wears jewelry?"

I touched the collar of my shirt on instinct. "Well, yes, but it's not *doing* anything." I hopped over the nearest bed and then sauntered over to my own. "I mean, it just rests on me until I want it to do something."

"*Want it to do something*?" Nasbit asked. He sat on his bed and fluffed his pillows. Then he carefully removed his boots. "What does that even mean?"

The others turned their gazes to me. They each held a hint of suspicion behind their eyes, as though they didn't quite trust me to tell them the truth. After Sorin's statements in the hallway, I didn't blame them.

I grabbed Vivigöl, making sure it was still around my neck, and tightened my fingers around the abyssal coral. It was as cold and hard as metal, but with a rough texture. I imagined the weapon as a trident—like how Deimos had wielded it. Magic pulsed through the object.

Vivigöl *click-click-clicked* as it changed shape. The pieces around my neck and across my shoulders shifted and reformed. In a matter of moments, it went from gaudy jewelry to a gold trident worthy of a Death Lord. It wasn't massively heavy, but it was *sturdy*, and I had lowered my arm. The three tines were sharper than any I had seen before.

"By the good winds," Raaza muttered as he dropped the sheets and leapt over his bed. He approached Vivigöl, his eyes wide. "And it really *changes shape*? Just like that?"

"My mimic magic was infused into it," I said. Then I half-heartedly swung it around. "I told you back in class it can change shape."

"I... didn't believe you. Seeing it in action is a different story."

Nasbit's eyes were so wide, I feared they would fall off his face. Sorin scooted to the edge of his bed, his gaze on the golden weapon. Even Knovak, who seemed like he wanted to be disinterested, couldn't bring himself to look away.

Twain twitched his ears. With a mischievous smile, he gestured to an unclaimed bed with no sheets. "Use it! Break the bed with Vivigöl."

"I don't know..." I swished the trident through the air a second time.

Raaza nodded once. "Do it. I want to see this in action."

"Yeah," Sorin said with half a smile. "No one is using that bed, anyway. Show us how powerful that weapon is."

"*Do it, do it, do it*," Miko said as she jumped up and down on Raaza's bed. Her fox eyes were wide, and fake fire flashed from her paws with every bounce. "*Do it!*"

"C'mon, Gray. Show us."

"*Do it!* I'm losing my mind waiting!" Miko dramatically threw herself on the mattress, acting as though she had died. She just lay there, unmoving, her tail flopped behind her.

"Okay, okay," I said, holding my hand up. "I'll do it." With my breath held, I gripped Vivigöl with both hands and approached the unoccupied bed.

Then it occurred to me that I didn't really know how to use tridents. I mean, obviously you would stick the pointy tines into your enemy, but that didn't help me demolish the bed. Was I supposed to stab the mattress until it was nothing but a mess of feathers and fluff? Or chop it in half? Perhaps it would be better if I had an axe or a sword...

Vivigöl *click-click-clicked* as it once again changed shape in my hands. This time, it morphed from a trident into an elegant longsword. The blade was nearly three feet in length, which was far longer than I would've expected, and the cross guard of the weapon was flared out on both sides, creating six spikes that were just as sharp as the blade itself.

"Oh, amazing." Sorin stepped close and stared at the weapon over my shoulder. "Gray, I like this."

It was still gold, but it had a rough tarnish to the coloration. It was interesting, to say the least. Gold wasn't a metal used for weapons because it was too soft. But this wasn't gold, it just had the same appearance.

"Do you know how to wield swords?" Raaza asked.

I almost laughed at the question. "I know how to make candles," I quipped. Then I swung the blade. It sliced through the air with frightening speed. If I wasn't careful, I'd cut myself on the damn thing. "Uh, maybe everyone should stand back."

Knovak leapt to the other side of his bed. Nasbit ducked close to the ground, like somehow, I would cause an explosion. Even Raaza took drastic measures and hid behind his wardrobe.

Only Sorin remained close. He stepped backward, but he remained within lunging distance.

"You've got this," Twain said from my bed. "Make that bed pay for being... uh... empty?"

After a nervous chuckle, I tightened my grip on Vivigöl and then swung downward, hoping gravity would aid my power. The blade effortlessly sliced through the air, and when it hit the bed, it cleaved the mattress like butter. But then Vivigöl struck the solid wood frame and went halfway through before getting stuck.

I tugged, found it wedged in there, placed my foot on the edge of the frame, and then yanked back. Vivigöl came out, leaving a perfectly clean slice through half the bed. Even with my lack of skill and strength, it was enough to make this bed unusable.

"Excellent," Raaza whispered from the side of his wardrobe.

I swung again, aiming for the same spot, and the bed shattered clean in half. It happened so quickly—and the blade *clanged* on the ground so loudly—I startled myself. I dropped Vivigöl and leapt backward, running into Sorin's solid body. He grabbed me, like he had known this would happen.

"It's okay," he said.

After a deep breath, I nodded.

Vivigöl...

It remained a sword for only a short period of time. While everyone watched, it *click-click-clicked* back into its trident form, as though it was more comfortable like that than as a sword.

Miko perked up her head. "Do it again! Mess up that whole bed! And then another one!"

"Th-They're actually Academy property," Nasbit said. He hurried over his bed and into the area around mine. "I think Gray should pick up his foul weapon and wear it again. And we should hide any evidence we destroyed something."

"Didn't you also encourage this?" Raaza asked with a sneer.

"I admit nothing." Nasbit motioned to the bed. "Hurry. Before someone comes in here to investigate that calamity!"

Knovak peeked out from around his bed. He stared at the broken bed for some time, never muttering a single word.

"I thought Vivigöl would be... magical," Sorin said as he patted my shoulder. "Nothing really special happened. It was just an extra-sharp blade."

I shrugged as I bent down to pick up the weapon. "Apparently, it amplifies magic. I think, if Twain had transformed into something, I could've used some magic through it, if that makes sense. I'm not sure, though. I haven't experimented much."

As Raaza picked up splinters from the shattered bedframe, he glanced over. "You should experiment. Constantly. I want to see what that thing can really do."

Nasbit frowned. "You should curb your bloodlust, Raaza. Not everything needs to be violent. Perhaps Gray can make the weapon transform into tools."

"What kind of *tools*, ya blowhard? A weapon is already a kind of tool. A tool of war. And self-defense."

"Well, um, perhaps a hammer? Those can be used to build great buildings, or even assist with chiseling a beautiful statue."

"Oh, yes. I like that. Hammers cave in skulls quite easily." Raaza snapped his fingers at me. "Make it turn into an epic hammer."

Knovak darkly chuckled. "Or why not an *icepick*? A great tool for both picking at ice, and killing a man."

"Yes." Raaza laughed with him. "The hat-boy gets it."

"Hey!" Knovak barked. He stepped out from his hiding place and crossed his arms. "I'll have you know those hats were designed by a great fashion designer in Thronehold."

"Uh-huh. Whatever, hat-boy. Just keep coming up with deadly tools and leave all your thoughts about clothes for another time."

Nasbit nervously chuckled as he stepped closer to Raaza. "Now, now. We should all calm down and focus on hiding all our tomfoolery. What if someone sees this?" He knelt and grabbed some of the feathers from the mattress. "They said we could rearrange the dorm, not obliterate it."

After a dramatic roll of his eyes, Raaza knelt and went back to cleaning. I glanced down at my weapon and thought of it as the necklace it had been before. Vivigöl clicked into place, wrapping around my arm, then my neck, and then settling onto my shoulders so it wouldn't limit my movement.

Sorin watched the whole time with a critical eye. When he realized I was staring, he merely smiled.

"Maybe you should go take a shower," he said. "Unless you're tired? We should try sleeping in our new arrangement."

"I think our sleep will be exactly the same as any other night," I muttered.

"You never know. Maybe you'll feel protected and safe, and that will help."

I shrugged. "Maybe."

"Then, c'mon." My brother threw himself back on his bed. "I, for one, am looking forward to having no more troubled nights."

That would be great.

I took a seat on my bed and smoothed the bedding.

Perhaps it would happen.

CHAPTER 8

THE HEADMASTER'S SPEECH

When I awoke, I was surprised that I wasn't in a dream. No strange voice, no bizarre torture device, nothing trying to kill me—it was just a normal night sleeping.

Strange.

Everyone got ready for the day, dressing in our clothes and then putting on our uniform robes. Knovak left early to shower, saying he would meet us for breakfast, but I swear he never looked at me, not even a single glance.

The rest of us went to the dining hall. At the door, before we were allowed in to get our food, there were professors giving everyone instructions.

"Once you're done eating," a professor said as I walked by, "you're to head to the central courtyard. Headmaster Venrover will be making an announcement to the entire Academy."

That piqued my interest. I knew what it would be about, though. Professor Helmith had tipped me off.

What did Professor Helmith think of everything that was happening? I wanted to speak with her about the specifics of the protections.

With Twain in my arms, I gathered food and sat down at a table with my brother and Nini. Today, they had bread, fish, and soup for breakfast. I had made sure to get extra helpings of the tilapia for Twain, who had licked his lips the entire time I fixed the plates. When I sat down, he leapt from my arms and practically slammed his whole face into the dish.

Sorin smiled at me. "You're feeling good, right? Safe and secure?"

"So safe," I sarcastically muttered. "So secure."

Nini swirled her soup in her bowl. "Oh, Gray, remember how Professor Helmith brought in a guest speaker to teach us about true forms for mystical creatures?"

I chewed my bread and nodded.

"Maybe we can suggest they bring in a guest speaker about mimics? I thought it might help you out if you had someone *specifically* trained with your magic, you know? Since yours is so different than the rest of ours."

Sorin's eyebrows shot for his hairline. "Nini, that's such a good idea."

Her cheeks reddened—almost to the color of her hair—and her gaze fell to her food. "O-Oh, it's not that good. It's just a normal idea."

"No, it's inspired. Right, Gray?" My brother nudged me with his elbow.

"It's definitely a good idea," I said. "And even if it was a *normal* idea, it's still much better than *no* idea, so I don't understand why you wouldn't take some pride in it." I chewed some more of my food. After I swallowed, I asked, "What made you think of it?"

"Sorin has been really concerned about your magic, and I wanted to help, so I thought this was probably the best way to do that." She fixed her glasses, perching them higher on her nose. "Hopefully the professors will know someone who is a powerful mimic arcanist."

Sorin and Nini...

They were so concerned about me, I was the subject of their discussions. I was lucky to have them in my life, but at the same time, I was making them worry. That wasn't ideal. But at least Nini's idea was something I could work toward. A master mimic arcanist could probably help me improve faster than other arcanists.

The rest of breakfast was quiet and quick. We finished, and then headed for the central courtyard.

Twain rode on my shoulder as we traveled down the main hall, his belly distended from all the fish he had eaten.

"Breakfast is my favorite meal," he said with a tiny burp.

I patted his orange head. "Try not to toot in class, and I'll be happy."

"*Hey!* That happened once. You don't have to remind people."

I smiled as I scratched his large ears. "Don't worry. Next time, I'll blame it on Brak."

The courtyard was in the middle of Astra Academy, and square in shape. A massive square filled with beautiful plants, winding walkways, small brooks, and four gorgeous statues. I remembered being wildly impressed the first time I saw it. It was a place for kings.

When Sorin, Nini, and I reached the courtyard, I was reminded how many students attended the Academy, though. The once quiet space was filled with a few hundred arcanists and their eldrin. Chairs and benches littered the courtyard, giving people places to sit and relax. Many arcanists opted to sit in patches of lush grass. They almost looked as though they were enjoying a picnic.

Nini's reaper floated behind her, a gloomy eldrin unlike everyone else's.

Most people shifted to allow us through. Some even whispered and pointed at Waste, like they hadn't ever seen a reaper so close before.

Sorin walked nearby, his shadow flickering around his feet. I wondered if Thurin was agitated by the crowds, but I kept my questions to myself.

There were stone walls on all four sides of the courtyard, with windows and balconies overlooking the greenery and decorations. The headmaster would likely stand on the main balcony—the one that attached to his office. I walked until I had a clear view of it, then I sat down on a stone bench. Nini sat on the other end of the bench, and Sorin sat near her feet. He was so tall, and wide, that Nini could easily place her hands on his shoulders.

He tilted his head back until he could look her in the eyes. She stared down at him and giggled as she grinned.

It was so cute, I was almost jealous.

The only thing not cute about the scene was the reaper with the scythe hovering just a few inches away. He added an air of spookiness to the otherwise picturesque atmosphere.

The hundreds of students engaged in all sorts of conversations, but their words were so numerous, and at all levels of volume, that it was impossible to make out any one person's words. The jumble of noise

SHAMI STOVALL

grated, and after a long sigh, I focused my attention on the bright blue sky overhead.

For half a second, I had the urge to mount a dragon and take to the clouds.

I shook my head.

I had never ridden a dragon in my life. What a strange thought.

A wave of silence swept over the crowd, quieting people in a ripple that originated at the headmaster's balcony. He stood at the railing, his tall stature making him easy to spot.

Headmaster Venrover had hair as black as midnight, and he allowed it to grow long. It contrasted with his tanned skin, and complemented his dark eyes. Everything about him screamed *elegance* and *poise*. Unlike arcanist warriors, who had physiques for fighting, he was clearly a man who wielded a pen and not a sword.

He wore a black vest and shirt, and a long blue-and-silver robe that covered everything else. On his chest, the four symbols of the Academy were stitched over the breast: a globe, a sundial, a star, and upside-down gates.

"Greetings, students," the headmaster said, his voice articulate and loud enough to hear from across the courtyard. Today he sounded tired, but his tone retained the same confidence I always heard from him.

He was an odd man to read, sometimes.

Venrover's eldrin walked out onto the balcony with him.

Nubia.

She was a beautiful sphinx with a lioness's body, the wings of an eagle, and the head of a woman. Her golden fur had the hue of honey, and the feathers on her wings glistened with inner health.

Unlike normal sphinxes, however, she had two human eyes, and a third eye on her forehead which always remained closed.

When she sat by his side, a group of girls by the balcony gasped and pointed.

Nubia was popular, apparently.

"I've gathered you all here today to make several announcements." Headmaster Venrover smiled wide enough that I could see it from my seat on the far bench. "The first is that the Academy's Menagerie is empty. We will be sending some students on an expedition to save some mystical

66

creatures from highwaymen who have made camp at the base of our own mountain range."

That was surprising news, but not entirely unexpected. Sometimes vile individuals captured mystical creatures to kill them and sell their body parts. In other cases, they stole creatures just to sell to wealthy nobles who didn't want to look for them out in the wilds.

And it was stealing—a lot of mystical creatures already had homes and caretakers, like the hippogriffs of my home island. The hippogriffs were cared for by the people of Haylin, and sometimes pirates or raiders tried to take the hatchlings from us, just because there was good gold in it.

"The third-years will be handling this assignment," Venrover stated.

His sphinx spread her wings, and the students cheered. I joined in the clapping, though I was disappointed I wouldn't get to see a bunch of highwaymen get punched in the face.

Once everyone calmed down, Headmaster Venrover said, "My next announcement has to do with the structure of the Academy itself. I've hired architects—and powerful artificers—to increase our defenses. However, Astra Academy is not made of coin. We are funded by donations from powerful arcanists, and in order to gain additional funding, we will be holding a fundraiser."

The mere mention of a soiree sent a spark of excitement through the students and their eldrin. A fairy in the crowd fluttered high into the air, spewing glitter the whole way.

The headmaster held his hand out and frowned. "The fourth- and fifth-years will be helping put on the event. It will be the perfect opportunity to meet influential arcanists before you graduate, and you can help the Academy by showing off everything you've learned."

Ah. Yet another event I wouldn't be taking part in. How lovely.

But I thanked the good stars I wasn't included. The last "party" I had gone to had been a disaster. I didn't want to go to another one anytime soon.

"The last announcement I have is for the first- and second-years." Headmaster Venrover gestured to the far end of the courtyard, probably off toward the training fields beyond the wall. "We will be having a festival of skill for all the newer arcanists. You will be required to enter one of the many competitions, but fear not. There will be something for everyone."

That news garnered more questions than the first two. Everyone immediately glanced around, as though trying to find all the first- and second-years in the crowd.

Sorin turned to me with a smile. "This will be really interesting."

"If you say so," I said. I scanned the crowd.

Ashlyn still wasn't back at the Academy. She was the only other student I liked to compete against. I didn't want to do anything against my brother, honestly.

Twain nibbled my ear. I shot him a questioning look.

"I know who you're thinking about," he whispered. "And I'm sure she's okay."

"I wasn't thinking about anyone." I pulled him into my lap so he couldn't mess with my ear. "Just focus on the announcement."

Twain huffed, like he knew I wasn't being truthful.

"Fine," I whispered. "I *was* thinking about Ashlyn, but keep that to yourself, all right?"

"She's fine. Definitely. I doubt she was even hurt during that whole explosion at her cotillion."

"That's not what I'm worried about..."

Last I saw her, she was engaged to be married to some scumbag. Would Ashlyn get married before returning to the Academy? Before I had a chance to convince her father I was a valid candidate for his daughter's hand in marriage? One she would prefer, if she was telling me the truth...

"Those are the end of my announcements," the headmaster said with a flourish and slight bow. "Now, enjoy your classes and please look forward to the many events we have planned."

CHAPTER 9

HIERARCHY OF VIOLENCE

Today, our class was *Combat Arts*.

After the headmaster's speech about the changes to Astra Academy, I walked with Sorin, Nini, Nasbit, and Raaza through the long halls of the Academy until we reached the doors that led to the training fields.

Knovak was already there with his unicorn. He opened the door and allowed us through, but he muttered things to himself. Something along the lines of, *I'll get better*, but I couldn't make out all his words. Knovak didn't even glance up when I walked by.

I thought it would just be the six of us in class, but someone waited for us just at the edge of the grass outside. I recognized her immediately, even from behind. Phila had the longest hair in our class—it went to her waist—and it glistened a vibrant strawberry blonde. When she turned around, her hair fluttered outward, like the skirt of a giant dress.

With a smile, Phila said, "Oh, there you all are. I was beginning to worry I had forgotten our schedule."

Her robes were held tightly around her body. The chilly morning air whipped by, and Phila shivered. She was rather thin, and she didn't much care to spend time outside.

Phila's eldrin, an elegant coatl, slithered around her feet. His name was

Tenoch, and he was a five-foot-long corn snake with white and orange scales. His colorful wings resembled a parrot's, and he draped them around Phila's sides, as though attempting to shield her from the weather.

"Is this better, my arcanist?" Tenoch asked.

Phila nodded once—but she didn't stop shivering. "You're so kind to me, Tenoch. I don't deserve you."

"Nonsense, my arcanist. Come. Let's find the professor straight away. If you start exercising, I'm sure you'll heat up."

Phila's coatl hugged her with his wings, and she scooped up his snake body into her arms. It was awkward, but they managed after several flaps of Tenoch's wings. "You don't need to be worried about me," Phila said with a smile. "I'm fine."

I glanced around, hoping the other two members of our class were nearby. Unfortunately, I didn't spot Ashlyn or Exie.

I wanted to say I wasn't worried, but instead, I said, "I can't wait to see what *Professor* Leon has for us today."

The others chuckled at my joke as we all stepped onto the grass field. It stretched out before us, surrounded by a track for running, with several pieces of equipment in the center for training our muscles or specific combat arts. Javelins, weights, bows, and fake swords were kept on a wood rack, ready for our class should the need arise.

Everyone glanced around as we all stomped across the field. Captain Leon was usually here before us. Instead, a hazy fog lingered around the field, as though clouds had settled onto the Academy and taken up residency on the edges of the grass.

It was odd. Astra Academy had controlled weather—what were these rebellious clouds doing?

"Oh, there you all are," a voice from the clouds said, wafting over us with the morning breeze. "I was wondering when the headmaster's speech would conclude."

A man stepped out of the cloud cover around the field.

His posture was upright and confident, though he wasn't that tall, perhaps a few inches under six feet. He had a well-balanced and athletic build, and he didn't wear the school uniform—just a shirt tight enough to hug the muscles of his physique and a pair of loose trousers.

The man didn't even wear shoes.

It reminded me of Professor Helmith's aversion to shoes.

This strange man also kept his head perfectly shaved. I saw every dent and odd crease in his scalp. Most people had a slightly wonky head, but hair kept that fact hidden.

The man's arcanist mark was also on full display. It was a seven-pointed star with a serpentine dragon woven through the points. Well, a dragon and... some clouds.

A nimbus dragon.

"I'm Professor Jijo," the man said as he walked toward us, his movements fluid, displaying a combination of agility, control, and power.

The instant Jijo said that, a dragon snaked its way out of the clouds. It was a creature with six short legs with bird-like talons. And while the nimbus dragon had no wings, it flew through the air with ease regardless. Its blue scales shimmered with the vibrancy of a summer afternoon sky, and its mane was made of wisps of clouds, constantly morphing and flowing, as if it were made of living vapor.

Nimbus dragons were among the smallest of the dragons, at least according to Professor Helmith. She was right—the little dragon sailed over and landed on Professor Jijo's broad shoulders without difficulty. It was about the size of Phila's coatl.

"This is my eldrin," Jijo said as he came to a stop in front of the class. He scratched the dragon's chin. "He's a nimbus dragon by the name of *Cirrus*."

"It's a pleasure to meet you," Cirrus said, his voice airy and light. I almost missed it.

"Hello," Sorin said, waving.

The shadows around his feet stirred. "Greetings," Thurin said from the depths of the darkness.

No one else said a word.

Professor Jijo half-bowed to the class and then motioned to the field. "I apologize for my late arrival to the Academy. I was away on business, and only recently could I return to my post here at this illustrious institution." With a smile, he added, "Headmaster Venrover told me all about this *eventful* year. It's a shamed I missed it."

"Trust me, you didn't want to be here." Nasbit forced a nervous laugh. "But the headmaster is making sure it never happens again, so that's good."

Jijo held up a finger. "Well, as your combat arts instructor, I'm going to give you all the tools to defend yourself, in case something unspeakable happens again in the future."

Phila raised her hand barely above her jawline.

The professor's dark brown eyes were sharp. He quickly turned to face Phila. "Yes? Oh, and please tell me your name, so that I might commit it to memory."

"I'm Phila Hon," she said. "Um, but I was wondering... Do we need to learn *combat* per se? What if I would rather learn magic I can use in constructive ways?"

"Phila Hon..." The professor slowly walked around the seven of us in class. He rubbed his chin, and his dragon—still perched on his shoulders—did the same. "Do you know who is in charge here?"

Phila's eyes grew wide. "Hm? What do you mean?"

"Let me rephrase. What would happen if an arcanist tried to rob another arcanist?"

"Rob?" Phila blinked. "I suppose knights or other arcanists would arrest the criminal."

Her coatl nodded along with her statement. "That's right. The knights would do something."

"And what if the *knights* tried to rob someone?" Professor Jijo walked a full circle around us and then stopped. "What would happen then?"

"Well, it would depend where it happened. Maybe the queen of the empire would step in. Or maybe another powerful arcanist. Like the Warlord of Magic." Phila brushed her long hair with her fingers. "Isn't that the proper way? My mother said it was best to leave such matters to the governing arcanists."

"What happens if the *Warlord of Magic* decides to rob someone?" Jijo asked, diving deeper into his hypothetical.

The whole class was silent for a long while.

Raaza snorted. "We met him once for a class. He didn't seem like the type who would rob people."

"It's just for this thought experiment," the professor said, smiling.

"What would you do if the Warlord of Magic robbed someone? What if he was robbing one of *you*?"

Sorin crossed his arms. "Well, uh, I would try to stop him if he was hurting anyone in this class."

Jijo snapped his fingers and pointed at Sorin. "Ah. There. You're making my point for me. You see, the person in charge is *whoever is at the top of the hierarchy of violence.*"

With a playful twirl of his hand, he manipulated the clouds around the field until most cleared away, giving us all better visibility.

"If you had no way to fight back, you would be at the complete mercy of whoever was the strongest individual," the professor said. "You must *never* allow yourself to fall too low on this hierarchy of violence. You must strive to keep yourself as high as possible—so that you can always fight back, just in case. Who knows? Perhaps the person in charge abuses their authority."

Raaza's expression shifted from neutral to shocked. It was as if someone had hit him in the face with a wet fish. He stood a little straighter and even raised his hand.

Again, Jijo noticed immediately. "Yes? Your name, please."

"I'm Raaza Luin. But... go back to what you were saying... You think it's right to fight back? What if... What if we can't win against the Warlord of Magic? Shouldn't we just let him rob us? So we can live another day?"

Professor Jijo chuckled. Then he held his hand against the small of his back and lifted an eyebrow. If his head weren't shaved, he'd likely have oily black hair, like me and Sorin—judging by his dark eyebrows.

"Raaza Luin—there will be moments in your life where hiding will only make things worse. The reason you should study combat arts is so that you always have the *option* to fight back. If you never have the option, you will be ruled through fear and tyranny. Perhaps not now, but eventually."

"I agree," Raaza whispered, practically in awe.

"So, I *do* have to learn combat?" Phila asked, her gaze downcast.

Professor Jijo chuckled. He stepped away from the class and waved his hand again. A few clouds formed across the field. They became white bubbles of mist. "You needn't worry, Arcanist Hon. Our practice today will be against these clouds and nothing more."

Phila patted her coatl eldrin. "Well, my hands are soft." She glanced down at her palms. "And my arms are... *delicate*."

"And I'm not a fan of physical competition," Nasbit interjected. "If we're bringing up complaints."

"Who are you?" The professor created seven cloud bubbles, one for each student.

"Nasbit Dodger."

"Ah. I see. Nasbit Dodger—fear of competition is understandable, but it can also be a boon. When you compete with others, you are forced to reflect on yourself. If you win, you can reflect on your strengths. When you lose, you can critically examine your weaknesses."

"I still don't like it," Nasbit murmured.

His stone golem nodded its boulder head.

Jijo chuckled. "Fair enough. Perhaps, before this year is over, I can change your mind." He pointed to the bows on the rack. "Today, we will have no competitions. Instead, I will teach you all how to use a bow and arrow. *Then*, I will show you how to use your bow with your evocation."

"Our magic?" Nini asked, her voice soft. "B-But some of us don't have evocations that can be used like an arrow."

While some people could evoke fire and use it on an arrow, Nini and Sorin both evoked *terror*. Nini was right—how were they going to use that as a projectile weapon?

"I'll show you once you're good with a bow," Jijo said. Again, he motioned to the equipment. "Trust me. I'm familiar with the magics of a reaper. I know your limitations, and your hidden strengths. Come, come. Show of hands—who here has fired a bow?"

No one raised their hand.

If Ashlyn were here, I knew she would be the only one with her arm in the air.

"What was your name, reaper arcanist?" Jijo asked.

"Nini Wanderlin," she replied.

"Ah. Good, good, Nini Wanderlin. Trust me, once I've finished my lessons with you all, the bow will be your new favorite companion."

I set Twain on the grass. He stared up at me with a frown. The grass still had dew on the blades, and I knew it had to be wet to the touch.

"You'll be fine," I whispered to him.

Twain huffed as he awkwardly walked to the edge of the field. The other eldrin followed suit, giving all their arcanists plenty of space to practice with their new weapons. Tenoch clapped his wings, encouraging his arcanist as much as possible.

Sorin and I walked together over to the weapon rack. Neither of us had ever picked up a bow. Technically, we had used a crossbow when we played around with the city guard one afternoon, but our father had yelled at us afterward, and it never happened again.

I grabbed one of the bows and spun it around, examining it from all sides.

It was crafted from supple yew wood, and polished smooth. The slender curved frame seemed higher quality than anything we would need, and I grazed my fingertips across a small portion.

The bowstring, taut and purposeful, stretched the length of the bow, and was woven with delicate threads of something shimmeringly silver. It was almost ethereal.

"Gray?"

I flinched and turned to my brother. "Yeah?"

"You're staring at that bow like it's your honeysuckle."

My face heated, and I turned away from him with one forceful stomp. "What's wrong with you? I'm doing no such thing."

"You were, though. You sure you're okay?"

I pushed him aside as I headed for the professor.

The bow...

Somehow, I knew it was more than high quality. It was exceptional quality. And I liked it. That was weird—since I never had thoughts about bows before—but right now, I felt excited to try it out.

I wanted to shoot something.

CHAPTER 10

JARMAKEE

Professor Jijo's nimbus dragon leapt from his shoulders and shot through the air. He flew low to the ground, the emerald grass tickling the scales of his underbelly. Then Cirrus slowed his flight and dragged some of his talon-like claws through the dirt, creating seven firing lines for everyone.

Once finished, Cirrus glided through the air, returning to his arcanist within just a few seconds.

He was fast. Faster than any creature I had seen before. Perhaps his small size made it easier to whip around.

Jijo patted his eldrin. "Thank you, Cirrus. Now then. Everyone pick a firing line and stand there."

We all complied, but it was obvious that only Raaza and I were excited. I jumped into position, and Raaza took a step up to the line next to me. He held his bow at the ready, and even flashed me a smile.

Sorin whispered with Nini until he took a spot on the other side of me. Nini went to the line on Sorin's other side, her hands shaking. She didn't seem to like her bow at all.

Phila held hers like it smelled bad, and Nasbit had a permanent frown.

"When firing a bow, you need to learn the importance of *back tension*," Jijo said matter-of-factly. He walked over, grabbed a bow off the rack for himself, and then picked up a basket full of arrows around the backside. As he walked over to us, he smiled. "Your back muscles, especially the ones around your shoulder blades, are the most important when firing these types of bows."

His nimbus dragon leapt off his shoulder and gracefully glided to the grass. Cirrus smiled and held his serpentine head high as his arcanist spoke.

Professor Jijo removed his shirt in one quick motion.

Phila gasped, but stifled her noise a moment later.

The professor had several runes across his skin, most of which were black. They were in bizarre, vein-like designs. It almost looked rotted, but at the same time, the lines matched up with the grooves of his muscles.

And his physique was rather defined.

Professor Jijo turned so his back faced us. He held his bow, and tensed the muscles of his back, perfectly demonstrating what he had been talking about.

"See?" Jijo rotated his shoulder slightly to show us the tension. "Now, there are two ways to draw your bowstring. You can pull to your chin, or you can pull past your head. For today, keep one arm straight, and with your draw arm, pull your bowstring until you can touch your chin with the side of your thumb."

Everyone watched, completely silent, as the professor did everything he said. He drew the bow.

"When aiming," Jijo said, his eyes on the distant cloud bubbles he had created, "you must make a conscious effort to hold the bow at full draw using only your back muscles. Let your arm, shoulder, and hand muscles become as relaxed as possible."

Sorin glanced down at his bow. He effortlessly lifted it and then drew the bowstring. When Nini saw him trying, she did the same, but her arms shook with effort.

I held my bow tightly in my hand. My eagerness to try surprised me. Since when had bows become so fascinating?

Jijo had no trouble keeping the bow at full draw, even as he continued his lecture. "Back tension is important because it stabilizes the shot. The stability of your back muscles surpasses that of your arm and shoulder muscles due to their shorter length, inherent strength, and proximity to the spine."

I rubbed my shoulders. Most of what he was saying was interesting, mostly because I had never thought about it before.

Professor Jijo loosed the arrow.

It sailed through the air and struck a cloud bubble with ease. The cloud burst outward from the force of the arrow in a satisfying *puff*.

"You should hold the arrow with two of your fingers," Jijo said as he walked over and passed out two arrows to each of us. "Your pointer finger and your middle finger. Aim with both eyes open, and just attempt to strike a single cloud."

His nimbus dragon waved his tail around until the cloud target reformed in the exact same position as before.

Jijo motioned to our targets. "Go ahead, then. Fire a single arrow. Take it slow, if needed."

Raaza and Sorin both held up their bows and nocked an arrow. Raaza pulled back, his thumb to his chin, and immediately fired. His arrow shot off between the cloud targets, a complete miss. He cursed under his breath and grabbed his second arrow.

Sorin, on the other hand, drew the bowstring back and waited. He took a solid thirty seconds to aim and then fire. His arrow, at least, swiped the edge of a cloud target, puffing out misty vapors. Sorin smiled and then turned to me.

"Did you see that, Gray?"

I nodded. "Yeah. Impressive."

"I might be a natural." Sorin glanced over at Nini. "It's not as hard as it looks. You can do this."

Nini poked at the rim of her glasses. "I don't know. My eyes aren't the greatest..."

"Your glasses help with that. Go on. I'm sure you'll be great."

Emboldened by his encouragement, Nini sheepishly smiled. She picked up her arrow, carefully nocked it, and then held it with two fingers, just as Jijo had instructed. When she drew the bowstring, she struggled, but not for long. Once her back was straight, and her muscles tense, she managed to hold the draw long enough to aim.

With her tongue caught between her lips, Nini fired her bow.

The arrow sailed over and *just barely* missed one of the cloud targets. It was so close to the cloud, a wisp of white vapor twirled away from the target as the arrow shot by.

"Almost," Sorin said as he slapped one of his knees. "I told you! Not so hard. You can do this."

Raaza—who had nocked an arrow and aimed while I hadn't been paying attention—fired his second arrow. He struck a cloud target in the side, exploding half of it away in a delightful *puff*. The professor reformed it afterward.

"Very good," Jijo said. "C'mon now. Everyone else try. The bow won't hurt you."

Nasbit sighed. "He hasn't seen me practice with weapons before... I could hurt myself in a pillow fight."

My brother rubbed his hands together. Then he glanced over to me and lifted an eyebrow. "Gray? Is something wrong? You haven't tried yet."

My heart beat harder than before. I picked up my bow, nocked an arrow, held the bow out with one arm, and then grabbed the bowstring just as the professor had said. But something didn't feel right. When I drew the string, my body screamed at me—like I was doing something wrong.

I lowered the bow, my muscles practically twitching in anticipation.

What was wrong?

I felt restless, like I was rolling around in bed, unable to find a comfortable position to fall asleep. Something about my stance, my hold, and the arrow didn't *feel right*.

Nothing felt right.

Sorin returned his attention to Nini—to cheer her on as she drew her second arrow—and while everyone was seemingly preoccupied, I just stared at the bow in my hand. Although the professor had made it very clear what I should be doing, I didn't want to fire the arrow using his method.

Instead...

I held up the bow with one arm, and then reached *behind my head* with my draw arm in order to grab the bowstring. I felt bizarre doing it— but it also felt *right*. And instead of grabbing the arrow with my pointer and middle finger, I grabbed it with my pointer and thumb.

Raaza stared at me in utter disbelief, his mouth hanging slightly open. I looked ridiculous. I knew I did.

What in the abyssal hells was I doing?

But when I drew the bowstring—pulling until my hand reached the back of my head—I felt confident. More than confident. I felt *in my element*. I knew what I was doing. The target seemed easy.

I let loose my arrow.

And my shot struck the cloud bubble dead center. The target exploded in a blast of misty vapor, swirling around.

"What was *that*?" Sorin asked, bewildered. He stared at me, then glanced at the fizzled cloud, and then back to me. "Gray? Did you just fire that bow... from behind your head?"

Everyone stopped what they were doing to glance over. I didn't blame them. Even *I* wanted to gawk at my strange archery display. What had I done? Was it a fluke?

Raaza snapped his fingers and then pointed at the second arrow resting by my feet. "Do it again. C'mon. I wanna see it again."

After a short exhale, I knelt and picked up the arrow. Then I held the bow out, and again, drew from behind my head. It just... felt more natural to do it this way. Drawing the bow with my arm in front of me didn't seem right.

I nocked the arrow, drew the string, and then took aim.

After a single breath, where I steadied myself, I fired. The arrow flew through the air and struck a second cloud bubble square in the center. My eyes widened, and I held my breath. What was this?

Professor Jijo, his attention on the cloud, slowly panned his gaze over to me. "What was your name?" he asked, his voice low.

"Gray," I said as I lowered my bow. "Gray Lexly."

"I see." Jijo walked over, his expression set to something unreadably neutral. "Gray Lexly—I thought you said you had never fired a bow."

"I haven't." I shook my head. "I swear."

The professor stopped once he stood in front of me. He motioned to the bow, and then to the cloud targets. "You fired those arrows using *jarmakee archery*."

"What is that?" Sorin asked.

Raaza stepped closer. "Yeah. What he said. What is that? It's *real*?"

"Jarmakee is an ancient form of archery used by the most skilled of dragon arcanists," Jijo said, his attention still on the far cloud targets.

"But why?" Raaza flailed one arm behind his head. "Why would *anyone* fire an arrow like a lunatic with their arm all wonked out of position?"

Jijo returned his gaze to the class. His voice, distant in all regards, was almost too soft for me to hear correctly. "Jarmakee is the advanced style of archery used for firing *down*. You see, back tension is very important in archery, and if you lean over—say, while riding on a flying dragon—you will lose all the tension in your back. *But*, if you fire with your arm behind your head, you can maintain a taut back, even while leaning over in your saddle. Even while firing downward."

No one said anything. When the wind rushed by, it howled, sending a shiver through half the class.

"Jarmakee was once also taught to castle defenders," Jijo continued, his voice gaining more volume as he spoke. "They would lean over the castle walls and fire down on invaders. If they used the jarmakee style, they retained all their strength when firing."

"I've never seen anyone fire like that," Nasbit chimed in. "And I've been to *many* archery contests." He nervously rubbed the length of his bow. "Are you sure it's a real style?"

"It's ancient, like I said." Jijo stared at me, his expression hardening. "Ever since the use of crossbows and pistols became commonplace, all advanced forms of archery became obsolete. There's no reason to teach jarmakee anymore. Firing a crossbow from a dragon's back is much easier than firing an old-fashioned bow."

My throat dried as I glanced down at my hands.

An ancient form of archery used by dragon arcanists? Although I didn't want to admit it, I already knew why I had fired the arrow like I had.

Death Lord Deimos had been a sovereign dragon arcanist, and then become an abyssal dragon arcanist. He must've learned that archery style.

Which meant... the fragment of his soul was having an effect on me, and more than just dreams.

CHAPTER 11

NOT AS THEY APPEAR

"Well," I said, "Professor Helmith showed me this archery style in my dreams." I shook out my hand and rotated my shoulder. "I didn't think I could learn things like how to use a bow, but I guess I was wrong."

The others stared at me, their eyebrows raised. A few of them eventually nodded and accepted my lie. Why wouldn't they? No one knew what I did in my dreams with Helmith. And why would I lie about this?

The truth was... I didn't want them to think I wasn't in control of the situation. If Deimos's soul was influencing me, then I was a risk. No one would trust me. But if I had learned archery from Helmith, no one would be worried.

"Professor Helmith told me all about her tutelage in your dreams," Jijo said. He stroked his chin. "But I was unaware she was skilled in such archaic archery styles..."

Raaza snapped his fingers and turned away from me. "I need to figure out how to learn things while I'm sleeping... I'll fall behind at this rate." He stared at the distant cloud targets, his eyes set in a harsh glare.

The only people who didn't seem to readily believe me were Sorin and Knovak.

It was painfully clear that Knovak thought something was wrong. He eyed me, his lips pressed tight, but he said nothing. He took hold of his bow and returned to his archery.

And I didn't dare look at Sorin for longer than a second or two. I avoided making eye contact at all costs. If we locked our gazes, he would see right through me. Sorin would know. He just would.

And he would be so disappointed.

Jijo, thankfully, stepped forward to save me from this awkward moment. He held up his hands. "Now, I know that was exciting, but we must focus on our studies." The professor waved his arm, and the cloud targets lifted, ascending at a quick pace until they were about twenty feet in the air. "Jarmakee is for firing arrows downward. It's useless if your target is above you."

Jijo's nimbus dragon darted through the air, zipping over to the equipment stand and gathering more arrows. Before I even finished taking a breath, the dragon slithered through the sky and made his way to each student in class.

Cirrus dropped off two more arrows for everyone.

Then the dragon swooped over to his arcanist's shoulders.

"Thank you, Cirrus," Jijo said.

"Of course." The dragon held his little head high, his bright blue scales a dazzling sight in the light of the morning sun.

When I picked up the arrow and glanced upward, my gut twisted in a knot. Something about firing above me didn't sit right. I *tried* to hold the bow the normal way—like the professor had demonstrated—but it was obvious my body thought that was terrible.

It was the equivalent of trying to push my hand into an open fire. My body anticipated terrible things, and tensed in preparation.

Sorin did everything as instructed. He pulled the drawstring to his chin, took aim, and then fired. His arrow broke a cloud, and then sailed in an arc until it hit the other side of the training field. With a frown, he glanced over to me.

I looked away and pretended to fidget with my second arrow. I watched him at the edge of my vision, waiting till he turned away before I did anything else.

The others in our class were busy with their own archery skills, no longer interested in whatever I was doing. Raaza successfully fired his bow twice. Nini nocked her arrow, but only after my brother encouraged her with a thumbs up.

"You can do it, my arcanist," her reaper called out.

With a slight grin, she took aim and managed to swipe part of the cloud.

"This is ridiculous," Nasbit muttered. He glanced up at the clouds and then glowered at his weapon. "I mean, they can't fail me out of the Academy if I just refuse to do this one thing, can they?"

Phila nocked an arrow and fired. She seemed to have forgotten all about the professor's speech about a steady back, and the importance of keeping her muscles taut. Her arrow didn't even reach the clouds above us. It sailed in a tiny arc and plunked onto the grass, not even really puncturing the dirt.

Phila pouted.

Then she glared at her bow, took aim again, and to my amusement, she evoked wind. Phila was a coatl arcanist, after all. They were masters of air, at least according to Professor Helmith.

When Phila evoked the wind, it carried her arrow straight, guiding it faster and straighter than anyone else's shot. The arrow pierced the cloud.

And then it kept sailing.

That was probably dangerous. Everyone stared, watching as it went.

When would it fall?

It took a few moments, but the arrow eventually tumbled back toward the mountains. I hoped there was no lone student or professor out in the trees beyond the training field. Getting hit by a random arrow would be a story, for sure. Perhaps an interesting obituary.

"That was amazing," Phila said with a giggle.

Professor Jijo shielded his eyes from the sun with one of his hands. He stared at the distant trees as he said, "Now, Arcanist Hon, I did say we would work on evocation and weapons once we were familiar with the weapons themselves. Skipping a step in your training isn't recommended. Familiarity with your bow is required to become a truly talented archer."

Phila tugged on a few locks of her long hair. "Oh. Yes. You did say that." She held her bow close. "I apologize, Professor. I'll attempt to learn the bow without magic first."

Cirrus flew around, passing out more arrows. I wondered why he didn't give us a whole bundle, but it occurred to me that the professor probably wanted to watch us closely—see how we improved with each shot. He didn't want us to go too fast.

"Nasbit," Phila said as she turned to him. "This is actually really fun." She snuck a glance at the professor. When the man had gone closer to Raaza—far from her, she lowered her voice and added, "Maybe you should try it with your evocation."

Nasbit slowly turned, his eyes narrowed into a sardonic glare. "Phila. I evoke *rocks*. This really isn't my strong suit." He frowned, his hate for this whole lesson rolling off him in waves.

With another giggle, Phila walked over to Nasbit's training area. She stepped close to him, and even reached out to grab his bow with her own hands, wrapping an arm around Nasbit's back.

"W-What are you doing?" Nasbit said, cringing, his face growing pink.

"I'm helping." Phila held the bow with him, trying to angle it upward.

It was rather awkward, to be honest. Nasbit clearly didn't know what was happening, and he just *stared* at Phila as though she were going to bite him at any second.

Phila either didn't notice or didn't care.

"See, hold it up, and just pull the drawstring. It's fun! I was surprised." She smiled as she finally looked over at him. "I think you'll like it, too. Come—we'll do it together."

"I-I can do it myself." Nasbit swallowed hard, but he didn't really fight to get out of Phila's hold. She eventually acquiesced and released him, but Nasbit never relaxed.

Phila pointed to the clouds. "I know you can do it, Nasbit. If *studying in your dreams* can make Gray a good archer, then your proven ability to study and learn anything should help you here. I bet you'll be the best archer in our class." She clapped her hands once, her smile genuine.

It was obvious to me that Nasbit didn't know how to take any of this.

His face brightened to a new shade of red. He sputtered something, stared at his feet, and then stared at the cloud targets above. "I mean, I could, yes, study, but..." He rolled his hand, struggling to find words.

"Just try," Phila said.

Nasbit, backed into a corner, nocked an arrow, and then pulled on the drawstring. He brought his hand to his chin, but his shoulders quaked.

Was the strain of the bow too much? Or was he just *that* nervous? I couldn't tell.

Nasbit shot his arrow.

It sailed up...

And *just barely* reached the bottom of the cloud target.

Then it tumbled back down to the training field and landed limply on the emerald grass.

"See?" Phila softly clapped. "That wasn't hard."

Nasbit chuckled, his face still as red as before.

"You shouldn't move your hand," Knovak called out to him, breaking his silence since class had started. "If you let your hand follow the string, you're going to weaken your shot."

Professor Jijo pointed to Knovak. "That's correct." With a curious smile, he asked, "But didn't you say you weren't familiar with archery?"

"Many members of my family practice," Knovak said. "I watched them. I didn't study it, but I attended a few competitions. I think I gleaned a thing or two."

Everyone seemed like they were enjoying the lesson, even if, at first, they had seemed like they would hate it. I wanted to enjoy the moment as well, but my thoughts continually slipped back to my apparent ability to fire a bow.

I had never learned an ancient form of archery.

Perhaps I should tell someone.

But whom?

Professor Helmith was ill, her husband had made it clear he wouldn't allow any more harm to come to her because of me, and I didn't know any experts on *the abyssal hells* or *Death Lords*. Who else was there to turn to?

Would the headmaster know what to do? He always seemed to go out of his way to help.

I raised my hand.

Professor Jijo snapped his attention to me instantly. "Yes, Arcanist Lexly?"

"Would you mind if I went back inside for a moment?" I rubbed the base of my neck. "I want to speak with the headmaster about learning things in my dreams. I didn't think it was possible, and I think I need to discuss it with him."

"You discuss things with the headmaster?" Jijo slowly lifted an eyebrow.

"Gray has been in a lot of trouble," Knovak interjected. He lowered his bow. "I mean, for a student. Strange things happen to him all the time. I think he should go see the headmaster... If that's what he wants."

Jijo nodded once. "I see." When he returned his attention to me, it was with a hard seriousness that hadn't been there before. "If that's the case, I will accompany you to the headmaster's office."

"Don't you have class to teach?" I asked.

The professor snapped his fingers. His nimbus dragon flew from his shoulder and then landed in front of the other students.

"I will bear this burden," Cirrus said, his tone all business. "Nothing will happen to our charges, my arcanist. I will instruct them with all my ability and heart."

That was dramatic.

Sorin stood a little straighter. With a rhythmic cadence to his speech, he proudly proclaimed, "*In a class where arrows fly with grace, where bows are held in steady embrace, there lies a tale of students bold! They seek wisdom, their dreams unfold, they stand united, their hearts aflame, all seeking to acquire an archer's name!*" He held his weapon high in a theatrical display of learning, I supposed.

"You just came up with that?" Nini smiled as she spoke. "I couldn't rhyme anything if my life depended on it."

Thurin, from the edge of the field, shifted through the shadows. "My arcanist practices the art of wordplay. Soon, he will become a master."

Raaza rolled his eyes.

The professor held out his arm and gestured to the Academy. "Come," he commanded. "Let us walk together to the headmaster's office. I have a few questions for you while we make the trek."

Chapter 12

Funding

"You can't leave without *me*," Twain said.

My mimic ran across the grass, practically bounding, until he reached my feet. I scooped him into my arms and held him close. "I wouldn't dream of leaving you behind."

Twain purred. "Good. We're partners. Now and forever."

With a grin, I carried him toward the Academy, and the professor came along.

I knew nothing about Professor Jijo except what I had seen of him today. He was a stranger, and I remained suspicious, but the man walked alongside me as though we were chums.

He kept his hands behind his back as he walked, a slight smile on his face as he admired the landscaping. Once we entered Astra Academy, Jijo turned his attention to the decorations on the walls, the scenes beyond the windows, and plush rugs that he walked barefoot across.

I thought he had forgotten he wanted to speak, but then Jijo voiced a question.

"Where do you hail from, Arcanist Lexly?"

"The Isle of Haylin," I said.

"How is your family? Are they well?"

I mulled over the question as we traversed the empty hallway. Finally, I replied, "They're fine, I guess."

Professor Jijo waited for a long period of time, as though he wanted me to elaborate. I wasn't sure what he wanted, though. I had only written my family a few times, and I didn't know much about the happenings of the island.

"Did your father or mother teach you a family trade before you became an arcanist?" Jijo asked.

That was a strange question.

"My father is a candlemaker," I said, trying to hold back a sigh. "He makes wax candles, scented candles, and all that sort of boring stuff."

"Boring stuff?" Jijo sounded amused, which irritated me for some reason.

But it also got me thinking about my parents. Normally, I didn't like to discuss them, because why would I? But Jijo seemed different. He sounded as though he wanted to get to know me better, which was rare.

"My father is boring by nature. He never innovates or goes anywhere." I shrugged. "And he does the same routine day in and day out." I pointed to the window. "In this kind of weather, he will dip wicks in hot wax till the night. That's what he's doing right now. I guarantee it."

"I see. And your mother?"

"She died," I said, curt. After a quick breath, I added, "She died giving birth to me and my brother."

Professor Jijo's smile faded. "My condolences."

I said nothing in response. I wasn't sure what to say about it. After silence descended upon us again, and before we started up the stairs to the next story, I asked, "Why did you want to know?"

"I was just curious as to your background. It might explain why you picked up archery in your dreams—without ever having practiced physically."

I darkly chuckled. "No. I'm just some no-name kid with a pathetic apprenticeship in a skill no one wants." After a long moment, I said, "My father *could have* become a lantern designer, or something interesting, but he never does anything worthwhile."

Professor Jijo rubbed the point of his chin. "I suppose."

"Right?" I held Twain close and shook my head. "I wish he would've taken us places. We never left our island! He just kept us there to rot. And he *never* would've taught me something like archery. That would've been too *bold* and *innovative*. My father makes cowardly decisions."

"Oh? Cowardly decisions?" Jijo stopped at the top of the staircase. Then he turned to face me, so I stopped too. "That's not what I heard."

Not what he heard?

I narrowed my eyes at him. What did he mean by that?

Jijo frowned. "You just told me a sad tale about a man who had a pregnant wife, the mother of his children—the love of his life. Then she died. Tragically, and suddenly, in a moment that should've been filled with happiness."

I held my breath, caught off guard by the professor's low tone and distant gaze.

"And then you said that same man decided to never change a thing in his life. He became a man who chose *safety* and *familiarity* over *risk* and *danger*." Jijo met my gaze, his dark eyes softer, almost filled with sadness. "Your father probably wanted to protect his family from any more unnecessary tragedy."

"I..." My throat tightened.

Jijo said, "So, *no*. I wouldn't say your father was cowardly." Jijo turned on his heel. "But I would say that one of his sons has yet to mature." He continued down the second-story hall, heading for the headmaster's office.

His speech left me reeling.

I had never thought of my father in those terms. But when Jijo made those observations, I knew he was right.

My father had been so afraid of losing us, that he picked safety over everything else.

"Gray?" Twain whispered.

I swallowed back my irritation with myself. In that moment, I felt like such a child.

"Yeah?" I asked, my voice tight.

"Aren't you going to follow the professor?"

"R-Right."

I headed down the hall, walking faster and silently chiding myself. When I got back to the dorm, I would pen a letter to my father.

I would apologize.

Then I cursed myself as I returned to Jijo's side. I had only known this professor for less than an hour, and I had already made a fool of myself. My father didn't deserve the hate I had thrown at him.

What was wrong with me?

We walked until we came to the portion of the hall with several offices. The headmaster's door was ajar, and Jijo slowed his pace as we neared.

"You might want to clear away your gloomy expression before we speak to Headmaster Venrover," Jijo said. "And kicking yourself over a few comments isn't the way to make amends. Corrective *actions* are the only cure for mistakes."

Twain twitched his whiskers and glared at the professor, like anyone who dared to make me unhappy was clearly a villain of the highest order. I patted his head, soothing him a bit. "Look, I'm sorry," I said. "I never should've spoken poorly about my father."

"Now, now," Jijo said. "Like I said. Actions are—"

"We're *tired* of your excuses," someone bellowed from inside the headmaster's office.

Both Professor Jijo and I went quiet. We glanced over at the door, though it wasn't open enough to see inside. Should I close it? Jijo didn't move.

"You can't keep doing this, Venrover," the same person said, forceful and gruff. A man, one with an obvious anger problem. "Astra Academy is on the mountain range claimed by the Argo Empire. It makes *sense* for all the arcanists schooled here to be hired by the Empire. We'll give you all the funding you need to make this place safe—you just need to stop sending arcanists off to all these other countries."

"First off," Headmaster Venrover said, his voice loud, but not as much as the other man's, "arcanists from several countries attend this prestigious Academy. Secondly, I send them nowhere—the arcanists who graduate choose their own careers from the countries, guilds, and mercenary groups who offer them positions."

"You could make it a *requirement of attending* that arcanists serve the Empire. Not *forever*. Just for a short while after graduating. The queen is being *very fair* with this offer."

"I disagree," Venrover stated, his tone heated. "I won't make indentured servitude a requirement for attendance."

"Then you won't get any more funding from the crown."

The chilly silence after that statement bothered me. I glanced over at Jijo. He stared at the partially opened door, his expression neutral. Did he want to hear this?

"Oh, that got you quiet, didn't it?" the angry man asked. "Then you finally understand. The Empire won't stand for our coin to go to the instruction of arcanists who will never benefit us."

"That is a narrow-minded way of perceiving things," Venrover stated.

"Either change your policy and attendance requirements, or find your funding elsewhere." After another short period of silence, the man added, "But I doubt all your wealthy friends can pay for your improved defenses *and* the crown's share of annual upkeep. I wouldn't be surprised if this Academy closes its door forever under your poor leadership."

"If you have nothing else to say, I suggest you leave. You're not one of the Academy's benefactors, and you're not a student, so I daresay your presence here is tantamount to trespassing."

A second later, the headmaster's door was thrown open. A portly man with a puffy shirt, black knickers, and a gold vest stomped from the room. His black hair was tied back in a tight ponytail, and his arcanist mark—a seven-pointed star with a unicorn woven between the points—was positioned in the middle of his long forehead.

The unicorn arcanist stomped his way between me and Professor Jijo. The man grunted out something I didn't understand before hurrying down the hallway and finally to the stairs. Jijo glanced over his shoulder and watched for a long moment before he returned his attention to the headmaster's office.

"Well, here we are," Jijo said as he motioned me forward. "Think not of any other vexations. Let's just focus on the task at hand."

I nodded once and then knocked on the headmaster's open door.

"Enter," Headmaster Venrover called.

Professor Jijo and I stepped into the modest office space.

Headmaster Venrover had an impressive desk that dominated most of the room. He also owned several bookshelves, a large couch I could sleep on, a low table covered in parchment, and a rug in the shape of a sphinx.

The headmaster's sphinx eldrin, however, was nowhere to be seen.

The ticking of a clock built into the far wall drew my attention, but only for a short moment. It was so quiet in the headmaster's office, the ticking was the only thing I heard.

When I returned my attention forward, I squinted back the barrage of light streaming in through the far window. Venrover stood behind his massive desk, his long inky hair shining in the beautiful light.

I always forgot how lithe the headmaster was. He was a ghost of a man up close. So thin.

When Headmaster Venrover turned to face us, he forced an awkward smile. "Ah. Professor Jijo. It's a pleasure to see you." Then the man glanced over to me. "I hope this isn't a reprimand moment."

Jijo stepped forward and slightly bowed his head. "Pardon the intrusion, Headmaster. I overheard the matter of funding. I had no idea the Empire would be so aggressive."

"I don't think you need to worry," Headmaster Venrover said. "I have a few more meetings with prominent arcanists, and I think we can make do without assistance from the crown."

"Of course."

I said nothing. This type of dilemma—where the Academy got its funding—was completely foreign to me. Professor Helmith had said that, during Astra Academy's construction, the world serpent arcanist had created a mountain range on the north-western border of the Argo Empire. He had also expanded the Sellix Islands to connect with the mainland—so they could grow more food—and as a result, the country expanded more than anyone had anticipated.

The mountain range was between those two countries. The Argo Empire never liked that, for whatever reason, so it didn't surprise me that they wanted more control over the area.

"What was the other reason for your visit?" the headmaster asked.

Professor Jijo motioned to me. "Arcanist Lexly wishes to speak to you about the potential of dreamweaving and learning while one sleeps."

The headmaster returned his attention to me. He rubbed the arcanist star on his forehead—the one intertwined with a sphinx. It seemed cracked. Or... not right... whenever I stared for a long period of time. Like there was a second image underneath that I couldn't quite make out.

"Well," Venrover muttered, "I do consider myself quite learned on the subject of dreams."

"Can we speak in private?" I asked.

Jijo cleared his throat and then stepped toward the door. "By all means. I shall return to class. I think they need me." With a quick turn, he walked out of the office and shut the door with a click.

Leaving me, Twain, and Headmaster Venrover alone in the room.

CHAPTER 13

STRONGER TIERS

Twain fidgeted in my arms as he twitched his large lynx-like ears. "Headmaster Venrover, why did you let that Empire arcanist speak to you like that? And who does he think he is, threatening you?"

"*Shh.*" I held Twain tight against my chest. "You shouldn't question him like that."

Venrover placed a hand on his desk, his long fingers gracefully grazing the grain of the wood. "There is nothing to be concerned about. This isn't the first time someone has attempted to strong-arm Astra Academy into doing what they wanted."

Twain bit my hand. I sucked in air as I loosened my grip. Able to speak again, my eldrin puffed up his chest. "I remember! People came to the Academy and demanded you close down the Menagerie. I was there—they wanted to take me away."

The headmaster chuckled. "Oh, yes. I had almost forgotten that incident." He smiled, though I could tell he didn't mean it. "I pay for the Menagerie out of my own personal coffers, but that didn't stop some people from demanding I sell all the mystical creatures held there to help fund Academy projects."

"What did you do?" I asked, now genuinely curious.

"Oh, I found funding in other places. I have plenty of powerful arcanist friends who don't mind helping." Venrover's expression melted into something I couldn't read. "Although, the Empire's support was the greatest... I'll just have to make sure some other arcanists are impressed enough with our students to donate."

While I didn't want Astra Academy to close—either due to financial hardship or attacks—I wasn't sure how I could help in the situation. I knew exactly *zero* wealthy arcanists. I couldn't even think of someone I could call on to help me make a sandwich, let alone keep an entire Academy afloat.

"Uh, I didn't come here because of that," I said. "I came here because today, while in *Combat Arts*, I used a bow for the first time."

"And he was *super* good at it," Twain chimed in. "So good. He used an ancient bow technique that impressed the professor and everything."

The headmaster said nothing.

"I think it has something to do with Death Lord Deimos." I held my breath afterward, hoping the headmaster would just know a solution to this problem.

And I hoped beyond reason he didn't see *me* as the root of all this trouble.

Headmaster Venrover grazed his fingers across the desk a second time. He seemed to mull everything over before he said, "Professor Helmith locked a piece of the Death Lord's soul away in your dreams... You see, a true form ethereal whelk arcanist—like all true form arcanists—gains a powerful new ability. And hers is to lock someone away in the realm of slumber. Forever."

Twain gasped.

I nervously chuckled. "She can put people to sleep indefinitely?"

"That's correct." The headmaster pointed to his temple. "I believe the Death Lord can't possess any part of your body because he's essentially sleeping. His knowledge, and his presence, are still part of you, however."

"So, learning things like *ancient bow techniques* is just a side effect of this?" I hoped nothing else would come of it.

The headmaster exhaled. "Well, *learning* something from him isn't what I imagined would happen." He met my gaze, his eyes cold. "I appreciate you telling me this, because I think I'll need to find a way to reinforce Professor Helmith's magic."

"Why do you say that?"

"Death Lord Deimos is an abyssal dragon arcanist." Venrover walked around his desk and stood in front of me. "You learned about the tiers of creatures, didn't you? Ethereal whelks are weaker than dragons, which means their magic isn't as potent."

"But true form creatures are more powerful than their base forms, right?" I asked, trying to recall everything I had learned in class.

The headmaster nodded. "They are... But I suspect abyssal dragons are creatures with magical abilities that affect the soul. Perhaps Death Lord Deimos is attempting to escape his dream prison, and his magic is slowly corroding Professor Helmith's."

I didn't like the sound of that.

Not one bit.

Twain glanced up at me, his two-toned eyes wide with concern. I gently patted his head. What was I going to do about this? The headmaster said he would try to find a way to reinforce Helmith's magic. He would come through for me.

Another thought crossed my mind.

"Uh, Headmaster?" I asked.

"Yes?" Venrover tilted his head slightly.

"Do you think I could visit my father on the Isle of Haylin? I... want to speak with him." Ever since Professor Jijo made his observations, I just wanted to apologize. I shouldn't have been so hard on my father.

"I don't think it's wise for you to leave the Academy," Headmaster Venrover stated. "There are people who worship the Death Lords who obviously have their sights set on you. And there are still gate fragments we haven't collected—which means your presence could activate them."

"R-Right."

That all made sense. But still.

I sighed.

Writing a letter to my father would have to suffice.

"We could invite your father to come to Astra Academy," Headmaster Venrover said. He tapped the point of his chin. "It's an expensive trip, but we have regular suppliers who take the Gates of Crossing every month. Your family could ride on one of those boats."

"Really?" I couldn't stop myself from smiling. "I would like that."

"I'll send a note to both the suppliers and your father on Haylin. It will be official."

That was kind of him. Perhaps I could show my father and stepmother around once they got here. It would shock them both—I doubted they had seen any building as large as the Academy.

"Thank you," I said.

"Yeah." Twain purred. "Thank you so much."

I headed back to class, my thoughts on the Death Lord rather than on archery.

As I walked across the grass of the training field, a pool of darkness slithered across the ground and then circled my steps. My brother's knightmare was cute, when I thought about it—an adorable puddle of black void. Twain watched the shadow shift about, his pupils growing larger like only a cat's could.

"Your brother is worried about you," Thurin said from the depths of the darkness.

"Tell him I'm fine," I whispered. "And that our father will be coming to visit."

"I will." Thurin's tone was rather matter-of-fact, almost too serious for our conversation. Then the knightmare slid across the ground with all the ease of a shadow, darting back to his arcanist.

Everyone still had bows, and they took aim at cloud targets across the field.

Curiously, three people I didn't recognize stood at the very far end of the field, observing the class. They all stood with arms crossed—all of them wearing the robes of second-year students. Who were they? I shook my head, not really caring. They had probably just come for some equipment and stayed to watch the class.

"Gray!" someone called out, breaking me out of my thoughts.

Phila waved to me, smiling wide. She pointed to her bow. "You need to try some of the techniques the professor is teaching us! Look."

She squared her feet, tensed her back, and then fired an arrow at a cloud a good thirty feet away. She evoked wind as she fired, carrying her arrow farther and faster than anything I had seen before. The arrow tore through the cloud with surprising accuracy and power.

Then Phila turned on her heel to face me as I walked over. "Did you see that?" she asked.

"I thought you hated the idea of using a bow," I muttered.

"Oh, I did. But that was before I realized how good I am with it."

"Evoking wind is a tricky magic," Professor Jijo said as he paced behind the class, never getting in the way of anyone firing. "Wind, by itself, is not typically seen as particularly dangerous until you can create gale force gusts. But that won't be for a long time—not until you train, and your eldrin grows older and more capable. So, while you only evoke *weak* winds, you can use it to make other things more dangerous."

"It's not *that* the wind is blowing, it's *what* the wind is blowing," Phila said with one finger up.

Jijo snapped and pointed to her. "Exactly. All projectile weapons, including pistols, can be enhanced with a bit of wind trickery. That will be our goal with you, young arcanist."

"Heh," Raaza said—louder than needed, obviously wanting the attention of the class. "Big deal. I can *make* my own arrows."

He waved his hand and evoked *fox fire*, a type of illusion that took on the physical properties of the object. The red flames flashed blue, and then disappeared to reveal an arrow in the palm of Raaza's hand.

He was getting a lot better with his magic. For a long time, the only thing he could create was gold coins.

Raaza nocked the fox fire arrow and then shot it at a cloud. He hit the side of the vapors, dispelling the target with a semi-skilled shot. Then he waved his hand again, created *another* fox fire arrow, and shot a second time.

Then he glanced over at us all with a smirk. "Seems more useful than some wind, if you ask me."

Knovak wore an expression that screamed, *Are you kidding me? That's it?* He huffed and dramatically rolled his eyes. "If wind is useful, then my magic should be twice as good." He aimed his bow and then fired.

Unicorn arcanists evoked force—just an invisible blast of magic.

When Knovak evoked his magic while firing, the arrow tumbled through the air, half-shattered, and then collided with the target in such an awkward manner, I wondered if it would've hurt anyone upon impact.

The class was silent for a few seconds afterward.

Then Raaza laughed. He even snorted, his chuckling became so hard.

Professor Jijo cringed a bit as he walked over and picked up the broken arrow. "Now, now. Wind works with projectiles because it eliminates resistance. The wind *engulfs* the arrow, and carries it along. Your *force* carries nothing—it just *pushes*. So, just like the arcanists who evoke terror, you shouldn't use your evocation with the projectiles. You should use your evocation on your target first, to weaken their ability to dodge properly."

Knovak's shoulders slumped slightly.

"Unicorns are also weaker creatures," Raaza chimed in, for seemingly no reason whatsoever. "Like, tier two? Maybe even tier one? Trying to combine their magic with any weapon feels like a waste of time."

Knovak shot the other man a glare that could kill.

But that didn't stop Raaza from chortling. He returned to using fox fire to create arrows.

Professor Jijo held up a finger as he paced behind everyone again. "Clever arcanists can use weaker magic to great effect. Never underestimate the power of creative thinking. Now, let's continue to combine our magic with our archery skills, shall we?"

I set Twain on the grass, grabbed my bow and another arrow, and quickly glanced around.

Raaza's fox fire *was* useful. The ability to infinitely create ammo whenever needed was a boon. But we already had all the arrows we needed here.

Nasbit's evocation was slow and terrible. He could create little pebbles? Or something? It wasn't useful.

Both Nini and my brother evoked terror. And if we were shooting at live targets—like highwaymen who were trying to rob us—their magic would be the best. I could terrorize the robbers and then shoot them while they were immobilized. But the clouds couldn't feel terror.

Knovak's force was even worse. And he did have the weakest eldrin here.

Phila's evocation was the best for this scenario.

I closed my eyes and thought about the threads of magic that connected me to everyone else's creatures. I tugged on Phila's coatl magic, and my forehead burned as a snake with wings appeared in my blank arcanist star.

When I opened my eyes, I noticed that Twain had transformed from an orange kitten into a corn snake with parrot wings. He was an exact duplicate of Tenoch.

With my new magic, I nocked an arrow, took aim at a cloud, and then evoked wind as I fired. Just like with Phila, my arrow was carried along and shot through the air without trouble. I blasted a cloud target, no problem at all.

"That was amazing," Sorin called out. "Gray, your mimic powers are really useful."

Again, Raaza huffed. "They're not *that* great."

But my shoulders twitched slightly, like my body wanted to go back to using the jarmakee style. I ignored the urge, determined to push the influences of the Death Lord away. Everything would be fine—I just had to continue learning.

CHAPTER 14

FIGHTING BACK

The sun set behind the mountain peaks, casting a warm golden glow across the sky. Learning the basics of archery had been more amusing than I had originally thought. The dying sunlight created long shadows over the field, but everyone still seemed enthusiastic about the subject matter, including the professor.

Professor Jijo clapped his hands, and we collectively lowered our bows.

"We didn't involve our eldrin today because we don't need any accidents," the professor said. Then he held up his arm and his nimbus dragon soared straight to him, landed on his elbow and perched there. "It takes time to master a new skill. Once you're more confident shooting, we'll incorporate your eldrin and their ability to evoke magic as well."

My brother raised his hand.

Jijo pointed to him before Sorin was even halfway done with the gesture.

"What about arcanists who merge with their eldrin?" Sorin chuckled as he added, "I'm not going to shoot Thurin while we're fighting as one. And together, I feel a lot... stronger."

The professor snapped his fingers. "That's exactly why. When reaper and knightmare arcanists merge with their eldrin, they gain additional strength and power. You will fire your bow differently—which is why you *must* learn the fundamentals first."

Even Captain Leon had seemed insistent on learning the fundamentals. He had us exercise whenever he taught *Combat Arts*. I wondered how useful training basic skills were, but considering both professors were talented arcanists, I figured they had to be correct.

"Did you see how well I did?" Phila asked as she turned to Nasbit. "I never imagined I would enjoy archery so much."

Nasbit glanced around, as though confused she was speaking to him. When it finally became obvious that she had spoken to no one else, Nasbit cleared his throat and said, "Archery competitions are quite the popular event. If you wanted, I'm sure you could compete with the best of them."

"Maybe I will." Phila tapped her lower lip as she turned to glance over at her eldrin. The little coatl waited patiently at the edge of the grass. When she waved him over, Tenoch slithered across the grass, his parrot wings half open as he went.

"My arcanist," he said, practically breathless from his haste to reach her. "What a thrilling day! Until this class, you never seemed interested in practicing your evocation. Now you've done it so much! The professor really motivated you to improve your skills."

Phila giggled as she held her yew bow close. "I hadn't thought about it like that, Tenoch. That's a good point..."

Once everyone had put their weapons away on the training racks, I glanced to the far end of the field. The second-year students had remained throughout most of the class, watching as we did our training. They were gone now, but I wondered what had kept them around for so long.

"Are you ready, Gray?" Sorin asked, jerking me from my thoughts.

I nodded once. "Yeah."

"Why is Dad coming to the Academy, by the way?" My brother stepped close and lowered his voice as he asked, "You're not in trouble, are you?"

"No." I offered a shrug. "I just wanted to see him. And tell him everything that's going on."

Sorin stared at me for a long time. He was slightly taller, and after a few seconds of silence, it was all I could think about. Weren't we twins? Why couldn't we be identical?

"You *want* to see Dad?" Sorin finally asked, clearly baffled.

"Yes," I replied, curt. "It's not that weird."

"It's weird for you."

I rubbed the base of my neck. "Look, maybe I've had several near-death experiences lately and I just want to make sure I have nothing to feel guilty about, ya know? Just in case."

That sounded worse than I meant it.

Sorin frowned, his body tense.

But then Nini and her reaper, Waste, came over. She smiled as she fixed her glasses. "What a class." She grabbed Sorin's arm with both of hers. "Aren't you hungry?"

"I'm always hungry," Sorin muttered. Then he smiled down at her. "I hope we have some kind of fish for dinner tonight."

Nini giggled as she nodded in agreement. But then Sorin shot me a quick glance, obviously still worried about my wellbeing. I shrugged it away and then headed for Twain. He was curled into a tight little orange circle on the edge of the grass, sleeping so hard, he didn't even realize class was over. I scooped my mimic eldrin into my arms and he groggily blinked his eyes out of sync.

"Hm?"

"Time to go," I whispered. "And I need you awake and alert for tonight, okay? We're going to do some dreamwalking."

"Oh." Twain yawned and stretched, his little claws poking out of his toes. "You can count on me."

I barely paid attention at dinner.

We ate, and then we headed back to our dorms. Ashlyn and Exie still hadn't returned, which meant Phila and Nini headed off alone, leaving me, my brother, Raaza, Knovak, and Nasbit to our man cave.

Everyone disrobed, and we dressed for sleeping, but—for some reason—the others refused to switch off the lanterns. I wanted to experiment with Professor Helmith's dream-manipulating magic, but I also didn't want to do it in front of everyone else.

I sat on my bed, within the circle of beds, listening to the others talk, trying to engage as little as possible.

Twain clung to my shoulder, occasionally moving around with the awkward grace of a kitten, his rump sometimes in my face as he attempted to find a comfortable position.

My brother's knightmare stood like a hollow suit of armor by the door. Sorin kept his nose in a small notebook, writing notes on something, though I couldn't read what he was jotting down.

Raaza and his kitsune both sat on Raaza's bed. He whispered to his eldrin more than to the others, petting the little fox whenever the flames at her feet flared. Since it was *fox fire*, it burned nothing, not even the highly flammable bedding.

Knovak stood by his wardrobe, placing certain clothes together, as though planning out his week. His unicorn, Starling, pointed with his horn, gesturing to things that matched.

The only arcanist here who didn't have his eldrin was Nasbit. He poked through various books, most of which he had gathered from the library after dinner.

"What are you doing over there?" Raaza asked, eyeing Nasbit. "You've been reading the same page over and over again."

Nasbit glanced up from his book. "Oh. Well. I was reading about various forms of archery, including the bizarre style Gray demonstrated during class."

"You seem *really* interested in archery all of a sudden."

Miko swished her fox tail as she whirled around to face Nasbit. "Are you going to focus on learning the ways of the bow?"

Nasbit huffed a laugh. Then he stared at the book. "Well... I thought it wouldn't hurt to learn something. Perhaps I could use one of these styles... If Gray can pick it up from his dream, it shouldn't be too hard."

That surprised me. Nasbit wanted to learn to fire a bow?

My brother sat straight in his bed, his whole body tense. "Wait. Nasbit —are you interested in archery because Phila is? Are you trying to help her?"

"W-What? No. Of course not." Nasbit shifted around on his mattress until his back faced the rest of us. "I... I told you. I was reading up about the old technique Gray used. Nothing else."

Everyone else in the room exchanged glances. Knovak smiled coyly as he sorted another outfit. In a casual manner, he said, "I think Phila would like someone to practice with. She seemed eager to learn."

Nasbit said nothing.

"She doesn't want someone to practice with," Raaza chimed in, his tone much harsher. "She wants a capable arcanist who knows what they're doing. Trust me—Phila will have more respect for Nasbit if he shows up to class and *decimates* some clouds." As if to make his point, Raaza punched his pillow as he said the last few words.

His kitsune leapt on top of the wounded pillow afterward, playfully growling as she bit at the edges of the case.

"You're always so gruff and uncouth," Knovak said. He didn't even look at the other man as he continued, "Not everyone is as impressed with sheer violence as you are."

"That's right," Starling said with a snort and swish of his tail. "It's unbecoming."

Sorin scratched his chin and said, "You know, Knovak has a point. Raaza, why are you so excited whenever any of the professors bring up using our magic for fighting? You've been fixated on it since we arrived at Astra Academy."

"Tsk. *Apparently*, I'm the only one here who grew up in a world of strife," Raaza snapped. He touched the scars on his face. They weren't too deep, but one was over his eyebrow, and another over his lip—four in total, like claw marks. "All of you don't seem to understand..."

"Understand what?" My brother leaned forward. "Did someone hurt you?"

Raaza glowered at him. With a sneer, he said, "My homeland was absorbed by the nation of Sellix. *Everyone* there is fighting. We have a king, technically, but he's *weak*. All his generals run the show, and anyone with power just claims title and land, and no one can say anything about it."

That was interesting. On my home island of Haylin, nothing that dramatic ever happened. It was quiet and peaceful, with only one arcanist.

Raaza huffed. "All our *lords*"—he said the word with a hefty dose of sarcasm—"are just arcanists with wealth and power. They're not even confirmed by the king."

"That's not how it's supposed to work," Nasbit interjected. "The power of the crown is meant to confer noble status."

"I know, *fool*." Raaza grabbed his crumpled pillow and fluffed it for a minute. "I'm saying no one in Sellix cares anymore. Those with power—the arcanists who can fight—get to do whatever they want, and everyone else just stays quiet about it all. I figured, if I came to Astra Academy, and managed to bond with a mystical creature, I could learn to be powerful..."

Nasbit closed his book. "You want revenge?"

"I want those thugs masquerading as lords to take a long walk off a short pier," Raaza said, practically shouting.

Sorin held up both his hands. His knightmare even walked over, Thurin's shadow armor clinking with each step.

"Okay, take a breath," Sorin said in a calm and slow tone. "We don't need to yell. I think I understand why you're upset."

Knovak closed his wardrobe and then took a seat on his mattress. "Did a specific one of these so-called lords harm you?"

"I don't want to talk about it," Raaza whispered. His eyes were dark and distant as he rested on his bed. He stared at the ceiling as he muttered, "I just want to get stronger. I want to have control. I want to protect the people I care about."

The last bit resonated with me.

I needed to get stronger, too. For the same reason—perhaps more than Raaza. I had Death Lord cultists after me...

Nasbit set his book on his nightstand. "Perhaps we should all get some sleep."

"Good idea," I finally said, chiming in. "Let's snuff the lanterns and get some shut eye."

Twain chuckled, his little kitten body on my shoulder practically shaking with delight.

Thurin manipulated the darkness in the corners of the room. Tendrils of shadows slithered to the many lanterns and extinguished the flames, blanketing the whole dorm room in night.

Starling nickered as he trotted for the back window. He stepped onto the sill and then headed along the branch to the treehouse.

Once everyone was settled, I held my breath and waited.

As soon as they were asleep, I would transform Twain into an ethereal whelk... And then I would attempt to speak with Death Lord Deimos.

CHAPTER 15

CRACKS IN THE CAGE

It didn't take long for the others to fall asleep. My brother's even breathing, and Raaza's snoring, were telltale signs. Once I heard their symphony of slumber, I sat up on my bed and shook Twain awake.

He stretched, and yawned, and then rolled onto his back. With a paw, he patted his belly. "Scratch me," he whispered.

"It's weird when you command me like that," I said.

"Your little nails feel nice. My claws are too sharp."

I scratched his fuzzy tummy for a short moment before placing my eldrin on the stone floor. "Okay, enough. I need dream manipulation powers, so I'm going to transform you into an ethereal whelk."

Twain frowned, his whiskers drooping. "Fine. But at some point, I want to be a big dragon again. I like it better when I'm gigantic and intimidating." He twitched his ears and purred. "I was running around the Academy as an abyssal dragon when you were fighting Deimos. That was so fun."

"All right. We'll do it again. At some point. I promise."

Twain purred in response.

I closed my eyes, and felt the many threads of magic in the Academy. There were the standard eldrin of the people near me—and even the abyssal dragon, from Death Lord Deimos—but I had to really search for distant creatures. Astra Academy had hundreds of arcanists, after all, and many of their magical threads were a mystery to me.

But I would never forget Professor Helmith's.

Her ethereal whelk, Ushi, had transformed from an iridescent sea snail into her true form... And I couldn't wait to see Twain as a true form ethereal whelk. When I found the string of magic that led back to Ushi, I tugged on it.

My forehead burned as my arcanist mark shifted. I opened my eyes and watched as Twain's orange kitten body bubbled and shifted. In a matter of seconds, he went from small to medium sized. His fur hardened into a spiral shell, and his coloration changed completely. He resembled a puddle of water with oil across it—a rainbowy hue of magic and wonder.

He glowed rather brightly, which I hadn't considered. I glanced over my shoulder, hoping the others wouldn't wake. In my desperation to remain incognito, I grabbed Twain and pulled him under my blankets.

But Twain's body in the shell... was just a sea snail with tentacles.

That was the form of a standard ethereal whelk.

A true form ethereal whelk looked like a dream given flesh. It had the body parts of several animals, all merged together to form a single being of wonder.

But Twain wasn't that. He was a standard ethereal whelk, and it irritated me slightly. I grabbed his shell and rubbed the spiral shape with my palm.

"Why aren't you transforming all the way?" I whispered.

Under the blankets, with Twain's body glowing bright, it felt like we were camping all over again.

"I *have* transformed," Twain replied, his voice identical to Ushi's. He wiggled his tentacles. "See?"

"No—transform into Helmith's true form eldrin."

"Um. I don't think I can." Twain's snail body sagged. "This is the only form I can take."

I frowned as I turned him around, examining his shell from all angles. He was surprisingly light—like he weighed almost nothing at all. That made sense. Ethereal whelks could float through the air, and supposedly, they were made from nothing but light.

"If you were a true form mimic, do you think you could transform into a true form ethereal whelk?" I asked.

Twain used his tentacles to shrug.

That was disappointing. If I had access to Helmith's ability to permanently put someone to sleep, perhaps I could handle the Death Lord without involving anyone else. That way, Professor Helmith wouldn't ever have to put herself in danger on my behalf.

I needed to find a way to transform Twain.

But that would have to wait.

I rested back on my bed and placed Twain on my chest. "Okay, here's the plan. You watch over me while I sleep, and if anything happens, wake me."

Twain gently cuddled me with his tentacles. "I'll protect you, Gray."

I smiled as I patted his shell. Then I closed my eyes again and forced myself to drift off into the realm of sleep. Nothing about the process was new to me. I had dreamwalked hundreds of times before, so when I opened my eyes, I knew exactly what to expect.

Which was why I was shocked when the dream wasn't anything like before.

I sat up and found myself in a dark coliseum. Somehow—perhaps through dream logic—it was underground. The ceiling high above was dark and marked at a few locations with stones jutting down.

The stands were mostly empty, and I stood between two benches.

The oval coliseum had stands that overlooked the fighting pit in the center. It wasn't a normal arena, where the fighters were cheered and the stands filled with people from all walks of life. The arcanists in the pit came out of caged areas, their eldrin chained to them, so neither could leave easily.

In the fog of the dream, it was difficult to make out details.

I heard the rumble of booing, though. People threw things from the stands, their anger infectious. They hated the arcanists in the arena, and when the clash of iron rang out through the coliseum, there was cheering.

I rubbed the side of my head, confused by the spectacle. It seemed the audience *wanted* the gladiators to die. I had never heard of something like that. Most coliseums I knew of were for sportsman-like competition.

After I took a breath, I held up a hand. I could manipulate the dream

—and change my surroundings—but I paused once I realized the stone of the coliseum resembled the stone found in places through the Academy. Black rocks that shimmered as if perpetually wet were dotted throughout the coliseum. Some walls were made of the material, and even several of the benches.

That was odd.

The cheering and bloodlust echoed all around me. If I could see the fights, perhaps this would've been interesting, but all I sensed was the violence and hate.

"Mimic arcanist," a voice said, so gruff and hostile, it caused a shiver to shoot down my spine.

I turned on my heel and caught my breath.

A stone cage was built into the stands. It was bizarre, and clearly a product of the dreamscape. The bars of the cage were fused with the ground, and the three walls of the cell were attached to the stands and even the awning above.

The interior of the cage was steeped in darkness so thick I couldn't see the individual inside. Despite that, I knew who it was.

The cage was a representation of Professor Helmith's true form magic. Her ability to trap Death Lord Deimos in a permanent slumber clearly took the form of this imprisonment.

I walked to the stone bars, the dream coliseum solidifying more around me. The smell of sweat and burnt flesh permeated the space. Everything was cold, and the air thick. When I stopped in front of Deimos's prison, the scent of blood mixed into the aroma, creating a terrible musk.

What was this place? It didn't look like anything I had dreamt of before.

"Release me," Deimos commanded from within the cage. "Keeping me here only delays the inevitable."

He always sounded confident, no matter his situation or the hand dealt to him.

I ignored him, though. Instead, I examined the bars of the cage. Obviously, something about his presence was influencing me. I knew an archery style I had never even heard of, and my dreams were filled with foreign people and places. This was all Deimos's doing, I'd bet my life on it.

So I focused on the stonework of the prison, and it didn't take me long to realize there were cracks at the base of the structure. They spread across the stone like spiderwebs—tiny and subtle, but clearly there.

Was Helmith's magic not strong enough to hold Deimos? His abyssal dragon magic was powerful, just as the headmaster had stated.

What was I supposed to do about this?

"It's only a matter of time before I free myself."

I glanced up, shocked to find Deimos standing just a few inches away on the other side of the bars. This was the first time I was just *next to him*, like we were chums having a pleasant chat. He was just as intimidating as I remembered, his posture stiff, as though he were tense and ready to strike at any moment.

He wore armor made of white bone and dark gray metal. Up close, I realized it was intricately woven together, forming "scales" of bone that accented his formidable physique. The iron and crude steel were interesting in a horrific way.

Parts of Deimos's armor were just... hooked into him? I stared for a long moment, almost disbelieving what I saw. It was as if the armor had been sewn onto parts of his body. Was that to prevent it from being removed? Was that even effective? He wasn't actively bleeding, and I wondered why.

The Death Lord had his black hair slicked back, showing his arcanist mark. The seven-point star was laced with the creepy form of the abyssal dragon.

His eyes were dark—nearly black—but a hint of yellow circled his pupils. What a strange coloration.

Deimos didn't seem to mind me staring. He just met my gaze with something icy. In the resulting silence, I could've sworn he was bored with me.

I didn't know why, but the fact that he was taller—like my brother— bothered me more than anything else. I wondered if there was any way I could just kill him inside his cage, but I didn't know where to start. This was just a fragment of his soul, and I had fought it before. Even when I damaged him, Deimos seemed unconcerned.

"Mimic arcanist," he said again.

"Gray," I corrected. "My name is Gray."

Deimos clicked his tongue in dismissal. "Tch. Never choose your name if you can use a title instead, child."

Child?

Right. Deimos was ancient.

"Listen, *old man*," I said, unable to restrain my sarcasm. "Why don't you just sit tight and stop trying to break out of *this*." I gestured to the cage.

"I have promises to fulfill—arcanists to lead—and you're standing in the way."

With a chuckle, I said, "Obviously, no one wants you around. You were locked in the abyssal hells, and now you're locked away in a dream. Maybe you should take a hint and stop."

I knew being sardonic wasn't the best way to handle this, but what was I supposed to say? At least I could amuse myself while in this dreamworld. Then again, perhaps agitating him wasn't the best move.

Despite my goading, though, Deimos remained unfazed. He didn't even appear bothered or upset.

"I never relent," Deimos stated, his tone low. "That's why they're afraid—why they're *all* afraid—because they know they can never win."

"Well, I would really appreciate it if you at least took a break." I placed my hand on the cage and imagined it strengthening. Perhaps *normal* ethereal whelk magic could fix some of the cracks. "I didn't want to get wrapped up in this, ya know. You forced all this on me, and it'd be great if you just let me attend Astra Academy in peace."

I tried to manipulate the dream—this prison—to be stronger than before. However, the more I focused, the more I realized it wasn't working. Helmith's true form magic was just stronger than anything I had access to.

It was like trying to repair a brick wall with water. Splashing the holes in the structure wasn't going to do anything. It could even make things worse.

I removed my hand from the cage.

"Release me," Deimos commanded again. "And I'll leave you and your Academy alone."

I huffed a single laugh. "Nice try."

"I have no interest in your education or that pathetic institution. I must correct the balance of the abyssal hells—and then I'll take my rightful place as ruler. Just as I was promised millennia ago."

"Uh-huh." I rubbed my ear and then shrugged. "That's great. Look, you can't trick me that easily. I'm not letting you out of here. Ever. And once I find the magic to permanently seal you away, I'm going to use it."

I thought this would anger the Death Lord, but again, he made no indication that I had rattled him. If anything, it was the opposite. The man smirked.

"You got something to say?" I asked.

"You act as though I'm a fiend. It amuses me."

I shook my head. "You are."

"Believe whatever you want to believe, because I don't mind being the villain in your story—you're just a corpse in mine."

I huffed another laugh and then turned on my heel. Big talk. However, if Deimos ever got free, he would probably make good on that statement. If I managed to keep him confined, though... These were all empty threats.

The roar of the coliseum shook me. I had almost forgotten where I was. The dream maintained the details, right down to the thick and sour smells. This was more of a memory than a proper dreamscape.

Something Deimos once experienced.

However, there was a second reason I had visited my dream—more than just repairing the cage. I slowly turned back around, wondering if I had ruined my chance to get a straight answer.

Death Lord Deimos remained near the bars. He watched me with his keen gaze. What was he thinking?

"I have a question," I said. "You once... mentioned you would harm my mother's soul. I need to know—did you?"

CHAPTER 16

THE CLASS TOGETHER AGAIN

For a long moment after I voiced my question, Deimos said nothing. I figured he wouldn't answer me, so I turned away, cursing myself for not opening with the question first. I shouldn't have taunted the man.

"I did not harm your mother," the Death Lord eventually stated, surprising me.

I whirled back around, my heart hammering. "R-Really?"

"While it would be amusing to torment you with a lie about how I made her suffer, the truth is I couldn't find her soul. She was either reincarnated or was consumed by the elder creatures who dwell in the depths of the abyssal hells."

I stepped closer to the cage, my chest twisting in agony. "You don't know which?"

In a tone that bordered on bored, Deimos said, "I do not. I searched for her, hoping I could use her against you—to force you to cooperate— but I failed to locate her."

Flustered, and unsure what to do with my anxiety, I paced in a small circle for a moment. Then I ruffled my hair and rubbed the side of my neck. When I glanced back at the stone prison, the Death Lord still seemed completely disinterested.

"Why tell me that?" I walked back over to the bars. "Why not lie? I mean, what's there to be gained by just *telling me* what happened?"

Deimos lifted an eyebrow. Then he coughed a laugh. "It appears my thoughts are bleeding into your dreams, child." He motioned to the coliseum with a quick jut of his chin. "Eventually you will see if I'm lying. And if you catch me in a falsehood, all future threats become meaningless."

I hadn't thought of that. With a hesitant glance, I examined the bizarre dreamscape. This *was* Deimos's memory, at some level. Would I have dreams where he searched for my mother in the abyssal hells?

Death Lord Deimos placed a hand on one of the stone bars and glared down at me. "So when I say I'll make you regret holding me here, I hope you realize I mean every word."

Someone shook me awake.

In an instant, I was jerked upright, my consciousness ripped from the dreamscape and back into the waking world. It was so sudden, and startling, I almost shouted, but instead, I stared into a set of gray-blue eyes that resembled my own.

Sorin sat on the edge of my bed, both his large hands on my shoulders. I shook my head and pushed one of his hands away, fearful he would touch the shapeshifting weapon I kept on my body.

"Gray?" he asked. "Are you okay?"

I ran a hand down my face, clearing away a bucketload of sweat. Why was I so anxious? "I'm fine." Then I glanced around.

Everyone was awake. Nasbit, Raaza—even Knovak, who remained aloof, seemed concerned. I met their gazes and then spotted Twain, still in his ethereal whelk form, resting on the mattress next to me.

"What's going on?" I asked.

My brother furrowed his brow. "You tell us. You were thrashing around while you slept. When I checked on you, your skin was pale and you were sweating. Gray, you don't look well."

Twain wiggled his tentacles. "I was getting worried, too."

"Were you bothered by the Death Lord?" Nasbit asked. He grabbed his notebook, scooted to the edge of his bed, and held his pencil poised over the parchment. His brown hair was squished to the side, held up in an awkward wave. "I'll take notes about everything."

Raaza leapt to the foot of his bed, the only one of us who opted not to wear a nightshirt. I didn't realize until then, but the man had faint scars on his chest that matched the claw-like markings on his face. "Tell us what happened," Raaza demanded. "I need to know."

"You're not going to get possessed again, are you?" Knovak stood by his bed, his arms crossed over his silky nightshirt. "I mean, I think we shouldn't rule that out as a possibility. We should... probably have a plan in place in case something happens. A failsafe, if you will."

My brother ignored their commentary and gently patted my back. His eyes calmed me more than usual. They reminded me of our mother, and knowing she hadn't been harmed put me at ease.

"I had a dream about an underground coliseum," I muttered. "It was just... really intense." When I faced Sorin, I forced a smile. "Deimos was in the dream, but he didn't hurt me." I shot Knovak a glower. "And he's not going to possess me. You don't have to worry."

"I still think we should have a contingency in place," Knovak whispered. He glanced away, his shoulders stiff.

"Heh." Raaza dismissively waved his hand. "It's not like *you're* going to do anything if Gray is possessed. You were already defeated by Deimos, and unicorns are so much weaker than abyssal dragons."

"*I can get stronger,*" Knovak snapped. He stepped around his bed, his fingers digging into his biceps as he held himself. "You'll see!"

"Don't say things that are blatantly untrue. You'll never get strong enough to handle a master dragon arcanist."

Sorin stood and held up his hands. "C'mon. Enough of that. We don't need to argue amongst ourselves." He stepped between the many beds in the room, grinning at the others like he hoped they would do the same in return. No one did.

"I do think arguing is pointless," Nasbit eventually muttered.

"Yes. It is." Sorin clapped his hands once. "*Together we improve, achieve, and strive—in collaboration, our greatness shall thrive.*"

"That's how we'll defeat Death Lord Deimos," Raaza murmured, pointing to my brother. "Deimos will cringe to death hearing Sorin's rhymes."

Nasbit wrote something in his notebook. Then he slid his gaze over to

Raaza, a slight frown on his round face. "I enjoy Sorin's positive disposition and dedication to poetry. You shouldn't belittle it."

"Yeah," I said as I threw my legs over the side of the bed. "You're a grump when you wake up in the middle of the night, Raaza. Lay off my brother and take a nap, ya rube."

Twain giggled. "He reminds me of an angry porcupine."

After a short sigh, Sorin hung his head. I immediately understood his frustration. He wanted us to all get along, and it seemed we were having problems with that. Perhaps it was because everyone was woken up in the middle of their sleep...

It was my fault.

So I should make it better.

I stood. "Hey, listen." Then I glanced around, and I met everyone's gaze. "I really appreciate everything you all have done for me. Thank you all for waking me up and checking on me."

The others were quiet.

Twain's body bubbled and shifted until he melted back into his orange kitten form. The arcanist mark on my forehead transformed back into a blank star.

"You don't need to thank us," Nasbit said, breaking the silence. "I think we should work on our camaraderie—it may prevent disaster in the future. Raaza, that especially means you."

Raaza exhaled. After scratching some of the scars on his chest, he leaned back in his bed. "I've never shared a room with other people like this before. Actually... if I'm going to be honest, I've never been around this many people my age. I spent a lot of time working for thugs."

"It shows," Knovak quipped.

"Whoa, whoa!" Sorin moved over to Raaza's bed and took a seat next to the man. With a smile, my brother wrapped an arm around Raaza's shoulders and pulled him close. "You're in good company! You see, Gray and I have been together forever. Since birth. It can be hard sometimes, sharing a space with someone, but I wouldn't trade it for anything. You need to embrace all the fun times in life."

Raaza frowned, his eyes on Sorin's arm. He squirmed until he freed himself of my brother's grip. "Uh-huh. Well, I'll try. I suppose it would be better if I had... arcanist friends..."

"That's the spirit!"

I rubbed my face, my skin hot. Sorin was a little much at times.

But it was reassuring to hear he appreciated my company.

I had taken my father's love for granted, but it occurred to me then that perhaps I had taken my brother's for granted as well.

"Well, if nothing bad happened in Gray's dream, I suggest we all head back to bed." Nasbit set his notebook down on his nightstand. He glanced between us. "We all need a good night's rest if we're going to learn about mystical creatures tomorrow in class."

Oh, that was right. I had almost forgotten.

Tomorrow we would attend Professor Helmith's class, only she wouldn't be there to teach it.

Her husband would be.

In the morning, I headed for the classroom with everyone else. Raaza, Knovak, and Nasbit seemed tired, and I didn't blame them. Phila and Nini weren't, though. And the two of them chatted a bit as we walked, much to my surprise.

"I went to the library," Phila said, her eyes bright. "They have dozens of books on the subject of archery. Did you know that roc arcanists are some of the best archers and riflemen in the world? It's because of their wind evocation."

Nini tapped the tips of her fingers together. "Oh? Really? I... uh... I read about famous reaper arcanists, but I don't think I should share my findings in polite society."

I was about to chime into the conversation—and talk about how most reaper arcanists I knew of had been pirates or bounty hunters—but I stopped myself short when I spotted two individuals in front of the classroom door.

Ashlyn Kross and Exie Lolian—the last two arcanists in our class.

Ever since the disaster at Ashlyn's cotillion, I hadn't heard from her. My first thought was to run over and ask if she had married her sad sack of a fiancé yet, but I dreaded the answer. I still had hopes to convince her father I was a better suitor, but if she had already wed, that would be a moot point.

Ashlyn had her blonde hair in a tight ponytail, and she stood with her arms crossed and her feet set apart. From a glance, she seemed irritated. Or perhaps guarded. Her athletic frame and build almost made her seem like she was ready to pounce on the first person who got close.

Exie was the exact opposite. Her curly chestnut hair hung loose around her face. She had the smoothest, most lustrous skin in class, and an hourglass figure she decided to accentuate by wearing a belt over her robes. No one else did that, but Exie really wasn't like anyone else here.

Exie's eldrin, the erlking fairy, Rex, fluttered around her head. He was so small, he could fly through the halls of the Academy without a problem.

Ashlyn's typhoon dragon, on the other hand, was too large for that. Her dragon would likely be waiting for us in the classroom, since he would have to take the treehouse walkways to get anywhere.

Phila brightened when she saw the other two girls. "Ash! Ex! You're both back." She hurried over and gave the other girls a brief hug. Then she stepped away and lightly clapped her hands together once. "I was so worried neither of you would return."

"I don't want to talk about it," Ashlyn stated. The heat in her words was unmistakable. "For the record, my father tried to convince me to stay home, but then I reminded him that my brother wouldn't have stayed away from the Academy in a similar situation, and only *then* did my father allow me to return."

Exie fluffed her brown hair. "My father gives me whatever I want. I told him I wanted to return to class, and he sent me here straight away."

Phila nodded, and the instant Exie was done speaking, she said, "Well, I know Ashlyn's cotillion didn't go as planned, but I enjoyed everything beforehand. So much so that I went home, and told my family, and they agreed I could have my own cotillion. Isn't that lovely?"

Nasbit groaned so loud it almost startled me.

"I already had my cotillion," Exie stated as she rolled her eyes. "Why has everyone here waited so long? You're supposed to do it once you become an arcanist."

"We didn't really have them where I grew up." Phila then motioned to our whole class. "And I think it would be wonderful if it was just all of us for my cotillion—right here in the Academy. I don't want to risk any, um, villainous arcanists or bizarre gateways to the abyssal hells."

Ashlyn narrowed her eyes into a glare.

"Sorry," Phila said. "I didn't mean to speak poorly about your event."

"It's fine." Ashlyn turned sharply on her heel. "Let's just get to class." She motioned to the door. "I don't want to talk about any parties or celebrations. I just want to get this over with."

She never looked in my direction. It was obviously a purposeful decision. I silently cursed the abyssal hells, wondering what she was thinking.

Everyone filed into the classroom after her declaration, and I followed my brother inside. Ashlyn avoided my gaze, even as I walked by. That was fine—I'd speak to her eventually. Perhaps once I had all the Death Lord stuff under control.

CHAPTER 17

THE NEW PROFESSOR HELMITH

W e entered the classroom and ambled over to our seats.

The five long tables in class were familiar places, even if we hadn't been at Astra Academy long. I took my seat at the front table, placed Twain down, and then faced the chalkboard at the head of the classroom. The professor's desk was clear, and nothing had been written on the board.

After a big yawn, Twain curled up into a tight ball of fur and purred.

Knovak, Nasbit, and Raaza all sat together at another table, which was new. Normally they sat apart, but now it seemed they wanted to chat. Ashlyn, Phila, and Exie took their usual seats, all clustered together. Since Sorin, Nini, and I sat together, we left two whole tables open, making our class seem small.

The window at the back of the room had a walkway that led to the redwood treehouse. One by one, the larger creatures entered class. First Ecrib, Ashlyn's dragon, and then Brak, Nasbit's sandstone golem.

The stomp of Brak's steps really woke me. I sat a little straighter and turned around to catch sight of the golem lumbering over to its arcanist. Although Brak didn't have a face to emote with, it was clear from the way the golem sped up its steps that it wanted to be near Nasbit.

Brak stopped near Nasbit and then sat beside his chair. The golem fell to the stone floor with a *clunk*, practically rumbling Nasbit's desk.

"How are you?" Nasbit asked as he gently patted his eldrin. "Was the evening okay? Did you get along with all the other mystical creatures?"

Brak said nothing, but it was obvious Nasbit understood the golem's subtle gestures. When Brak tilted its head, Nasbit smiled.

"I'm glad it was pleasant," he said.

Made me wonder if they could speak telepathically to one another...

"What will we learn today?" Sorin asked as he placed his *Magical Bestiary* on the table in front of him. "I'm hoping we'll discuss true forms a bit more."

Nini poked at the rim of her glasses, her brow furrowed.

I glanced over my shoulder, only to catch sight of Ecrib staring straight at me. I was surprised, because of how aloof Ashlyn had been in the hallway, but Ecrib was clearly paying me all sorts of attention.

He was a large dragon hatchling—almost as big as a horse—with scales that came in every shade of blue imaginable. Fins dominated Ecrib's back, like he had stolen them from a whole gang of sharks. And when he moved, his sharp claws scraped the stone floor.

He was obviously a typhoon dragon, since he had no wings, and he had a set of gills, but I sometimes wondered what he would look like soaring through the clouds.

I met his stare for a long moment. Then I lifted an eyebrow.

Ecrib snorted, his pupils constricting into slits.

I shrugged in response. He discreetly pointed his reptilian snout to the classroom door. He clearly wanted me to get up so we could speak in private. Before I could act on that suggestion, the door opened inward to reveal our professor for today.

Professor Helmith.

Well, not *Rylee* Helmith. This time it was *Kristof* Helmith.

When he entered, everyone held their breath. There were no whispers or sounds of any kind as Kristof made his way to the professor's desk.

He wore Academy robes, but they didn't appear fitted for his body. He was too muscular for the outfit they had given him, and I suspected it was because they hadn't had enough time to get something tailored.

Professor Helmith had been injured, and Kristof had rushed back to the Academy to help, after all. This was all sudden and impromptu.

"Good morning, class," Kristof said, his tone confident, bordering on authoritative. "I will be your *Mystical Creatures* professor for the time being. My wife, Rylee, hasn't yet recovered fully, but rest assured, I'm quite knowledgeable on this subject matter."

He went straight for the chalkboard and wrote his name. Then Kristof wrote a series of points, the clack of the chalk on the board so hard, it sounded as though he was stabbing rather than writing.

"I'm not sure where Rylee left off, but I suspect she hasn't gone over the various types of dragons yet."

Ecrib perked his head up at the comment.

When Kristof turned on his heel, everyone sat a little straighter. The man had a neutral expression that showed neither interest nor boredom, and I wondered if he even liked the idea of teaching.

"As you can see," he said as he motioned to the arcanist mark on his forehead, "I'm a celestial dragon arcanist."

Exie made a noise that sounded like a cross between a gasp and an excited giggle. "Those are *so* rare!"

"They are," Kristof said matter-of-factly. Then he motioned to the back window.

A creature flew over the treehouse walkway, slow and steady, as though gliding on a leisurely breeze. It was a dragon—*Kristof's* dragon— but it was so large, I couldn't see it fully through the gigantic window.

The mighty beast had a body that resembled the night sky, with glittering stars and swirls of dark colors. It had a liquid-like form, where only a small portion was truly physical. I knew, because when the morning light passed through its chest and ribs, and spilled into the room, everything was covered in a watery shimmer.

The purple, blue, and indigo colors washed over everyone, and several people in class gasped in amazement.

The light filtered through the dragon's body in such a mystical way, it stole my breath. It was like staring up at the sun while underwater—the majesty of nature seen through a new lens. But that only lasted for a moment.

The celestial dragon flew off, allowing the sunlight to return in its full glory.

"Celestial dragons are mostly composed of starlight," Kristof said—again, his tone matter-of-fact, like this was all old news.

Everyone kept their attention on the back window, hoping to catch another glimpse of the massive, and wondrous, beast.

Kristof walked around the desk and continued his speech. "Celestial dragons are capable of teleportation, dream manipulation, and evoking crystals."

Dream manipulation?

I turned around in my seat, my heart hammering. I hesitantly raised my hand. When Kristof took note, he pointed to me. "Yes, Gray?"

"Can celestial dragons manipulate dreams like ethereal whelks?" I asked.

"They can, yes. However, unlike ethereal whelks, celestial dragons have no way to keep a person sleeping, or even induce sleep."

"But since it's a dragon—a tier four creature—celestial dragons are stronger than the whelks, right?" It hadn't occurred to me until this very moment, but perhaps I *could* strengthen the cage around Deimos...

Kristof nodded once. "Ethereal whelks vary in power based on the amount of magic they've consumed, but they're never as powerful as dragons or dragon-kin."

That made sense. Which meant I would just need to use Kristof's eldrin to help combat the Death Lord.

When I glanced down at Twain, he was smiling up at me.

Twain was already excited.

"I can be a dragon *and* help you," he whispered with a purr.

This was going to work out nicely. I would just have to try it out one of these nights when I had enough time to myself. Kristof's eldrin was so large, I doubted Twain could just transform into it while everyone slept in our dorm. The sheer size of the celestial dragon—even if it was mostly incorporeal—would lead to problems.

Perhaps at some point, when I had the showers to myself...

When it was obvious Kristof's dragon wouldn't be returning anytime soon, everyone turned back around and faced the chalkboard.

Exie fluffed her hair, but then realization struck. She leaned onto the table and widened her eyes. "Wait, you mean both you and Professor Helmith can manipulate dreams?"

Kristof's lips twitched into a slight frown. "I just said that, yes."

"Is that how you two met? You were dreamweaving together and then romance erupted?" Exie wistfully sighed. "That's beautiful."

"I... don't think we should be discussing that." Kristof turned and tapped his knuckles on the desk. "It's not important to the subject matter at hand."

"It's so adorable, though. Do you two share your dreams every night?" Exie softly exhaled as she practically melted onto her table. "That would be the most precious thing ever."

That comment seemed to quiet Kristof. He wasn't facing us anymore, but I got the distinct impression this was embarrassing him. Or perhaps he thought we were all randy youths who couldn't focus on a single subject.

Either or.

Although, I knew they didn't share dreams every night. Professor Helmith had seen *me* for most nights over several years. Clearly, she and Kristof did other things at night than just stare into each other's eyes while painting wondrous dreamscapes.

Nasbit cleared his throat and raised his hand. "Uh..."

After squaring his shoulders, Kristof turned around and pointed. "Yes?"

"I was wondering about dragons." Nasbit tapped his fingers on his textbook. "Not every variant is covered. For example, when I went to investigate *abyssal* dragons, I found nothing. Do you have information on them? I'd love to hear more."

"Abyssal dragons don't roam the countryside." Kristof returned to the chalkboard. "We're only going to discuss dragons you may have to deal with."

The room went dead silent after his statement. Kristof must've sensed the shift in mood, because he slowly glanced over his shoulder and examined everyone.

My brother leaned onto the table and muttered, "Gray, Nini, and I have all seen an abyssal dragon. In person." He waved his arms around, trying to convey how large it was. "And I saw its leg *cut off* from a portal closing on it." Sorin then rubbed the back of his neck. "I, uh, would like to learn more about abyssal dragons, too. Just in case we see it again—and it's angry about its missing limb."

Everyone waited, their eyes wide, as Kristof mulled over that bit of information.

Finally, our new professor said, "It's very unlikely you'll encounter the abyssal dragon again. But even if we do see one—" Kristof shot me a quick glance, and I sank a bit in my seat, "—you won't have to worry."

Raaza snorted back a single laugh. His kitsune leapt onto the table, her fiery paws bright, and also huffed out a laugh.

"I think it's our biggest worry," Knovak interjected. He patted his unicorn eldrin with a shaky hand. "Abyssal dragon magic is... powerful."

Kristof forced a smile. In a tone far fiercer and more determined than before, he stated, "There's more than one reason I'm here. *If* a Death Lord and their abyssal dragon appear, I'll be here to drive them back. I've been a mystic guardian for decades—fought the worst of the worst—and my celestial dragon magic has never failed me."

He held his hand out, and bits of sparkling dust emerged from the lines of his palms. The motes of magic drifted to the floor, but upon touching the stone, they exploded into crystal formations at least three feet high, sharp at the tip, and iridescent throughout. They crackled with power, practically sucking magic and moisture out of the air in equal amounts.

My eyes felt dry afterward, and I had to fight the urge to jump out of my seat.

This was his crystal evocation?

Impressive.

"I won't let any Death Lord harm the Academy." Kristof waved his hand, and the crystals broke apart into glittering dust before completely vanishing a moment later.

Nasbit rubbed his chin. He stared at where the crystals had been, and then turned his attention to the professor. "So... what if I'm just... *intellectually curious* about the dragons? I never said I wanted to fight them. I just want to know more about them."

That resulted in a long minute of silence.

Finally, Kristof sighed. "And that's a fair point. Unfortunately, we don't know much about the dragons outside of legend and myth." He returned to the chalkboard and began writing down the names of dragons in order of size. "So, while we can speculate, I don't have much to teach you. Instead of wasting time, I'll tell you all I know about the *other* dragons. Sound like a plan?"

The class muttered agreements and then pulled out their notebooks.

I felt the animosity our new professor had for me, especially in his speech and demonstration, but I shook off the feeling.

I would fix this. Now that I knew his dragon magic could help... This problem would be over shortly.

CHAPTER 18

IMPRESSIVE

After a riveting lesson on dragons, the time for our first break arrived.

Kristof set his chalk down and patted his hands together to clear the dust. He faced the class with a stern expression. "Your break begins now. I expect you all to take care of business and then be back in your seats before class resumes."

Murmurs of understanding lazily rolled through the room.

Sorin quickly stood, and Nini followed suit.

"We'll be right back," my brother said. Then he motioned to Nini with a tilt of his head. "We're going to... be right back," he awkwardly repeated.

I nodded once. "I heard you the first time."

Sorin and Nini headed for the door out of class. Nini's reaper silently hovered after her, practically a ghost. His scythe floated on the air, and the rusty blade almost chipped the doorframe, but Waste twirled the weapon to fit it just right.

I wondered how the reaper could see, considering he didn't have eyes. Or a face. Obviously, *magic* was the answer, but what kind of magic? Telekinesis? Or perhaps it was just invisible...

Exie and Ashlyn stood afterward, and then exited the room. Should I follow them? I decided against it.

Raaza and Knovak stood and walked to the back of the room. They peered out the back window, their necks craned backward in an attempt to get a better view of the sky. Were they looking for Kristof's celestial dragon?

With a playful giggle, Phila leapt from her seat. She walked over to Nasbit, her coatl eldrin close. Once by his side, Phila offered him a smile. Nasbit—who seemed at a loss for words—just grunted an incoherent greeting.

"My grandpa didn't want me leaving our family compound," Phila said matter-of-factly, and in my opinion, completely out of nowhere.

She wasn't talking to me, though. I sat at the next table over, but it wasn't like she was whispering.

Nasbit nodded, his eyes wide.

"So, I never got to go anywhere until I came of age." Phila maintained her bright smile. "But when I told my grandpa I wanted to go to the beach, he hired some men to move a bunch of sand and palm trees around until we had our own makeshift beach in the garden."

I almost laughed.

Phila continued, "I know you don't like cotillions, and I know Ashlyn's ended in misfortune, but it was still a shame you didn't join us."

With a nervous chuckle, Nasbit said, "Uh, well, thank you. I'm not sure why you're telling me this, though."

"I'm trying to say that, when I asked my family for my own cotillion, they said I had to remain at the Academy, but they would bring whatever I needed to have a wonderful time." Phila clasped her hands together. "So, I was thinking—what would it take to get you to attend a celebration? Is there a drink you love? A dish you prefer? Or perhaps an environment? We could get snow! I'm certain my family wouldn't mind bringing a whole bunch here."

I petted Twain and just listened to the conversation. I kept my attention on the chalkboard, attempting to hide my smile. Phila wanted Nasbit to attend her cotillion so much, she was going to turn the halls of Astra Academy into a winter wonderland?

Phila was either extremely kind, or she fancied Nasbit more than phoenixes fancied charberries.

"O-Oh, no," Nasbit mumbled. "I don't like the cold. Um. I don't need anything special. If it's important to you, I'll attend your cotillion. Just... don't expect me to dance. Or give a speech. Or socialize much, really."

"Speech?" Phila laughed into one hand. "I'm only inviting the arcanists of our class. Why would we need a speech?" She patted Nasbit's shoulder. "You're silly sometimes, but I'm so glad you'll attend. It would upset me if you were excluded."

"I'm pleased as well," her coatl said, fluffing his parrot-like feathers.

Nasbit tapped his fingers on the top of his table. "Oh. Good."

Then Phila hurried back to her seat, all smiles and joyful energy. Her cheery demeanor was a stark contrast to the book she opened, though. During our break, she read through *War Designs: The History of the Bow* and something about it seemed rather grim. Phila hummed as she read.

I was about to comment on all this to Twain, but before I could voice any of my thoughts, Ecrib snorted a bit of lightning. Then he turned and lumbered toward the back window, his scales glittering in the afternoon light.

Knovak and Raaza leapt out of the dragon's way as he climbed onto the redwood walkway. Then Ecrib shot me a backward glance. Did he want me to follow? If he did, why did he have to head to the treehouse? Heights weren't my favorite.

After a long sigh, I got up from my seat. Twain stood and leapt after me as I went straight for the window. The others in class seemed disinterested. Everyone took a seat to wait out the rest of the break.

I stepped up onto the windowsill and then out onto the wooden branch walkway. The wind howled by, taunting me with promises of falling. I shivered and attempted to not glance down. It had to be hundreds of feet to the mountainside below.

When were those architects going to change things around?

Probably not until Headmaster Venrover got his funding.

"Are you okay?" Twain asked with a tilt of his head.

"I'm fine. I just... get a little nervous around the edges." I pushed the dread from my thoughts as I headed along the branch. Ecrib wasn't difficult to spot. I slowly made my way over and rubbed my arms through my robes.

The walkway was wide, and the surface flat. Smaller branches grew off the main one, and I suspected I was perfectly safe, but my imagination clearly held a grudge against me. It made up all sorts of bizarre situations in which the wind threw me to my death.

Once I made it to Ecrib, I asked, "You want to speak?"

The typhoon dragon stood in the middle of the branch, his aquamarine scales flared. Then he pulled back his lips, revealing a whole row of fangs. "This is all *your* fault."

I lifted an eyebrow. "What's my fault?"

Twain puffed his orange fur. "Yeah! You better speak up."

"My arcanist's cotillion was ruined because of *you*." When Ecrib spoke the last word, a spark of lightning crackled around his mouth. "I don't know how or why, but I recognized the midnight waters that appeared during the celebration. Those gate fragments were activated because of your presence."

That was true.

I crossed my arms. "I didn't bring any gate fragments to the cotillion."

Ecrib growled. "My arcanist didn't tell her father all the details, and now things in her family are strained worse than before."

"It wasn't really my fault," I said, trying to keep my voice low.

But...

It kinda was.

Just like Professor Helmith's injuries.

"I'm not the one trying to kill me," I said, my tone sardonic. "Trust me, I don't want any of this either."

"You need to fix it," Ecrib glowed.

"How?"

Ecrib lowered his head until one of his eyes was close to my face. "My arcanist is precious and wonderful. No person here is worthy of her."

I said nothing, waiting for the dragon's condemnation.

"But..." Ecrib slowly lifted his head, his fins relaxing over most of his body. "For some reason, your presence makes her happy. Not her family. Not her brother—and especially not her fiancé. I don't care what it takes.

I want my arcanist to be happy." Again, he flashed his fangs. "*Make it happen.*"

I held up my hands. "Whoa, whoa. I can't just... undo what happened at the cotillion."

"You can at least try."

"Look, I had plans, but..." Then a thought struck me. "Wait, her father is upset that everything went wrong at her cotillion? And Ashlyn didn't get to show off in front of a bunch of nobles?"

Ecrib nodded once. When he snorted, more lightning sparked from his nostrils. "He wanted to announce his daughter's entrance into the arcanist world. But it was a disaster. Now he and Enki are quite enraged."

"Enki?"

"*My* father." Ecrib placed a clawed hand on his scaled chest. "He's my arcanist's father's eldrin."

Oh, right. Ashlyn's father had a giant typhoon dragon eldrin. Perfect.

"Okay, listen to this." I held up my hands, trying to pantomime all my thoughts. "The headmaster is allowing the first- and second-year students to show off in a little competition. How about we try to help Ashlyn win most of whatever takes place." I made gestures of her winning and people cheering.

"Will her family see this?" Ecrib asked.

I stopped all my examples and half-shrugged. "We can invite them. Apparently, that's possible. My father is showing up to the Academy at some point, and Phila is allowed to have her cotillion here. I'm sure if Ashlyn asked the headmaster to invite her family for the competitions, and they saw her win a few things, it would be impressive. Maybe we should just... I dunno... Suggest the headmaster invite tons of people. Maybe sell tickets. He needs funding, right?"

Maybe a *lot* of people would show up. The more, the better.

Ecrib glowered down at me as he obviously mulled over the proposal.

I liked this idea—because it would allow me to show off as well. Perhaps I still had time to show off in front of Ashlyn's father and convince him I was amazing.

"This may work." Ecrib snarled a bit as he added, "But if it doesn't, you *will* do something else to make this right."

"Or what?" I asked, more as a joke than anything.

Ecrib flared his scales and practically lunged at me. I leapt back, holding up my hands, and nearly stumbled. Caught off guard, with panic flaring in my thoughts, I didn't even realize when I tugged on Ecrib's thread of magic.

Twain bubbled and morphed until he was an identical copy of Ashlyn's familiar. My forehead burned, and I rubbed the mark.

Twain stepped between me and Ecrib, his own scales flared.

"Back away," Twain growled, his voice identical to Ecrib's.

The typhoon dragon calmed his anger and twitched the tip of his finned tail. "I won't allow my arcanist to be upset. I'll do whatever it takes to ensure she gets what she wants."

He sounded so serious—and proactive. Perhaps Ashlyn was more upset than I originally figured.

"I'll try my best to make things right," I said.

Which seemed good enough for Ecrib. He huffed, stomped around Twain, and then headed back to the window that led to our classroom. After a moment to dwell on the situation, I carefully turned on my heel and patted Twain.

"Thanks," I said.

He nodded once before reverting to his normal form. As a little kitten, he nuzzled the side of my leg. "We should hurry. I think our break is almost over..."

CHAPTER 19

UNSKILLED

I n the middle of class, while Kristof wrote yet another list of dragons found in desert regions, Twain closed his eyes and blatantly fell asleep. However, as I gently petted my eldrin, I had a thought.

I raised my hand, and even though Kristof had his back to the class, he glanced over his shoulder and narrowed his eyes. "Yes, Gray? You're curious about dunes?"

"No, actually, I was wondering about mimics." I motioned to Twain's sleeping form. "Do you know what it takes for a mimic to gain its true form? And what does a *true form mimic* look like, anyway?"

Most of the class grew still and quiet. Apparently, I wasn't the only one interested in that question.

"I'm glad you asked," Kristof drawled. He returned his attention to the chalkboard and wrote something else about the desert landscape. "Rylee wanted to bring in an expert on shapeshifters to give you all an in-depth lesson. You see, her uncle is very knowledgeable on the subject of mimics and doppelgängers. He'll be here to give you a special seminar."

"When?" I asked.

"A few weeks from now, hopefully. So, while his lecture will no doubt delight the class, why don't we all take notes on pyroclastic dragons, shall we?" Kristof continued writing on the board. "Remember that dragons are the most powerful of mystical creatures, and—"

"Besides god-creatures," Nasbit chimed in.

"—and the god-creatures are all dead, so I thought I didn't need to include the caveat," Kristof drawled. "So, *as I was saying*, dragons are the most powerful, and their abilities often trump other creatures with similar powers. The fire from a dragon will often eclipse that from a will-o-wisp."

I zoned out, my attention on Twain.

Whenever he became true form, we'd be more powerful than ever. Would we be able to take on any dragon arcanist? I hoped so.

After most students had gone to bed, I went to the showers with Twain. The washroom was empty, as most arcanists preferred to wash after a tough day outside, or in the morning. Some went in the evening, but they were rare.

The washrooms were separated by boys and girls, but I assumed both were just as grand. Glowstone chandeliers hung from the vaulted ceilings, keeping the place bright. Plumbing kept the water running, even though we were positioned on a mountain, which was the greatest magic of all, if I was being honest.

But the best part was the size. The whole washroom was gigantic. There were showers, tubs, changing areas, and racks for towels. Everything was open and clean—and would definitely accommodate a celestial dragon.

At least, I hoped.

"Ready, Twain?" I whispered as I shut the door behind us.

My mimic squirmed in my arms. "I'm *super* ready. I'm gonna be the best dragon ever." His voice echoed off the tile floors and drifted up to the chandeliers.

"Good," I muttered.

I set Twain by my feet and then walked over to a tub. Each one was large enough for a fully grown man, so I stepped inside and then rested my head back on the edge. Once positioned for sleeping, I glanced over at Twain.

My eldrin sat on the tile floor, his eyes wide, his pupils both giant circles.

"Dragon time," he whispered with a smile.

I smirked as I closed my eyes. The threads of magic around the Academy were... more numerous than before. Fortunately, I could tell them apart. Each string that led back to my classmates, or the ones associated with my professors...

Kristof's dragon was easy. His thread of magic seemed stronger than the ones around it. That made sense.

I tugged his thread and then opened my eyes to watch Twain transform. His kitten body bubbled and shifted, and I held my breath as he grew larger. Outward went his fur, until it shimmered into a translucent jelly-like body. Twain grew into a large dragon—one that practically filled the whole washroom. I had to lean away, even though I was still in my tub.

His body was like a bubble of thick water sparkled with the stars themselves. The light from the glowstone chandeliers twinkled through his chest and wings, casting the washroom in liquid ripples that shimmered across the walls.

Twain's wings were just as translucent, but they were clearly just for show. His body seemed almost weightless, just like the ethereal whelks. His eyes glowed like stars, and when Twain turned his attention to me, I sat a little straighter.

He was so... mystical.

"Do you like being a dragon?" I asked.

He nodded once. "Oh, very much." His voice was regal and deep—or perhaps *refined* was the term.

I drummed my fingers on the side of the tub. Then I rubbed my forehead. I had been so curious about Twain's transformation, I hadn't felt the sear of my arcanist mark changing. That was new.

Then I glanced around. Normally, with ethereal whelk magic, I would put myself to sleep. But Kristof was right—the celestial dragon couldn't do that. So what was I supposed to do now? Wait until I was sleepy?

"Gray, don't be foolish," I whispered to myself. "You're a mimic arcanist. You—theoretically—have *all* the magic."

Even if a celestial dragon couldn't put someone to sleep, that didn't mean *I* couldn't.

"Hm?" Twain asked with a tilt of his giant dragon head.

I glanced up at him. "I'm sorry, buddy. I'm going to transform you into an ethereal whelk, put myself to sleep, *and then* transform you back into a dragon."

Twain visibly pouted. His whole nebula body squished down a bit, in a way that was far more adorable than a dragon his size should be.

"It'll only be for a moment," I said.

With a dismissive wave of my hand, I felt for Helmith's magic and then tugged on her thread. Twain went from a celestial dragon who filled the washroom to a floating sea snail the size of a human head in a matter of seconds. His body shrank and squashed itself into a spiral shell with iridescent coloring.

Small octopus-like tentacles hung from his body, wiggling in the air.

"Quickly," Twain said. "I don't want to be like this for long!"

Using the ethereal whelk's augmentation, I forced my body into a deep slumber.

I opened my eyes in the dreamscape. This time, there was no coliseum, or bizarre torture device statues. It was a cold and barren rocky wasteland— the type of valley found at the base of lifeless mountains.

Where was I?

The sky was as gray as my name, and I shivered back the cold. I saw no plants, no people, or even any sunshine in the sky. Instead, I spotted Deimos's prison affixed to the rocky ground, his cell blending with the dream, as though he had always been trapped here.

As a terrible wind howled by, I walked over to his prison. With each step, I focused on the magical threads all over again. Then I picked out the celestial dragon and changed Twain back into his desired form. Although I didn't see Twain in the dream, I knew that, in the waking world, he was a beast who once again filled the washroom with his massive body.

Once I reached the Death Lord's cage, I stopped.

He was there, lurking in the depths of the darkness, just out of my sight. There was practically a void at the back of the cell where he liked to dwell.

I placed my hand on the prison.

The cracks were noticeable, but thin. Perhaps I could patch them? Celestial dragons had the ability to manipulate dreams, after all. This *had* to work. Deimos wasn't even at full strength—this was just a fragment of his soul—so Kristof's fully grown eldrin would counteract everything.

I hoped.

It worried me that Deimos had said nothing, though. He was normally so talkative.

"What's that? No threats of death for me today?" I quipped. "Are you feeling sick?"

Deimos stirred from the darkness. He stepped closer to the bars, his expression not one of irritation—but of boredom. He said nothing as he observed me.

"Afraid?" I asked as I motioned to my arcanist mark. The celestial dragon was woven between the points of the star.

Death Lord Deimos slowly lifted a single eyebrow. "Is there a reason I should be?"

"You don't recognize my eldrin?"

"I do not." He clicked his tongue in mild disinterest. "Tsk. Some sort of dragon, given the shape. A variant born long after my time."

I flexed my fingers on the stone of his prison. "It's going to be your undoing."

That seemed to interest Deimos. He stepped closer to the bars and smiled, his attention fully on me. "Is that so?"

"Celestial dragons can manipulate dreams—far better than an ethereal whelk. I'm here to fix your prison, and then resume my life of normal classes." I matched his grin. "So, you're basically defeated."

Deimos didn't miss a beat when he asked, "Then what're you waiting for? I can't wait to see your *epic triumph*." His tone oozed with contemptuous sarcasm. I would know—I loved sarcasm.

I returned my attention to my hand. Again, I flexed my fingers, feeling the smooth rock beneath my grasp. The stone prison *felt* magical, likely because it was completely made using Professor Helmith's true form ability.

Would I be able to repair it?

I had to envision it. That was the key to magical manipulation.

No room for doubt. I just had to act. That was the key. Confidence.

"Heh," Deimos said. "You're all bluster, child." In an icier tone, he added, "If you have the gall to face me and throw taunts, you better have the spine to back up your claims."

His words spurred me into action. I imagined the dream changing—the cage changing—and then willed it so.

In an instant, the dreamscape warped. My arm and hand burned from the use of magic. It hurt so much—seared my insides—I shouted and leapt backward.

Dragon magic...

The whole dream changed. Without warning, and all at once. It was far more thorough and faster than anything I had seen Professor Helmith do.

Boulders exploded into trees. The ground transformed into a swamp. The distant mountains became plains of purple flowers. Rainbows shot through the sky, slicing through clouds.

And then, in typical dream fashion, weird things seeped into the mundane. Horses pranced out of rivers that formed between trees. The rainbows turned on each other. They fought to dominate the sky. The temperature became cold.

But worst of all, a part of Deimos's cage shattered.

Two of the bars cracked and splintered, bursting inward and creating a hole. The outer shell of the prison crunched inward, creating more spiderweb cracks, and deepening the ones already there.

Helmith's magic weakened...

The only noise in the dreamscape was the callous laughter of Death Lord Deimos. He stuck his hand through the broken bars. He couldn't fit his body through—thank the good stars—but his arm slipped through without a problem.

"What a wonderful display," Deimos said with a dark chuckle. "You're all power and no skill. Delightful."

I cradled my arm close to my chest. It still hurt. Kristof's celestial dragon magic was too strong for my young mimic powers.

The bizarre dreamscape rippled and shimmered all around me. I shook my head and allowed my connection to the celestial dragon to fade. My arcanist star reverted to its usual unadorned self, and everything around me melted.

That was when...

I awoke in the washroom tub, my heart hammering.

"Gray?" Twain asked as he leapt onto the rim of the tub. "Is everything okay? You seem scared."

Dammit. I rubbed my face, clearing away the sweat.

I had made everything worse.

CHAPTER 20

MY FATHER

I returned to the dorm saddled in dread.

When I rested on my bed, Twain snuggled close. The others were either already asleep or quietly on their way, and paid me little mind. Once the lights were snuffed, I stared off into the darkness, unable to fall asleep.

It felt like eternity until the dawn broke through the gloom. The first rays of dawn trickled in through the massive window, and I sat up before the others could even wake. Twain, who hadn't slept either, got to his four feet and stared at me with concern in his large eyes.

"Everything will work out," Twain whispered. "Professor Helmith is here. Even if something bad happens, she can fix it like before. You're still okay."

A soft tapping at the door to our dorm caused me to tense. I glanced over, my eyelids heavy. When I went to rub my chest, my fingers grazed the bizarre shape-shifting weapon around my shoulders. Vivigöl. I shook away its presence from my mind.

Or maybe... it was making things worse? I gave serious thought to removing it from my body.

Instead, I stood from my bed and headed over to the door. I slowly opened it to find someone dressed in Academy robes.

"Hello?" the man asked. He was long in the face, and his tone jittery. "Is Gray Lexly here?"

"I'm he," I muttered as I rubbed my eyes.

"Your father will be joining us this morning. He's due to arrive at the docks in front of Astra Academy."

Already? That was fast. Headmaster Venrover wasn't one to put off tasks, it seemed.

"Thank you," I said.

"You should go now, if you wish to see him as he arrives, that is." Then the man bowed his head slightly and turned away. With hurried steps, he went straight for the staircase, never offering me a second glance back.

He had things to do, it seemed. Or classes to attend.

If I went now, perhaps I could get my father and still make it to class on time. What did I have today? I thought my class was with Professor Ren... in *Magical Fundamentals*. That wasn't my strongest subject, which meant I probably shouldn't ignore it.

But I needed to see my father.

I returned to my bed and quickly changed. Then, before the others woke, I went to my brother's bed. The shadows around the floor moved when I approached.

My brother's knightmare lifted out of the darkness, forming a partial suit of plate armor. The shadows themselves formed his cape and the metal of his hollow body.

"I heard everything," Thurin said, his haunting knightmare voice quiet enough that it didn't wake the others. "You should grab breakfast while I wake my arcanist."

"Thank you," I whispered. After scooping Twain into my arms, I jogged to the door. "I'll meet you two just outside the main doors to the Academy. Try not to be late."

The morning rays of sunshine invigorated me. I ate my pastry and waited for Sorin to arrive. Twain pawed at my leg, and I gave him a bit of the berry frosting on top of the breakfast treat. He purred as he consumed it all.

Sorin and Thurin exited the Academy's massive front doors. My brother smiled wide as he made his way to my side. Despite being woken early, he was as bright and chipper as ever.

"Good morning, Gray," he said.

I handed him a pastry. "We should hurry if we want to get to class on time."

Sorin took a bite of his food and then glanced around. "The headmaster isn't here to greet Dad?"

"Why would he be? He's busy trying to get funding for the Academy, remember? I'm sure we're perfectly capable of giving our father a tour."

"Hm."

Sorin, gobbling his food like a starved man at the gallows, swallowed the last of his meal, and we headed for the long staircase down to the lake. The mountain winds were enough to cause me to shiver, and the staircase was hundreds of steps to the docks.

After a couple steps, I had to carry Twain. He was too small to make it all the way down by himself.

The Academy's lake had no real rivers or way to get to the ocean, but five gigantic Gates of Crossing were positioned in the mirror-like waters. Captains sailed ships through the teleporting rings on a regular basis to bring the Academy supplies. I wondered which ship my father had caught a ride on.

Sorin caught my gaze. "Are you okay? Thurin told me you didn't sleep at all."

Ah. His snitch of an eldrin. Knightmares didn't sleep, so of course he just watched me.

I held Twain close. Sorin didn't want me to lie to him...

"I became a celestial dragon arcanist," I whispered, "and attempted to *deal with* Death Lord Deimos on my own. But it backfired. I think I made things worse."

Sorin's eyebrows shot for his hairline. "R-Really?"

"Yeah."

He stopped on the step right in front of me and then placed a hand on my chest. "We should go tell Professor Helmith. She can help, can't she?"

I shoved his hand away and then walked around him, continuing my descent to the lake. "Not yet. It's not... It's not too bad yet."

"Why not?" Sorin followed behind me, his tone filled with concern.

"She's still recovering. I can't ask her to deal with a Death Lord while she's barely able to stand." I stared at the steps as we continued, my thoughts dark. "She could die, Sorin."

"What about telling the headmaster?"

"I already told you. *He's busy.* He's trying to make the Academy more defensible. Because of me. And he doesn't even have the right magics to help. I mean, maybe he could find an arcanist, but I'm just a burden on him. On everyone."

Sorin took several steps at a time until he was right next to me. He frowned as he stated, "You're not a burden."

I couldn't stop myself from sarcastically laughing. I didn't even look at my brother when I said, "Ashlyn's cotillion was ruined because of me. People at the Academy were put in danger. Professor Helmith is bedridden. *C'mon.* Even *you* can do the math."

Sorin didn't have anything to say after that.

"I don't think you're a burden," Twain whispered.

I petted his head. "And that's good, but if Kristof finds out I messed up the prison holding Death Lord Deimos, I... don't know what he'll do. Probably something terrible. So, for the time being, we just have to keep this to ourselves."

"Until when?" Sorin whispered.

"If I ever think I've lost control of the situation... I let them all know then."

After that statement, we descended the stairs in silence. Sorin glanced away from me, his gaze searching the distant horizon. He took deep breaths until we reached the base of the stone stairway.

"You don't have any poems or rhymes to cheer me up?" I asked, trying to lighten the mood.

"No," Sorin said. "I know you think they're stupid. I didn't want to irritate you—not when you're going through so many problems."

That statement cut worse than any dagger. I turned to him, angrier at myself than anything. Words caught in my throat. Unable to think of what to say, I quickly glanced out over the lake. The smooth surface reflected the rising run. It glittered with the cold beauty of the mountain setting, dampening my anger.

After I took a breath, I once again faced my brother. "Sorin, you shouldn't change yourself for anyone—not even me. And I don't think your poems are stupid. I just... think they're strange sometimes, okay?"

My brother rubbed the side of his neck. With a shrug, he said, "Well, I don't think I've been doing a good job with my poetry, as of late. I say words, and they rhyme, I guess, but it's not *meaningful* like the poems that inspired me in the first place."

"Why haven't you told me about this?"

Sorin lifted an eyebrow. "You've been going through so much lately. I didn't want to bother you with my small things."

"Sorin, I don't care if you need help folding laundry, you can *always* come to me, okay?" I gently punched his arm. "I'm not going to lie to you, and you're not going to hide your problems from me, got it?"

Although I hadn't said much, it seemed to brighten Sorin's day. He smiled wider than before. Then he cleared his throat and spoke in dramatic fashion. "*A rift once vast, a bridge now grows. Reconciliation, the tale now shows!*"

"That one wasn't bad," I said. "Not entirely sure what it means, though."

"It means we're closer now than ever before." Sorin slapped my arm. I almost dropped Twain as I stumbled to the side. My mimic eldrin puffed out his orange fur in irritation.

"I do have one other problem..." Sorin huffed a nervous laugh. "And I never thought I would say this, because I've never been popular with the ladies, but..."

As if the universe wanted to interject itself into the conversation, someone shouted from the stairway. Both Sorin and I turned toward the voice. Nini came hurrying down the steps, her reaper floating behind her. Halfway down, she nearly slipped, but Waste reached out with his red cape and grabbed her arm.

Although he was a creepy reaper, Waste gently and effectively pulled her back onto the steps, brushed her off, and then motioned for her to continue, all without saying a word.

"Th-Thank you," Nini said to her eldrin.

I gave Sorin a sidelong glance. "Are you having problems with Nini?" I whispered.

"No," Sorin replied, his voice equally low. "Everything with her is great—she's my honeysuckle. It's, uh, something else. I'll talk to you about it later." Then my brother waved and motioned for Nini to join us. "What're you doing up so early?"

"I got up to come see you," Nini muttered as she made her way down the last of the steps. She was breathing hard by the time she reached us. "I got your letter saying you were heading to the docks. I figured I would join you." She threw her arms around my brother in a quick hug.

I was almost jealous. I wished Ashlyn were here with us.

But I kept that to myself.

When Nini stepped back, she offered me a smile. "Good morning, Gray."

I nodded.

Just then, the Gate of Crossing activated. We all stopped everything to watch the arrival. The gigantic circular artifact lit up, the rizzel etchings along the side indicating it was a device for teleportation.

A ship sailed through, one I had never seen before. I wasn't an expert on the vessels that came to Astra Academy, but I figured my father would've hitched a ride on a cargo vessel. The ship that headed for the dock was a smaller, faster craft meant to carry a limited number of passengers.

A strange choice.

There were two masts adorned with white sails, but also oars for rowing through calm waters. A few men steered the ship until it reached us. Sorin immediately stepped forward to help them tie everything down. Then he grabbed the gangplank and set it up the dock.

"It's really neat your parents are coming to visit," Nini said to me. She wore her robes and large jacket both, giving her a much wider appearance than most arcanists at the Academy. But she also wore a bright smile today, and it infected me a bit.

"I'm glad our father came today. I could really use some good news."

And then I spotted my father, and my stepmother, on the deck of the ship.

My father was hard to miss. He was a tall man with a gut large enough he could pretend to be pregnant. He usually wore an apron, but today he was dressed in his finest vest and slacks. Had he dressed up to see us at the Academy? That thought warmed me a bit.

His dark hair was swept back, and his skin was extra tanned from the summer sun.

My stepmother stood next to my father, holding his arm tightly with both of hers. Her eyes were always watery, but today they almost seemed on the verge of tears. She wore a blue dress, more frumpy than alluring, though I suspected she had made it herself, just for this occasion.

Her lip quavered, and it slowly dawned on me that she *was* crying.

"Gray?" Twain whispered. "What's wrong?"

I stepped forward, my throat dry with panic.

A sailor on the ship—a lithe woman with a harsh gaze, a tight leather jacket, and a bandana wrapped over her forehead—stepped close to my father and shoved the barrel of a revolver against his temple.

"Gray Lexly," the woman said, her voice raspy. "Get on the ship—or your father's life is forfeit."

CHAPTER 21

NULLSTONE RESTRAINTS

Thurin leapt from the darkness around my brother's feet. The knightmare stood tall, with such a menacing appearance, even the woman with the revolver to our father's head flinched in apparent fright.

The woman scoundrel grabbed my father's arm and pressed her weapon deeper into his temple. "If you try anything, I'll shoot. *That's a promise.*"

It would take a fraction of a second for her to pull the trigger and kill our father. Even if Sorin or Thurin used their terror evocation, it was too great a risk. Likewise, Nini and her reaper stood close. Waste twirled his scythe, but didn't move to attack.

Everything was silent and tense. When my stepmother cried, she did so without making a noise.

I held up my hands. "I'll get on the ship, so don't hurt anyone."

The scene was so tense, every step I took felt like a monumental gesture. Sorin watched me, his gaze hard, his hands balled into fists. Nini reached her hand out halfway, like she wanted to stop me, but couldn't bring herself to interfere.

I slowly made my way onto the gangplank with Twain following behind me. The wooden board creaked underfoot, sending a shiver of anxiety throughout my body.

No one spoke.

Once closer, I realized the villainous woman was sickly in appearance. Her complexion was wan, her eyes sunken into her skull, and her cheeks shallow. Her brown hair had all the allure of mud, and she had enough piercings on her ears to replace all the nails on this boat, if needed.

The revolver she held was from down south. The Norra Revolvers were famous for their stopping power. Apparently, a few clever arcanist gunsmiths had developed them with the purpose of creating more exciting Magi Crosses—deadly duels between arcanists.

I stepped onto the deck of the ship, my hands still up. "You've got me," I said. "Now what do you want with me?"

The woman smiled, revealing her yellowed teeth. "Give us the soul fragment of Death Lord Deimos, and we'll let you all go."

We?

I subtly glanced around. The ship had a crew of ten people, each armed with a Norra Revolver—some with two. Most of them had bandanas over their foreheads, and I wondered if there were any arcanists among them. Even this woman kept that hidden—perhaps their eldrin were below deck.

The scumbag readied her finger on the trigger of her revolver. I held my breath, my heart out of control with worry.

"You're his followers?" I asked, trying to keep my tone calm while I gathered some information. "You're trying to save Deimos?"

Twain pressed his body against my leg, his claws out. Did he want to fight? I could transform him into an abyssal dragon, but it would take a few seconds for him to shift. By then, my father would be dead...

"We don't follow *Deimos*," the woman hissed, spittle exiting her mouth off the last word. "We have always been faithful to Death Lord Naiad—the *first* and *true* Death Lord of the abyssal hells. Give us Deimos's soul, so that we might shatter it."

Death Lord... Naiad?

I didn't know who that was. Nor did I care, frankly.

With a single nervous laugh, I said, "Listen, lady, if I knew how to give you Deimos's soul, I would. I hate the man just as much as you all. Maybe more."

"We were told you were harboring Deimos," the woman shouted. "*Release him.*"

"If I could, I would—I swear it."

My father stared at me, his face twisted in fright. He held my stepmother close, and then whispered something only to her. Probably a comforting statement, as she didn't shake as much afterward.

I didn't know what to do to solve the situation, though. As far as I knew, there was no way for me to hand over Deimos's soul.

He was just trapped in mine.

One of the ship's crew, a man with a marble stone leg, as though it had been petrified by some sort of cruel magic, stepped forward. He wore boots, but that didn't stop the heavy weight of his marble leg from *clunking* on the deck with each step.

"I told you, Bevia. In matters like this, you can't expect a simple solution." He spoke with a garbled tone, like his throat wasn't right. Or perhaps he had smoked since he was an infant and accidentally swallowed a cig, but never managed to get it out of his windpipe.

The cutthroat woman—Bevia—shot the stone-legged man a glare. "Gather the nullstone, Vinnie. If the boy can't give Deimos up, we'll just have to take him by force."

Nullstone?

My heart stopped for a moment. Nullstone was a bizarre naturally occurring material that negated most magics.

Not *powerful* magics—like the ones wielded by dragons—but almost all other forms. Dragons were the special exception to most limitations, at least according to Helmith.

Nullstone was one of the few ways to negate the abilities of mystical creatures, and old-timey poachers often used nullstone cages to take baby creatures away from their nests.

I had never seen nullstone, but I knew all about it from Professor Helmith.

The crew members hurried below deck and then returned with torso-sized cages, the bars of which were as thick as fingers and made out of bluish-black rock. They also carried shackles—complete with a set of keys.

The nullstone had a distinct *sensation* I felt as they brought them forward. Like a sponge soaking up water.

Only the water was my magic.

"We can't go with them," Twain whispered as he gazed up at me.

I shook my head, trying to indicate we didn't have much of a choice at the moment.

Thurin hovered close to my brother, and I secretly wished the knightmare would just slink away as a shadow and get help. Unfortunately, knightmares weren't prone to run from enemies.

Even Waste could've gotten away, but the deadly reaper stayed as close to Nini as possible without fully merging with her. Was he protecting her first and foremost?

I stepped forward. "Let everyone else go. If you want Deimos, I'll even help you get him. I don't even want to be involved in this."

"No, *boy*, that's not how this works." Bevia kept her revolver on my father. "You're *all* coming with us now."

"I won't let you harm them," I said, rage at the edge of my thoughts and actions.

"*No one will get harmed so long as you comply*. But the arcanists of the Academy can't know what's happened here. They'll try to stop us." She growled something to the crew, and then offered Nini and Sorin a cold glower. "You two. On the ship."

Sorin hesitated. He exchanged looks with Nini, and I hoped they would just run.

"Your father," Nini whispered.

Sorin didn't reply, but he did give her words thought.

Unfortunately, they both reluctantly walked up the gangplank, their eldrin in tow.

Once aboard, the crew moved forward with the nullstone cages. Thurin, being malleable shadow, was forced into a cage, where he promptly deflated, his armor becoming rather static. Waste was the same, though his scythe just wouldn't fit into the confinement. It was kept outside, but his blood-red cape just sat inside the nullstone cage, practically lifeless.

My brother and Nini were placed in shackles, and so was I.

Then they grabbed Twain. My mimic thrashed in the arms of his captors, hissing and spitting as though they were about to neuter him.

"Don't hurt him," I shouted.

One of the thugs grabbed my shoulder and held me back as they threw Twain into a nullstone cage. He continued to flail, even when confined, his fighting spirit practically overflowing out of his tiny prison.

"You're not going to get away with this!" Twain shouted, his voice a hissy growl. "I can eat you! I-If I were bigger, that is. Which I can be!"

The stone-legged man groaned. "We have two star shards left, Bevia. *Two.*"

"That's all we need," she said as she motioned to some of the crew. "Now tie these two mortal sad sacks up."

Men grabbed my father and stepmother. They didn't bother using nullstone. My parents had no magic, after all. They used rope to bind their hands and ankles, and then made them sit against the ship's railing, where they bound them to the actual vessel.

Bevia ripped off her bandana and revealed the arcanist mark etched into her forehead. She had a seven-pointed star with the image of a worm wrapped around the points.

"We have what we need," she said. "Now ship out!"

The crew rushed to carry out her orders. They untied the ship, pushed away from the dock, and used oars to guide the ship across the smooth surface of the mountain lake. As they worked, Bevia's eldrin slithered out onto the deck.

It was a repulsive creature that resembled a cross between an earthworm and a swamp leech—only five feet in length and thick enough to consume a small child. Its leathery-looking skin, faded of all color, shimmered with slime as it made its way over to its arcanist.

It was a *mireem.* A little bog-dwelling mystical creature that Professor Helmith always lovingly described as *putrid.*

The beast had a circular mouth filled with fangs, and four little eyes on the top of its worm head.

"There's my little Bentley," Bevia said in a sickeningly sweet voice. She grabbed the squishy cheeks of the mireem and playfully wobbled him around. Then Bevia leaned over and kissed the mireem between a set of its eyes. "You're such a good boy, watching all our captives."

The mireem, Bentley, wagged the tip of his tail. The mireem didn't speak, and I wondered if he even could. Perhaps he just didn't want to.

Vinnie walked across the deck, his stone foot creating his own tempo. *Thunk. Thunk. Thunk.* Every other step. The man would have trouble outrunning a croissant, but I feared there was more to him than he was showing.

"We can't keep *all these people*," he said as he waved an arm, gesturing to the ship. "Students at Astra Academy are arcanists from noble families. We'll have an army pursuing us—and then the followers of Deimos will learn what we've done!"

Bevia scoffed as she stood straight. The wind swept her muddy hair back as the ship picked up speed. The sails filled, and we would soon teleport through the Gate of Crossing.

"We don't need to worry about this," Bevia said. "Once we get to shore, we'll litter the beach with their bodies. We can make it look like a mugging. The students were *out and about*, heading to Anchor Isle, but then tragedy struck. All we need is Gray Lexly."

"You said you wouldn't harm them," I said, my voice loud.

Sorin and Nini turned to me, their eyes wide.

One of the crewmen still held my shoulder, preventing me from just charging this villainous woman and throwing her off the damn boat.

"They don't have anything to do with this," I continued, each word louder than the last. "Just leave them at Anchor Isle. None of us come from noble families."

"*Shut up*," Bevia hissed as she turned on her heel. "You're a liar, and a vessel for Deimos. As soon as we reach the temple, we'll cut you up, extract *all* the souls you're harboring, and you won't have anything else to worry about."

Then she stepped forward and—with the revolver held tightly in her fist—backhanded me.

I had never been struck by a revolver before.

My vision went black as I tumbled to the deck, unconscious.

Chapter 22

Now Choose

"Get up."

My head throbbed in agony.

Obviously, I hurt—I had just taken a weighted punch straight to the orbital socket—but it was worse than that. The recent events played through my mind, clawing at my subconscious.

The villains had moved me. Where was I now?

Although my eyes were closed, I knew I was lying on a hard, damp surface. I felt it. On my body, on my cheek. It was like lying on a moist plank of wood.

"Get. *Up*."

I fluttered my eyes open and took a deep breath. The scent of salt water flooded my nose and stung my sinuses. With all the strength I could muster, I pushed myself off the ground and sat up. What had happened to my shackles?

While holding my breath, I glanced around.

I wasn't on a ship anymore.

I was in some sort of cave. A wooden platform, built over an underground river, was the only manmade structure I noticed. Several nets filled with glowstones hung from the cave wall, illuminating a small portion of the underground, but that was it. Darkness reigned supreme in either direction down the small river.

After rubbing one of my eyes, I spotted a cage "growing" into the cave wall.

Then I realized this was a dream.

It was Death Lord Deimos's cage. It was still cracked, and some of the bars were missing, all from my failed attempts at reinforcing it.

My body ached as I got to my feet. Deimos haunted the corner of his prison, his body a mere silhouette of shadows.

"Finally," he growled. "You manage to stand."

"Were you yelling at me to stand?" I asked, my voice practically a croak. Even my throat hurt.

I examined my surroundings. Our voices echoed up and down the cave, but there was no one else here to disturb with our argument. We were alone in the bizarre and damp dreamscape.

A few glowstones faded, dimming the lights. I had never seen, or heard, of that happening before. That was the result of dream logic, obviously. Glowstones could lose their magic here, to heighten the nightmarish atmosphere.

"*Wake up*," Deimos commanded, "and get us out of this problem."

"*Get us out of this problem?*" I repeated, and then shook my head. "I'd rather hand you over to those bloodthirsty lunatics and be rid of this whole situation!"

The Death Lord didn't have a retort for that.

More glowstones faded. The cave grew darker than I liked.

"I didn't ask to be part of this." I glared at the wooden platform beneath my feet, wondering how I could possibly fix this problem. "I didn't want to fight an abyssal dragon arcanist, I didn't want to be hunted in my dreams by freakish monsters, and I certainly didn't want cultist thugs hurting me and my family. *I want none of it.*"

I ran a hand through my hair, the pain of my nails digging into my scalp all too real.

"You've never sounded more childish," Deimos stated. "You can't pick your battles. You can only decide how you will handle them."

I snapped my gaze to his silhouette in the corner of his prison. "You can go straight to the darkest corner of the abyssal hells."

"Are you done whining? Because if you are, then you should *wake up* and deal with this. Before you lose that option."

I stepped up to the cracked bars, my rage fueling all my words. "What am I supposed to do? I can't just *deal with it*. They have my brother! My parents! *Even Nini.* They're going to kill everyone, and I don't have a solution for that."

Deimos darkly chuckled. "They'll also kill everyone if you do nothing. If the consequences are the same regardless, best to choose action over inaction."

I placed my hand on his cage and shook my head. "I *can't*. I don't know anything about fighting. They all have revolvers and everyone in shackles. *I'm just here, dreaming, like a useless lump on a log.*" After a long exhale, I stared at my feet again. "I don't want to give up—I never want to give up—but I always had options before. I don't have... any ideas this time around."

Professor Helmith had helped me in the past. Or Sorin. Or someone.

And everyone who had helped me was now injured or in danger. Because of me.

I closed my eyes. Why hadn't I gotten stronger faster? Why couldn't people just leave me alone for *two seconds* while I improved my skills?

"You always have options," Deimos whispered, his tone serious.

"Like what?"

"Kill. Them."

I took a ragged breath. "I told you. I don't know how. Twain can't transform while he's in his nullstone cage. What am I supposed to do?"

"Even if you only have a broken plank stolen from a sailing vessel, you can riddle them with splinters and puncture flesh with rusted nails."

With half a smile, I managed to quip, "What a pep talk."

More glowstones went out. The darkness crept ever closer, and it was difficult to make out the details of the wooden planks just underfoot. For some reason, the cave felt colder as well, as though the light was also my source of warmth.

Death Lord Deimos slid his hand out of the cage. His gauntlet was crafted of steel and bone, and practically clawed at the fingertips, the sharp razor-edges capable of cutting flesh, no question about it.

"Let *me* handle this," Deimos whispered. He held his hand palm-up—inviting, yet somehow sinister.

"*No*," I snapped as I stepped away from the cage.

"It isn't just *your* life they'll take. This fragment of my soul is also in peril. We have a common enemy. If you can't slay them—I will."

"But..."

I couldn't. What would happen if I let Deimos have control again? He had almost killed Knovak last time, and attempted to gather all the gate fragments so he could reopen the abyssal hells. Saving my life wasn't worth risking of all that.

But saving Sorin...

My brother was always there for me. I couldn't leave him when he was in danger.

And my father...

I never even got my chance to apologize. This had all happened so fast.

Was allowing Deimos control worth saving their lives? Was the chance things could get even *worse* worth helping them all?

"You have a choice," Deimos said. "Die, and free yourself of this pain —and all the things you cried about *not wanting*. Or fight, and make them regret harming your kith and kin." He flexed his fingers, the metal of his gauntlet scraping. "I know *my* decision."

"My brother..." I slowly reached for Deimos's gauntlet, but I stopped halfway. "Twain... Everyone else. You have to promise me nothing will happen to them." Saving them would be worth any price I could pay.

"I understand the need to protect your twin," Deimos said. "He was with you at your birth, he should be with you at your death."

I kept my hand out, but I didn't move it. "*Everyone* else."

Deimos stretched his fingers ever so slightly. "You have my word."

After a moment's hesitation, I placed my hand on his gauntlet. Death Lord Deimos grabbed my wrist and stabbed his claw-fingers deep into my flesh, pain lancing through my arm. It ended a moment later, and a dark feeling of power filled me.

The last of the glowstones died.

And I felt my eyes fluttering open again.

My heart beat steady against my chest. Voices danced around me, two people talking in the distance. When I opened my eyes, I realized I was on the ground. Sand and dirt mixed together, and the smell of the ocean filled the air.

The midday sun shone through a canopy of leaves above, creating pillars of light that illuminated a small woodland area.

I sat up, my head clear, my anxiety dead.

"We can't kill the reaper arcanist," someone said. "Or the reaper, either."

"You keep saying that," the woman—Bevia—barked. "Why?"

"Don't you know nothin'? Reapers are creatures that embody death itself. If you kill one, *you die in turn*. It's called *the King's Revenge*."

Bevia scoffed. "That's just a myth."

"It's no myth."

I felt strangely aware of everything. My breathing. The forest. The... the fish in the ocean? That was new.

"Okay, we won't kill them here," Bevia said, her boots crunching leaves as she walked. "We'll take them with us all the way to the temple. We'll let someone else deal with the reaper arcanist. Some poor schlub from town."

When I stood, I realized my hands were still shackled in nullstone. I also spotted the ship that had come to kidnap me. It was beached on the dark sands of the coast not far from where I stood. At least two hundred feet away, half in the water, half on land.

Eight of the shady crew members patrolled the vessel. My brother and Nini and were on the deck, unharmed. Our eldrin remained in the nullstone cages. None of them moved or attempted to get free. My father and stepmother had to be below deck.

I turned on my heel and stared off into the woods, my heart rate increasing.

Bevia and Vinnie milled around between the trees. They both held silvery shards as large as their fingers.

Gate fragments.

They were bits of the teleporting gate that led to the abyssal hells. Those sinister pieces were activated by my presence, and last I had seen, allowed souls to escape into the realm of the living. These "souls" took ghoulish forms. Or perhaps they were monsters. I never got a straight answer. All I knew was that the gate fragments caused terrible things to happen, and these lunatics were obviously trying to use them.

Bevia and Vinnie didn't turn to face me.

I suspected they were too engrossed with their conversation to notice my movements.

"He's definitely the one we're looking for." Bevia twisted her fragment around. "See? Look at how they shine." The fragment glittered with magical power in her hands.

Vinnie held his fragment close. "We shouldn't stay here much longer. We should take Gray's body, gather up as many of these gate pieces as we can find, and ship off before the sun sets on the horizon."

Ah. They were using my body to find fragments on this shore.

This was where they had planned to kill everyone. That thought sent rage through my veins. I reached my cuffed hands up and tugged the collar of my shirt down enough to expose Vivigöl.

I grabbed the weapon, surprised at how much... control... I had. Hadn't Deimos said he wanted to handle this? But his actions weren't taking over.

With my grip tightening on the abyssal coral, the weapon *click-click-clicked* into shape. It transformed from a bizarre piece of hidden jewelry to a sword with a dark golden hue.

And then—with expertise I had never possessed—I sliced through the chain holding the cuffs together. Nullstone still remained on my wrists, however, as the cuffs wouldn't slid off past my thumbs. I placed a hand on one, and then pushed magic through my being.

Normally, nullstone prevented magic use.

But not *dragon* magic.

And the sickening blue glow that emanated from my palm was the evocation of the abyssal dragon. My raw magic crept into the cuff and then shattered it into dust, like a window being thrown into a grinder.

I touched the second cuff and did the same.

Then I took a moment to stare at my new weapon, and marvel at my freedom. I had thought Deimos was going to possess me fully, like he had at Ashlyn's cotillion. But that wasn't the case.

It was like... Death Lord Deimos was guiding my actions.

I felt his influence, and his magic, all throughout my system. Even his thoughts crept into mine, permeating my mind.

He thought about...

Death Lord Naiad.

She had become the first Death Lord, and never left her post. Instead, Naiad had turned her power and rage against her fellow Death Lords. Naiad had killed them to steal their magic and control the largest section of the abyssal hells.

How bizarre. I shook the intrusive thoughts away.

Death Lord Naiad wouldn't be adding my strength to her own.

"I don't think there are any more gate pieces here," Vinnie said, drawing my attention back to the present.

"Then let's head back to the ship." Bevia turned and stormed through the woodlands, her gaze falling to me only a second later. With wide eyes, she stared. First at my arms, then at my weapon.

"*You*," she said. "You're Death Lord Deimos."

I didn't know what had given it away, but I couldn't stop myself from smirking.

"You came here to claim my soul?" I asked. Or perhaps it was Deimos —the words came without much of my thoughts. With a flourish of my wrist, I twirled the sword. "I can't wait to see you try."

CHAPTER 23

I Tried To Warn You

Bevia stepped in front of Vinnie. The man with the stone leg blubbered something and then threw himself behind a tree with the haste of a panicked woodland animal spotting a bobcat.

"We're going to get your soul one way or another," Bevia said with a cruel smirk.

She pulled her revolver and fired. No time for aiming—she drew from the hip and shot. The bullet tore through my Academy robes, my shirt, and then through my chest, all with such force, I staggered backward, almost unable to keep my footing. For a split second, I panicked—what if the bullet pierced my heart? What if I bled out?

A burning sensation of pain flooded my mind.

But then another set of thoughts took over. My panic was washed away with a sense of dark amusement.

Information came to me in small fragments. Abyssal dragons drew their magic from souls. They grafted souls to their bodies and then used them, like someone using bullets in a gun. Each soul could be "used up" to quickly repair their flesh, or give them a boost in strength. But when they ran out, they would need to replenish their supplies.

And when I glanced down, I noticed blood blooming across my clothing—but then it stopped. The hole in my chest, just below my heart and through my ribs, was filled with a bright blue *gel* that was made from the very souls I had just thought about.

Abyssal dragon magic had saved me.

Deimos was using it... channeling it through my body. Because his soul was in mine, and his magic still worked through him.

My arcanist mark on my forehead remained blank. I didn't have the mark of the abyssal dragon. This was all Deimos.

I ran a hand over my injury.

"What was that?" I asked, my tone harsher than I ever spoke naturally. "Some sort of projectile weapon?" Only, it wasn't *me* speaking. It was Deimos. He spoke through me.

"It's a firearm," *I* said—to myself, basically—answering Deimos.

Bevia stared with wide eyes, her eyebrows rising. I definitely appeared insane.

"Enough games," Deimos said with my voice.

But it was *me* who readied the sword. Again, I had thought the Death Lord was going to take over, but it seemed he couldn't. Spurred by his desire to end this fight, I ran forward, Vivigöl firmly held, the weapon still in sword form.

Bevia opened fire again. This time, she shot at me four times. Two of the bullets pierced my flesh—one through my chest, one through my arm. The bullets were *powerful,* and I stumbled each time one of them struck me, almost knocked off balance by the sheer force of the revolver.

And while it hurt, the abyssal dragon magic flooded my body, stopping the blood flow and immediately repairing the damage.

Once close enough, I lunged and slashed with my blade. The abyssal coral—golden and beautiful when it caught the rays of sunlight—was stained red as I cut through Bevia's gun arm. In one fell swoop, I had *disarmed* her, literally. She screamed and tumbled backward. Then she hit the ground on her back, blood gushing from her missing limb.

Then, without thinking, I drew back Vivigöl, and the weapon *click-click-clicked* into the form of a trident—Deimos's preferred weapon.

I stepped forward, my heart racing fast. My thoughts centered around *ending the fight*. I had to ensure Bevia couldn't hurt me, or anyone I cared about, anymore.

But before I acted on my own grim thoughts, Bevia waved her

remaining hand in front of her. *"You'll pay!"* She evoked a muddy liquid from the creases in her palms, splashing it everywhere. Her evocation struck the trees, the detritus on the ground, and even my pants and legs.

Within a couple of seconds, the liquid dissolved everything it touched.

Mireems, and their arcanists, evoked a type of dangerous acid. It liquefied living material, turning it into pudding.

Bevia evoked more of her horrible acid, but instead of standing still, I expertly dodged aside, without any conscious thought on my behalf.

The trees she struck with her magic began to sizzle and melt, becoming a terrible ooze. The bits of her acid on my body burned my legs, but the abyssal dragon magic once again stopped the damage and repaired everything.

"Die!" she yelled, preparing to splash more of her acid.

I slammed the trident's three tines down on her chest, piercing her heart and her lungs in one brutal strike. Vivigöl effortlessly cut into her, but afterward, the barbed tines didn't easily come free. My hands shook as I stepped away, my breathing ragged.

Bevia gargled a cough and then went lax. The mark on her forehead faded slightly.

It had been... so easy.

"Aren't you concerned about your brother?" I asked—Deimos asked—and I snapped my attention to the boat on the shore.

Without giving the death another thought, I yanked Vivigöl free and headed for the vessel. I didn't want to fight anyone. I hadn't started this. I had specifically said I *didn't want* this. Before I fought anyone else, I'd give them a warning.

One last warning.

To leave me alone.

I ran across the beach. Normally, I had trouble with my breath if I ran too hard, but this time, I took in air with each alternate step, inhaling through both my nose and mouth, taking in as much oxygen as possible. It seemed... different. And instinctual. No one had taught me how to properly run for any distance, but now I had that skill.

I leapt up the gangplank of the vessel, and appeared on the deck before any of the villains had time to prepare themselves.

A man standing near the top of the plank reached for his revolver. On instinct, I lifted my trident and took aim for his throat. I could've *easily* stabbed him through his windpipe, but I held back, remembering my desire to issue a warning.

Instead of just ending the man's life in an instant, I twirled Vivigöl around and bashed the shaft of the trident straight into his noggin. The strike created a *crack* sound that filled the air and made me empathetically cringe. He collapsed to the deck, unconscious.

"Gray!" Sorin shouted.

He and Nini were shackled to one of the masts, their eldrin, and Twain, in nullstone cages nearby. Sorin had been sweating—probably because of the harsh midday sun over us—and his robes were soaked under his armpits. Nini, who kept herself swaddled, had a red face and a tired appearance.

The rest of the crew, still startled and caught off guard by my presence, stared on in horror.

I stepped closer to my brother.

Sorin sucked in his breath, his expression shifting from elation to horror. "You're not Gray," he whispered.

He knew instantly. Of course he did.

"What's going on?" Twain asked from within his cage.

Instead of explaining, I turned my gaze to the startled men who followed Death Lord Naiad.

"Surrender now," I said, icy and confident. "Or I won't hold back."

No one listened.

Three of them drew their guns, and four others pulled knives. When the first man lifted his revolver to fire, he made the terrible mistake of taking a second to aim. That brief hesitation cost him. I threw the trident, and the tines sank through his soft neck.

Unfortunately, the weapon didn't go all the way through. Despite having expert skill with a trident, of all things, I hadn't thrown it hard enough.

"You're weak," I said—Deimos said to me, using my own mouth.

"Stop chucking your weapon around," I replied once again, speaking to myself.

But that was when the abyssal dragon magic coursed through my veins. Another soul was consumed, and it enhanced my physical body, giving me strength even when my puny muscles couldn't.

I leapt at the man with my trident, yanked the weapon free, and then took a bullet to the back. I stumbled forward, my teeth gritted.

"Gray!" Nini screamed.

I whirled around on my heel, and Vivigöl *click-click-clicked* into some sort of chain whip. The weapon was still gold abyssal coral, but now it was long and flexible, the links of the chains barbed and dangerous.

I didn't know how to use a whip. If I tried, I'd likely cut myself from my arms down to my toes. But right now—channeling Deimos's expertise —I knew exactly what to do.

With my new power, and skill, I easily lashed the chain whip and struck the gunman straight across the face. That kind of precision shocked Sorin and Nini, who both gasped. I whipped a second time, striking the man in the same spot *again* before he could really react.

By the abyssal hells—my skill even shocked *me*.

"You know how to use a whip?" I asked as I pulled back the weapon and lashed another gunman, gouging his arm from his elbow to his shoulder. He yelled and hit the deck.

"I'm a weapons master," Deimos replied with my own voice. "My techniques have been forged in the fire of three wars."

When three men ran at me with knives, my first thought was—I couldn't possibly defend myself. How was I supposed to fight three goons who were all armed?

The first man slashed with his five-inch knife.

But then I acted without conscious thought. I grabbed his wrist, twisted hard, and he yelled, dropping his knife in an instant. I whipped around, kicked the legs out from under the second man—who hit the deck so hard, one of his teeth exploded out of his mouth—and then twirled my chain whip around so fast I caught the third man across the face.

Blood splattered across the ship, and the man grabbed at his ruined nose and eyes, screaming to the sky.

Their agony gave me pause.

They were... scared of me.

"Don't lose focus," Deimos said to me.

With a powerful stance, I gripped Vivigöl tightly and turned my attention to the last two men, who had yet to attack. They trembled, both unwilling to move forward.

Then the mireem, Bentley, shot up from below the deck. The hideous worm-leech drooled acidic magic from his circular mouth lined with fangs.

"You killed her," Bentley said, his voice basically gurgles and spits. "*You killed my arcanist.*"

I was surprised he was capable of speaking.

The monster shot for me.

Vivigöl transformed into a halberd—a stylized axe blade at the end of a long pole. I thrust Vivigöl at the deranged mireem. I sliced through a portion of his mouth, and the beast screeched as he slithered away.

Then he vomited acid across the deck of the ship. With a sneer, I turned to Twain. He watched from within his nullstone cage, his big ears perked. I wanted him with me.

I leapt over and slashed the top of his cage. The abyssal coral Vivigöl was made of wasn't drained of its magic when it struck the nullstone. Abyssal coral and nullstone were both naturally occurring elements, and I wasn't sure how to identify which was "more potent," but it seemed the coral just wasn't going to react to the nullifying properties of the stone.

The instant Twain was free, he leapt from the ruined cage. And although he regarded me with some suspicion, Twain ran to the space between my legs.

"Let's kill this monster," he said.

Using my mimic abilities, I quickly searched for a thread of magic. All I felt was Deimos's abyssal dragon and the mireem. It seemed I couldn't draw from sources that were under the constraints of nullstone...

I tugged on the mireem's thread.

Twain bubbled and shifted until he, too, was a nauseating worm-leech.

Thankfully, I didn't lose Deimos's magic. No—it was the opposite. I still had Deimos's abyssal dragon powers, *and now* I had the magic of the mireem. When the monster vomited more acid, I took the strike. Now, thanks to the mireem magic I had stolen, I was immune to the damaging effects of the acid.

It still corroded the ship. And most of my robes.

But not my flesh.

Then I held out my hand. When I used my evocation, I thought it would be the acid, but I was mistaken. The abyssal dragon's evocation—raw magic—blasted from my palm and blew through the head of the enemy mireem, disintegrating his flesh and killing him within an instant.

I shuddered and took a step backward, my heart fluttering as realization hit me.

That was all me.

The magic—the power—I had control of it.

When I glanced around the half-melting deck, and spotted the bodies of the men I had killed, the reality of the situation finally sank in. The injured sailors leapt off the side of the boat and fell straight into the water or hit the sand of the shore.

"Gray," Sorin shouted, returning my thoughts to the immediate. "Gray. Snap out of it. Fight Deimos! Resist!"

Nini glanced between me and my brother. "G-Gray? Deimos? What's going on?"

Twain transformed back into his mimic form, his little kitten gaze locked on mine.

"I..." But I didn't know what else to say. I shook my head. "We need to make sure Father is okay." After a long exhale, I stepped close to Sorin. "Here. I'll free you both. And your eldrin. We should also... make sure those sailors don't get too far. And the gate fragments... We need those."

I had almost forgotten about them. They were still in the woods, probably releasing monsters into the world.

But the thoughts in my head centered around how the runaway sailors would report everything to the other followers of Death Lord Naiad. And I couldn't allow that to happen.

CHAPTER 24

REAPER CHAIN

Using Vivigöl, I sliced through Sorin's and Nini's nullstone restraints. Then I turned my weapon on Thurin's and Waste's cages. Once free, the mystical creatures sprang back into shape, their invisible and hollow bodies taking form under the armor and cloak respectively. Waste's scythe snapped back to his "hands," floating around his blood-red cape.

Thurin immediately dove into the darkness, and then lifted as a shadowy suit of armor around my brother. They merged and became a single being, one that lived and died together. Thurin wasn't a complete suit of armor—I saw parts of Sorin's body through the missing pieces—but he was whole enough to make my brother seem intimidating.

Sorin, with his knightmare, waved his gauntleted hand.

The darkness answered his call, and thin tendrils of shadow sprang up from the deck of the boat. They were like black ropes that moved with a life of their own.

And they all shot for *me*.

Disbelief caused me to hesitate. The tendrils latched on to my legs and arms, attempting to hold me in place. Death Lord Deimos had skills for this. My mind screamed at me to act. I should use Vivigöl to cut myself free of the knightmare magic, and then end the source of my troubles.

Despite that, I kept my body from acting.

Sure, I had the combat knowledge to free myself, but I refused to fight my brother. When his tendrils tightened their grips around my wrists and ankles, I let them.

"Release my brother, fiend," Sorin and Thurin said together, their voices intertwining in a harrowing echo.

Nini straightened her glasses, her hands shaky. "Is Gray not himself?"

Waste floated close to her. "My arcanist, allow me to add my strength to yours." He folded his red cloak body around Nini, merging with her like Thurin had merged with my brother.

Nini and Waste were now a single being, their magic amplified through their unification.

And while those two stood against me, Twain huddled between my legs, his orange fur on end. He growled and slightly hissed at the shadows, but he didn't swipe at them. When he glanced up at me, he seemed scared —or just worried.

I hated seeing him like this.

"I'm okay, Sorin," I said as his restraints slowly coiled further up my limbs. "You don't need to do this. I'm in control."

"Our enemies are escaping," Deimos said through me.

Could Sorin, Twain, and Nini tell it wasn't me who had spoken? Or did they think it was just me?

Sorin didn't release his shadowy hold on my body, but he did falter for a moment. Finally, he asked, "Gray, what's going on?"

"The Death Lord is just letting me borrow his skills and magic," I replied. "To get us out of this situation."

"You... don't seem like yourself."

I chuckled. "Deimos is in my thoughts. But only a little bit."

Twain twitched his large ears until they were perked straight up. "*What?* That sounds terrible!"

"If we don't move now, our enemies will escape," Deimos growled, his irritation clear in my voice. "Stop explaining yourself to these simpletons and do what must be done."

Nini, Twain, and Sorin all stared at me.

They knew *that* wasn't me. I wouldn't call any of them "simpletons," and I never really spoke with such a rough timbre. My throat would hurt afterward if Deimos said any more of his angry statements.

I motioned to the beach with a jut of my chin. "Those sailors who took us hostage *are* fleeing. And the stone-legged man, Vinnie, in the woods had gate fragments. Deimos is right—we need to stop them."

"You and Death Lord Deimos speak as one?" Nini asked, her voice tangled with Waste's. "Interesting."

For some reason, my mind filled with information about reapers. Was this Deimos's knowledge?

Reapers were special mystical creatures born of death. They spawned from the energies of souls leaving living bodies and gained more power from each death they personally caused. Once they were strong enough— once their *chain of life* was complete—they could finally achieve their true form.

The chain...

A small gold chain hung from the folds of Waste's body. It had five golden links, but only three of them had names etched onto the strange metal.

I tightened my grip on Vivigöl. Something about the chain reminded me of the abyssal coral my weapon was made of.

Deimos seemed to regard the reaper with respect. He thought of it as an *agent of the abyssal hells*, and somehow, felt Waste was an ally. Which was an odd thought.

"We should listen to the wisdom of the Death Lord." Nini turned to face the forest. "One of us should handle the stone-legged man, and the other two should search for the two men who went in opposite directions."

My brother reluctantly waved his hand. The shadow tendrils around my arms and legs vanished in an instant. The darkness melted away, leaving me free. I rotated my shoulders, thankful I didn't have to fight my brother.

Twain frowned. "Gray..."

I leaned down and patted his head. "I told you. I'm fine."

"Nini," Sorin said. "You head to the woods. Gray and I will run down the men on the beach. Just shout if you need us."

"All right." Nini grabbed her scythe in both hands and then hurried down the gangplank.

My father and stepmother were still below deck, but they could wait a few more minutes while we cleaned everything up. I wouldn't want to distress them with all the violence.

Once alone, my brother faced me fully. "Gray…"

"I'm fine," I repeated.

"You're not fine. This isn't natural or normal."

I didn't have a rebuttal for that.

Sorin continued, his voice still interwoven with Thurin's, "Don't worry. After all this is finished, I'll help you get rid of the Death Lord's influence. I promise."

"Thank you, Sorin."

What I didn't say, because I didn't want to have an argument, was that I didn't think Sorin could help me. *I* was the one who had weakened Professor Helmith's cage, and *I* was the one who had accepted Deimos's help when he offered. I was also the one running the show. How would my brother help me now? This was my problem, and I'd have to solve it myself one way or another.

Sorin stepped into the darkness and traveled like a puddle of black liquid across the deck, over the railing of the ship, and then down onto the beach. He stepped out of the shadows and onto the sands, his boots getting splashed by the waves.

Before I could follow, Twain leapt in front of me.

"Gray?" he whispered.

"I really am okay," I said.

"Can I help you?"

I knitted my eyebrows. "What do you mean?"

He pawed my boot. "I'm your eldrin. You have Deimos's magic, right? Transform me into something useful."

I didn't have many options, but both the knightmare and the reaper were interesting. If I merged with my eldrin, would that block Deimos from supplying me with his knowledge and magic? I decided to try.

After closing my eyes, I quickly tugged the magical thread that led to my brother's knightmare. Twain bubbled and shifted and then transformed into an exact duplicate of Thurin, including the knightmare's feathery cape.

"Perfect," Twain said, his voice now dark and haunting.

He dove into the darkness and then sprang up around me. The cold power of his shadow armor crept into my body as we merged. It was a strange feeling, because now I had Deimos's thoughts *and* Twain's in my mind all at once.

"*We can do this,*" Twain said telepathically.

"Quickly," Deimos barked, using my mouth. "You have wasted vast amounts of time on *nothing.*"

I wasn't as naturally gifted with knightmare magic as my brother. Instead of shadow-stepping onto the beach, I just walked down the gangplank, similar to Nini. I'd rather look competent than make a fool of myself.

Sorin was already chasing after the man who had run north along the beach. The other man had gone down, down the coastline, his footprints gradually being erased by the slow lap of the waves across the sands.

But...

I felt the man.

Well, not *him.* I felt his life energies. The beat of his heart. The strength of his breath. Abyssal dragon arcanists could tell when creatures were close to perishing. They could also gauge how healthy someone was. Bizarre powers. Useful, though. In a creepy way.

I ran down the beach, Vivigöl in hand. The weapon *click-click-clicked* until it transformed into a trident once more.

The man frantically glanced over his shoulder, his eyes practically bulging from his skull when he realized I had given chase. His scrawny legs picked up pace, but the abyssal dragon empowerment made me faster than a normal man.

I ran him down like a nemean lion does its prey.

The tine of the trident could've easily pierced the man's flesh, but instead, I used the weapon more like a club. I battered the man's legs from the side in one vicious swing, toppling the man over. He hit the sand face-first.

Content I had caught him, I leisurely sauntered around his position on the beach and then pointed Vivigöl at the side of his neck.

"Why are you serving Death Lord Naiad?" I asked.

The thug threw both his arms over the back of his head. "I don't! I'm a mercenary! They paid me—*they paid me.*"

He sounded sincere.

Which was disappointing. It meant this lackey wouldn't know any valuable information. He was just a hired gun.

"Kill him, and let's move on," Deimos said, though it was odd to hear my own voice whenever he spoke.

"There's no point," I replied—to myself. "He's just some stooge."

"There's always a point. And it's to send a message. If none of Naiad's flunkies return, not even the hired muscle, then sellswords in the future will think twice about accepting offers from her."

I mulled that over for a second.

"Besides," Deimos continue, "if his soul comes to me, I can torture it."

I shook my head. "There are hundreds of mercenary companies in nations all across the world. Just because one failed doesn't mean they'll all cower. And torturing the man definitely won't help anyone."

"Then take him captive. Anything to prevent his ilk from harming us further."

"Fine."

Although I had killed several men on the boat, those men had been actively attempting to take my life. *This* sad sack was trembling in the sand, obviously afraid for his life. Taking him prisoner and handing him over to the authorities seemed a fair alternative.

I grabbed the man by the collar and yanked him to his feet. He blubbered something, but didn't fight me as I dragged him back to the ship.

Despite my mercy, a part of me already felt like a cold killer. I chalked that up to Deimos's influence. He had no qualms with slicing through a dozen individuals like they were chunks of bread. I felt it in the cold way he analyzed our surroundings.

Even now, if I concentrated on my thoughts, I heard the whispers of his machinations. He wanted to return to the woods and fill the stone-legged man with shallow holes, slowly bleeding him to death, until he told us everything we wanted to know.

I threw the mercenary onto the deck, tied him to a mast, and then thought about Nini.

With Twain still a knightmare protectively wrapped around my body, I ran for the wooded area near the beach. My brother slipped through the darkness and met me at the tree line. A few feet into the woods, I stopped.

Nini, still merged with Waste, stood by a large thicket, not far from us.

Three gate fragments sat at her feet, flickering with magic. Three corpses were also chopped to bits around the forest. They were shambling zombies brought through to the land of the living through the gate fragments.

But they were dead again.

And Nini had three more chain links.

No, wait...

She had four. The last one had the name *Vinnie Kalkos* written on the golden metal.

CHAPTER 25

BACK TO THE ACADEMY

S orin and I glanced around.

While Nini stood protectively over the active gate fragments, she clung to the reaper scythe with white-knuckle intensity. Her eyes were large and round as Sorin and I hurried to her.

"What happened?" Sorin asked, his voice a mix of his and Thurin's.

Nini took a shallow breath. "Th-There were monsters. I cut them down. Another appeared. *And then the man leapt at me.*" She practically tripped over her words in her haste to speak. "I d-didn't mean to. I was just trying to get rid of the beasts. I thought— I didn't know—the man would lunge!"

Thurin unmerged from my brother. The knightmare melted away, like the shadows were ice under the heat of a summer sun. Once free of the darkness, Sorin stepped forward and placed both his hands on Nini's shoulders. "Are you okay?"

She nodded, but her wet eyes threatened to spill with tears at any moment.

My brother slowly hugged her. He rubbed Nini's back, his fingers sliding over the bloodred cloak of the reaper. Nini took deep breaths and rested her head on Sorin's collarbone.

"Pathetic," I whispered.

Well, it wasn't *me*. Deimos clearly had little empathy.

I gritted my teeth. "Nini has had a hard time," I muttered under my breath. "She accidentally killed someone."

Deimos replied, "She's a reaper arcanist. *Obviously*, she has killed before. And it will only get easier as her power grows. There is no need to feel sullen."

I didn't reply. Would Nini want stronger magical death powers? She talked about her brother's death like it was the worst moment in her life. But as I glanced around, watching the zombie bodies ooze into puddles of water and basically vanish, I wondered...

When she merged with Waste, did *he* have a killer instinct that made slaying enemies easier? Like I had with Deimos's skills?

One of the gate fragments flickered with a pulse of magic. Salt water gushed out across the floor of the forest, and out of the puddle rose a corpse-like entity. It was humanoid, but so bloated with water, every inch of its blue skin sagged. The sunken eyes and waterlogged face of the monster looked as though someone had taken a plank of wood and bashed it several times across the beast's nose.

Despite that, the bones of the fingers were exposed and sharpened. It clawed its way to a standing position and then reached for me.

I grabbed Vivigöl. It clicked as it shifted into a long, golden sword. Before Sorin or Nini could react, I slashed the freakish monster straight across the chest. Water gushed from the injury, and the creature staggered backward. With skill I had never possessed before, I swung down with a powerful overhand swing, cleaving through the beast's shoulder and disarming it.

The zombie *thing* toppled to the ground, more briny water splashing from its body.

Then it stopped moving and began to dissolve.

I had seen these strange undead before, when I had gone camping with the rest of my class. They came from the gate fragments, but they weren't mystical creatures, like ghouls. Professor Helmith had guessed they were fragments of humans given form through some sort of foul magic.

I assumed it had something to do with the abyssal hells.

And they were obviously some sort of soul, because when Nini slayed them, she gained another chain link, though it had no name. What did that mean? Nothing good, clearly.

"*I can't maintain this anymore*," Twain said telepathically to me, his voice strained.

His knightmare body melted off me. Then he bubbled and reformed into a small orange cat. His large ears twitched as Twain scratched himself all over.

"I don't like being hollow," he said.

I chuckled. "I bet. That must be strange."

Twain was getting better and better at maintaining the shape of another creature. Apparently, the older he got, and the more refined his magic became through use, the longer he'd be able to hold shapes. Days. Weeks.

"Gray," my brother said, drawing my attention.

"Yes?"

"I'll grab these fragments and help Nini back to the boat. Can I trust you to free Dad and Mum?"

"Why wouldn't you be able to trust me?"

Sorin stared at me for a long while. His eyes—the same gray-blue color as mine—spoke volumes.

He didn't like the fact that I had channeled Deimos somehow. He didn't like that I was still doing it. And that I wasn't worried or actively trying to stop it.

"I'm fine," I said. "And I'll go get our father."

"And Mum." Sorin held Nini close. "Don't forget her."

"I won't."

How could I forget? What did he even mean by that? Before my brother could say anything else, I turned on my heel and headed for the boat. As I jogged my way to the gangplank, I transformed Vivigöl back into the jewelry shape that clung to my shoulders and neck. I tucked the weapon away, thankful to feel the cold touch against my skin.

"W-Wait up, Gray!"

I stopped, one foot on the gangplank, and glanced over my shoulder.

Twain ran to catch up with me, his little paws leaving adorable prints on the beach as he went. He huffed as he reached my feet.

"You almost left me," he said, a touch indignant. "When did you get so fast?"

I shrugged. "I don't know. It's just... easier to run."

"Pick me up."

With a smile, I scooped Twain into my arms. He purred as we both headed onto the ship, crossed the deck, ignoring the tied-up mercenary I had left on the mast, and then went down into the hold.

The place was a mess. It looked as though the mireem had gone crazy after his arcanist's death. The blasted creature had smashed up barrels and bags, spilling rations of jerky and fresh water everywhere.

My father and stepmother were at the far end of the hold, tied simply to the bulkhead.

"Gray?" my father asked, his eyes wide.

I ran over to him. "I'm here." My hands shook as I undid his restraints. Then I turned and undid the ropes around my stepmother's wrists. Her eyes—always watery—spilled tears as she threw her arms around me.

"Oh, Gray. W-We were so worried about you." She tightened her hold around my neck and then sobbed onto my shoulder.

I didn't know why, but I hadn't been expecting this. My stepmother and I had never been particularly close. In my heart, I always thought of my real mother, and how she died when I was born, and that if I loved my stepmother, it would somehow be a betrayal to her.

My mother had sacrificed everything to bring me into this world. If I loved another as a mother, would that be an insult to her gift?

But I couldn't stop myself from hugging my stepmother back.

"Everything is going to be okay," I whispered.

"What happened?" she asked in a soft voice.

"I dealt with the... people. No one will be hurting you two anymore."

Deimos's presence lingered at the forefront of my thoughts. He seemed... preoccupied with thoughts of his own mother. At that moment, while I held my stepmother, he was wrapped up in old emotions.

I released her, and my father immediately yanked me into a bear hug.

My father was larger than me. Like Sorin, he was nearly six inches taller, and his body was large. His gut stuck out, and his arms were thick and hairy. He practically enveloped me.

And I wanted to give him a hug back, but...

I shoved him away, hatred rushing through me.

"*My father is a monster*," I growled through clenched teeth.

No. That wasn't me.

It was Deimos.

His intense anger seeped into all other parts of my being. Deimos despised *his* father, and with each beat of my heart, his hate became my own.

"Pull yourself together," I murmured under my breath.

"G-Gray?" my father asked, his eyes wide.

I hugged myself, and dug my fingers into my forearms. "I... I'm sorry," I managed to choke out. "I'm not myself." With a shaky hand, I ran it through my hair. "You wouldn't believe what I've been through..."

Both my father and stepmother waited. They didn't move, they didn't even breathe.

Once I had everything under control, including Deimos's irrational rage, I exhaled and stepped close. Then I held out my arms.

"Sorry," I whispered again. "And I don't just mean about *this*." I glanced around at the dank hold. "I mean about everything. I... didn't make things easy as a son. And I should've been... more grateful. For everything you provided Sorin and me. I should've—"

I wanted to keep going, but my father cut me off with a second bear hug. I didn't even see it coming. He just wrapped his arms around my body and pulled me into him again.

"Don't spout all this nonsense now," he said, tightening his squeeze. "I couldn't be prouder. My son, an arcanist, saved us from these cutthroats? And look at you. A man."

Despite Deimos's general disgust for my father, I wrapped my arms as much as I could around my father's rotund body. "Sorin helped with everything."

"Course he did. Course. You two have always been inseparable."

Then we parted. I wanted to apologize again, but he patted me on the shoulder and gave me a stare that told me he was on the verge of raw emotion. I motioned to the ladder up. "C'mon. We should take this ship back through the Gate of Crossing. We can go straight to the headmaster. We can tell him what happened."

"Right. Smart. We'll do just that." My father held out an arm for my stepmother, and then the two of them headed for the deck.

The voyage back to Astra Academy only took a few hours, but by the time we arrived back on the mountain lake, it was after noon, and the sun was beginning its descent.

I handed off the captured mercenary, and then went up the long stairway to the Academy.

Once back in the castle-like building, we headed straight for the headmaster's office, which overlooked the central courtyard. Headmaster Venrover allowed us in without question. My father and stepmother sat close to his desk, while Sorin and I stood on either side of them.

Nini stood at the back of the room, her gaze on the floor the entire time. Waste kept himself partially draped over her shoulders, and she hugged the cloth of his cloak to her chest. I had never seen her so quiet.

My brother explained everything, for which I was grateful.

I didn't trust myself to speak, lest Deimos make a comment.

"—and that was when Gray fought off the kidnappers," Sorin concluded. "He and Twain managed to get us free, and we ran down some of the fiends, but they were mercenaries."

"And the ones in charge—the arcanist and her assistant—claimed to follow Death Lord Naiad?" Headmaster Venrover asked, one eyebrow perfectly raised.

"That's right."

"Oh, how dreadful." My stepmother grabbed my father's arm. She was so small compared to him. "What is the world coming to? People worshipping Death Lords? It's worse than pirates. I thought we were done with those dark ages."

My father pressed his lips into a hard, straight line. "This morning was filled with dozens of bad omens, but I ignored them all. I should've scheduled this visit for some other day."

The headmaster forced himself to smile. "Ah, Mister and Missus Lexly, why don't you stay with us for a few weeks while we sort this all out? We have quarters for visiting guests."

"I have a candle shop to run," my father promptly said.

"I can pay for the loss in business, of course," the headmaster replied, never missing a beat.

"O-Oh. I see." My father rubbed his chin. "Then we'll gladly take you up on your kind generosity."

Headmaster Venrover slightly bowed his head. "Good to hear." Then he gave Sorin, Nini, and me a quick glance. "While I have arcanists investigate this tragedy, why don't the three of you head to Doc Tomas's office? For healing."

"I'm fine," I said.

Sorin jabbed a finger into my chest. "Are you sure? You look... not good."

I glanced down. Twain did the same.

My robes had holes through them, my white shirt was stained crimson with my own blood, and my pants appeared as though they had been dragged through three mud puddles. I agreed with Sorin. I looked "not good."

Funny, the headmaster didn't seem that concerned with my appearance. He hadn't even seemed bothered by the copious amounts of blood.

He was a strange man. But I didn't have time for that.

"I'm no longer injured," I eventually said.

The headmaster replied with a single nod. "Very well. Why don't you return to class, then? But don't hesitate to take care of yourselves. If you need to rest in the dorms, you may."

I hesitated.

While Sorin had recounted what had happened, he had completely omitted the part about Death Lord Deimos. Then again, the headmaster already knew about the soul fragment—and its ability to give me skills. Did I really need to explain these new details to him?

It was better not to make everyone worry.

"Thank you, Headmaster," I said. I picked up Twain. "Which class do we have again?"

Sorin lifted both his eyebrows. "*Magical Fundamentals*, remember? With Professor Ren?"

"Right."

The three of us left the headmaster's impressive office, but Nini did so without so much as a word. Once we were in the hall, away from everyone else, she finally released her reaper's cloak. The gold chain rattled out of the folds of the reaper's body. It clattered as it swung through the air, hanging like a deadman's noose.

"Have you been holding that this whole time?" I asked.

Nini didn't reply.

Sorin placed a gentle hand on her shoulder. "Nini?"

"What am I going to do, Sorin?" she whispered as she turned to stare up at him. "I can't go back to class. I'll just... I'll just go to the dorm. And stay there."

"Why?"

She motioned to the chain, her eyes wide and glassy. "Do you see this? Everyone will know, Sorin. *Everyone will know.* I killed someone else. L-Last time this happened, I was shunned, and disowned, and everyone hated me." Nini grabbed Waste's cloak. "What am I going to do?" she whispered into her eldrin.

The reaper draped himself over her once more, as though offering a comforting embrace.

Sorin turned to me, his gaze hard.

He wanted me to think of something.

"What can we do, Gray?" he asked under his breath.

Obviously, murdering individuals was against all codes of laws in every nation—except in the cases of self-defense, wartime, or direct orders from monarchy. In this instance, Nini had defended herself from a madman who was going to kill us all.

But I understood why she would be upset.

The rest of our class hadn't been there to see what had happened. The only thing they would see was that Nini's chain had gotten longer. And some people in our class had already treated Nini poorly because she was a reaper arcanist.

I mean, no one really *liked* reaper arcanists. They were murderers, inherently. But some of the class had warmed up to Nini—like Phila. Would Phila distance herself once she saw the chain?

CHAPTER 26

CLASS CHEMISTRY

"My arcanist," Waste said, his voice stronger and louder than I had ever heard before. He kept his cloak tightly swaddled around Nini. "I have grown more powerful. Those in this Academy will see that. And the smart ones will admire your newfound abilities."

I hadn't noticed until then, but Waste was... different.

Scary different.

His scythe had been dull and rusty before. Now it seemed to be crafted from fresh steel, and rather sharp. The ends of his cloak were more frayed than before, like someone had ripped at the edges, giving him a sinister hemline.

Not only that, but his cloak was thicker, and an inch or two longer.

The more reapers killed, the stronger they became.

Nini stroked Waste's bloodred fabric. "I don't want them to hate me."

"They won't hate you," Waste darkly muttered. "They will fear you."

Nini's lip quavered. Clearly, that thought wasn't helping at all.

"Reapers are sacred," Deimos said through me, curt and cold. "They're one of the few creatures allowed to roam the realm of the abyssal hells, and the only creatures permitted to bring soul fragments to the final gates. Even the elder creatures won't impede their path. You should be proud, girl, not sniveling. Those who shun you have just forgotten their place."

Both Nini and Sorin stared at me for a long while. Nini had to adjust her glasses.

My brother grabbed my arm. "Gray—if you're in control, you need to stop this now. I don't think you need the Death Lord's power any longer."

"Right." I rubbed my temple. "I'll do that."

If I knew how.

Which I didn't.

Twain stared up at me. I held him with my other arm, cradling him close. He said nothing.

"Look, I have an idea." I gestured to the hallway. "We can't get rid of Waste's chain, but we can hide it."

"It hangs off of him," Nini said, pointing to the links.

"We're not going to hide it *physically*. We're going to hide it with magic, which is clearly superior."

"How?" Sorin asked.

I held up a finger. "Let's just go get Exie. She's an erlking arcanist. She has *illusions*. We can cover the chain. We can make it look like something else... Or at the very least, cover the name on the link, and say she just killed weird abyssal zombies."

Everyone in class knew that was how Nini's chain had gotten longer before, and no one seemed to care.

Sorin stepped closer to me and lowered his voice to a whisper. "Uh, can we ask anyone but Exie? Literally anyone else."

"Why?" I whispered back. "We don't have tons of options here, Sorin."

"Well... Remember how I told you I had *relationship problems*?"

Ah. Right.

Exie really wanted Sorin for herself. Had she made overt moves to get him and now he was feeling uncomfortable? That didn't surprise me. Sorin was as steady and true as the sun's path through the sky. Perhaps *other* individuals could be tempted away from their significant others—but not Sorin.

I nodded toward Nini, who had gone back to fidgeting with Waste's cloak. "Look, we can get an illusion or Nini can hide in her dorm," I said. "You pick."

Sorin shook his head. "First, you should change. It'll also give us all some time to think."

I held up one hand. "All right. Nini, wait at the end of this hall. Sorin, head to our classroom—it's almost time for a break. I'll change and meet you there."

My brother nodded. Nini didn't look as confident. She clung to her eldrin and bunched her shoulders at the base of her neck, as though trying to take up the least amount of space possible.

Although they both remained silent, I took off down the hall and headed straight for the first-year dorms. Twain clung to me as I jogged through Astra Academy. When we passed the massive windows, I caught sight of other classes taking place outside. Magic flew through the air— fire, lightning, and what appeared to be shooting stars.

They were older arcanists, I could tell. Their magic was more refined and powerful.

But I shook my head and slowed my pace once I was closer to my destination.

The enhanced strength and speed from the abyssal dragon magic was waning. It was a short burst of power for the price paid. It seemed inefficient. Or cruel. But I also pushed that from my thoughts.

"Deimos," I said. "I don't need your assistance anymore. How about you go back to slumbering now, hm?"

Twain twitched one ear. "Do you seriously think that will work?" he whispered.

I hoped it would.

"Feh," Deimos said through me, clearly amused. "Our agreement had no terms for duration. And with this channel, I can see the world you inhabit more clearly than before. I won't go back to that prison."

I ran a hand down my face. "Curse the abyssal hells..."

"What a foolish thing to do," Deimos shot back.

I was glad I was alone in the hallway except for Twain. My split personality was starting to hit new highs I wasn't comfortable with.

Nini was afraid of all the death she had brought, but it was nothing compared to the power I had used against our enemies. I had killed before —only once. At Ashlyn's cotillion.

My hands shook a little when I thought about that.

So I didn't.

"Listen, Deimos," I whispered to myself, "at least keep your commentary to a minimum. Obviously, Death Lord Naiad somehow knows of your presence. How? How did she know? How did her followers know to come get me?"

I had given this some thought on the sail back to the Academy, but I hadn't come to any real conclusions. Death Lord Deimos's followers had *also* known when I would be attending Ashlyn's cotillion, which meant there was someone spreading information about what was happening in my personal life.

This had to stop. And if Deimos made himself known to *everyone*, it would make searching for the one leak difficult.

If only a small number of people knew about Deimos, I could easily go through them and discover who had discussed my parents' arrival at the Academy.

"Just stay quiet," I said.

Deimos didn't reply. I didn't know if that was him being sarcastic, or if he was just following orders, but it bothered me that he didn't outright agree.

I ran the rest of the way to the dorms, went straight for my bed, opened my personal chest of clothing, and changed. Would my ruined clothes be mended? I hoped so. I left them hanging on the end of my bed so the housekeeper would find them.

Then I dashed down the halls until I reached my classroom, and just as I had suspected, everyone else was funneling out to take their break. Sorin was already waiting, and he approached the students before me.

I stood at least ten feet from the door, hoping Professor Ren wouldn't notice me and ask me why I hadn't been in class. Then Ashlyn stepped out into the hall, followed closely by her typhoon dragon. She took one look at me and strode over, her confidence—and irritation—on full display.

I straightened my posture as she approached. Her dragon loomed behind her, all intimidation.

"Gray," Ashlyn said in a harsh whisper once she was by my side. "*Where have you been?*"

With a casual shrug, I replied, "I got kidnapped. No biggie. I'm fine now. Thanks for asking. How's your day been?"

Clearly, Ashlyn wasn't amused by my sarcasm.

"Where have you *really* been? The professor was asking about you, and Ecrib said you had some sort of crazy scheme and—"

"We actually got kidnapped," Twain interjected, no mirth in his tone.

Ashlyn swallowed the last of her words. She hardened her gaze and slowly narrowed her eyes. "Explain, then."

"It's a long story, and I have to do something before I get back to class." I took her hand and offered her a playful smile. "How about I regale you with all the details tomorrow morning? Before class? Outside, in the beautiful morning mists?" Then I rubbed her knuckles.

Ashlyn didn't immediately jerk her hand out of mine. She waited for a long while, staring at me intently. Finally, she tugged her hand free of my grip. "Fine. In the morning. At least an hour before sunrise." Ashlyn gave me a pointed look that said, "*You better be there.*"

I lifted an eyebrow and tilted my head to the side, basically saying—without any words—"*Of course, I wouldn't miss it for anything.*"

Her typhoon dragon snorted, and a spark of lightning flickered from his nostrils. Ecrib didn't seem like he enjoyed my company at the moment. I gave him a sardonic salute as he turned away.

Sorin made his way over to my side, Exie in tow. Her erlking silently fluttered through the air, orbiting her head as though he was bored. What was his name? Rex. Right. Rex the erlking. He had his little arms folded across his chest.

"And where are we going?" Exie asked. She fluffed her curly brown hair. It shimmered with health and extreme amounts of care. "Class will start again soon."

"Um," Sorin said, obviously cringing internally. "Well, I need your help."

Exie's green eyes widened. She stepped closer to Sorin and delicately touched his shoulder. "Ah. I see. You came to me because I'm the most beautiful and talented arcanist in our class, is that it?"

"Uh, sure."

"I thought so!" Exie giggled. "I'd love to help you, dear."

Dear.

I cringed.

"Good." Sorin nervously rubbed his hands together. The shadows at his feet fluttered, and I figured his knightmare was silently encouraging him. "I'd also really appreciate it if you kept this a secret."

Exie's expression practically glowed. She cupped her own rosy cheek. "Hm. Interesting. I won't say no..."

"So you promise you won't say a word?"

"I promise."

Sorin gestured to the hall. "Come with me, okay?"

Exie walked beside him with a smug little smile, and I trailed behind. Ashlyn gave me glances over her shoulder, and I did the same. We had this silent language between us, and I knew she was worried about me.

By the abyssal hells—*I* was worried about me.

But I would handle it.

As I thought that, Deimos's impressions crept into my thoughts. He seemed determined. About everything. And his willpower briefly infected mine, giving me this righteous confidence that nothing would stop me if I put all my effort and mind to a task.

Was Deimos always that confident? It seemed tiring.

Yet, also very useful.

It didn't take us long to find Nini at the far end of the headmaster's hallway. Headmaster Venrover's office door was still shut tight, but light shone from underneath, and I wondered what he was discussing with my parents.

Sorin immediately went to Nini. He turned to face Exie as he said, "I was hoping you could use an illusion to help Nini."

Exie stopped dead in her tracks. She kept her stance stiff, and a smile in place, but all of it was tense. "Hm. You said *you* needed my help."

"I do." Sorin took Nini's hand. "Nini is my honeysuckle, and if she's in distress, I'm in distress."

Oh, clever. I had wondered how he would logic his way out of this. It was romantic, I'd give him that much, but I knew Exie didn't like this development at all.

She held a hand up to the bottom of her chin. Then she gave Nini the once over. "Look here, my illusions can't fix garish choices of style, nor can it fix someone's slumped posture, or their meek personality."

"Is this you being polite?" I quipped. "I'd hate to see how you speak to your enemies."

Nini held on to the cloak of her reaper tighter than ever.

"*Exie*," Sorin said, his tone restrained. "Nini doesn't need help with any of that." He wrapped an arm around her. "What she needs is privacy."

Exie stared at him with a half-lidded glare of sarcastic disbelief. "Uh-huh."

"Can you illusion the chain on her reaper so people won't see it?" Sorin stepped aside and grabbed the chain from the folds of the cloak. The gold links practically sparkled. Especially the ones with names on them.

Exie recoiled in disgust. Even her erlking sneered and fluttered away, his tongue poking out of his lips.

"She's killed again?" Exie whispered.

Nini's lower lip trembled.

"She had to," Twain said, perking up from my arms. "We were attacked. And kidnapped! Nini helped us."

I petted my eldrin. That was a good point.

Exie glowered at us. "If her actions were so righteous, why does she want to hide them?"

Also a good point.

"That's why I said she needs *privacy*," Sorin calmly stated. "She just doesn't want people to know. And that's not a crime. Please—can you help her? I... I would be in your debt."

Exie's expression instantly changed from sour to intrigued. She relaxed as she strode over to the reaper, and while she clearly didn't want to touch Waste, she did examine the chain with a keen eye. "I can't make things invisible, but I can hide the name. Or perhaps make the whole thing look like a ribbon. It might be suspicious, then."

"Just hide the name," Nini whispered.

Exie rotated her hand through the air. An illusion of light shimmered over the name on the chain, hiding it from the world.

"I can't hold this forever," Exie said as she backed away. She placed a single hand on her hip. "If you want to permanently hide it, I suggest you purchase an illusion trinket."

"A trinket?" Sorin asked.

"A minor magical item," I said. "But we need star shards for that. Which are expensive. Even a small item would be way more expensive than we could afford."

Exie folded her arms over her chest. "Well, I can reapply the illusion every morning before class. But I won't do that *forever*." Then she fluttered her lashes at Sorin. "Just for a few weeks, while you think of another solution. Does that sound acceptable, Sorie?"

Sorie?

I wanted to vomit in my mouth.

"That's fine," Nini muttered. She stepped between Exie and Sorin, and then rested her cheek on my brother's chest.

I didn't know if she did that on purpose, or if she was just in need of comfort. Either way, it didn't sit well with Exie.

"Very well, if you don't need my services anymore, I'll be heading back to class." Exie turned and then flounced down the hallway without another word, her erlking giving us cold glares as he flew by.

"Remember that you promised to keep this between us," Sorin called out after her.

"I remember." Exie didn't even glance back. She continued on her way, anger in her steps.

"And thank you!"

Exie slowed a bit, visibly cooling off. She still didn't turn around, though.

Sorin turned to me. "Thank you, too, Gray. I can always count on you to come up with good ideas."

I shrugged. "Eh. Don't mention it."

Nini held my brother with a tender hug. Then she gave me a weak smile. "Thank you, Gray."

I waved away her comment. "We should probably get to class as well." I hefted Twain higher into my arms. "Let's at least *pretend* today has been normal, shall we?"

CHAPTER 27

DREAM PARTY

Everyone settled into their seats just as the break ended.

The others in class glanced at Nini's reaper as he floated by, his chain rattling. No one said anything, thankfully. Perhaps our plan had worked.

Professor Ren stood at the front of the classroom with enough pomp and swagger for three boats full of swashbucklers. He leaned against the front of the desk and regarded the whole classroom with a smirk. His bright red hair had been slicked back.

"Glad some of you could make it," Professor Ren said, glancing over at Sorin, Nini, and me.

The man was classically handsome. He stood tall, had plenty of muscles, and flaunted everything in a classy, but blatant way. He wore his robe open with a half-buttoned shirt, exposing some of his rune-covered skin. The runes were glittering tattoos of pure power, just like Professor Helmith's. Ren had runes of red and blue, many of which were shaped like fire.

Normally, his chest was left uncovered, but today he had bandages over a large majority of his body. He was still injured, then.

Professor Ren had been the only other professor to face Death Lord Deimos while I had been possessed, and Ren had nearly died. Unlike

Professor Helmith, who had been injured in the fight and was still bedridden, Ren was already back on his feet.

Professor Ren gave me a weird sidelong glance. "How are you today, Gray? Feeling okay? Like yourself, and no one else?"

Some of the others in class chuckled at the joke.

Knovak didn't.

And neither did I.

If Ren knew the truth, I suspected he would've thrown me out a window.

"I'm fine," I said.

Professor Ren kept his smirk as he walked over and slapped me on the shoulder. "Don't worry. I'm back on my feet, and the headmaster has all sorts of plans to improve security. You'll be as safe as a bug."

I met his gaze and nodded once.

Obviously, Professor Ren didn't know I still had a problem. Whereas Sorin could tell something was wrong with me from a single glance, Ren didn't know me well enough. He suspected nothing.

"Thank you," I said.

Then Ren turned to face the rest of the class. The man had piercings along the edges of his ears—at least half a dozen on each. They glittered in the light of a late afternoon, especially as he began pacing around the classroom.

"As I was saying—the real key to enchanting your body with runes is to know your magical weaknesses. You want runes that will complement your abilities. Take mine, for example." Ren held out his arm and grimaced. He rubbed the bandages over his body before continuing. "I have phoenix runes that allow me to light my webs on fire."

Professor Ren pointed to his arcanist mark. It was a seven-pointed star with a spider woven between the points.

Ren was a treasure cache spider arcanist.

I glanced around, looking for his eldrin.

There he was. In the corner of the room, near the ceiling, clinging to the walls through the use of copious amounts of webs.

The metal spider was at least three feet tall, and his legs were needle-sharp. The whole damn creature—Trove, his name was—appeared to be made of metal and raw gemstones. He sparkled up in his corner, watching the class like a creepy spectator.

Sorin raised his hand.

Professor Ren turned to face him. "Yes?"

"When will we learn about *trinkets?*"

"That's later in the curriculum."

Sorin nodded. "Uh, could we maybe... alter the curriculum? I think learning about trinkets would be more interesting."

Professor Ren chuckled. "And you want to rearrange the whole lesson plan based on what *you* find interesting? I mean... Sheesh. We need a new lesson on narcissism before we do anything else, clearly."

Nasbit also raised his hand. When he was called on, he said, "I think a practical lesson on trinkets would be fascinating."

"M-Me, too," Nini quietly chimed in.

Ren pinched the bridge of his nose.

"Will we learn how to make trinkets as part of our studies?" Sorin leaned onto our table. "I was hoping we could make one ourselves."

"That would be mighty expensive," Nasbit whispered.

Professor Ren held up a hand, and everyone went quiet. "We *will* make trinkets, but that's the lesson of the year. Everyone makes their first trinket, and you get to keep it."

"What if we can't pay for the materials?" Raaza interjected. "I'll never be able to afford a single star shard."

The professor shook his head. "The Academy will be paying for all the materials."

"Heh." Raaza leaned back and snorted. "No wonder the headmaster is desperate to put on a fundraiser. He's bleeding coins."

Professor Ren held up a single finger. "Headmaster Venrover specifically went out of his way to make sure any arcanist could get a proper education here, regardless of background. That's why he maintains the Menagerie, and why he feels it's important for the Academy to cover the costs of materials."

"What if he runs out of funds?"

Ren nervously chuckled. "That's why he's putting on a fundraiser. Don't worry—plenty of wealthy arcanists believe in Headmaster Venrover's vision. Everything will be fine."

I didn't think anyone *had* been worried, but when Ren said it like that, I became a little anxious. What would happen if the headmaster failed to secure the coin necessary for the Academy? I wondered...

Night settled over Astra Academy, bringing with it a cool and calm atmosphere I desperately needed.

Everyone retired to their dorms, and I curled up on my bed, ready for the day to end. Unfortunately, the others had *questions* about Sorin's, Nini's, and my disappearance. Fortunately, my brother was more than happy to explain everything.

"That was when it happened." Sorin stood and dramatically held out his arms. "On the beach. We had to fight for our lives."

Moonlight and lanterns kept the dorm dimly lit. All the beds, still piled around in a circle, felt like a cushy cave with all the sheets draped overhead. Nasbit, Knovak, and Raaza all rolled around on their mattresses. Only Raaza, Sorin, and I had our eldrin. The others were in the treehouse.

"Then what happened?" Knovak asked.

"Gray used his *shifting weapon* and *mimic magic* to defeat all the villains." Sorin stood straighter, a proud smile blooming across his face. "He saved our parents, and Nini and me."

"Did he use any strange archery skills?" Raaza quipped.

Sorin shook his head. "No. And once they were all defeated, we sailed ourselves back to the Academy. It was quite the adventure."

Knovak, who was smoothing his silk sleeping shirt, stopped midstroke. He glanced up and turned to face me. "Gray... You defeated all those thugs? By yourself?"

"Yup," I muttered into my pillow.

"But you don't know how to fight. You told us that before. You never had any training."

I froze in place, unwilling to even breathe. Why did Knovak have to remember that detail?

"Did... Death Lord Deimos take control of you? Or did you somehow use his combat arts to defeat those fiends?" Knovak spoke with fear in his words. He rubbed his arms. "He is *powerful*."

I rolled onto my back and stared at the ceiling. What was the point of lying? There wasn't much. They all knew about Deimos.

"Yeah," I whispered. "I channeled Deimos's abilities to help in the fight." Then I sat up and held out a hand. "But don't lose your mind over this. I was in perfect control. Everything is handled. Nothing went wrong."

Knovak wrung his hands, his gaze falling to the floor. For a prolonged moment, he grew tense, and I wondered if he would be outraged to the point of shouting. Finally, he stood from his bed.

"Maybe we should... destroy this presence in your mind." Knovak glanced around at the others. "All of us. It's just a *fragment* of the Death Lord, after all. We should be able to handle this."

"Not *you*," Raaza spat. He also stood from his bed. "You're a unicorn arcanist. Sit down and let the more powerful arcanists handle this."

Knovak glared, though he didn't argue. He balled his hands into tight fists, his muscles never relaxing. How often could one man be told he was weaker than everyone else before snapping? I suspected I would learn the answer before I graduated at this rate.

Nasbit grabbed his notebook and then clapped his hands. That was surprising enough that everyone turned to face him.

"Gentlemen," he said in a faux courtly manner. "I suggest we try something else." Nasbit turned to me. "If you can channel Deimos's *skills*, perhaps you can channel Deimos's *knowledge*. You said Death Lord Naiad's followers attacked you, correct?"

I nodded.

"Then perhaps you should tap into your connection with Deimos and learn all you can about this foe, hmm?" Nasbit held his pencil over the third page in his notebook. "While we're at it—why don't we learn about *all* the Death Lords who still remain in the abyssal hells? That sounds like a plan, yes?"

That was a good idea, but I wasn't entirely certain how to go about executing it. If I focused on Deimos's emotions and thoughts, they came to the forefront of my own. If I thought about the Death Lords, would Deimos's knowledge then come to me?

I scratched my chin and concentrated.

"Wait." Sorin leapt over to my bed, smiling wider than I would've expected. "Gray. You told me—for years—all about your time in the dreamscape with Professor Helmith."

I lifted an eyebrow. "Okay?"

"I, uh..." He rubbed the base of his neck and glanced away as he said, "I'm not saying I was *jealous*, but I did think it sounded fun. Mostly because you said it was!" He turned back to me, his smile right back in place. "Can you use your mimic magic to put us to sleep? So we can venture into the dreamscape with you? And maybe... see some of these memories and places you speak of?"

"Whoa, you can do that?" Raaza asked.

Knovak perked back up, his eyes wide.

Even Nasbit scooted to the edge of his bed, his interest in the subject matter plain for all to see.

Raaza motioned to everyone. "We can all go? Into a dream?"

"We could have... *a dream party*." Sorin whispered the last few words like they were a secret no one should ever hear.

"First off—don't call it that." I playfully shoved his shoulder. "It should have a more impressive name. And secondly—Twain can't maintain his form as another creature for *too long*, so we can only do this for a handful of minutes."

Twain turned me, both ears twitching. "This could be fun! I'll try really hard to maintain the form longer."

Raaza's kitsune leapt up and down on the mattress. While she bounced, she said, "I'll stand watch!" Bounce. Bounce. Bounce. "If someone knocks on the door." Bounce. Bounce. "I'll wake you up!"

"We can call it a *dream jubilee*," Sorin said, fanning out his fingers.

I groaned and shook my head. "Somehow, that's worse."

"A *dream expedition*," Nasbit chimed in. He penciled that down. "Since we're exploring things, you see." He tapped the pencil to his lower lip. "Or perhaps... *dream odyssey*. Hmm."

Sorin snapped his fingers and pointed. "Oh! I know. We're going on a *peregrination*." He spoke the last word with dramatic flair.

Knovak laughed out loud. Raaza frowned deep enough his face contorted.

"What is that?" Raaza barked. "I've never heard that word."

Knovak rubbed his eyes. "Oh, it's an *old* term for a meandering journey. *Peregrination.* Where did you even learn that, Sorin?"

"I've been reading a lot of books on poetry." Sorin shrugged. "I've really expanded my vocabulary, I think."

"I like it." Nasbit scribbled out 'dream expedition' and wrote down 'peregrination' in its place. "If Gray can handle it, we'll embark on this peregrination and learn about the Death Lords. I'll write everything down, and then we can analyze everything."

"Smart," Sorin said. He stood and then patted Nasbit on the shoulder. "I'm glad you switched dorms to this one. We're really getting somewhere now."

Nasbit rolled his pencil between his fingers, his face pinker than before. "Oh. W-Well. I do try very hard when I get invested in things... Thank you so much for noticing."

Despite the fact that I wanted to rest, I slipped to the end of my bed and pulled Twain into my lap. "Okay, we'll do this. But not for long, like I said. And if anything terrifying or revolting comes to light, I reserve the right to terminate the dreamwalking right then and there."

Knovak rubbed his hands together again. "What if Deimos attacks us in our dreams?"

"That won't happen." I held Twain close. "Okay, ready to become an ethereal whelk?"

"Not my favorite," he said. "But I can."

"Good. Because we have a dreamscape to create."

CHAPTER 28

PEREGRINATION

I had never attempted anything like this before.

Everyone relaxed in their beds, waiting for me to put them to sleep. But there was a slight problem. In the past, I had forced myself to sleep just fine—but inducing slumber in *others* was a type of magic I hadn't even learned yet in class.

Augmentation.

We had learned evocation—the ability to *create* magic, like fire and bursts of wind—and we had learned about manipulation—the ability to *control things* that already exist in the world, like water or dreams—but we hadn't yet gone over augmentation.

From what I had read, augmentation was filling something with our magic to change it.

And this was a problem because I had to use ethereal whelk magic to augment the wakeful state of everyone else.

How was I supposed to do that? When I had put myself to sleep, it had been intuitive, similar to breathing. But now, faced with the reality of everyone waiting, I hesitated.

"It's one of the most basic forms of magic," I whispered to myself—Deimos whispered, actually.

His comment left me tense. Deimos knew what was causing me

anxiety? Obviously. He was inhabiting my body. Despite that knowledge, it still left me uneasy.

"I don't know how to do it," I replied in a quiet voice only I could hear.

"Force your magic into the object—or person—and allow it to permeate. Much like water soaking into a rag or how the heat of the sun penetrates your skin."

It was... awkward... taking magical lessons from Death Lord Deimos. Why was he helping me, anyway? Did he *want* me to walk through his memories and gather knowledge? Or was he just helpful by nature?

I snorted back a laugh at my own joke.

Deimos was anything but helpful.

"What's taking so long?" Raaza asked.

"Nothing," I replied.

I walked over to my brother first. He was the perfect person to practice on. Sorin wouldn't say anything if I struggled to use augmentation properly for the first time.

After I placed my hand on his shoulder, he glanced up at me. The shadows around his bed stirred, and I knew Thurin watched my every action.

"I'm ready," Sorin said.

I nodded. "Hey, uh, do you know what knightmare magic does when you augment something?"

"When I augment someone else, it gives them night vision. When I augment myself, I can step through shadows." Sorin motioned to the books stacked up near his chest of clothes. "I've been reading about them in my bestiary."

I quirked a smile. "And augmenting yourself is easier?"

"Way easier. I haven't mastered augmenting others at all."

At least I had the same troubles as other arcanists.

With my fingers gripped around his bulky shoulder, I concentrated. Sorin's black hair had gotten longer since the first day we had attended the Academy. His dark locks sat in slight curls atop his white pillow. He stared at me with my own damn eyes, failing to fall asleep.

"Visualize the magic leaving your palm and flowing into your brother," Deimos said.

"I don't need your help," I quietly replied.

"Are you not a student? You should be overjoyed to take advice from a master."

I exhaled.

And then I did as Deimos instructed. I tried to imagine my ethereal whelk magic leaving my body and entering Sorin's. My brother continued to stare, and I wondered if I would just fail this task altogether.

Fortunately, that wasn't the case.

Sorin's eyes fluttered closed as the cool presence of my magic left my fingertips. In a matter of moments, Sorin drifted into a silent sleep.

"I did it," I whispered.

"You're too tense," Deimos replied. "Your magic will be sluggish if you remain as you are."

"Let me just have this, okay? This was an accomplishment."

No response, but I could tell he was unimpressed.

I wandered over to Nasbit's bed. He smiled as I approached, clearly excited. I touched him, and it took me several long seconds to use my augmentation all over again. Nasbit, too, slipped into slumber.

Once Knovak and Raaza were asleep, I rested on my bed, and forced myself to dream.

When I awoke, it was to pain flaring through my right arm.

I gasped as I opened my eyes, surprised to see I slumped against the bars of the dream prison Professor Helmith had created. Death Lord Deimos still had a firm grip on my arm, the claws of his gauntlet digging into my flesh.

Rivulets of crimson blood wept from the entry points of his fingers. It ran the length of my body, soaking my clothing in gore.

Although this was a dream, the pain still felt real. It didn't wake me or shatter my concentration—it was just a throbbing agony that left me feeling weak.

With a groan, I managed to get to my feet. Then I attempted to yank my arm from Deimos's grip. I cried out as he tightened his hold, the claws digging deeper than before, hurting worse than ever.

"*Let go*," I snapped.

Deimos stood on the other side of the bars, his body half shrouded in darkness. He met my gaze with an expression of amusement and said nothing.

Clearly, he was not going to release me.

That was fine. This was fine. Everything was fine.

I'd handle this eventually.

First, I needed to manipulate the dream. I had done this before, though in a limited sense. After a few short breaths, where I blocked out the dull ache and focused on my surroundings, I managed to sense the dreams of people nearby. Specifically, Knovak, Sorin, Nasbit, and Raaza. They were so close, it didn't even take much to alter their dreams with my ethereal whelk magic.

However, I was so inexperienced that I couldn't even sense people in the next dorm over. Not Nini, not Ashlyn—no one else.

Professor Helmith had made dreamwalking and dreamweaving look so easy. She had effortlessly woven dream after dream, protecting me from danger and never breaking a sweat.

This was probably the best manipulation training I had ever done in my life. Just pulling four other people into this dream took all my attention and consideration. When they arrived, it was like they had floated to the surface of water. They appeared from the ground and bubbled upward, wearing the exact clothes they had gone to bed in— sleeping tunics and trousers.

But...

Where were we?

It was a flat plain of grayish rock, with a sky as dull as the ground. There were no mountains or lakes or walkways or trees or vegetation of any kind. It was a void of rock and gloom. The only blemish was Deimos's cage, which jutted from the rock and appeared to be made of it.

Sorin was the first to stand. He stumbled until he got his footing, his bare feet slapping on the smooth rock surface.

"Gray?" he asked.

Once he spotted me, his eyes widened. He ran over and gave my arm a long stare.

"Are you okay?" he whispered.

"I'm fine," I breathed.

Sorin grabbed my arm. He smeared my blood across my skin, staining his own palms. He pulled one of his hands away and examined the crimson marks, his brow furrowed.

"You can get hurt here?" Sorin turned to me, frowning. "Gray... We need to stop this."

"I'm fine," I repeated.

"You're bleeding."

"It's just a dream, Sorin. I'm not bleeding in real life."

But this wasn't good. I knew it in my gut. Despite that, I didn't want Sorin to worry, so I put on a confident smile. Eventually, I'd figure this out, but for right now, we had a mission, and that was to gather information.

My brother stood close to me. It was then that Deimos stirred. The Death Lord growled some sort of curse, and Sorin leapt away, his body tense. My brother lifted an arm, as though defending himself, but when no attack came, he relaxed a bit.

"Deimos?" Sorin whispered.

The Death Lord chuckled.

Nasbit, Raaza, and Knovak slowly got to their feet. They groggily glanced around until they spotted the stone prison and wandered over. Like Sorin before them, they took stock of the situation and backed away.

"Is that who I think it is?" Raaza barked, pointing at the bars.

Knovak combed his sandy brown hair with his fingers, his hand shaky. "This is terrible. Worse than I feared. He's already attacked Gray. We should... We should fight him. Together."

I held up my free arm. "No. We're not doing that. Everything is okay. This is just how Death Lords shake hands in the abyssal hells. I'm not in distress. Nothing to see here."

I was half playful, half irritated. Why wouldn't they just believe me?

Nasbit ran to me and gingerly held the elbow of my injured arm. "Oh, no." He frowned. "Deimos is hurting you, Gray. What can we do?"

"I'm all right," I said, practically yelling. "You can stop fussing over me."

Nasbit hesitantly released my arm. His frown deepened.

"Are you infants done?" Deimos asked, his voice gruff and cold.

Raaza threw his arms up, one hand held flat, as though he would chop the Death Lord if he drew near. It was as hilarious as it was pathetic. However, I understood his need to have a weapon. There was nothing here, and he was in a set of sleeping garments. We were all defenseless.

Good thing Deimos was trapped, or else this would've been a bloodbath.

Everyone held their breath in silence.

Deimos huffed. "You came here for knowledge, did you not? *Then let's begin.*"

"What, you have somewhere to be?" Raaza quipped. He slowly lowered his chopping hand. "Seems like you're trapped and have all the time in the world."

Deimos growled. "The boy said he couldn't maintain this magic for long. Or are you so thick you've already forgotten?"

The boy.

Did he really just call me *the boy*?

"Are you eager to share your knowledge with us, uh, Mister—er— Lord Deimos?" Nasbit anxiously smoothed his short hair. "Or do people say *Your Grace*? Your Excellence? What is the proper way to address a Death Lord?"

"On your knees, begging for your life," Deimos replied, his tone frighteningly serious.

Sorin placed a hand on my shoulder. "Guess what we're *not* going to do. Ever."

Knovak, Raaza, and Nasbit had paled, though. Each of them took another step away from Deimos's prison, leaving me and my brother the only ones close to the bars.

"I don't care how you nincompoops address me," Deimos said, more levity in his words this time. He smiled a cruel smile. "What matters here is that we use our time wisely."

"So you *do* want to share your knowledge with us?" Nasbit tapped the tips of his fingers together.

"Correct."

"But why?"

"Because I have a misguided hope you will tell others. All the waking world should know what I'm about to divulge."

Deimos wanted us to tell people? That was interesting.

"Where should we start?" I asked.

Deimos squeezed his fingers into my arm. "At the beginning. With the first Death Lord. This was a time before civilizations truly took shape—the world was as feral as it was bloody."

His touch, and his words, stirred memories to the forefront of my thoughts. I was seeing what Deimos said, but only faintly and without focus. Did he want me to manipulate the dream to show these images?

I tried.

I wasn't very good, but I tried.

The smooth stone plain rippled and shifted. Forms of armies took shape, like pieces on a playing board. Soldiers clad in pteruges—defensive leather skirts—fought each other in a battle with three sides.

"There were three peoples," Deimos said, the gravelly tone of his voice softening as he recollected the tale. "The Hevron, the Ayless, and the Tharagins."

None of these nations still existed in our day and age, which just spoke to how ancient Deimos really was.

"The Ayless were warriors without peer," Deimos whispered, his voice filled with reverence. "Each of them trained in deadly arts. Those who couldn't make it through their training were harvested to feed their finest warriors."

The dreamscape rippled again, but I refused to envision that. The stone landscape went flat.

Knovak rubbed his arms. "The Ayless ate people?"

"They were master wendigo arcanists," Deimos continued. "And they won nearly every war."

"Why tell us about this?" Sorin whispered.

Deimos scoffed. "You're talkative for students. No wonder you know little." He snapped his other gauntleted hand and continued. "Naiad was one of the Ayless. Their elite warriors would burn their scalps so their hair would no longer grow, and they would scar themselves in sensitive areas, to kill their ability to feel pain forever. Naiad was one of them."

Nasbit softly gasped.

The dream shifted as I imagined that, and stone figures of men and women hacking away at themselves until they were chiseled into perfect warriors played out before us.

"Naiad was the first to discover the pathway to the abyssal hells, and the first to bond with an abyssal dragon."

"Who was ruling over the abyssal hells *before* her?" Nasbit interrupted. "Was it just mass chaos?"

Deimos exhaled. "There are aspects of life that are a mystery. Naiad claims there was something else ushering souls, but once she took up the mantle, it ceased to be. Since no one else witnessed her claims, they may as well be reality. Once the first Death Lord took their place in the world's order, they became a cornerstone of life."

Nasbit pondered this for a long while.

I wondered as well.

Deimos ground his teeth. "We learned then that Death Lords have a sacred duty. Souls descend to the depths, and the abyssal dragons separate them into two categories. Souls that will reincarnate, and souls that will delve deeper, never to be seen again."

"I wish I had my notebook..." Nasbit patted at his waist but found nothing in his pockets.

"Abyssal dragons also graft souls to their flesh, as punishment to individuals who caused great harm to others. The souls give the dragon power beyond their normal limits."

This information *really* excited Raaza. He looked as though he was about to start clapping. "I wish I had that," he muttered to himself.

Deimos exhaled. "This strength was meant to give the Death Lords full domain over the abyss. In a land of souls, they are infinitely powerful, but in the realm of the living, only the souls they carry with them can be used. Death Lords basically cannot die so long as they have souls on their dragons, which makes them too powerful for normal arcanists to handle."

The smooth rocks around us shifted into a nightmarish landscape. Rivers of souls, walls that formed a labyrinth, and far-off monsters roamed the land. I couldn't create many details, but I tried.

The others watched the strange rock sideshow as Deimos continued.

"The proper order of nature is for the Death Lords to serve their time in the abyssal hells, and *then* return to finish their life in the realm of the living. As reward for your years of toil—alone and away from the world—they are given land to govern until it finally their time to pass."

Rulership in exchange for years of thankless toil? I wasn't sure if it was worth the trouble.

Deimos waited for a moment. When he spoke again, his tone was thick with contempt. "Naiad guided souls for a time. The second and third Death Lords did the same. All was well."

But no story ever just ends happily like that.

"However, Naiad didn't want to stay in the abyssal hells. She exited and came to the lands of the living, to fight in the Second Hevron War, after Ayless was mostly decimated in the first."

I felt Deimos's anger through our connection in my arm.

"What happened?" I asked.

"That was the end of the war—the moment Naiad took to the field, no one could stand against her. Armies retreated. Naiad fled back to the abyssal hells, where she regathered her strength, harvesting souls like she once harvested the weak."

Sorin stepped closer to me. While everyone else exchanged worried glances, Sorin just hardened his expression. He seemed determined—more so than I had seen him before.

When the stone statues morphed to play out a scene with an abyssal dragon, Raaza watched intently, his eyes wide. He liked this part, apparently.

An abyssal dragon was a gross creature with dead scales and flesh, wings made of screaming souls, and six eyes that moved independently of one another. The stone version in this dream crushed the other soldiers.

"Other arcanists bonded with abyssal dragons," Deimos whispered. "And most of them stayed in the hells where they belonged. Centuries passed, and when it seemed war was brewing again, Naiad returned."

"Seems like cheating," Nasbit commented.

Deimos snorted. "The Third Hevron War was brutal."

The stone armies clashed, and one of the nations ceased to be.

Deimos ran his fingers across the bars of his cage, creating a *clack-clack* sound. "I fought in it as a sovereign dragon arcanist. It seemed Hevron would easily win. But then, to even the odds, *all* the abyssal dragon arcanists took to the field... Two arcanists from Ayless, two from Hevron, and only one from Tharage. The Death Lords were impossible to fight. They never died. Never tired. Never *stopped*."

"They're just all fighting each other in the mortal world?" Knovak asked, indignant.

Deimos ignored him and continued with the tale. "But then, Naiad crushed her fellow Death Lord—the only one fighting for Tharage. She grafted *his* soul to her dragon, ending his life once and for all. It gave Naiad great strength... and a deep-seated lust for more blood."

CHAPTER 29

BEDTIME

"So, the only people who can kill a Death Lord... are other Death Lords?" Sorin asked, his voice low.

Deimos nodded within his prison. "The ability to rip a soul out of a body is the key to ending a Death Lord's magic."

The stone figures of two dragons clashing shook the whole dream. They weren't very detailed, since my manipulation was so lousy, but it was enough to get the picture.

Deimos returned his gaze to my terrible pantomiming. "Once Death Lord Naiad killed their abyssal dragon arcanist, Hevron seized its opportunity. We marched into Tharage, exterminated their people, and set their lands ablaze."

They were going all out, it seemed. Every nation for themselves.

Deimos sighed. "People were getting desperate," he whispered. "But I had won against Tharage. After that, I murdered my father and took to the field with a banner made of his flesh, defending our burgeoning empire from followers of Naiad. My strength gave others hope."

"This is getting intense." Knovak turned to me. "Didn't you say you would end the dream if it got too bad?"

"We haven't learned much about the Death Lords who still exist," I said through gritted teeth. "C'mon. We can handle a little more."

"After the war was over, and the Ayless had retreated, I was to bond with the sixth abyssal dragon, but I refused." Deimos grabbed the bars of his prison. "The only person I trusted was my twin brother, Zahn. To this day, he is the sole arcanist I depend on, and we both agreed I should have the *seventh* abyssal dragon."

Sorin shook his head. "Oh, Professor Zahn? The one who tried to kill us?"

Deimos nodded once. "The same."

"Wow."

"But the world was changing. Three more became Death Lords while civilizations rose from the ashes of long wars." Deimos grew frustrated, our connection causing me to develop some of that feeling. "But Naiad continued meddling with the natural order. Her disregard for her role as Death Lord led to what scholars called a *Turning of an Age*."

That sounded epic. And important.

"The very sky trembled, and deadly crystals rained to the ground," Deimos whispered. "There was so much destruction that god-arcanists had to rise to power in order to combat the calamity. All nations, and all god-arcanists, blamed the Death Lords for the devastation..."

"I definitely blame them," Knovak quipped.

Raaza snorted out a laugh.

"Those other nations implored the god-arcanists to seal the gates to the abyssal hells, preventing anyone else from entering—or leaving. It was a heinous act that disrupted the very flow of nature."

"Sounds like a good move, actually," Sorin muttered.

Nasbit shook his head. "Didn't you hear Deimos? It sounds like *Naiad* was the one doing things improperly. The whole world shouldn't be punished for her actions." He tapped his chin. "But... The first god-arcanists... Was it *Astros* who sealed the gates? He was known as *The Warden*, and his abyssal kraken ruled the dark depths."

"It was," Deimos intoned.

"Fascinating."

Deimos ignored the last comment. "Abyssal dragons need an arcanist to help with the sorting of souls—without their efforts, all souls descend deeper and deeper, and none are reincarnated."

"Don't we already have multiple Death Lords?" Sorin rubbed his chin. "Why do we need more?"

"As the world grows larger—as more people are born—so grow the duties of the Death Lords. But now only four remain. Naiad has killed the others and added their souls to her dragon."

"And this is... bad?"

"*Abyssal dragons continue to be born,*" Deimos shouted. "And they are left to the darkest abyss, where they feast on souls and turn into elder creatures—monsters who hate all life, and want to consume it. Naiad and Umbriel have built *armies* of the damned, and they grow more powerful with each passing year."

"Umbriel?" Nasbit asked. "W-Wait... What about Death Lord Calisto? My uncles tell stories about him all the time."

"Annihilated," Deimos said flatly. "Naiad slaughtered him *and* his dragon."

No one said anything.

What were we supposed to say?

"Death Lord Kallikore has instead made friends with the elder creatures who dwell in the darkness. He even has a phoenix dragon on his side." Deimos darkly chuckled. "He fights against Naiad and Umbriel, but he's gone mad. Naiad intends to kill us all. She believes—erroneously—that if she collects enough Death Lord souls, she will ascend to the status of a god-arcanist herself."

All the previous god-arcanists were dead, from what I understood. Or at least, their eldrin were dead. Maybe *they* still lived, but they had no more god-arcanist magic. If Naiad did become a god-arcanist, who would stop her?

Raaza crossed his arms. "And if Naiad does kill the rest? What happens then? I mean, who cares if she's a god-arcanist trapped in the abyssal hells? Still trapped."

"If the abyssal hells are left unfixed, all souls will be obliterated upon death, and magic will begin to fade from the world... until only oblivion awaits us all."

Oh, wow.

"Is that all?" I asked with a laugh. "Sounds like it's mighty damn important it gets fixed, then."

Deimos narrowed his eyes in sardonic hatred, as though he had been shouting this from the beginning and couldn't believe no one was listening.

"Continue," I said.

"Wait," Raaza interjected.

Our stone surroundings flattened. Everyone turned to face Deimos.

Raaza stepped forward. "Don't *you* have an army of the damned? Why not just fight Naiad yourself?"

Deimos's lip curled in disgust. Then he shook his head. "Zahn, my clever brother, concocted a plan to reopen the gate, and to set things straight. I was to exit the abyssal hells, take my rightful place as ruler, and then build an army to rival Naiad and Umbriel's."

"Really?"

"I put all my effort into communicating with Zahn—and finding ways to send things to him and vice versa. There are still pathways, just too weak to allow an arcanist to venture through. And we would've opened the gates, and put everything in its proper place, *except our efforts were ruined.*"

Deimos once again tightened his grip on my arm.

What did he want me to say? I wasn't going to apologize for *not dying* to help complete his gate.

"Why didn't you just tell people?" Nasbit asked.

"No one believes this is a problem," Deimos said. "They believe if the gates are sealed, all the troubles of the abyssal hells will *stay* in the abyssal hells."

Nasbit nodded along with his words. He gave them a long, thoughtful moment before he asked, "Do you have proof? About the whole oblivion thing? So we can convince people to help?"

Deimos didn't reply.

I suspected there was no proof. It was like saying, "*If it rains too hard, the valley will flood!*" How are you supposed to prove that ahead of time? Sure, once it rains, everyone will see, but until then, it was just speculation.

Perhaps Deimos was wrong. Maybe nothing bad would happen.

But...

I felt his conviction through our connection. He wasn't lying. Deimos meant every word he spoke, and genuinely seemed concerned.

"Things have become dire," Deimos said, bitterness in his voice. "For centuries, I have focused on helping Zahn in what little ways I could. I had no time to create an army of my own. After his Gate of Crossing was shattered, I used my astral projection to spy through the gate fragments, hoping I could salvage his plan."

Knovak raised his hand—like we were in class, the dunce—and Deimos turned to him with the deepest of frowns.

"*What is it*?" Deimos growled.

"What is *astral projection?*" Knovak asked as he slowly lowered his arm.

The Death Lord tensed, his irritation becoming visible. "Abyssal dragon arcanists can partition their soul into many pieces and send them from their body. I can see what's happening through this soul fragment, even though my body is far from here."

"Ah. Okay. That's how you got yourself stuck here. You astrally projected through a gate fragment and then into Gray's body..."

"*Correct.*"

Nasbit braved the distance between us. He walked over to the stone prison and nervously tapped the tips of his fingers together. Then he glanced up at Deimos.

"Uh," Nasbit muttered. "How long do we have before we all get sucked into oblivion?"

Deimos narrowed his eyes. "Not until Naiad finishes consuming the other Death Lords. We could have days, years—centuries. Until then, the abyssal dragon arcanists still do their duty."

"Oh, whew." Nasbit let out a great, long sigh of relief. He clutched the front of his shirt. "I was so worried. The tension and anxiety were killing me. B-But it sounds like there's time to deal with this." He wiped sweat from his arcanist mark on his forehead.

"*Tell someone,*" Deimos growled. "Preferably someone with power and influence."

"Of course." Nasbit glanced over at me. "Right, Gray? Although... who would we tell?"

I hesitated. We had a problem. Someone was spying on Astra

Academy. They knew about me, and Deimos, and even the gate fragments. They were clearly using this information in an attempt to get me—or Deimos's soul—and they weren't playing fair or nice.

"We should tell everyone," Raaza said, throwing his arms into the air. "Anyone who will listen!"

Knovak nodded. "I agree."

I shook my head. "Listen, if *I* were an insanely evil lunatic with murdering tendencies, I would manipulate the information once it was out there. I'd make Deimos look like the villain, and get people on board with capturing me—and then keeping the gates sealed forever."

My brother frowned. "What're you trying to say, Gray?"

"I'm saying... We should compile all this information, and then we should *only* hand it to people we absolutely trust."

Raaza snorted. "Like who? The headmaster?"

I didn't know the headmaster that well. He seemed well intentioned, and maybe he had a kind heart, but I wasn't certain. Headmaster Venrover was also a little off. He didn't react to things like normal people did. He was cold. Or distant. I wasn't sure which.

"We should give the information to Professor Helmith," I whispered.

She was warm, brave, intelligent, and capable. Helmith had also been attacked by the followers of Zahn and Deimos, so she wasn't part of their little cultish gang. She had even fought Deimos just to save me...

Professor Helmith was, without a doubt, trustworthy.

She would know what to do.

My thoughts of her must've stirred into the dreamscape, because our surroundings shifted, even without my dreamweaving. The sky transformed into a vibrant midnight blue, sparkled with thousands of stars. The ground sprouted lush green grass, and a babbling brook of glittering water flowed next to Deimos's prison.

This was a tranquil setting I was all too familiar with.

Images of Professor Helmith and me materialized only thirty feet away. We were having a picnic underneath the starlight, a wide variety of tarts laid out across a red blanket.

She was as beautiful as ever, her black hair shimmering, her smile radiant. I was... younger. Thirteen, it seemed, and I stared at her the entire time, even when she offered new tarts for me to taste.

It was a memory we all watched.

And the others definitely *watched*. They stared with wide eyes, taking in the scene with a smidge of confusion that blossomed into realization.

"This is what happened between you and Professor Helmith?" Sorin asked. "She made wondrous dreams like this for the both of you?"

I nodded.

Even Deimos seemed intrigued by the setting. He stared at the phantom memories of Helmith and me.

"That woman..." Deimos whispered.

Raaza broke the quiet tranquility with a single, mocking laugh. "Oh, no wonder you're so infatuated with her."

"I'm not *infatuated*," I snapped.

"Uh-huh." Raaza gestured with a sweep of his arm. "The scene says otherwise."

Then, everything shattered.

The sky, the ground, our surroundings—a blast of magic slammed through the dreamscape, ruining the memory and knocking out the color. The only thing not affected was Deimos's cage.

A voice boomed over the blank area—one I recognized. It was the *other* Professor Helmith.

"What's going on here?" Kristof shouted.

CHAPTER 30

MISTY MORNING

My concentration left me.

The whole dream ended, and all my augmentation on the others ended in an instant. When I awoke, it was to the feeling of a hundred butterflies battering their way out of my guts. I sat upright, my heart out of control.

Twain, as a kitten, was on my lap, his eyes huge.

"What happened?" he asked.

Miko, the little kitsune, jumped around Raaza. "Nobody came into the room. I was keeping watch, I swear."

Raaza grabbed his eldrin and tucked her under his blanket. She gave a muffled *blarg* as he threw himself down on his bed and held still. Was he pretending to be sleeping?

Knovak rubbed his face clear of sweat, took one look at Raaza, and then did the same. He swaddled himself in his blankets and rolled over, trying his best not to breathe too deeply.

"You two can't be serious." Nasbit shook his head. "If the other Professor Helmith comes to check on us, he's going to know you're not really sleeping."

But Raaza and Knovak didn't say a damn thing.

My brother sat up on his bed and turned to me. While the others seemed more concerned with hiding themselves, Sorin maintained eye contact as he asked, "Are you sure you're going to be okay, Gray?"

"Yeah." I held my eldrin. "You don't need to worry."

Twain purred.

Sorin threw off his blankets. The darkness around the posts of his bed stirred. "If you need me to speak to Kristof, I will. He seemed angry, like he might yell at you, but... You should probably just get some rest."

I didn't know why, but his willingness to deal with Kristof made me smile.

On the Isle of Haylin, they had a saying. *It's not the length of time someone knows you, it's their willingness to help that makes them a true friend.*

Twain, Sorin—to a lesser degree, the other arcanists in my class... Ever since I had my problems, they kept stepping up to help me.

I was touched.

It made me want to help them in turn. Genuinely help them. And I wasn't prone to such feelings.

"I'll handle this," I whispered to Sorin. "Don't worry. It's not like Deimos is hurting me or something."

Loud banging on the door to our dorm ended our conversation. Sorin slowly turned his attention to the racket. Nasbit shuddered and then *also* wrapped himself in his blankets. He wasn't as good at pretending to be asleep as the others, which amused me, but I doubted they would get in trouble.

I got up from my bed, Twain in my arms.

"Maybe it's a ghost," Twain playfully said as I carried him toward the door.

"I'm not that lucky."

When I opened the dorm door, Kristof Helmith was standing just on the other side. He stared at me with a cold and emotionless expression, though his tightly balled fists gave away his mood.

"Gray." Kristof took a single step back. "Can I speak with you out in the common room?"

I exited the dorm and walked with him a few paces to the nearest couch. We didn't take a seat. No, that would've been comfortable. Instead, Kristof wheeled on me.

"What did I tell you?" he asked through clenched teeth. Before I could sarcastically answer his rhetorical question, Kristof continued. "*I told you not to get involved in the dealings of the Death Lord!* You're putting everyone at risk. *You're putting Rylee in danger.*"

"I—"

But Kristof wouldn't let me get a word in. He threw his arm out, angrily gesturing to the dorm. "I saw that dream! What was that? Deimos? His prison? Rylee? What're you telling him? Don't you see how dangerous this is? You shouldn't even be weaving dreams. *You should allow me and the headmaster to handle this.*"

"I didn't see either of you when my family was in danger," I growled under my breath. "And I'm *not* going to put Rylee in danger."

Saying her first name...

I didn't normally do that. Her name didn't roll off my tongue right.

Kristof pointed at me. "Stop."

"Stop *what*?" Twain sardonically asked. He puffed up his orange fur in my arms.

"Stop *all of it*. Headmaster Venrover has closed off the Academy. No one is coming in or out of the Gates of Crossing. All the professors are staying here on campus, even if they would normally leave. So *stop messing with things you don't understand*. It's a simple rule—most arcanists manage to follow it just fine."

I took in a deep breath and then exhaled. What was I supposed to say to that? No? I wouldn't follow the rules? Of course I would follow them.

"You know not who you threaten," I whispered—Deimos, really—in a tone that could only be described as *chilling*.

Kristof glared at me. "What was that?"

"Nothing. I'll be on my best behavior." I kept my words controlled.

Kristof stared into my eyes for a long while. Then he took a step back. "Good. Because I had originally come to tell you that Rylee would like you to attend the fundraiser dinner. You and your family, since they're here for the time being. Do you think you can handle that without looking like a fool?"

Something about his tone irked me.

But I was being good.

"I'd love to attend," I said.

"It'll be in a few weeks." Kristof turned on his heel. "We'll both see you then."

"Will Professor Helmith be okay then?" I asked before he could get too far.

"She should be recovered by then, yes."

He didn't even glance over his shoulder as he said it. On the one hand, I admired his dedication to hating me. On the other hand, I despised the fact he thought I would put Professor Helmith in danger.

"He's that woman's husband?" Deimos asked, his question in my own whispered voice.

"That's right," I replied.

"If you want to impress her, you should slay that man and offer his heart as a token of your affections."

I snorted back a laugh. "I hope you don't regularly dole out relationship advice."

Twain twitched his large ears. "Hm. On that note..." He yawned. "Maybe we should sleep for real."

I patted his head and then headed back into the dorm. Sleeping sounded great.

I rose before the sun did.

Ashlyn had wanted to talk, and I wanted to explain, so this was the perfect time to meet. Plus, the misty fog around Astra Academy was beautiful in the morning. That was why I had suggested this time.

I stood at the edge of the training field, Twain at my feet. It was cool out, but not freezing. Something about the Academy kept the temperature at bearable levels, which I appreciated.

As I waited, the mist wasn't as dazzling as it usually was. The fog was thin, and the atmosphere was damp and sad.

Perhaps someone else would've shrugged this off—or considered it a bad omen—but I was done being held captive by the whims of circumstance.

I'd make my own good omens.

Twain glanced up at me, his ear twitching, as though he had the same thought I did.

I closed my eyes, felt around for the threads of magic, and decided to tug on Ashlyn's typhoon dragon string. Twain leapt away from my feet as his body bubbled and shifted into a large, horse-sized dragon with shimmering blue scales. Long fins protruded from every part of his body, and he was rather intimidating.

I rubbed my forehead where my arcanist mark shifted.

"Okay, let's spruce this place up," I muttered to myself.

Typhoon dragons could manipulate water. When I waved my hand, the mist in the air answered my summons, shifting with the movements of my fingers and palm. The fog swirled, practically shimmering.

Twain snorted. He waggled his dragon tail, as if enjoying it. His little nub of a bobcat tail couldn't wag like this dragon one. He also manipulated the fog.

We clumped it together around us just as the first signs of daylight sparkled over the nearby mountaintops. The wondrous and ethereal feeling of the cool mist, mixed with the warm glow of day, created something romantic.

At least, I hoped it would feel romantic to Ashlyn.

As if summoned by my thoughts, Ashlyn emerged from the mist like a wraith—silent and practically otherworldly. Her dragon wasn't with her, and I suspected that was because he was so large and recognizable. She wore her Academy robes, and her blonde hair was tied back in a neat braid.

She gave Twain a double take, as though she thought he was Ecrib for a split second. Twain waved, giving away his identity immediately. Ecrib wasn't a waver.

I smiled as Ashlyn approached. "Good morning. You look beautiful, as always."

She obviously hadn't been expecting that. Her next step was stuttered, and her face shifted to a slight pink. Then she hardened her expression. "Gray. You know I'm betrothed. That's not the most appropriate morning greeting."

"You want me to stop?"

Ashlyn didn't reply.

Instead of pressing the issue, I tucked my hand into my pocket and withdrew a few pages of notes. Then I handed them over. "So, here are Nasbit's notes on the situation."

Ashlyn took them with a look of confusion. "Situation?"

"About me and the cultists. Death Lord Deimos." I hadn't included the dream party, because was that really needed? It wasn't. And I still didn't want anyone figuring out I knew so much. So I kept all those details hidden. If Ashlyn needed to know anything else, I'd tell her personally.

"And you're okay?" She lifted an eyebrow as she glanced up at me.

"Something like that." I stepped closer and shrugged. "But none of that is important at the moment. Right now, I want to talk about your future. Our future, really."

Ashlyn kept her eyebrow raised, like it was now permanently fixed in to that position. Then she shoved the paperwork into her pocket. "Ecrib told me all about your scheme."

"I'm not talking about my scheme." I waved away her comment. "I'm talking about what *you* want. You came back to the Academy all haughty and angry."

"I was *not* haughty and angry."

I pointed to her, indicating she was making my point. Ashlyn crossed her arms—her own sign of defeat. She was cute when she was disgruntled.

"Why are you just going along with what your father wants?" I asked, completely serious. "You hated your cotillion. You hate your fiancé. Who just goes along to get along like that?"

Ashlyn had held her breath as I bombarded her with questions. Only once I was done did she allow herself to take a breath. Her shoulders remained tense as she spoke. "You wouldn't understand."

"Try me."

"*Everyone* in my family expects me to be a failure," Ashlyn immediately responded.

That hadn't required much coaxing. Which was good, because I was all ears.

"My brother was amazing—is amazing," Ashlyn said with a sigh. "When I was younger, and I didn't match his performance exactly, everyone started to say it was because I'm the second born, or because I'm a girl, or because my mother was sick while she carried me." Ashlyn dug her own fingernails into her arms. "And as an arcanist from a noble house, everything I do reflects on the *whole* house. I can't do anything without someone saying, '*Look how far the Kross family has fallen.*'"

I listened to her words, fully absorbing everything.

Ashlyn glared at the ground, the mist swirling around us, keeping us in a chilly bubble of sparkling dew as the sun slowly lifted over the distant mountaintops.

"You just don't understand." Ashlyn exhaled. "Everyone is expecting me to fail. My aunt even said I'm probably not talented enough to find an arcanist worthy of taking the Kross name. She said I should probably just marry into a different house." Ashlyn spoke the last sentence with contempt.

I didn't know much about nobles, but since arriving at Astra Academy, I understood surnames carried a lot of weight. Ashlyn's fiancé was a leviathan arcanist with no noble family. If he married Ashlyn, he would take *her* surname, and become a member of the Kross family.

Marrying away from the family was only reserved for weak members—people the noble family wanted to purge.

"Your family really wants to get rid of you?" I asked.

I just... I couldn't believe it.

Ashlyn continued to stare at the grass. "That's what it feels like sometimes."

"They're insane."

She glanced up and met my gaze.

Twain huffed and stomped his little kitten foot. "Yeah, I'm with Gray! They're cuckoo. You're amazing."

Ashlyn relaxed her shoulders as she glanced away. Her cheeks pink, she muttered, "Thank you." She took a moment before continuing. "Not *everyone* in my family dislikes me. Ever since I bonded with Ecrib, they've started to change their minds. They think I'm worth something now. But... if I mess up... I'll just prove all my doubters correct. So, if I continue to succeed, I'll prove them wrong."

"Who cares if you prove them right if you're not going to be happy at the end?" I shrugged. "I mean, do you even hear yourself? You're going to bed your fiancé—what's his name?"

"Valo," Ashlyn dryly replied.

"Ugh," I said as a gut reaction. "Sorry. I probably blocked it from my memories to avoid the active trauma of hearing it said aloud."

Ashlyn stifled a laugh.

"So, like I was saying—you're going to go to bed with *Valo* just to make your *aunt* happy? Your aunt isn't the one who is going to wake up to Valo's crusty face. It's *you*."

Ashlyn rubbed her nose. The mist was cold, and the tips of her ears had paled a bit. While Twain was still transformed, I motioned my hand through the air, to create a sphere around us where the fog would just float around.

"You're... really talented at making the mist look pretty," Ashlyn said.

"I learned from Professor Helmith." I shrugged. "She would manipulate dreams in all the best ways. Every time I imagine manipulating magic, I think about her."

"Huh." Ashlyn stepped closer to me. "Gray," she whispered, her voice more tender than before. "I know I have plenty of resources and magic and willpower, but still... I feel trapped. It's hard to explain. Like no matter what I do, I'm going to disappoint someone."

"Just don't disappoint yourself," I replied. "That's the real key, I think."

A small smile quirked at the edge of her lips. Then Ashlyn met my gaze, her blue eyes gorgeous in the morning light. "Ecrib said you had a scheme, and while I admire your willingness to show up Valo's crusty face, I think you're in over your head."

"Why's that?" I asked. "You don't trust me?"

"I heard most of the clubs are putting on the competitions during the Academy's exhibition. Tournaments. Archery competitions. Sword skill displays. Stuff like that. I don't think you're going to measure up to some of the second-year students."

I actually had to hold back a laugh. "Oh, I think I'm going to have a major advantage in those types of competitions. Just... I feel sorry for the other competitors."

Twain snickered as he transformed back into a kitten. Then he ran to my feet, my forehead burning a bit as my star reverted to its normal blank version.

The fog receded, returning to a dull state.

Ashlyn, obviously in the dark about my newfound skills, slowly nodded. "Uh-huh. You really think you'll win a few competitions?"

"Definitely," I said, no mirth in my tone. "The real question is... do you think your family will consider that good enough to consider me?"

Ashlyn bit her lower lip. "I'm not certain. But maybe, if one of the professors spoke highly of you."

"Then leave everything to me." I patted my chest. "I'm the type of man who's going to help people now, all right? I've got this—no need to worry."

CHAPTER 31

CLASSES

Our next class was *Imbuing and History*.

Once everyone was seated, our professor, Piper the rizzel arcanist, strode into the classroom all confidence and smiles. Which was highly unusual. Normally, the first bit of Piper's class was *Silent Sustained Reading*, or as Raaza playfully put it, *Hangover Hour*.

Today, she wore a lightweight dress made out of the brightest white silk I had ever seen. Her robes were barely on, and her black hair was done up in an elaborate bun, exposing most of her long, slender neck.

Her rizzel, Reevy, leapt up onto the front desk, his little chest puffed out. His ferret body was long, and his white fur matched Piper's outfit. His silvery stripes were beautiful, and Reevy smoothed his coat before coughing to get everyone's attention.

"Class," Reevy said as he clapped his front paws together. "Your favorite professor has arrived."

"Which one of you ever said she was your favorite?" Raaza whispered to the rest of us.

Piper sat on the edge of the desk and then crossed her legs, but she took a while to do so, carefully smoothing her outfit and fixing every last strand of her hair. Then she smiled wide for the class.

"Everyone, pay attention," Piper said, her voice hard-edged.

All the arcanists in class sat a little straighter.

"What's going on?" Phila whispered. "This is quite peculiar."

Piper pointed to her eyes, and then pointed to the rest of the class. "Someone told me you asked *Professor Ren* about making trinkets. Is that true?"

"Is that *true*?" Reevy echoed, his voice angrier than his arcanist's.

Everyone in class exchanged glances, including all the eldrin. Even Brak, the stone golem with no eyes, "glanced" over as though this were an unbelievable fantasy.

"I asked about the trinkets," Sorin finally admitted. He stood from his seat. "Is something wrong?"

Piper narrowed her eyes at my brother. "*I'm* your professor of Imbuing and History. Is your education so terrible that you don't remember what imbuing is?" Before Sorin could reply, Piper continued. "Imbuing is the art of making magical items—trinkets and artifacts. I'm the professor you should be speaking about that with."

Sorin gave me a sidelong glance.

His thoughts were written all over his face.

He was thinking—*but you barely ever teach us anything.* And he probably thought Professor Ren had a better chance of getting him the item he wanted.

But my brother was too nice to say any of that. Instead, he glanced back at Piper and rubbed the back of his neck. "I apologize, Professor. Um. Can you—"

"Oh, don't apologize," Piper said, cutting him off. She smiled and waved for him to sit down. "You've actually done me a huge favor. Sit, sit."

My brother hesitantly took his seat.

Piper smiled. "Now, class, what I need from you is to work diligently today. All right? And talk about how much you love history. And imbuing. If you all can do that, I'll overlook your blunder and obvious lack of magical knowledge."

"You want us to talk about how much we love history?" Exie asked with a sneer. "Who even does that? No *real* person would."

Nasbit, who had been smiling ear to ear, slowly deflated.

"Why?" was all Raaza managed to bark.

Reevy pointed his little ferret-like paw at him. "Listen, *you*—no one gives my arcanist any lip today, got it? We have a special mission."

A soft tapping at the classroom door drew everyone's attention. Today had some weird energy to it, which I found amusing.

Piper quickly leapt off her desk and then fidgeted with her outfit.

Before she went to answer whoever was knocking, Piper squished herself up in the front until she had acres of cleavage. Only then did she stride over and lazily open the door.

"Oh, hello, Professor Ren," Piper said, her smile genuine. "Come in, come in!"

Ren stepped into the classroom. "Thank you, Piper." He waved to everyone. "Hello, everyone." Ren pointed to me. "Still yourself, right?"

I nodded once. "Last time I checked."

His treasure cache spider scuttled into the room, the metal legs clicking across the stone floor with each step. The spider said nothing, even when Reevy waved to him.

Piper walked over to the desk and practically giggled. "Oh, class, this may come as a surprise, but Professor Ren was so impressed with your desire to make magical items that I managed to convince him to help me discuss their creation. Together." She pointed at herself, and then at Ren. "Jointly. We're a team."

"A *great* team," Reevy said, his voice filled with faux cuteness.

"Right," Ren said, giving Piper a bizarre glance. Then he stood on the other side of the desk and folded his arms. His robes were open, like they usually were, showcasing his muscular body. He didn't seem to care that Piper kept sneaking sideways peeks.

Maybe he didn't even notice, actually.

"Okay, class," Piper said, way cheerier than normal. "Are we ready to continue our lessons?"

Nini raised her hand. When Piper pointed to her, Nini fixed her glasses and said, "Before we talk about magical item creation, can we please finish the lesson on the God-Arcanists War? I *love* how much knowledge you have—it's really opened my eyes to how amazing history and stuff can be."

Professor Ren rubbed his chin and smiled to himself, as though impressed with something.

Piper, making sure she was out of Ren's line of sight, gave Nini a small thumbs up. She then walked over to the chalkboard and scribbled a few words down. It became apparent she was writing all the god-creatures and their order of appearance.

"We'll recap this really quick and then move on to item creation," Piper announced.

While her back was turned, Sorin whispered, "Why did you do that, Nini?"

Nini half-shrugged. "I dunno. I like seeing Piper happy. She seems nicer."

Reevy clapped his little rizzel paws. "Everyone, take notes! This will be on the test."

I wasn't so sure if I liked this version of Piper. But I did as I was instructed. At least I would learn something.

Free days at the Academy were rare.

We were *supposed* to pick clubs, or be social by visiting islands beyond the Gates of Crossing, but all gates were closed until further notice. No one was allowed to leave Astra Academy, currently.

Which was strange. That meant there were *way* more arcanists out on the training field. Clubs met and practiced, but I didn't care about them. I picked out my own corner of the field and started to exercise.

"Are you sure you want to do this?" Twain asked.

I jogged in place, lifting my knees high each time. "Yup."

"You're a mimic arcanist. You have access to all the magics in the whole Academy. You don't also need to be big and buff." Twain examined himself. "And also, I don't want little cat abs."

I laughed between heavy breaths. "You can just sleep until it's time for magical training."

"No, I don't want to miss anything."

"What would you miss?" I sat in the lush grass and did a single sit-up. "There's nothing going on."

Twain pointed with his nose. I followed his gesture until I caught sight of Knovak. He was training, too? Knovak and his unicorn were running laps around the field, both of them rather fast. Faster than all the other runners, it seemed.

I hadn't known he would be out here.

That was fine. The training field was large enough for everyone. And by my count, there were at least twenty other arcanists out here. More magic streaked across the sky like whimsical fireworks. Wind, lightning, and even pink flower petals.

It made my sit-ups interesting, to say the least.

"Maybe I will take a little catnap..." Twain gingerly stepped across the grass. He curled up on a patch of clover, tightly balling his whole orange body. Then he slowly closed his eyes and used the afternoon sun as his blanket.

After ten more sit-ups, my stomach ached. I had to rest in the grass and stare up at the sky, my heart beating hard.

"You're as weak as a maggot," Deimos said through me, his tone low.

I chuckled, even though it hurt my stomach. "Translation—I suck. Got it." After a deep breath, I did five more sit-ups. Then I forced myself to stand. Once I felt confident, I went for my own run.

Even with Deimos's skills, my run didn't last long before I had to decelerate to a jog.

"You're so infirm, your children will be born misshapen," Deimos said.

"I get it," I said between huffs. "I *really* suck."

"Tsk. You should use the words as fuel for your training."

"You *want* me stronger?" I asked.

"If Death Lord Naiad, or her followers, attack you, then you must be strong enough to defend yourself—with or without my magic. And right now, you are little more than a waterlogged corpse."

"Wow, really inspirational." I choked out a laugh. "A few minutes of talking to you, and I'm already wondering how much nightshade I would have to ingest to put myself in a permanent coma."

Deimos, to my surprise, found that amusing.

I was going to go for another lap around the field when something caught my eye.

Three arcanists had stepped in front of Knovak and his unicorn and stopped him from running. They were larger than Knovak, both in height and muscle, and when they stepped close to him, Knovak backed away.

I wasn't an expert on body language, but I would say Knovak wasn't having a great time.

Were the other arcanists asking him to get off the track?

What was going on?

And while my previous response would've been to sit on the sidelines and observe, that wasn't going to be me anymore. If Knovak needed some backup, then that was what he would get.

CHAPTER 32

COMBAT SKILL

I jogged over to Knovak and the three who were surrounding him.

I hadn't realized until I got close, but all three arcanists had the same mark on their foreheads. They were all *nixie* arcanists—water fairies, basically. The nixies were tiny, and they fluttered around the heads of the three boys, their bodies made of water.

Nixies were often considered cruel, at least according to Professor Helmith. They had little mouths, and the water could shape itself in any way, but the nixies chose to have fangs.

How quaint.

"I'm allowed to use the track," Knovak stated.

His unicorn, Starling, moved forward and puffed out his chest. "Yes. You ruffians should step away now."

"Ruffians?" the first arcanist said. He sneered as he swept back his lush auburn hair. He wore his second-year robes like they were a judge's uniform. They were crisp and flowing around his thin body.

"How dare you call us that," the second arcanist chimed in. He was just as judge-like as the first, his black hair done in curls, but he was much heavier set.

The third had stains across his robes from weeks of rolling through the grass. "We're nobles," he said, his speech thick with saliva. He was much stronger than the other two. His biceps were threatening to burst the seams of his sleeves.

All the nixies hissed and called Knovak names. *Peasant. Lowborn. Deadweight.* Their voices were squeaky and cute, but also filled with the hisses of snakes.

"Captain Leon said I was allowed to use the track today," Knovak stated, forceful and clear. "Stand aside." When he tried to go forward, the first arcanist blocked his path. "I mean it, Roy."

The thin one—Roy, I supposed—smirked. "You're not going anywhere. I don't care what Captain Leon says. We don't want your pathetic presence on our track." He smacked his two friends on the chest. "Harriot and Perana agree. Don't you?"

Harriot, the round one, swiftly nodded, his curly hair bouncing with each gesture.

It took Perana a second to agree... He was clearly as sharp as a sack of soup.

I stepped onto the track, between the three nixie arcanists and Knovak. That seemed to surprise everyone. Even Starling's eyes widened as I interjected myself into the confrontation.

"Gentlemen, gentlemen," I playfully said, holding up my hands. "What's the problem? I mean, I know your large friend here needs a good portion of the track, but surely there's enough room for all of us, right?"

Harriot grew red in the face. He frowned so hard, his chin wrinkled.

"Get out of here, *fool*," Roy said. He dismissively waved his hand. "This is a matter of principle."

Before I could mock them for their complete lack of principles, Knovak placed a hand on my shoulder. "They don't want me to train because I'm a unicorn arcanist. They want to win the races during the Academy-wide competitions, and they've been harassing me not to participate."

"That's not true," Roy snapped.

Harriot nodded. "That's right. The competitions have nothing to do with it."

"*Nothing to do with it,*" the nixies echoed.

Perana held up a beefy finger. "We don't want *lowborns* on our track."

"That's right!" Roy pointed at me, and then at Knovak. "If you all weren't attending Astra Academy, the headmaster wouldn't need to hold a fundraiser for coin. It's people like *you*—charity cases—who hurt *all of us*. You should realize you're a burden and stay to yourselves."

"I thought you three said you were nobles?" I asked, knitting my eyebrows in exaggerated confusion.

Harriot angrily smoothed his robes over his gut. "We are! I'm of the Hackett family, thank you very much."

"I've never seen a group of stooges act *less* noble," I replied with a shrug. "You all are twenty-four eggs short of a dozen, and have less manners than a corpse."

"*What was that?*" Perana growled through clenched teeth.

Knovak hesitantly stepped to my side. "Gray, please. We shouldn't get into fights. The *noble* thing to do would be to turn the other cheek and—"

I met his gaze, and Knovak stopped speaking. "I've got this," I said. Then I motioned to the track. "Just keep practicing. These thugs won't bother you anymore."

The three nixie arcanists all grew tense and agitated. They clearly didn't like that I was talking about them like they were losers.

Even though they were obviously losers.

Knovak must've sensed my intentions, because he grimaced as he whispered, "Don't do anything you'll regret."

"Hmph! Ruffians deserve no mercy," Starling interjected. He swished his mane and then pranced back onto the track. "They are the epitome of rude."

Perana removed his outer robe, revealing even his muscles had muscles. Whatever he lacked in brains, he made up for in brawn.

He stepped closer, puffing out his chest as he did so. "I'm going to smear your face across the track."

"I can't wait to see you try," I said. Or maybe it was Deimos.

It was probably both of us.

Perana threw a punch. A wild and telegraphed slugger that would've sent me straight to the moon—if it hit. I ducked just in time, the skills I was "borrowing" from Deimos kicking in like a second set of instincts.

It was just like the fight on the boat with the followers of Death Lord Naiad...

If combat was a combination of agility, strength, skill, and strategy, then Deimos was giving me infinite *skill*, which was more than enough to completely overwhelm anyone with average abilities.

I knew just what to do in a fight, period. With a quick step forward, I got within inches of Perana and then slammed the heel of my palm *straight up* into his nose, shattering it back into his face.

Blood exploded onto his shirt.

The man yelled and grabbed his face with both hands. His eyes watered so much that tears streamed down his bloodied face.

That was it—fight over. Perana was basically blinded, and with his nose aching, he obviously couldn't concentrate.

His nixie flew at me, yelling the whole way. It evoked little ice crystals and threw them like darts. I lifted an arm, and a few pierced my sleeves, cutting my skin, but it was hardly noticeable.

Once the nixie was close, I backhanded the blob of water, and it broke apart midair.

The nixie would be fine. Its watery body would reform without much trouble. However, the shock and awe of my brutal attacks were too much for Roy and Harriot. Both arcanists lost all the blood in their face, their eyes as circular as gold coins.

Harriot found his courage, though. He stepped forward and threw a weak punch, his knuckles covered in magical ice. I sidestepped out of the way, and then grabbed his outstretched arm. I wasn't strong enough to throw him to the ground—even if that was Deimos's first instinct—but that didn't matter.

I slammed his elbow so it bent in the wrong direction.

Harriot let out an undignified yowl.

Once again—the fight was over. Harriot cradled his arm and scurried back to Roy. Then the two nixie arcanists fled with their eldrin.

"They abandoned you," I said to Perana, whose eyes were still watering uncontrollably.

The man grumbled into his hands, blood sputtering down his chin. Then he, too, turned and ran off.

Perana and Harriot would be fine. They were arcanists, after all. They would heal.

Well, maybe their *egos* wouldn't heal, but the rest of them would.

Knovak and his unicorn, Starling, came jogging back. They stopped on either side of me and watched as the three nixie arcanists ran off the training field and headed for the Academy.

"You're not worried they'll report you to Leon?" Knovak whispered.

"No," I said. "Then they'd have to admit they were beaten by a *lowborn*, and they would never live that down, obviously."

Starling snickered as he swished his beautiful tail. "They're afraid of losing a race to a unicorn arcanist, and I can't wait to make that nightmare come true for them. Unicorns are rather fast, I'll have you know."

"I'm aware," I said.

Knovak turned to me and partially smiled. "I was worried because of, uh, you know. What's happened to you. But obviously my fears were unfounded. Thank you, Gray. For helping."

I nodded once. "Don't mention it."

There was a pleasant feeling that came along with helping. And I was going to chase it.

Time at Astra Academy went faster now that nobody could leave.

I sat in class, watching the morning light shift to the glory of a beautiful afternoon, wondering where all our time had gone. The *other* Professor Helmith stood at the front, writing charts on the chalkboard about mystical creatures. We were supposed to be taking notes on the differences in power between the tiers, but my mind was elsewhere.

Twain snoozed on the table in front of me, half his body covering my notebook.

"Most arcanists have a mark on their forehead," Kristof said as he wrote. His chalk scratched on the board with each harsh stroke he made. "This mark always contains a star—formally known as the *star of magic*—and it typically has seven points."

My brother diligently wrote notes. Nini did the same, her reaper occasionally glancing over her shoulder to "look" at what she was writing. Waste had no visible body, but he acted as though he had a face like anyone else.

"There are times when an arcanist will get a star with *nine* points,"

Kristof muttered. He wrote it on the board. "This only happens when a person bonds with a unique mystical creature."

Nasbit raised his hand.

Exie didn't wait, though. "What do you mean?" she blurted out. "What is a unique creature?"

Nasbit slowly lowered his hand, rolling his eyes in the process.

The professor stopped writing, but he didn't turn around to face the class. "Unique creatures are just that. *One of a kind.* They aren't born through fable or normal progeny means—they are created once, through strange processes that aren't replicable." Then Kristof turned around, his gaze meeting mine.

I sat a little straighter.

Twain snorted as he woke up. "Huh?" he said loudly. "What's going on?"

"We were going to have a guest speaker today," Kristof said. He narrowed his eyes. "His name is Ryker Blackwater, and he bonded with the *Mother of Shapeshifters.* His eldrin is unique, and supposedly, the source of all shapeshifter mystical creatures."

Twain's ears perked up. Then he glanced around. "R-Really? Where is this Mother of Shapeshifters? I want to meet her."

"Due to the fact the Gates of Crossing are closed, Ryker and his eldrin won't be joining us today."

I slumped a bit. "Oh."

"But—" Kristof resumed his writing, "—he will be at the Academy's competitions and the fundraiser dinner. So, there might be a chance to meet him yet."

Raaza shot his hand into the air. Despite not being called on, he asked, "Are these unique creatures stronger than normal mystical creatures?"

"They seem to vary in strength," Kristof said. "But there is one thing they all have in common. They can all produce offspring that are their own type of mystical creature. For instance, the Mother of Shapeshifters gives birth to mimics and doppelgängers."

"But not another Mother of Shapeshifters."

"Exactly."

Everyone settled down after that.

Except for Twain, who vibrated with such intensity, he looked as though he would explode. When he turned to face me, I understood his unbridled excitement.

He wanted to meet his mother.

"We will," I whispered.

Twain vigorously nodded along with my statement.

We just had to wait for all the celebrations.

Morning on the training field invigorated everyone. We did stretches out in the fog, everyone reaching for their toes or twisting their bodies to loosen up.

Combat Arts training was today. Professor Jijo had yet to arrive, but the field was already set up with racks of wooden weapons. Swords, spears, hammers, clubs, and pikes were all sorted into groups. Apparently, today we would learn the fundamentals of melee combat.

Nasbit did his stretching near me.

Nasbit's stone golem, Brak, *also* stretched, but it was comically ineffective. The human-shaped pile of boulders didn't have any muscles to loosen. Despite that, Brak copied everything Nasbit did, including touching its stone feet.

"I have all the notes compiled for Professor Helmith," Nasbit muttered between torso twists. "You can give her the paperwork and tell her all about the trouble in the abyssal hells whenever you're ready."

"At the fundraiser," I whispered to him.

"Hm? Why then?"

"She invited me to it, so I figured it would be easy to give it to her then."

Nasbit nodded once. "I see."

Once a few people were done with their stretching routine, Phila practically danced around the class. Her coatl fluttered alongside her, his red-orange scales beautiful, his feathery wings spread wide.

"Oh," Phila said as she came to an abrupt halt. "Remember that my cotillion will be taking place this coming free day!" Phila giggled as she glanced between everyone. "You'll all attend, won't you? The headmaster said we could have it in the grand lounge."

"What's the *grand lounge?*" Raaza asked.

"It's a nice sitting area with tables and a fireplace." Phila swished back her strawberry-blonde hair. "I wanted it to be more snowy, but we're not allowed to leave the Academy proper, and the headmaster doesn't want us bringing anything in from the mountains."

"I'll be there," Nasbit said with a smile.

Phila softly clapped her hands together. "Oh, excellent."

Before anyone else could confirm or deny, Professor Jijo stepped out of the morning mist. His nimbus dragon was on his shoulder, his eyes big.

Jijo rubbed his bald head and smiled at the class. Today, he wore a sleeveless shirt that clung to his muscular body. It showcased the many black runes he had enchanted across his skin. What kind of magic did that give him?

"Hello, class," Jijo said as he walked over to pick up a wooden sword. "Today, we will learn the basics of melee combat." He pointed to my brother. "Most importantly, as a knightmare arcanist, you should decide on the weapon you fancy."

"Why is that?" Sorin asked, pointing to himself.

"Knightmare arcanists typically forge weapons from the darkness of their eldrin. A personal weapon—something they are skilled with. You haven't done that yet, have you?"

Sorin glanced at the liquid shadow moving around his feet. "No. I haven't."

"Then you should make sure to test out all these weapons today, to get a good grasp of them." Professor Jijo smiled.

His nimbus dragon leapt from his shoulder, flew through the air, and then landed on the grass near the wooden weapons. He pointed with his tiny dragon claws.

Jijo quickly swirled the wooden sword around in his hand. He knelt into a combat pose, and then thrust forward. Afterward, he straightened his posture. "Melee fighting is not a skill you can train by yourself. You need a partner." He turned to us. "So partner up."

Nasbit immediately lifted his hand.

Jijo gestured to him with a calmness that betrayed his infinite supply of patience.

"There are nine of us in class," Nasbit said. "May I sit out and observe for this class?"

"No."

"B-But there's an odd number, and—"

"*I'll* be someone's partner." Jijo grinned as he glanced between us.

Raaza motioned to me with a jut of his head. "Partner with Gray, Professor." He and his kitsune snickered afterward.

I tensed, mostly because I didn't really want to fight the professor. I wanted to learn the fundamentals of melee combat. One day, whenever I learned how to purge Death Lord Deimos, I wouldn't have all these extra skills, so what better time to learn them for real?

"Very well," Jijo said. He motioned to the wooden weapons on the field. "Everyone grab a weapon. Any is fine. The fundamentals for any weapon are the same, and from there, I will teach you the skills associated with each."

I walked over to the various weapon racks and glanced between them.

CHAPTER 33

MELEE TRAINING

The pike was a thick piece of wood with a massive point at one end. It seemed deadly. When I reached for it, however, Deimos spoke to me.

"Don't be a fool, child," he whispered. "Your sparring opponent has a sword. A pike is meant to deal with mounted enemies. You will be at a severe disadvantage."

I moved my hand over to the hammer. Unlike the other wooden weapons, it had a flat metal head on the head, at least the size of my fist. It also seemed dangerous.

"Your incompetence knows no bounds," Deimos growled when I reached for it. "Your opponent also wears *no armor*, which means he relies on agility. Maces and battle hammers are heavy, and thus *slow*, and are meant to rip a hole in even the thickest of metal."

"Tsk." I crossed my arms. "Which should I take, then?" I whispered to myself.

"A whip."

I sarcastically motioned with my arms. "Do you see a whip?"

"Whips are perfect for disarming opponents and maintaining a safe distance from attacks."

"Unless you can materialize one out of the abyssal hells, we're going to have to stick with lumpy, dumpy, or sad sack," I said as I pointed to a sword, spear, and club.

"Then *dumpy* it is," Deimos quipped.

I picked up one of the spears. It was six feet in length and surprisingly lightweight. The tip was pointed, and the shaft sturdy without being too rigid.

The others in class moved around me, grabbing weapons they thought were interesting. Sorin picked a sword and held it aloft. "This is my legendary blade," he playfully proclaimed.

Nini held a hand over her mouth as she giggled.

"*This is a blade of moonlight grace,*" Sorin continued. "*With every swing, foes it'll erase.*" He swished the wooden practice sword. Then he bowed to Nini. "My lady, will you be my partner?"

Her face grew as red as her hair. "S-Sure." Then she picked up her own sword and made the same swishing movements.

Exie rolled her eyes so hard they almost popped out of her skull. Fortunately, it didn't appear as though either Sorin or Nini had seen. They were too busy being content together.

Raaza huffed as he grabbed a hammer. "Bashing skulls time." He glanced over at Nasbit. "C'mon. Me and you."

"Why me?" Nasbit balked.

"You have a golem, right? Hammers beat rocks."

Nasbit frowned and stepped away from Raaza. "Um. No, thank you." He hesitantly glanced over at Phila. "I, uh, was thinking that..."

But Knovak leapt into his line of sight. "Have no fear. I'll be your partner." He quickly picked up two swords, and handed one to Nasbit.

"Ah." Nasbit's shoulders slumped. "Well... Okay."

Raaza huffed and then turned his attention to Ashlyn. She had picked a spear as well. Was it because *I* had? Or did she just think it was an interesting weapon?

"Hey," Raaza said to her. "Partners?"

Ashlyn glanced at me, and then back to Raaza. "I suppose."

Phila and Exie were the last to choose. They stood around the weapon racks, glancing between each. Exie placed her hands on her hips.

"Rex," she said to her eldrin. "Pick one for me."

Her little erlking fairy tapped his tiny lip and then pointed to a sword. "Elegant ladies sometimes wield rapiers," he said.

"Rapiers?" Exie grabbed the wooden sword and glared at it. "This is basically an over-glorified soup ladle." She huffed and flounced over to the training field.

Phila held out a hand. "Exie, wait! Are we going to be partners?" But Exie never replied. After a long exhale, Phila returned her gaze to the weapons. "I suppose she has no choice." Phila hefted one of the spears with both hands. "I wish we had bows again..."

The morning wind picked up, taking more of the fog with it. The clear sunshine streamed down over the green field. Professor Jijo walked out to the center and then pointed to places in the grass.

"Everyone face their partner." Jijo held his wooden sword at his side. "Combat, especially close-quarter combat, can be taxing on you both mentally and physically. That's the first key to success—*conditioning*. You must *condition yourself* to handle such stress."

Everyone did as they were instructed. Sorin and Nini faced each other. Raaza and Ashlyn did the same. It took Exie and Phila a little bit to actually get lined up. Finally, Knovak and Nasbit, since Nasbit was dragging his feet about everything.

"Physical conditioning requires exercise," Jijo said matter-of-factly. "Mental alacrity only comes from awareness and calmness of mind. Best to hone your control."

The nimbus dragon flew to the edge of the field and lifted his head to watch everything.

"I'm going to teach you footwork and fighting styles, but the real key to winning in combat is to remember two things." Jijo held up a single finger. "First, do *not* become predictable. No falling into a rhythm when you fight, no using the same thrust or strike over and over again. The more predictable you are, the easier you are to defeat."

Raaza paid close attention.

Jijo held up a second finger. Strangely, it was his pointer finger and his pinkie. Who did that?

"Second," Jijo said, "is about identifying the enemy's pattern. Most amateurs rely on their basic fighting styles, and if you can exploit their movements, you should. For instance, a thrust with a sword requires the attacker to put all their weight on the front foot."

Jijo demonstrated by slowly stepping forward with his right foot and then dramatically thrusting at me. Everything was casual, and the wooden blade stayed inches from me, to allow everyone to see the motions.

"If you know the opponent will thrust, it's best to come at their arm from the side, since they're leaving themselves exposed." Jijo demonstrated by tapping his own extended elbow. Then he turned to me. "Now, how about you help me, Arcanist Lexly? I'll thrust, and you strike at my arm from the side."

"All right," I said.

We stood a few feet from each other. The rest of my class watched from the side of the field. Even their eldrin, who were gathered close, observed the practice.

Jijo thrust his wooden sword, but his movements weren't slow at all. The man came at me, and Deimos's instincts kicked in. I sidestepped and then twirled the lightweight spear around with shocking precision.

I didn't aim for Jijo's elbow, like he had instructed. Instead, I struck his wrist.

Deimos's thoughts... his memories... For some reason, I felt his old combat training lessons from when he was younger. His instructor had said to always aim for the weakest point. The wrists. The ankles. Points that would render the attacker helpless faster.

I struck Jijo so hard, there was a *crack* of sound as the shaft of the spear hit him right where his hand met his arm.

Jijo sucked air through his teeth and dropped his weapon.

Half the class gasped. The other half grimaced.

Well, except for Raaza, who couldn't seem to hold back a smile. Had he recommended me to spar with Professor Jijo because he was *hoping* something like this would happen?

Jijo's nimbus dragon flew over, but the professor waved it away. Without a word, the dragon returned to his post on the edge of the field.

"I'm sorry," I forced myself to say.

Professor Jijo's smile shifted into something harder than before. "So, not only do you know rare and ancient forms of *archery*, it seems you know a thing or two about being a lancer."

"Barely." I shrugged. "It was just a lucky strike."

"I know skill when I see it."

Jijo bent over, picked up his sword, and then slashed up from the ground, straight at my face.

It happened so suddenly, I almost didn't register it as an attack. Again, Deimos's second set of instincts kicked in. I leaned away—barely in time —and the tip of the wooden blade grazed the tip of my chin.

I stumbled backward, shaken.

Professor Jijo stood up straight, the training sword held tightly in his hand, his dark eyes so focused on me, it bordered on intimidating.

Everyone else was so tense, I swore they weren't breathing. They watched, some of them with their mouths half open.

Sorin and Twain took a couple of steps forward, but they both stopped, as though not sure if they should get involved.

"Uh, Professor," Sorin finally said. "Shouldn't we move onto the next lesson?"

But Jijo didn't take his eyes off mine. I gripped the spear with both hands, one higher up, one lower. It was all Deimos's knowledge. He seemed *very* familiar with the weapon.

And Jijo took note of my hand positions, his eyes calculating and never losing their intensity.

"You're no lancer?" he said, his voice both serious and playful. "What an interesting statement to make."

Professor Jijo lunged at me—which was, I had to admit, rather startling. He was much faster than I had thought he would be, and I reacted defensively. He slashed with the practice weapon, and I blocked with the shaft of the spear, knocking his strike away.

But defending myself hurt my arms.

Jijo had put *all his strength* into that strike. My spear cracked on the shaft, and his sword wobbled. Neither weapon was built for such intensity.

Without missing a beat, Jijo whirled on his heel and struck at me a second time—this time aiming for my neck. It took all my personal speed and strength to defend myself again, but I managed it.

The *clack* of our weapons was surprisingly loud and rang out over the whole training field.

Jijo slashed a third time.

I blocked, my arms hurting again, but this time I jumped backward, putting distance between us. Then I slammed the shaft of the spear on my knee and shattered it into two pieces. It had been instinctual—from Deimos.

"Why?" I asked myself. "Why would I ruin my own weapon?"

"His plan was to break your weapon on the fourth attack," Deimos whispered to me as I leapt backward a second time. "Didn't you watch him? He struck it three times in the same location, weakening the structure."

If Jijo's sword had blown through the shaft of the spear and hit me in the face, it would've been lights out for me. By breaking it myself, I now had two smaller wooden weapons, and I had destroyed his plan.

Professor Jijo didn't seem to care. "Talking to yourself?" he taunted. "That's a waste of breath in a battle." Jijo rushed at me—something about his intent gaze told me he *wanted* to win this fight no matter what.

What was his problem?

When he got close, I knocked away his thrust with one stick, and with the other, I swung for his wrist again. Jijo was prepared. He dodged away, and then leapt at me again, barely giving me room to breathe.

He was just *faster*.

And when Jijo switched hands from right to left, he swung harder, too. He managed to strike me hard in the shoulder. It hurt—it felt like the man was aiming to bruise my bones.

I hit the ground and tumbled through the grass, my teeth gritted so hard, I might have chipped a tooth.

While Deimos gave me plenty of skill, it couldn't make up for my general lack of speed and strength as compared to Professor Jijo.

"Gray!" Twain called out.

My mimic bounded over the grass and ran to my side. He purred as he nuzzled my cheek.

I patted his head and stood with a groan. "I'm fine."

Twain turned to glare at Jijo, his ears all the way back.

The professor had eased up on his intensity. He lowered his weapon and backed away from me, his casual smile returning to his face. "Well, I'm mighty impressed with your talent. Obviously, you shouldn't be lumped in with the others. I'll have to train you personally."

"You're skilled, but not enough to instruct me," Deimos replied.

Of course, to Jijo, it just looked like it was *me* being brazen and arrogant.

Professor Jijo tightened his grip on the hilt of his practice sword. "We'll have to see about that." Then he faced the rest of the class. "Sorry about that, everyone. Why don't you all try the thrust and follow through? Once you've taken turns, we can move on to more advanced stages of understanding."

The rest of the class hesitantly entered the field in pairs. They did their training, but everyone kept a watchful eye on Jijo and me. I suspected they thought we would break out into fighting at any moment.

But I didn't want that to happen. Instead, I practiced the moves just as Jijo instructed, completely ignoring Deimos's whispered comments of disinterest and disgust.

CHAPTER 34

PHILA'S COTILLION

"Spears are best used in groups," Jijo said as he went from arcanist to arcanist. He spoke loud enough for everyone to hear, even all the eldrin, who watched from the side of the field. "Historically, spearmen would stand behind the vanguard. Those in the front held swords and shields, and would create a defensive wall. The spearmen, with their reach, would thrust forward beyond the shields of their allies to kill enemy soldiers."

Everyone went through their training motions. People with swords practiced swinging, while people with spears practiced thrusting. Their sparring partners would block and do nothing else.

"Arcanists are unique, however," Jijo said. He waggled a finger. "They can use their magic to give them an advantage, which means they can fight individually, with almost any weapon. Some arcanists are physically tougher, or faster, or have deadly evocations that synergize with their weapon of choice to create a winning combination."

Phila stopped mid-swing. "Like my wind evocation and the bow?"

Jijo nodded. "Yes. Exactly."

"What should I do?" Raaza asked. He, also, stopped his training.

"You have fox fire, don't you? Unlike normal illusions, which aren't tangible, you are a *jack-of-all-trades*. You can create any weapon you want.

Even if disarmed, you can materialize a *new* weapon and continue fighting."

"Really?"

"It also means you can afford to be reckless. Throwing weapons, especially, are dangerous because you run out of ammunition. But kitsune arcanists never need to worry about that."

Raaza glanced down at his hands. Then he returned his attention to the professor. "But I don't know how to make solid weapons. All I can make with my fire are coins and little orbs. Simple things."

Jijo motioned to the field. "The next step of our training is to incorporate magic. Why don't you take a break and focus on making a simple dagger with your fox fire?"

"What should *I* do?" Knovak blurted out. "Raaza is my sparring partner. Am I to sit around while he practices?"

"You're a unicorn arcanist..." Jijo rubbed his chin as he mulled over the question.

He thought for a long, and awkward, amount of time. Raaza chortled under his breath, and my brother shot him an actual glare.

Sorin could be intimidating when he wanted.

That quieted Raaza, who dragged his feet as he went out into an empty portion of the training field.

"You should probably wait a bit," Jijo finally replied.

"Let me guess, *I'm too weak*," Knovak practically spat. "Unicorns are only *tier two*."

Jijo shook his head. "Weakness is a state of mind, young arcanist. You can do many things to overcome a poor starting position." He pointed at Starling, the little unicorn foal. "You need to wait because you can't yet ride your eldrin."

Knovak glanced over and stared for a long while. "Oh."

"Unicorn arcanists are best suited to learning spears and halberds, so they can fight from the saddle. Bows are also a good option, but those may take years to master." Jijo smiled as easily as ever. "I would suggest you start there, and once your eldrin is a tad larger, you can learn to fight from horseback. Or... *unicorn*back, as it were."

This news seemed to excite Knovak. He held his head a little higher as he walked around the training field. He even went and swapped out his weapon for a spear.

I had a new spear as well, and I patiently waited for the professor to finish his speech to the others. When Jijo walked over to me, I thought he would offer me some more words of wisdom.

That was a mistake.

He swung with his wooden training sword, aiming straight for my head. Deimos's combat instincts were a gift from the good winds, because I never would've been able to block that strike if it weren't for his skills.

The *clack* of our wooden training weapons startled the others.

Before anyone said anything, Jijo tossed the sword to his left hand and struck at me again. I blocked again, but this time, I shifted my weight and managed to knock the sword away rather than full-on blocking, which meant my spear wasn't as damaged.

"You're getting predictable," Deimos said, his tone one of playful warning.

Professor Jijo leapt away from me, his gaze intense.

Jijo knew something was wrong; he obviously just couldn't piece it together. And I wasn't about to tell him I had Death Lord Deimos's abilities. That would just get me in all kinds of trouble. No, I would keep that to myself.

"I'm very surprised with your level of skill for someone your age," Jijo said, keeping his voice low. "Perhaps, sometime soon, we shouldn't hold back while sparring."

"Who's holding back?" I laughed. "I mean, this is me at full potential."

"No, it's not. Neither of us are using our magic."

That was... a good point.

But I definitely didn't want to fight my professor using my magic. That would get too intense, I felt it in my bones.

"Maybe," I finally said.

Jijo lifted his sword and held the hilt with a tight grip. He was about to lunge again, and I braced myself for the conflict. But, out of nowhere, Jijo gasped and practically leapt into the air.

Twain was on his ankle, his little kitten fangs sunk deep in Jijo's flesh.

My eldrin didn't let go, even as Jijo shook his leg with the force of an elephant's trunk.

"Wait!" I ran over and pried Twain from him. "Sorry about that. I'll have a talk with him."

Jijo smoothed his clothing and frowned. "Yes, well, please do that, Arcanist Lexly." He then turned on his heel and left me alone with my mimic.

I glanced down and met Twain's stare. "Thanks."

He twitched his whiskers. "No problem. He was being mean to you, I could tell."

I cuddled Twain close, but when I glanced over at Jijo, it felt as though Deimos had strong feelings about the man. Were they in some sort of rivalry? It seemed like it.

"He's a descendant of the Ayless," Deimos said through me.

"That's unlikely," I replied, basically talking to myself.

"I recognize his swordsmanship. Only the Ayless were obsessed with teaching themselves the art of ambidextrous fighting."

Twain narrowed his colorful eyes. "What is *ambidextrous*?"

"It means they fight with both hands equally," Deimos curtly replied. "It's a rare and difficult skill to master. Most never bother."

Jijo was throwing his sword around from his right hand to his left. And it had caught me off guard, even with Deimos's skill. That would be a fantastic ability to have, but I dreaded even writing my name with my left hand... I couldn't imagine fighting with it.

But Ayless was an extinct nation, wasn't it?

Then again... Death Lord Naiad was from Ayless. Did that mean Jijo had some sort of connection to her, even if tangentially?

I hoped not.

I was awake in bed, staring at the ceiling. It was well beyond midnight, but the sky refused to cooperate. The moon glowed with pride, and the stars twinkled as though they were the coming of a second sun.

It was pleasant, and made the whole dorm room feel awash in mystical light. Flecks of dust twirled through the air above me, dancing to slow music no one could hear.

Twain slept on my chest. Although it was mildly uncomfortable, and prevented me from rolling over, I didn't have the heart to push him off. I was soft, as Deimos liked to remind me. I didn't care, though. Twain was my eldrin. I'd care for him no matter what.

The others were asleep as well. Nasbit snored, and my brother's bed creaked under his heavy frame. Occasionally, Raaza's kitsune, who refused to leave the dorm for any reason, would sneeze a puff of flame.

I glanced over at Sorin, wishing he were awake so I could speak with him.

For some reason, it stirred Deimos's thoughts and memories.

"You miss your brother?" I asked.

He had a twin, just like me, after all.

"Zahn is my only true companion—the one I can trust," Deimos replied, solemn.

"He did make a super special Gate of Crossing to reach you." I chuckled to myself. But then I glowered at the ceiling. "You know, now that I think about it... Aren't two gates required to make a functioning Gate of Crossing? Does that mean you have one?"

"No." Deimos's memories fluttered for a bit, his thoughts focusing on abyssal coral. "My brother is far cleverer than any artificers you know, child. He made a Gate of Crossing linked to my very soul."

Ah. Right. I remembered Zahn screaming that when he had tried to kill me. He had crafted a Gate of Crossing that somehow linked with Deimos himself. It had transported the Death Lord straight to the Astra Academy basement.

Now the fragments were out of control...

I thought about asking how Zahn had done it all, but I realized I didn't have much information on magical items. Instead, I stared at the ceiling and wondered innocuous thoughts.

"Do you think Zahn is still looking for you?" I asked.

"Of course he is."

I smirked. "Even though he failed? I mean, it was a pretty embarrassing defeat in the basement. Better to just tuck his tail and hide forever."

"He has only failed once he decides to quit," Deimos stated. "And we share an unbreakable will. Zahn will never relent—and neither will I. That means it is only a matter of time before he summons me to the realm of the living."

"I guess that means I have something to look forward to," I quipped.

I wasn't excited, though. Fighting Zahn a second time sounded awful. At least this time I knew he was a mimic arcanist. Whatever terrible plot he had, he couldn't fool me with that one a second time.

Content that everything would be okay as long as I stayed in the Academy, I closed my eyes. Things were starting to look pleasantly normal.

Classes came and went.

One afternoon bled into the next.

When it came time for our next free day, I woke up refreshed. I was going to train from sunup until sundown, but then I noticed *everyone* was awake, and it got me curious.

"What's going on?" I asked as I rubbed the crust from my eyes.

Nasbit grabbed his silk shirt and nicest trousers and carefully dressed. "It's Phila's cotillion today, don't you remember? She invited the whole class."

"Oh, right..."

Attending another cotillion hadn't been high on my priority list. Ashlyn's had been rather catastrophic. Then again, it would be nice to spend time with Ashlyn outside a classroom setting. We hadn't done much of that since she returned to the Academy.

"Do I need a gift?" I asked as I dressed myself.

Ashlyn's cotillion hadn't required I bring anything, but I suspected some people had. I didn't know much about party etiquette, though.

"Where do you think you're going to get one?" Knovak asked with a sneer. "You think Astra Academy just has a gift shop?"

Raaza threw on a tunic and then waved away the comment. "Where is he going to get the coin? That's my question."

"I wrote Phila a poem," Sorin said. He had dressed long ago and was already waiting by the door.

Nasbit neatly combed his brown hair until it was just perfect. "I paid one of the artificer students to craft me something to give to her." He smiled as he said, "So I didn't have to go anywhere to get the gift."

"Well, la-dee-da." Raaza rolled his eyes.

"I should've thought of that," Knovak said. "Hm. I hope Phila isn't upset with the Gentz family because I didn't arrive with a gift."

Once I was ready, I headed over to my brother. Twain, still groggy, loped along after me. "Where is the cotillion?"

"In the grand lounge," my brother said. "Haven't you seen it yet?"

"Nope."

"It's *massive*. The fireplace is so big, you could raise a family inside it."

That did sound large. Now I was anxious to see. I opened the door to the common room, and the others exited with me. Nasbit carried a wooden box shaped like a chest, which he kept close to his side. Even the box the gift came in looked expensive.

CHAPTER 35

THE GRAND LOUNGE

The grand lounge was just that—grand. Magnificent and imposing in appearance. Stupendous.

The walls were covered in illusioned tapestries, and each long piece of magical cloth hung from the ceiling all the way down to the floor. And it was quite a way down. The vaulted ceilings were at least thirty feet above us.

And the tapestries didn't really show images... They were of beautiful ethereal landscapes. Right now, every wall was a shimmering illusion of a mystical forest. Glowing blue mushrooms, ripe lemons hanging from perfect branches—there were even streams of water that elegantly flowed throughout the setting.

Couches, plush chairs, and even small tables were placed around, but the centerpiece of the lounge was a fireplace. It stood tall, carved from ancient stone as gray as a stormy night. Towering statues of mystical creatures flanked the hearth—one was a majestic sovereign dragon with horns that resembled a crown, and the other was a nemean lion with claws as sharp as knives. Both seemed almost alive, their eyes flickering with an enchanting radiance.

The flames within the hearth danced with an iridescent brilliance, weaving together colors I didn't think were possible for fire.

Sorin slapped my shoulder the instant he laid eyes on it. "Gray, do you see that?"

"I see it," I said.

"I told you this place is amazing."

The fireplace crackled with energy.

Gleaming glowstone chandeliers hung overhead, suspended by shimmering chains, casting light that played on the polished marble floors. Soft tunes emanated from an unseen location, like ghosts were playing us a soothing symphony that encouraged relaxation and contemplation.

The aroma of rich cocoa lingered in the air, reminding me of my hunger.

Phila, Ashlyn, Nini, and Exie all sat in front of the fireplace. No one else was around, which was almost a shame. The grand lounge could easily accommodate a thousand people, so seeing only a handful made it feel sad and empty.

"Oh, there you all are." With a smile, Phila waved us over to the couches. "You're just in time for breakfast."

She giggled as she pointed to a massive table. It was low to the ground, which meant people would have to sit on the floor or on pillows in order to eat at it. That was fine—the food on top of the table made any discomfort worth it.

Bowls filled with fruit were at the four corners of the table, including some charberries, blueberries, and golden apples. Whole plates of baked sweets were in the middle, some piled so high, they were damn near two feet tall. Honey trickled down off a couple of croissants, glistening in the light of the fireplace.

Plump sausages were arranged in neat stacks on a dozen different plates. Everyone had their own plate, utensils, and a cup of piping-hot cocoa.

Had the Academy provided all this? Or had Phila's family?

I took a seat. Sorin sat next to me, and Nini sat on his other side.

When Phila sat, Ashlyn and Exie were the first to take seats on either side of her, much to Nasbit's obvious chagrin. He sat with Raaza and Knovak, as though they were a barely acceptable alternative. He set his gift box on the table next to his empty plate.

Twain, Thurin, Miko, Rex, and Waste were the only eldrin here, currently. Twain and Miko, cute little eldrin, sat on top of the table, and no one said a word.

But when Waste, the reaper, floated close to Nini, Exie balked at his presence. The clatter of his chain signified his displeasure, but Waste moved away and hid himself in a dark corner, looming with all the presence of a murderer.

Rex fluttered over Exie's head. He never seemed to grow tired. Or if he did, he never complained.

Brak, Ecrib, and Tenoch entered the grand lounge from a window hidden behind the illusioned tapestries. They walked off the branch of the tree house and then sauntered inside. Brak's stone golem legs stomped each step of the way. Ecrib slid over the last bit of the distance, reminding me of an otter on its belly.

Tenoch was the happiest. He spread his coatl wings and slithered over to his arcanist.

"Tenoch," Phila said with a squeal of delight. "You didn't miss anything! Look, I saved you a special sausage." She grabbed a plate and showed her eldrin the food. "Just for you."

"Thank you, my arcanist," Tenoch said, the tip of his tail twitching in apparent happiness.

Before anyone dug into the food, Phila stood at the head of the long table. Her smile never left her, and she was practically the embodiment of summer happiness and warmth.

"Now that everyone is here," she said, "we can begin!" Phila motioned to the tapestries.

The one magical forest shimmered and shifted into a winter wonderland. Rolling hills of snow, skies filled with an aurora, and frosted pine trees were everywhere. Although we had a fireplace with roaring flames, I swore the whole lounge grew colder.

Actual snowflakes wafted in from the windows hidden by the tapestries. At first, I thought it was some sort of illusion, but the icy flakes melted whenever they got too close to the fireplace. Were mystical creatures outside, evoking ice to make Phila's cotillion exciting?

"I've never really been to the snow," Phila commented as she sat back down. "So I thought this would be a fun theme for my cotillion. And of course, I had to avoid a beach theme or a princess theme, since Ashlyn and Exie took those."

Had they been friends for a long time before attending Astra Academy? It seemed like it, though I hadn't asked.

"It's beautiful," Ashlyn said.

Exie nodded and smiled. "Yes, I quite approve, given the circumstances."

While everyone scooped food onto their empty plates, Nini glanced over at Sorin. In a whisper I almost couldn't hear, she said, "I've never had a cotillion."

"Do you want one?" Sorin asked.

"I... don't know how to go about it. My family has... disowned me."

"I'll talk to our professors." Sorin wrapped an arm around her. "If you want one, I'll see what I can do to make it happen."

Nini fixed her glasses, but I suspected it was to hide the glow of her pink cheeks.

The food was good. Probably too good. I had one bite of that sausage, and I realized every other sausage I had ever had in my life was crap. *This* was a real sausage.

The cocoa had a rich and creamy texture. I took a sip, but then I downed the whole mug because I didn't want to stop drinking.

Twain stared at me with a playful show of disapproval, his eyes narrowed in judgment. I cut up a sausage and fed him a bite.

He practically melted. "So good," Twain said with a purr.

Everyone's silence, followed by soft moans of delight, told me they were all enjoying their food as well. Phila took dainty bites, and occasionally stopped to feed her eldrin. Tenoch had no arms or hands— just wings and a snake body. Phila took the time to spoon him more sausage whenever she paused from her own meal.

Nasbit, once finished with his honey pastries, dabbed his lips with a soft napkin and then cleared his throat. The rest of the class glanced over. "Uh, Phila, for your cotillion..." He scooted the wooden box across the table in her direction.

"Is that a gift?" she asked with a tilt of her head.

"Yes. I thought you might like it."

Phila waved away the comment. "Oh, Nasbit. You shouldn't have."

Then she leaned over, grabbed the box, and placed it next to her plate. "I actually have a surprise for everyone."

"For us?" Raaza balked.

"That's right."

Phila stood, and her coatl perked up. Together, they walked over to a large couch and then dug around behind it. Phila and her eldrin withdrew several small wooden boxes, each tied shut with a colored ribbon.

Snickering as they returned to the table, Phila and Tenoch went around to each arcanist and handed out the boxes.

"This is for you," Phila said, handing me a box with an orange ribbon.

It was the size of a fist, and just as fancy as Nasbit's.

"What is it?" I asked as I hesitantly took it from her.

"A gift."

"Why are you giving *me* a gift? It's *your* cotillion."

Phila walked over to my brother and handed him a box with a black ribbon. "I wanted you all to be surprised. And I love giving gifts. I thought this was the perfect combination."

She handed Nini a box with a red ribbon.

"Th-Thank you," Nini stammered.

"No, thank *you* for joining us at my cotillion." Phila handed Ashlyn a box with a blue ribbon. "It's not every day you get to attend Astra Academy. I want everyone to remember it as fondly as I will. And my father used to say, *you have to make your own wishes become realities*, so that's what I'm going to do."

"Very wise," Tenoch said. He used his snake tail to hand Exie a box with a pink ribbon.

Phila handed Raaza a box with a green ribbon, and Knovak one with a white ribbon. But when she got to Nasbit, she giggled. Phila handed him the last box—one with a gold ribbon. It sort of matched the golden flecks found in his sandstone golem.

"I'm so glad you joined us," Phila said to him.

Nasbit couldn't seem to find his words. His cheeks were red, and he nodded, but otherwise he didn't respond.

"I was going to give these out later, but since *you* gave me a gift, I figured now was the time." Phila smiled a little wider as she went back to her seat. Then she picked up Nasbit's gift and gently caressed the outside. "Shall we all open our gifts at the same time?"

"Sounds good to me," Raaza said, turning his upside down and then shaking it next to his ear.

Sorin opened his gift first. He pulled out a silver chain necklace with a pendant that resembled a musical note and a shield. The same shield woven into his arcanist mark on his forehead.

He turned it over in his hand. When he grazed the musical note, a soft melody played from it, one that sounded as though it was made with string instruments.

"What is this?" Sorin asked, his eyes wide.

"My aunt called it a *Muse Necklace*," Phila stated. "It's a trinket made from—"

"*It's a trinket*?" Raaza interjected, his tone bordering on outraged. "You mean, a star shard was used to make it?"

Phila nodded. "That's right."

"A musical *necklace*? Someone used a star shard for *that*?"

"People use star shards to use the Gates of Crossing..." Phila tapped her bottom lip. "And they're just used up then. I thought this would be nice. I had these commissioned when we got back from our camping trip. All your gifts were mailed to the Academy, and I've just been holding on to them. I knew exactly what I wanted."

Sorin glanced up from the necklace. "You had this made specifically for me?"

"You love poetry, yes? Every good poet needs to have the music of his soul to speak his words properly."

Tenoch nodded as he flapped his feathery wings. "Also very wise, my arcanist."

Sorin slipped the necklace on. When he touched the music note a second time, the melody ended.

"Thank you," he said, his appreciation genuine. "It's lovely. I've never owned a trinket like this before."

"I have a trinket," Raaza whispered, crossing his arms. "I won it from Captain Leon."

But no one commented.

Knovak was the next to open his gift. His unicorn, Starling, clopped to him and glanced over his shoulder, his horn glittering in the light of the fireplace. Knovak withdrew a pendant that was shaped like a bird holding a coin.

"Is this the Gentz family motto engraved on the back?" Knovak asked, his eyes wide.

"That's right." Phila placed a hand on her cheek. "It's a trinket that allows you to see in the dark. I thought it would give you comfort if you were ever on another camping trip."

Knovak held the pendant tightly in his grasp. "Thank you."

I was curious now.

My box was calling to me.

I picked it up, untied the ribbon, and glanced at the contents.

Chapter 36

A Personal Rune

T nside was a vial.

I picked it up and held it in the firelight. The inside was filled with a dark powder.

"It's *occult ore dust*," Phila proudly said. "You can enchant yourself with a rune as long as you have that, and an arcanist with the magic you want to permanently affix to yourself."

Raaza practically leapt onto the table. "You gave that to *Gray?*"

"Well, he is a *mimic arcanist*. I thought it was fitting. He can be whatever he wants. Now his gift is whatever he wants as well."

"Extremely wise," Tenoch chimed in.

Phila grabbed her coatl eldrin and hugged him close. "Oh, stop that, Tenoch! You're embarrassing me. You don't need to keep saying it."

"But it's true, my arcanist. It's why I bonded with you. After all, you were the wisest of the individuals who attempted my Trial of Worth."

The others opened their gifts, and much to the elation of everyone involved, they were all trinkets. Nini was given a magical quill; Ashlyn received a bracelet that brightened to illuminate small spaces. Exie showed off her necklaces, which apparently made her eyes and hair glow slightly. Raaza was given a trick belt buckle—it could hide something within, and not be detected through normal means.

But I barely paid attention to any of that. I focused on the vial. Occult ore allowed someone to enchant their skin with a rune—one of the glittering tattoos some of the professors around the Academy had.

If I could give myself one magical ability for all time, what would it be?

I wasn't sure.

What would be the most useful for a *mimic arcanist*? I already had access to almost every magical ability out there. Twain could transform into anything.

When it came time for Phila and Nasbit to open their boxes, I paid more attention.

"You go first, Nasbit," Phila said.

"Oh, I insist *you* go first. It's your cotillion." Nasbit fidgeted with his box. "I hope you like it."

Phila opened her box and half-gasped. Both Ashlyn and Exie leaned over to get a better look. Phila eventually—and carefully—reached in to withdraw a golden ring. It was crafted, with loving detail, to be a coatl. A snake biting its own tail, and the wings tucked to the side. The whole ring was slender and feminine, and Phila slipped it on immediately.

"It's so beautiful," she whispered.

"It-It's not a trinket," Nasbit said, his tone apologetic. "But I thought it suited you."

Tenoch flitted his forked tongue out once. "This is... a very wise gift."

"I love it," Phila said. She held out her hand, showing the ring off to everyone around. "Do you all agree? It's beautiful?"

Nini clapped. "It is!"

For some reason, I thought Exie would stare on in jealousy, but that wasn't the case. She smiled just the same way she secretly smiled over Sorin. I wondered, in that moment where everyone was having so much fun, if Exie was friends with Phila because she saw Phila's true inner beauty, just as she saw Sorin's.

Exie liked beautiful things, after all, and Phila had a kind and generous soul. More than I had even originally suspected. She had done all this? For us? On *her* cotillion? Who did that?

"Open your gift now, Nasbit," Phila said.

Nasbit gingerly untied the ribbon and then opened his box. He withdrew a gold necklace, similar to Sorin's. The pendant, however, was in the shape of a globe. It sparkled with inner magic.

"What does it do?" Nasbit whispered.

"It stores memories," Phila happily announced. "I know you love taking notes, and learning so many things, so I thought I should get you something to help with that. This trinket can store up to fifty important moments. Isn't that neat?"

"It's wonderful." Nasbit immediately slipped it on over his head. "Thank you so much, Phila."

"I'm so happy you like it."

Sorin stood from the table. Everyone glanced over. I had forgotten— he had said he wrote a poem. I should've known this moment was coming.

"I've written you a little something, Phila," Sorin said. He touched his *Muse Necklace* and started the soft melody of violins.

"I can't wait to hear it." Phila scooted around until she was comfortable, her eldrin coiled in her lap.

Sorin took a deep breath. When he spoke, it was with passion and rhythm, more than I had ever heard before. Combined with the music, it was damn near an experience.

"In an Academy with rooms aflutter in snow, there dwells a girl with a heart aglow. Beside her until the end, a feathered eldrin, her coatl, a faithful friend.

"Through sunlit days and moonlit nights, they weaved a tale of shared delights. Their bond, a song of trust and grace, a beautiful pairing forged in this sacred place.

"And when the world grows dark, and awfully cold, their love's warmth will them enfold. For in their presence, joy is found, both wonderful, true friends profound."

When Sorin finished, no one spoke.

A moment later, the others clapped, and I joined them. Sorin had really given that poem everything he had. It was a delight. I almost couldn't believe I thought this, but... I almost wished he had more poems on him, so he could entertain us all day.

Phila's cotillion was better than I had thought it was going to be. We ate, received gifts, told stories, and some people laughed so hard their sides hurt.

Then it all went downhill when Phila insisted we dance.

The music in the grand lounge shifted to something slow and romantic. Most everyone groaned when Phila pushed the table out of the way so we could use the spot in front of the fireplace for our dancing. The only people *not* upset were Sorin and Nini. The two of them stood, and even though Nini was blushing hard enough to be seen from the moon, they both held hands and swayed in front of the fireplace.

I couldn't dance. Thankfully, Ashlyn already knew that.

I walked over to her and her typhoon dragon and held out my hand.

Ashlyn gave me a pointed look, as though to remind me she was betrothed, but this time she didn't voice the words. Instead, Ashlyn took my hand. I thought I would lead her to a spot in front of the blazing fire, but instead, she led *me* over to an area near the stones of the outer fireplace.

Ashlyn took one of my hands, placed it on her waist, and then held my other hand with hers. She stepped forward. I stepped back. The entire time, I maintained eye contact with her, searching her blue gaze for some sort of hint as to what she wanted from me.

"Nervous?" Ashlyn playfully asked.

"Me? Never."

"Your palm feels sweaty."

"It's the fire in the fireplace," I said with a shrug. "Besides, why would I be nervous now that I'm doing exactly what I wanted to do?"

A smile sprouted at the corners of Ashlyn's lips. She rolled her eyes as though I were being too corny, but I could tell she loved it.

Exie, Raaza, and Knovak sat off to the side, each of them taking up their own couch. When Phila motioned for them to pair off, all three gave each other sideways glances. Then they shook their heads in unison. No one wanted to move.

Nasbit nervously hovered around the fireplace until Phila headed in his direction. Then he straightened his posture and held out his hand. Phila gave him a slight curtsy. "What a gentleman. Thank you."

"Oh, no, thank you," he said. So awkward. I almost felt bad for him.

But Phila either didn't notice or didn't care. She happily danced with him by the fire, smiling the entire time. Nasbit did his best to lead, but it was rather slow, like he had just learned the moves to this dance earlier this morning.

And when it was all over, I could've sworn Nasbit used his necklace to capture a moment in time.

Phila's cotillion lasted all day.

Once it was over, dinner had already concluded for the rest of the Academy. Most arcanists were on the way to their dorms, their eldrin already tucked away in the treehouse.

I went to the dorm, but only for a moment. I gathered the notes Nasbit had written, and then I headed back out. My original plan had been to give these to Professor Helmith at the fundraiser, but things had changed. Instead, I headed through the Academy, intent on seeing her before I went to bed.

As I walked with Twain by my side, I wondered how Helmith would look.

"What did you do to Professor Helmith?" I asked, my voice quiet and barely echoing in the hall.

Twain glanced up at me in confusion.

Deimos replied with, "The woman who temporarily trapped me with you? I tore at her soul when I wielded Vivigöl against her."

That was what I had been afraid of.

"She'll get better, won't she?" I asked.

"She will. As long as she doesn't face a Death Lord again anytime soon."

I chortled. "Why's that?"

"Abyssal dragon arcanists manipulate souls. If I were to fight her again, while she was weak, I would effortlessly destroy her."

That thought got me angry, much faster than anything else. I kept my rage to myself, though. What use was it yelling at myself in the middle of an empty hallway? Instead, I quickened my step, intent on seeing Helmith to make sure she was okay.

Once I finally reached her door, I had calmed enough to be happy again. Phila's cotillion had lifted my spirits. Everyone's spirits, really. It had been so pleasant, and upbeat. Just like Phila herself.

I lifted my hand and then hesitated.

"Did *you* enjoy the cotillion?" I asked.

Twain vigorously nodded. "Oh, I did."

"Sorry, not you."

He pressed his ears flat against his head. "You need to stop doing that. I keep thinking you're speaking to me."

"Your tiny celebration was an amusing distraction from my otherwise dull existence as a parasite on your soul," Deimos replied, all apathy.

I rubbed my chin. "So, you *did* enjoy it?"

"Mildly."

"Are you just jealous you didn't get a gift?"

Deimos didn't reply to that one. I suspected he didn't like my sarcasm as much as I liked it.

"We're practically friends now," I said with a chuckle.

"Your delusions will be your undoing."

That made me genuinely laugh. "I think you need more friends, Dee. Can I call you *Dee*? I think good friends like us need nicknames for one another."

His annoyance spiked through my thoughts. Deimos *really* didn't like the nickname. Which amused me. It was difficult to get under the man's skin. His confidence was a shield that prevented him from caring about most of what I talked about.

Instead of provoking him further, I knocked on Helmith's recovery room door.

"Come in," she said from the other side.

The room was brightly lit this time. Several stained-glass lanterns hung in the corners, giving the whole room a fun and colorful feeling.

Professor Helmith sat on the edge of her bed, a book on her lap. Her tanned complexion had returned, her black hair once again lustrous and beautiful, her indigo eyes brilliant. The shine of her glowing arcanist mark really highlighted her beauty.

"Gray?" Helmith asked with a smile. "What're you doing here?" She glanced to the hallway behind me. "Is Kristof on his way back? I asked him to get me a few things from the library."

"I didn't see him." I stepped inside and closed the door. I hoped he wouldn't bother us.

"What can I do for you?" Professor Helmith moved her book to her nightstand and then patted the mattress for me to sit.

I did as she requested. The bed squeaked when I sat, but I didn't care. Instead, I handed Helmith the notes Nasbit had written. "This is everything I found out about Death Lord Deimos and the things happening in the abyssal hells."

Helmith took the paperwork. She placed that on the nightstand as well. "Kristof told me you continue to investigate, even though he asked you not to."

"I'm sorry," I whispered. "I'm done now, though. That's why I came to give you that. I think... something bad is going to happen. And someone should do something." I turned to face her. "But I think people who are loyal to the other Death Lords are here in the Academy."

Helmith's eyes widened. "Oh? Like Professor Zahn was?"

"Yes."

"I do, too."

Hearing her say it was both a relief and a burden. A relief because I wasn't crazy, but a burden because now we had to deal with it.

Well, we'd deal with it in due time. Right now, I had another request for her. I reached into my pocket, withdrew the vial of occult ore dust, and held it up in the multi-colored light.

"Professor?" I asked. "Phila gave me this as a gift."

She glanced over. "Occult ore? That's very kind of her. Are you planning on enchanting yourself?"

"Yes."

"What kind of magic are you going to permanently take? Keep in mind, you can only enchant yourself so much."

I held the vial tightly in my grasp and stared at my own fist. "I thought... Well, I'd like it if *you* enchanted me. With your true form ethereal whelk magic."

CHAPTER 37

BE YOUR BEST SELF

P rofessor Helmith laughed. I hadn't realized how much I missed her velvety mirth. But why was she amused? I thought, asking for her magic was a sentimental gesture.

"Gray," she said. "You shouldn't take *my* magic. Your mimic can copy ethereal whelks."

"But what if you're not around?"

Helmith shook her head, her inky hair fluttering as she did so. The sparkle of her own pink runes was painfully obvious to me now. The swirls on her shoulders made me curious.

"I would be a terrible professor if I enchanted you with ethereal whelk magic."

I lifted an eyebrow. "Why's that?"

"Because, as your professor, I should be encouraging you to be the best version of yourself." Helmith placed a delicate hand on my shoulder. "Gray—you need magic that helps you in a permanent way. It needs to synergize with your current skill set. My magic doesn't do that."

She made sense, but I had already thought this over. Since Twain could copy any mystical creature, what was the point of runes for me? Nothing was too critical or interesting. At least, not that I could think of.

"Do you have a recommendation?" I asked.

Professor Helmith nodded. "I do. My uncle will eventually be here—whenever the headmaster allows him into the Academy. He's the *Mother of Shapeshifters* arcanist."

"We learned all about him in class," I said.

Twain leapt up onto the bed and purred. "Could my mother *empower* Gray with her magic?"

"I'm not sure," Helmith muttered. "But a unique creature can craft a unique rune." She chuckled. "And that would help you more, I imagine."

I hadn't even considered the Mother of Shapeshifters arcanist. Would he help me? Would he enchant me with his magic if I just walked up and asked?

Helmith smiled. She usually knew what I was thinking. "My uncle will help, don't you worry. I'll ask him nicely. He never tells me no."

He sounded nice. Actually, from what I had seen, everyone in Helmith's family was kind. I wondered if it was genetic, or if they all just got lucky.

I stood from her bed. "Thank you. You're right... I think that would make for a better rune. I hadn't even thought of it." After I made my statement, I tucked the vial of occult ore dust into my pocket. Professor Helmith always looked out for me. Always.

"You should get some rest," she said.

"I will."

I headed for the door, and Twain followed. When I grabbed the handle, I stopped and glanced over my shoulder. "Actually... I had one more thing to ask you."

"What's that, Gray?"

"Will Ashlyn's father be attending the Academy competitions? Or the fundraiser? I know the headmaster is limiting people, but surely arcanists will be able to attend those?"

Professor Helmith laced her fingers together and mulled over my question, as though sifting through her memory to locate the answer. After a short while, she smiled. "Headmaster Venrover will allow individuals into the Academy for those events, so I suspect the archduke will join us, yes."

That was good to hear.

"Would you mind... talking to him about me?" I asked, trying not to sound awkward. This was a bizarre request, but Ashlyn said that professors needed to talk me up.

"Speak to Archduke Kross? About you?" Helmith tilted her head.

"Yes. And not about how you helped me fight a soul catcher in my dreams. I mean, could you talk to him about... what a promising future I have? And how, well, competent I am?"

I was about to add a bit about what an awesome man I was, but this line of requests was getting a little too weird. That would be enough to prove to Ashlyn's father I was someone worthy of his daughter.

I hoped.

"Oh, I see." Helmith stifled a giggle. "The archduke isn't a man who impresses easily, but I'm sure I could put a good word in. I'll have Kristof do the same."

"Well, maybe not him."

I doubted Kristof wanted to say anything nice about me.

"But thank you," I said as I opened the door. "I really appreciate you taking the time, even though you're still recovering."

"Of course."

Then I exited the room, shut the door behind Twain, and headed back for the dorm, wondering what a rune from the Mother of Shapeshifters arcanist would even do.

Class with Professor Ren was always amusing. Mostly because, out of all our professors, he was the easiest to get off topic. He never seemed to mind answering ridiculous questions.

He wrote on the chalkboard about the existence of magical phenomena, but most of the class was bored with the subject. Even Ren's treasure cache spider, which had taken up a spot in the corner and built himself a little web, looked as though he had fallen asleep.

"So, remember how we dealt with mushrooms that had elemental effects?" Ren asked, his back to the classroom.

"Professor?" Exie said as she half-heartedly raised her head.

"Yes?"

"Can you teach us about *augmentation*?" she asked. "I think it's outrageous we haven't had a proper class on that yet."

Professor Ren slowly turned around to face the class. He swept back his red hair, giving himself more time to contemplate her request. "Listen, I already got in trouble for discussing imbuing with you all when that isn't even my subject. Professor Jijo should be teaching you augmentation, sound like a plan?"

"But Professor Jijo was gone for the first part of the year." Exie rolled her eyes. "Captain Leon taught us about evocation and manipulation, but since Jijo came in, it's like he's started our class back from the beginning. He's just going over boring weapons and fighting."

"It's not boring," Raaza muttered with a glare.

Nasbit wobbled his hand back and forth.

After a long sigh, Ren crossed his arms over his chest. "All right. Here's the deal. I'll tell you, but we keep this to ourselves, all right? One small session on how to augment things with your magic never hurt anyone."

The entire class perked up immediately. Nasbit pulled out his notebook, Nini smiled widely, and even Ashlyn seemed excited. Since Deimos had already told me a bit about augmentation, I was less excited, but still interested. Everyone else's abilities were my abilities, after all. It would be good to know them.

Professor Ren erased what he had been writing and wrote two new things on the board.

"Augmenting yourself, and augmenting other things or people usually result in different effects." Ren stopped writing for a moment. "With some creatures, usually the weaker ones, the effect is the same whether used on themselves or others, but the general rule is that your own magic affects you differently. Got it?"

The class happily wrote that down.

Ren turned around and glanced between everyone. He sighed as he stared at Sorin and Nini. Then his attention slid to me, and he sighed a second time, only harder.

"What's wrong?" Sorin asked.

"Well, you all have... bizarre creatures." He pointed to Sorin. "When you augment yourself, you step through shadows. When you augment others, you give them the ability to see in the dark. However, it's the middle of the day." He motioned to the glorious sunshine streaming in through the back window.

"Oh," Sorin said.

"It'll be hard for you to practice here." Ren shuddered when he pointed to Nini. "And reapers are... quite, uh, *interesting*. When they augment themselves, they step through blood, rather than shadow."

Nini tapped the tips of her fingers together. "Hm. Yes. You told me that before. I didn't really know what you meant."

"If there are puddles of blood around—even splatters on the walls, really—you can move through them. *However*—" Ren really emphasized the word, "—we *definitely* can't test that out here in the classroom. I'll get fired immediately."

"What happens when I augment someone else?" Nini asked, her voice hopeful.

"You give them an immunity to fear effects," Ren replied. "Which can be helpful in some situations. Not many... but some."

Everyone in class whispered between themselves. Were they upset by Nini's disturbing abilities? Or just anxious to test out their own?

Professor Ren glanced at me and frowned. I waved away his concerns.

"I know, I know," I said. "I'm a mimic arcanist. I only augment things when Twain is transformed."

"That's not entirely true, actually."

With a lifted eyebrow, I sat a little straighter. "What do you mean?"

"Mimics can augment themselves." Ren tapped the side of his head. "You see, mimics can take on the form of items, both mundane and magical." He shrugged. "The mimic augments itself to change shape."

"Into what?" I asked. "A treasure chest?"

Ren chuckled. "Anything, really."

Anything? I glanced down at my pencil and notebook. Then I gave Twain a pointed stare. He met my gaze with his own, like this was the last thing he ever wanted to do.

"I'm not turning into a notebook," Twain finally said.

"We need to practice." I pushed the notebook closer. "C'mon. This should be easy."

"No."

"Just for a few seconds."

"Never." Twain turned away, his ears back. "I will not be something as undignified as a notebook."

Nini giggled into her hand. Sorin leaned back in his chair and shook his head. Both were clearly amused by my eldrin's obstinance.

"Enough of the weird mystical creatures," Exie said. She tapped her table with her pencil. "What about the rest of us who have normal creatures? What do erlkings augment?"

Professor Ren walked around the front desk and leaned onto it. He had to think for a minute, which meant he probably wasn't *as* familiar with erlkings as he was with other creatures. "When they augment other people, they make it so they can see through illusions," he said. "When they augment themselves, they temporarily gain immunity to magics that cause instant death."

Raaza half-gasped. "Really? That's so amazing."

"That's all?" Exie practically sighed. "I wanted it to be more useful."

"*How is that not useful?*" Raaza sounded like he was about to lose his mind. It caused some of the others in class to chuckle to themselves.

Nasbit scooted forward in his chair and raised his hand. When Ren pointed at him, he sighed. "I read that stone golem arcanists augment their own strength, becoming both rather durable and powerful... Is that true?"

"Why wouldn't it be true?" Ren asked, clearly baffled. "Do you think the textbooks would lie to you?"

"N-No. I was just hoping I would get something else, other than strength."

Raaza dragged his hand down his face. "What's wrong with all of you?"

"I can allow other people to breathe underwater," Ashlyn said. "I thought that was useful, though it has few combat applications."

Their constant bickering only made me laugh. While it was interesting to gain an immunity to instant death effects—wouldn't that be an amazing rune?—I decided I would stick to Professor Helmith's advice. The Mother of Shapeshifters was a unique creature, and her unique abilities would be something to have.

I just needed to wait a bit longer.

Another week.

Another free day.

Normally, most everyone in my class had a club or activity they did on their free day, but today was different. The training field was busy. Several first- and second-year students were out doing their own practice routines. Knovak jogged around the track, Nasbit had his stone golem in the center of the field, Phila practiced with a bow, and I went through my entire exercise routine.

There were others—arcanists who I wasn't familiar with—including a group of people who were all tossing iron balls across a measured sandpit, and a few pegasus arcanists who seemed to be playing tug-of-war with a thick rope.

As Knovak and his unicorn jogged by me, some random arcanist from one of the groups shouted, "*Unicorns are trash.*"

"*You're* trash," Knovak shot back. He stopped on the track and balled his fists, his face reddening.

"Nice one," I quipped. "They'll be thinking about that insult for days."

"What else am I supposed to do?"

I shrugged. "Just ignore them. They're not getting physical with you anymore, right? You're being your best self—you don't need those people's acceptance. If they're just throwing words, let them suck a lemon."

Knovak exhaled. His unicorn pranced around him.

"He's right, my arcanist," Starling said. "We are above the riffraff. We don't need their cheers—we just need to make sure we don't lose to them in a race."

Knovak stroked Starling's mane. "You're right. I just need to keep practicing."

I wanted a day where I didn't have to deal with anything, but then I caught sight of some people approaching Phila. Were they going to harass her, too? Was there no end to the pettiness of the arcanists in the other years?

But then one of them produced a beautiful bow from behind his back and handed it over.

It made me curious, so I walked over.

CHAPTER 38

COMPETITIONS

"This is such an elegant bow," Phila said as she examined it from every angle.

The wood was some sort of black yew, with limbs that curved and a riser that had been fashioned to look like a snake. The string glittered in the daylight, which told me it wasn't made out of the standard hemp like all our practice bows. It was probably silk, or some sort of magical component.

The man standing next to Phila was her same height, just much wider. He had the type of shoulders that could carry an ox, and his face was so broad, he could've fit another mouth on it, easy.

But not another pair of eyes, because the man's nose dominated every part of his face above the lips. Not in a pleasant way—he had obviously broken his nose when he was younger, long before he had the healing power of an arcanist. That sniffer went in three different directions like a meandering stream.

His arcanist mark was a seven-pointed star with a winged snake intertwined. And not a snake with feathered wings, like the coatl—it was a snake with bat wings.

He was an amphiptere arcanist.

"Do you like it?" the man asked. "I heard you recently had your cotillion, and I wanted to help commemorate the event."

"That's so thoughtful of you, Legott." Phila smiled as she hugged her bow. "Thank you so much."

Legott brushed back his chestnut hair and smiled wide. He flexed a bit as he did, showing off the muscles barely contained by his too-small tunic.

I stepped closer, interjecting myself into their conversation with my physical presence. They stopped speaking and stared. I nodded, unconcerned with their silence. "Hey, Phila. Nice bow."

Twain hopped through the grass around my feet. "Eh. It's an okay bow."

"I think it's lovely." Phila motioned to Legott. "It's another gift. I'm so lucky."

Legott frowned at me, obviously irritated by my presence. He offered Phila a smile and then gently took her hand to kiss her knuckles. Once he was done with *that*, he said, "I'll see you at the upcoming archery display. I hope you'll use my bow." Then Legott turned on his heel and strode off toward the targets.

"You know him?" I asked.

Phila shrugged. "I've seen him around the Academy. I think we've spoken. And he was at Ashlyn's cotillion."

Ah. Some noble arcanist, then.

"Well, I need to practice some more before all those competitions," Phila said. She didn't even wait for me to acknowledge her statement. She took her fancy new bow and hurried for the targets as well.

I was surprised at how eager she was to learn archery. Then again, with her magic, she would make a fantastic archer.

The stomp of Nasbit's stone golem alerted me to his approach long before anything else. I turned around, allowing the afternoon breeze to wash over me as I smiled. Nasbit and Brak stopped a few feet from me, and I realized Nasbit's shirt was soaked from his armpits down to his belt.

"Did you see that, Gray?" he whispered.

"See what?" I asked.

"Phila's gift." Nasbit sighed. He wiped sweat from his face and then dried his hands on the front of his trousers. "See, Gray... This is why I hate competitions." His voice grew quieter as he muttered, "Just when I think things are going my way, someone swoops in to show me up. I could be playing a game, and someone else has to prove they're better than me... Or maybe I like someone, and then *someone else* walks in and proves I'm nothing."

"Who?" I gestured with a shrug of my shoulder in Legott's direction. "That walking nose? You think he's showing you up?"

"Did you see him?" Nasbit wildly waved his arm. "He has six abs, at least. *At least.*"

"You have, like, one *big* ab," Twain said, obviously trying to be helpful. "That has to count for something."

Nasbit leaned onto Brak. The stone golem didn't even move. He held all of Nasbit's weight and even patted him on the back.

"Phila is too beautiful and kind and wonderful to end up with someone like me." Nasbit rubbed his gut. His dead-eyed gaze barely saw anything, like he was deep in the darkest corners of his own mind.

"You like her?"

Nasbit rubbed the sandstone chest of his golem. "Of course."

"And you think she deserves someone equally amazing?" I patted my stomach. "Someone with six whole abs?"

Nasbit pushed himself off Brak. "Of course."

"Then stop wasting your time feeling bad for yourself," I said. "You have abs to chisel."

For a split second, Nasbit stood straighter, but it didn't last long. He slumped and then sighed. "Seems like a long and hard effort."

"You must not like Phila *that* much," I said.

Nasbit glared. "I like her."

"You know what my stepmoth—er, my *mum* once told me?" She and my father were still here at the Academy, and my thoughts drifted to them for a moment. "She said that when you find your soulmate, you'll know, because they'll make you a better person."

"Er, Phila isn't making me do anything. And that's good, because I'd rather not have someone ordering me around."

"No, dummy. It's not because they *force* you to be a better person... You do it yourself. Because they inspire you." I shrugged as I headed back to the field. "And if a *long and hard* effort is too much, then you weren't inspired at all, if you catch my drift."

"My uncles said I shouldn't do anything for the sake of a woman, because then I might do stupid things, and make a fool of myself. They said I should only do things for myself."

I stared at him, holding back my sarcasm. "Well, think of it like this—if you improved yourself, regardless of why, you've still improved, right? You'll keep that forever. You don't actually need reasons to do good things, but they're good fuel for your metaphorical fire."

My words seemed to sink in one at a time. Rather than waiting for him to come to the obvious conclusion, I left Nasbit to mull over everything. If he didn't want to try, he could always sit on the sidelines—no harm in that. But hopefully he would find someone who really inspired him to do great things.

He seemed like a man who could, if only he had the right motivation.

We sat in Kristof's class, watching him attempt to draw mystical creatures on the chalkboard. He wasn't the greatest artist I had ever seen, and he took *way* too long to draw the ferret-like body of a rizzel.

"It's much easier… to create artwork in dreams…" Kristof murmured to himself as he drew leaves on a little dragon. "It's important for you all to understand there are occasionally *variations* of mystical creatures from one species to the next. Red phoenixes and blue phoenixes have different magical abilities, but a rizzel with silver stripes and a rizzel with gold stripes are the *same* in terms of magic."

Most of the class wrote that down.

"Some creatures are like… cats. An orange tabby is almost identical to a calico tabby, except for the coloration."

Raaza raised his hand. He hadn't taken many notes, and it was obvious he wouldn't care if a golden-striped rizzel came flying through the window.

Kristof turned around. "Yes?"

"The Astra Academy competitions are coming up, aren't they? I don't know the rules. Or what all will be taking place." Raaza leaned onto the table. "I heard second-years discussing everything, and I think it's unfair they already know."

"Oh." Kristof sheepishly walked over to the professor's desk and opened the top drawer. He withdrew a small stack of papers and then casually walked around the room, passing one out to each student. "These should've been given to you a while ago. My apologies."

I took my paper and glanced over the details. It was some sort of letter intended for the families of students, which listed the many things taught at Astra Academy, and how the arcanists would demonstrate their skills.

It read:

Astra Academy
In Life, Through Time, With Magic, Till Death

Dear Esteemed Relatives,

I hope this letter finds you in good spirits. As the new academic year is nearing the halfway point at Astra Academy, it is my pleasure to extend my warmest greetings to you. We are excited to announce an upcoming event that promises to be a day of enchantment and camaraderie: the Astra Academy Tournament Day!

This celebration will allow our first- and second-year students to showcase their magical prowess and competitive spirit in a series of thrilling events.

The Academy will gather to witness and participate in five exhilarating events, each designed to test various aspects of our students' magical abilities. Allow me to provide you with a brief overview of the events:

Archery Competition: All first- and second-year students are instructed on the ways of archery. In this event, students will compete against one another to see who can achieve the highest score with a limited number of arrows.

Obstacle Course: Our students will race through a complex obstacle course laden with magical challenges. The first three to cross the finish line will be considered the winners.

Melee Sparring Spectacle: Students will engage in friendly duels, demonstrating their combat techniques and defense strategies. A small circle will be etched onto the ground, and the first to be knocked from it will be disqualified.

Eldrin Race: A true test of teamwork and coordination, this eldrin race requires students and their eldrin to work together to cross the finish line. The first three there will celebrate alongside their eldrin.

Professor's Bout: An event that highlights the incredible talents of our students by allowing them to use all their magical knowledge on one of our skilled combat professors. The professor cannot use magic, and must stay inside the circle while the students try to knock them out.

We invite all family members to join us on this special day to witness the magical prowess of our talented students and to share in the excitement that permeates our hallowed halls.

As always, the safety and well-being of our students remain our top priority. Rest assured that all necessary precautions will be taken to ensure a secure and enchanting event for everyone involved.

Adelgis Venrover
Headmaster, Astra Academy

"Why weren't we told about some of these things earlier?" Raaza demanded. He glowered at the paper. "Why weren't these mailed?"

"Since the Academy has been locked down, not much mail has gone out or come in," Kristof replied matter-of-factly. "And you're already practicing for this tournament when you study magic and take lessons from Professor Jijo. You shouldn't be too concerned about a minor—and friendly—competition between fellow arcanist students."

"Do we have to do *all* of these?" Exie asked. "I don't like the sound of any of them."

"You must do one, and you can do a maximum of three," Kristof replied.

That news sent a buzz through the room.

Obviously, I had to win three of these if I wanted any hope of being recognized as impressive by Archduke Kross. Which would I pick? Sparring. Without a doubt. I would win that easily. The eldrin race? No. Knovak obviously wanted to win that. If I competed with him, I would just add to his distress over his lower-tier eldrin. Archery? No. Phila would clearly participate, and even if I could effortlessly win, I'd rather she had her moment.

That left me with the obstacle course and the bout against a magicless professor.

Jijo. It was definitely going to be against Jijo.

And I could handle him if I had my magic and he didn't have his. Again, in the bag. I had this.

I raised my hand. "Professor? What's happening with everyone's families? How will they be able to see this?"

"They're arriving in the morning, watching the competitions, staying for the fundraiser dinner, and then leaving," Kristof replied. He resumed his artwork. "Only a certain number of people are allowed, and they're all being checked before they arrive at the Academy. We should all be perfectly safe."

My father and my mum should be there as well. Which meant I would get to impress everyone with my skills. That was perfect, considering the event was less than a week away.

CHAPTER 39

EVERYONE IN ATTENDANCE

I rolled around in my bed long after the lanterns had been dimmed. The night sky beyond the window bewitched me. Every day felt better than the last. I couldn't remember a time I was this happy before.

Sorin rolled around his mattress, a squeak echoing throughout the dorm whenever he did. I glanced over, and caught him fluffing his pillow. He stared at me for a long moment.

"Can't sleep?" he asked.

"I was going to ask you the same question," I replied.

My brother pulled his blankets to his chin. His feet became exposed for his efforts. "I'm just thinking about Nini." Sorin had a wistful tone that told me everything was all right between them.

He just missed her.

"Have you been writing her a million poems now that you have your new fancy trinket necklace?" I asked.

Sorin shook his head. "I gave it away."

"You *what*?" I propped myself up on my elbows. Twain, who always slept beside me on my bed, grumbled something before rolling back over.

"I gave it away," Sorin repeated. "Well, to be more accurate, I traded it to an artificer student. I gave him my necklace, and in turn, he crafted me an illusion-creating trinket."

The moment he spoke his words, it all made sense. I eased myself back onto my bed. "You gave it to Nini. To hide the name on her chain."

"Yeah."

Sorin...

My brother was too good sometimes. It made me realize I needed to be better. He was one of the few people who would give up everything for the people he loved. Would I be that selfless, if ever the time came? Would I live up to the standards set by my twin brother?

I placed my hand on my chest and gripped my sleeping tunic.

"Are you okay, Gray?" Sorin asked.

"Yeah," I whispered. "Just thinking."

"Don't think too long. You need to get all the sleep you can. The competitions and fundraiser are tomorrow."

Time slipped by quickly whenever I wasn't paying attention. I closed my eyes, ready to tackle the problems of tomorrow. "I'll get plenty of sleep." After a soft sigh, I asked, "What competitions will you be competing in?"

"The eldrin race, for sure." Sorin motioned to the darkness around his bed. It was basically a moat. "Thurin and I are an unshakable team. I'm not sure what it entails, but I'm certain we can handle it."

"You know Knovak is going to give it his all to beat you, right?" I lifted an eyebrow and met his gaze.

"If he *can* beat me," Sorin replied with a smirk. "Knightmare arcanists have a special bond with their eldrin that other arcanists just don't understand."

"Uh-huh." I dismissively waved my hand. "What about Nini? Same?"

"Yeah. We'll be doing it together." Sorin shrugged. "It's the only competition we'll be doing."

"Right. Then you better get some good sleep as well."

"I will." He tucked himself further into his blanket. "Good night, Gray."

"Good night, Sorin."

Sun painted the morning sky with shades of gold and pink.

All the first- and second-year students had to wake early to get to the training field. Twain and I made our way outside the moment we finished our breakfast, but only after I left Vivigöl in the dorm. I couldn't risk taking it with me.

All the fog and mist had been cleared away by the pragmatic Professor Jijo. His nimbus dragon swooped around the area, making sure we had a clear view of everything.

A gentle breeze carried whispers of anticipation. Although this was a small-time competition, mostly used as an exhibition of our skills to impress wealthy arcanists to fund the Academy even more, some people were taking this *seriously*.

Banners adorned with Astra Academy's symbol fluttered in the wind, casting a mesmerizing dance of colors around the four corners of the field.

There were two new structures out in the field that I hadn't seen before. The first was a pentagon-shaped stage. It was made of marble, and sectioned into five distinct zones with circles carved into the stone.

The second structure was a small stand for spectators. Currently, it was empty, but the stand had an awning, cushioned seats, and even several tables to hold refreshments. It was clear the headmaster suspected the spectators would number less than one hundred. The stand wouldn't fit much more beyond that.

Most of the first- and second-year students were out and about, helping set up. There were racks of practice weapons, a strange stone tunnel around a portion of the track, and obstacles set up on the rest of it.

Our guests hadn't even arrived, but everyone was helping Professor Jijo, Captain Leon, and Piper put everything into place.

I even spotted Maryanne Beets, the head of housekeeping. She was an engkanto arcanist. Her elf-like eldrin had telekinesis, which explained how so many of these structures had been placed around the training field on such short notice.

Maryanne wore giant white robes with a thick leather belt around her waist. She kept her sleeves rolled up to her elbows, giving her an odd look that somehow suited her. She waved her hands, and a small pile of bricks outside the field came floating over.

Telekinesis was a manipulation of force, it seemed. She quickly piled the bricks together to form another set of stands. This was for the students, obviously. It was a little less cushioned and a lot more draconian in nature. It would fit a couple dozen people, and Maryanne fashioned together large stands for eldrin, which was all the students really needed.

"Listen up, *students*," someone bellowed.

I turned, ready to start this whole competition.

Captain Leon stood on top of the marble stage, his cerberus next to him. Sticks, the three-headed canine, panted happily.

It had been a while since I last saw Leon. He had once been my *Combat Arts* professor, but now that he wasn't, I rarely saw the man.

He wasn't old, but his white hair and weathered complexion made him appear as though he had thirty extra years. Captain Leon wore silver armor that glistened with impracticality. This wasn't real armor—it was ceremonial armor that had cute little etching around every joint, and polish that could be smelled from half the training field away.

Leon placed his hands on his hips. "Our guests will be arriving soon. When they do, you will all take your seats here." He gestured to the brick stands. Then he pointed to the stage. "Each competition will be held one at a time. We'll have lunch in the middle, and once it's all over, you'll return to your dorms."

Most everyone grumbled acceptances.

"Students—remember to try your best. You represent Astra Academy, and today is the day you flaunt your skills!"

That garnered more of a happy response from the arcanist students.

I wouldn't be going to my dorm at the end of all this, however. Sorin and I were attending the fundraiser dinner, which I was actively looking forward to. The Mother of Shapeshifters would be there, after all...

The last of the obstacle course and the weapons were placed just in time for a horn to sound over the field. The first-year arcanists took seats on one side of the stands while the second-year arcanists took their place on the other.

Obviously, I knew everyone in my class, but I didn't really know many of the other students.

I recognized a few—like Roy, the jerk who bothered Knovak all the time, and Legott, the man who clearly fancied Phila. Other than that, I wasn't concerned about the others.

Sorin and Nini sat on one side of me. Ashlyn sat on the other. She had given me a sideways glance when she took her seat, as if daring me to say anything. I just smiled. Why wouldn't I want her to sit next to me?

"You're in the presence of the winner," I playfully whispered to her.

"It's going to be so embarrassing if you lose now," she quipped.

"Nah. I'll be fine. Just remember to tell your father how handsome I was while competing, and how all my children will obviously inherit my wonder and grace."

Ashlyn almost choked trying to hold back a laugh. I wasn't sure if she was laughing with me—because I was so over the top—or if she was laughing *at* me. I chose to think it was with, especially when her blue eyes sparkled with mischief.

Another horn trumpeted, and then a whole gaggle of individuals exited Astra Academy and headed down the stone steps toward the training field. They made their way across the manicured grass, each one dressed fancier than the last.

Velvet robes adorned with intricate embroidery and shimmering gemstones that caught the sunlight like captured stars were all on display.

Of course, Archduke Kross led the procession. He held his head high, like he wouldn't dare get his nose too close to the ground, lest he smell something foul. His dark velvet robes were accented by typhoon dragon scales around the collar. Obviously, his eldrin couldn't be here—not unless he wanted to crush everyone to death with his massive dragon.

Actually, as I glanced between the other attendees, I noticed *none* of them had their eldrin.

Was this a precaution the headmaster had taken? The farther away from their eldrin, the weaker an arcanist became in terms of their magic. Perhaps Headmaster Venrover wanted to prevent anyone from doing something shady by limiting their magic?

I noticed Valo, Ashlyn's fiancé, wasn't among the guests. Which was odd. He didn't want to see his future wife participate? Or maybe Ashlyn had requested he not show.

Once all the noble arcanists had taken their seats, the headmaster and most of the professors at the Academy entered the field next. Unlike the nobles, all the professors had their eldrin, including Professor Helmith and her true form ethereal whelk, Ushi.

She was the strangest creature here... She was the size of a fully grown human, but her body was an amalgamation of animal parts. Ushi had the shell of a whelk, the long body of a serpentine dragon, the talons of eagles, the face of a cat, and the tail of a lion. Her skin, shell, and "fur" were all an iridescent hue that glittered in the morning light, drawing all attention to her.

Kristof's celestial dragon elegantly soared overhead, the semi-translucent body sparkling. It was a creature with wings, but the dragon obviously didn't need them. Untethered by gravity, the majestic beast hovered in the sky above us, never needing to land.

Amid the professors were my father and mum. They wore fine velvety robes just like the nobles, though they were clearly uncomfortable.

"Gray, look," Sorin said as he elbowed me. "Mum and Dad!"

"I saw."

But I wasn't looking for them. I wanted to find the Mother of Shapeshifters. What did she look like? I... I didn't know. Would she be a cat, like Twain? Or something else? Maybe a giant tiger...

I didn't see any unusual creatures, though.

I *did* see an unusual woman. She was beautiful—the type of gorgeous that Exie aspired to be—with luscious blonde hair that went to her waist, and a walk that demanded attention in all the scandalous places. She held the arm of the plainest-looking man in the whole lot, as though he was her direct opposite. Someone who demanded no attention.

I wondered who they were.

More importantly, where was Helmith's uncle? I wished I knew.

Once everyone was seated, another horn trumpeted. I wasn't even sure from where, though I suspected it didn't matter.

The headmaster stood out in front of the stands for professors and nobles and spread his arms wide.

"Ladies and gentlemen, thank you for joining us today on this special occasion." Headmaster Venrover gestured to the students with an elegant flick of his wrist. "Our students have been working hard to develop their magic and skills. Today will be a friendly competition to demonstrate those abilities."

Soft clapping wafted up from the stands. Were they excited? Or half asleep? It was difficult to tell.

"The first competition we will witness is the *melee sparring*. Two arcanists will face off against each other with only their weapons and magic. No eldrin, and no trinkets or outside assistance. Once one arcanist knocks the other out of the sparring circle, the match is over."

The circles on the marble stage made a lot more sense now.

"Our first match will be between two first-year students." The headmaster chuckled. "Gray Lexly, the mimic arcanist, against his classmate, Raaza Luin, the kitsune arcanist."

There was a lot more clapping this time. Probably because of the promise of violence—who didn't want to watch two arcanists fight each other?

My brother clapped me on the back and whispered encouraging words as I scooted past him in the stands. Raaza stood and followed me down the brick steps, his kitsune on his shoulders. Twain followed at my feet, his ears straight in the air.

We both reached the edge of the marble stage at the same time.

Captain Leon and Astra Academy's resident doctor, Doc Tomas, stood by the stage. Unlike Leon, who was young and just looked old, Doc Tomas just *was* old. His body was lumpy and lopsided, and he had a beard that resembled a long rat's nest.

The arcanist mark on Doc Tomas's forehead was a seven-pointed star with a deer wrapped around the points. The golden stag. A creature of healing.

And the stag sat in the emerald grass of the training field, waiting to be called on if there was an accident, I would bet my life on it.

Captain Leon pointed to the weapon racks. "You can pick whatever weapon you want, and use any non-lethal magical skills you've acquired. Once the bell rings, you just have to knock the other out of the circle. Understand?"

"Yes," both Raaza and I said at the same time.

Together, we walked to the weapon racks.

Everyone watched, but I wasn't intimidated by the hundreds of eyes. I *wanted* to look confident and ready. I held my shoulders back and moved with purpose.

As I reached for the practice spear, Raaza glanced over at me, his eyes narrowed.

"You gonna cheat?" he whispered.

"What does that mean?" I asked as I took my weapon in both hands.

"You know what it means." Raaza took the hammer. "You going to use your *borrowed magic and skills,* or are you going to face me like a man?"

The only people in Astra Academy who knew about Deimos and my new abilities were the ones in my class. And Professor Helmith, plus the headmaster, I supposed. If I used Deimos's skills to win, no one would know but Sorin, Raaza, Nini, Knovak, Nasbit, Ashlyn, Exie, and Phila...

They wouldn't rat me out, but I could see now they would be irritated if I used my advantages against them.

But...

I had to win. I had to impress Ashlyn's father.

I tapped my fingers along the side of the spear, mulling over the possibilities.

"Of course you'll cheat," Raaza said, a hint of pomp to his tone. "You don't have to also lie to me by saying you won't." He shot me a glare. "But if you have any hint of a spine, you would face me as you are. Just Gray Lexly."

"Fine," I shot back. "If you want *just me,* it'll be *just me.*" I didn't need a Death Lord's power to beat one of my peers.

Raaza smirked. "Good. It'll be a real fight, then. Let's see which of us was paying more attention when the professors spoke about combat."

CHAPTER 40

EVERYONE READY

Raaza took his position on one side of the circle, and I took my place on the opposite side. Our sparring ring was only ten feet in diameter. Fairly small.

The marble was unforgiving, and a little slippery. Was that intentional? It would guarantee that all the matches were over quickly, that was for sure.

Raaza's kitsune, Miko, sat outside the circle, her foxy red fur glistening. Twain sat next to her. He was smaller, but much cuter, in my humble opinion.

"Your hubris easily controls you," Deimos said with my voice. "You fell for an obvious taunt and snatched defeat from the jaws of victory."

I shook my head, hoping no one in the stands noticed I was speaking to myself. "What a fantastic pep talk. I'll keep those inspirational words in my heart while I win *without* your help."

"Feh. I care little for your show of competency, but I will be disgusted if my vessel fails at such a simple task."

My vessel...

I almost punched my own face, that was how disgusted I was with that statement. But I took a deep breath and allowed it to slip from my thoughts. Captain Leon walked around the marble stage. The headmaster called out four other matches, Ashlyn versus Legott being one of them.

The pairs gathered on the side of the pentagon stage, each couple of arcanists stepping close to the other circles.

Ah. It all made sense now. They were prepping the sparring matches. Once Raaza and I were done, they would start the next, to get this over with faster.

"Ready?" Captain Leon shouted.

I nodded. So did Raaza.

A bell chimed.

I hefted my practice spear and swung. Raaza blocked it with a bash of his hammer. They were crude training weapons, and the *clack* of their collision reminded me how silent everything else was. The crowd. The other students. Everyone's eldrin.

They were all watching.

That kind of pressure could bother some people, but just as I let my anger with Deimos go, I allowed my anxiety to slip away, leaving me in the moment, facing my classmate—who I knew I would beat.

"Why are you smirking?" Raaza asked through gritted teeth.

I hadn't realized I had been doing it, so I forced myself to stop. "Sorry. Lost in thought."

"Yeah, well, let's get this over with."

I thought Raaza would rush at me, or something similar, but he surprised me. Raaza held up his hand, and a flash of fox fire burst from his palm. With a confident grin, he formed something in his hand and then threw it.

As a defensive measure, I held the spear up, but that was useless. Raaza hadn't thrown a weapon—he had used his fox fire to create sand. The tiny granules got into my eyes, stinging bad enough that I had to close them.

Curse the abyssal hells!

He had blinded me.

Raaza slammed his practice hammer into my gut. I clenched my jaw and groaned, but I wasn't knocked off my feet. The crowd gasped, and while I couldn't see them, I pictured everything perfectly in my mind's eye. They were still watching intently. This was the first sparring match of the day—the one all others would be judged by.

Raaza drew back.

He was going to hit me again.

Unable to properly fight back, I threw myself to the marble floor of the sparring arena. I lay flat on my stomach, and I suspected everyone thought I was already defeated. But that wasn't true.

No, I just needed Raaza to drag me.

Which he did, because he was predictable. And what had Professor Jijo said about predictability?

The more predictable you are, the easier you are to defeat.

The moment Raaza grabbed my wrist in order to drag me to the edge of the circle, I mentally tugged on the thread of magic that led to Professor Helmith's ethereal whelk. With my newly gained abilities, I augmented Raaza's wakefulness...

And put him to sleep instantly. He collapsed straight onto my body in an awkward slump, obviously fighting against my magic but failing.

To the crowd, all they saw was me throwing myself to the ground, Raaza grabbing me, and then Raaza falling asleep on the spot.

Well, they likely saw Twain transform from a kitten into a floating whelk, but that was neither here nor there.

I couldn't have started the sparring match with Twain as an ethereal whelk, or else Raaza would've known my tactic. Because I had waited—and had him grab *me*—I had guaranteed I would be able to put him to sleep.

Poor, predictable Raaza.

Well, he had surprised me. I hadn't been expecting the sand. That had been rather shocking. But I had dealt with it.

Although my eyes still burned, I pushed Raaza off my side and then stood. I carefully moved him to the edge of the circle and pushed him out. That was it. I had won.

The applause that followed caused me to flinch. The claps and cheers washed out over the perfectly manicured training field, infecting everyone with excitement. I turned to face the crowd of nobles and offered them a little bow.

"That's it," Captain Leon shouted. "Gray Lexly is the victor!"

"I told you I'd win," I whispered to myself.

"You have a love for deception that I don't possess," Deimos whispered back. "Perhaps I could learn something from you..."

"Don't get too excited to learn my deceptive techniques. We're going to win all our upcoming matches the old-fashioned way."

"Old-fashioned way?"

I chuckled as Captain Leon led me off the marble stage.

"We're going to use *stick-to-the-face* tactics," I quipped.

It was a straight elimination competition. As soon as someone lost, they were out for good. Raaza lost immediately, so he had no other bouts. Ashlyn won against Legott, so she would have another match, and so on.

Fortunately, there hadn't been many arcanist students who had signed up for the sparring matches. It didn't take long for me to get a second fight.

"Next up is Gray Lexly, the mimic arcanist, against Cuva Derra, the dierkes knoll dragon arcanist."

The crowd chuckled.

"Dragon arcanists are always the ones to win these competitions," someone from the stands said.

"Of course. It's the natural order of things. Dragons are clearly the strongest—they only bond with the best."

I hadn't thought of that. When I glanced around at the remaining arcanists, it *was* mostly people who had bonded with dragons. Even Ashlyn...

However, because we were all first- and second-year students, there was no chance anyone would have a *fully grown* eldrin, which could be huge, especially in the case of dragons. No, everyone had a small eldrin, and Cuva was no different.

His dierkes knoll dragon hopped onto the marble stage and scurried over to sit next to Twain. The little dragon was practically made of leaves. His wings were a vibrant green, his scales reminded me of the leaves of oaks, and his tail was long and flexible, like a vine.

He was about the size of Twain, too...

A tiny little dragon.

I stepped into the sparring circle.

"These dragons manipulate animals to do their bidding," Deimos said. "By itself, that isn't intimidating, but dierkes knoll dragons have a secret. Their *full moon aura* transforms all normal animals into lycanthropes—were-creatures with a deep-seated bloodlust."

Cuva, the dragon arcanist, stepped into the sparring circle from the other side. He was a man who looked like he had been born in the forest and raised by wolves. Hair grew from every spot on his body except for half his face, and his bulky frame wasn't hiding any of his bulging muscles.

And he carried a practice club like he had years of experience with the thing.

"I seriously doubt he's going to send a bunch of werewolves at me," I whispered.

Deimos's amusement rang in my thoughts. "You never know."

"Are you whispering to yourself?" Cuva asked, his voice as gruff as he appeared.

"It's a habit," I said back.

"Unusual." He smacked his club into his opposite hand. "Sorry about this. I know you're a first-year who has had some problems, but I'm not gonna let you win. My mother is in the audience. I want to make her proud."

I half-shrugged. "No, *I* should be apologizing to *you*."

"Why?"

"For embarrassing you in front of your mother."

His hairy, beard-dominated face reddened slightly. I did feel bad. Mostly because he seemed nicer than some other arcanists I had met.

"Ready?" Captain Leon asked.

Both Cuva and I nodded.

A bell chimed.

Cuva held up a hand. A gush of yellow pollen escaped the wrinkles of his palms and flooded the sparring circle. On instinct, I held my breath. I didn't know what this did—Deimos hadn't mentioned the dragon's evocation abilities—and I wasn't about to find out the hard way.

I twirled the spear around and then struck with it. Cuva knocked it aside with ease. He was powerful, more so than I had expected. Then he swung with his club. Fortunately, he didn't have the greatest aim. I dodged, but my lungs were already feeling the strain.

Without the ability to breathe, this was going to be a very short match. I couldn't mess around.

In a display of expert skill, I jumped to the side of Cuva when he lunged for me. Then I hit him in the back of the leg, and his knee snapped forward. He crumpled to the marble floor, and I slammed the shaft of my spear against his ear.

Why? Deimos's combat expertise told me that if Cuva's ear was ringing, he would be off balance for the rest of the fight.

Sure enough, the man struggled to get to his feet.

However, the pollen was hurting my eyes. My head spun, and I staggered backward, fatigue taking hold. What was in the pollen? I decided I didn't want to find out the hard way.

I closed my eyes, tugged on the thread of magic that led back to the dierkes knoll dragon, and transformed Twain into an exact replica of the little leaf pile. In an instant, the pollen no longer hurt my eyes.

I gasped in air, tasting the sweet nectary mist, but no longer suffering any ill effect. Most mystical creatures weren't affected by their magic, which was why I transformed Twain.

Cuva grunted as he swung his club again. I kicked at Cuva's weak ankle and then struck him square in the throat. Now that I could breathe, this was an embarrassingly one-sided bout. Cuva stepped backward, and I jabbed the spear at his neck. He flinched, and that was when I went for his ankle a second time.

Cuva fell and tumbled out of the circle.

I had won.

It wasn't elegant, but it did display my overwhelming fighting prowess. Cuva had been stronger than me, and his eldrin was more powerful, but I had won regardless.

"Wow," Captain Leon half-shouted and half-laughed. "Gray Lexly is the victor! *Again!*"

The pollen around me faded, and I had Twain transform back into a mimic. I coughed for a long while after, but I stifled most of it. I had to maintain a tough demeanor, and wheezing my lungs out wouldn't achieve that.

The audience clapped again, this time more discerning. Most of the nobles whispered and pointed at my mimic eldrin. Had they not seen a mimic arcanist before? I supposed they were rare.

"That pollen induces sleep," Deimos said.

I shook my head. "Wow. Way to warn me ahead of time."

He didn't respond.

"You're doing amazingly, Gray!" Twain shouted as he ran over to me. "One more match and I think you'll be the *winner-winner*."

Perfect. Because there was no way I was going to lose. Not while Archduke Kross was watching.

Damn, I was unlucky.

Out of all the people participating, I was only afraid of facing one, and that was Ashlyn. But who was my final opponent? None other than Ashlyn Kross.

I wasn't afraid to face her because I might lose—I was afraid because I knew what it meant to her to look good in front of her father. Ashlyn went completely out of her way to do her family proud, and seemed ashamed of herself whenever she couldn't meet their standards.

So, if I beat her as quickly as I had beaten Raaza and that other arcanist, what would her family think?

"Our first event is coming to an end," Headmaster Venrover said, addressing the noble arcanists in the stands. "As you can see, even within a few years of study, many of our students become rather adept at melee combat."

Captain Leon stepped onto the marble stage, his armor shining so brightly, it almost hurt my eyes. "Our last sparring match for the day is Gray Lexly, the mimic arcanist, against another one of his classmates—Ashlyn Kross, the typhoon dragon arcanist."

I stepped onto the stage, and Ashlyn did the same. Ecrib snorted as he walked over to the edge of the sparring circle and took a seat, his back straight, his head held high.

Twain was so comically tiny in comparison. It was like watching a butterfly take a seat next to a house.

As I was walking to the sparring circle, a strange lancing pain shot through my chest. It was brief, and gone a moment later, but it had hurt so bad, I stumbled for a single step. I grabbed my shirt and tugged at the collar, panic entering my thoughts.

Deimos's thoughts were troubled.

"Is everything okay?" I whispered to myself.

Deimos didn't reply.

Which was odd.

But the pain had vanished, so I supposed everything was fine. I walked up to the sparring circle and took my position.

CHAPTER 41

MOS

Ashlyn lifted an eyebrow.

I half-shrugged in return, letting her know I was okay. She lifted her practice spear and then motioned to my own. With a flurry of movement, I twirled it around. Ashlyn answered that with a frown.

She obviously wasn't looking forward to this, either.

"Ready?" Captain Leon asked. "Whoever wins this will be declared the champion of melee combat!"

Ashlyn nodded. I did the same.

A bell chimed.

Instead of leading with a blast of lightning, Ashlyn lunged with her spear. She thrust the wooden point straight for my chest. I sidestepped the attack and swung at the side of her knee. The moment I connected, Ashlyn sucked in air through her teeth.

She leapt backward, out of my striking range. Then she held up her hand.

I leaned away, ready to dodge, but no magic lightning ever shot out.

It was a feint.

Ashlyn swung wide with her spear, aiming for my shoulder. I was off-balance, since I had been waiting for a blast of lightning, but I was still fast enough to dodge her attack. I ducked under the spear and then stood straight.

She swung back the other direction, and I blocked with my own weapon.

Clack.

Ashlyn pulled back and attacked again, this time aiming for my neck. I blocked.

Clack.

And then I shoved her weapon away with my own. She stumbled backward a few steps, recovered, and struck with impressive might.

Clack. Clack.

I was surprised by her level of skill. Clearly, Ashlyn had practiced before. When I attacked, she dodged or blocked, and when she attacked, I parried and riposted. However, after a few strikes, it was clear to me that Deimos's skill set was much higher. His instincts were aggressive and brutal, and if I wanted to end the fight quickly, I could've.

But going through the motions like this...

Was teaching me a thing or two about combat. The way I placed my feet, the way it felt to balance my weight when I blocked—I had never experienced a teaching method like this.

However, there were no other sounds besides the clash of our weapons. No cheering. No cries. Everyone watched without saying a word. They were on the edges of their seats, intently focused on our personal duel. Was it because Ashlyn was from such a prestigious family?

She thrust the tip of her spear again—harder than ever before. I knocked it to the side with my own weapon.

Clack.

"I'm not just going to let you win," Ashlyn whispered, her breathing rough.

"Would you rather I lose?" I earnestly asked.

She smirked. "No. I don't want to be with someone who holds anything back."

"But, my skills, they're—"

"I don't care how you got them. You have them, and I'm going to rise to the challenge. *Don't hold back.*"

Her conviction made her... so attractive.

Then Ashlyn unleashed her magic—right at the moment I was least expecting it. Lightning erupted from her hand, and I leaned to the side, barely dodging the bolt of raw magical energy. The hairs on the back of my neck stood on end.

Deimos's combat instincts were unrivaled, though.

Ashlyn's shocked expression was priceless. She went from astonished to impressed in half a moment.

I managed to focus long enough to sift through threads of magic and decided to go with a strange choice. Phila's coatl was nearby, and it was what I wanted the most. My arcanist star burned, and a second later, I had Phila's magic.

Ashlyn sent another bolt of lightning. We were so close, since the sparring ring was so small, which meant there weren't many places for me to go. She aimed to my left, meaning I had to dodge to the right—and closer to her—which made me an easy target for her follow-up blast.

Fortunately, I had the coatl's ability to evoke wind. I sent a wave of air at Ashlyn before she could unleash her follow-up strike. She stumbled, her blonde hair flying, her eyes watering.

Then I swung the spear at the same knee I had targeted before. Professor Jijo's tactic of attacking the same spot over and over again had taught me a valuable lesson. Things break if you hit them enough times.

My weapon *clacked* against Ashlyn's leg, and she tumbled to the ground.

The crowd reacted to that.

People gasped, a few even pointed.

Ashlyn's father, Archduke Kross, stood from his seat. He moved to the edge of the stands, his gaze narrowed. "Ashlyn," he called out. "Pick yourself up. You're a member of the *Kross family*. Act like it."

Ashlyn nodded to herself. She murmured something under her breath and then forced herself to her feet, even though it was obvious her injured knee caused her pain.

"Her brother wouldn't have lost," someone else said, their voice loud enough to carry to the stage.

I already hated the fact I had to fight her. Why did they have to make it worse?

"I don't have to use Deimos's skills," I whispered to her. "I can just fight you with what I have. It'll be a fair fight then."

To my shock, lightning crackled across Ashlyn's body. It sparked and flashed, radiating from her and filling the air around us with static. All my hair stood on end, and the *pop* of electric power surged with each of Ashlyn's breaths.

"I don't need pity," Ashlyn said. "I don't want your *easy mode*. I want you to fight me with everything you've got."

When she unleashed her lightning again, I knew I couldn't dodge, not even with Deimos's instincts. The bolt of power was too charged, and too fast. Instead, I leaned into it. The evocation ripped through my body, tearing through my insides and burning my muscles.

My heart felt it the most. For a split second, I thought it would explode right out of my chest.

My vision went black, and when I managed to see again, I was on my stomach in the middle of our sparring ring. That was why I had leaned into the blast—to hopefully stay within the circle if I collapsed.

"*A reminder to not use lethal force,*" Captain Leon bellowed.

"That's my girl," Archduke Kross called out. "Finish this fight and do our family proud."

Ashlyn limped over to me, her injured knee obviously hurting more than I had expected. The crackling of her lightning had ceased, and I suspected that was the most powerful burst she could evoke as a first-year.

But there was a reason I wanted Phila's wind evocation.

I placed my palms on the arena floor and evoked wind. It shot me up into a standing position, and although I staggered backward a few steps, I was ready to fight. Ashlyn grimaced, clearly not having expected me to recover this quickly.

She held up a hand, but I shoved all the force and magic I had through my arm and hand, evoking a sudden *blast* of gale-force winds.

Her bad leg failed her.

Ashlyn hit the ground and tumbled out of the circle. A bell chimed over the training field.

"That's it!" Captain Leon bellowed. "The match is over. Gray Lexly is the winner!" He leapt onto the marble stage, stormed into the sparring ring, and grabbed my wrist. After he lifted it above my head, more cheering emanated from the stands, more so from the students, but a few from the others.

Archduke Kross sat back down, his expression aggressively neutral.

Ashlyn pushed herself to her feet. Her dragon leapt to her side and sniffed at her clothing, as if to make sure she was okay. She gently patted his snout.

When she glanced over her shoulder at me, we kept our gazes locked. I thought she would be upset, but Ashlyn's expression was more hopeful than anything else.

"I like that woman," Deimos said through me.

Captain Leon narrowed his eyes at me. "What did you just say?"

"Nothing," I replied. Once he released my wrist, I headed for the edge of the marble stage. Twain ran to be with me, his whiskers perked up, his ears tall. In a quiet voice, I said, "You seem distracted."

"You needn't concern yourself with me," Deimos replied.

He didn't elaborate further. The fragment of his soul wasn't busy—that was trapped within me—which meant his *real* self, in the abyssal hells, had to be dealing with something. That was unfortunate, but there wasn't anything I could do about that.

Captain Leon followed me onto the grass and then motioned for me to join the professors in the stands. "Take a moment, Gray," he said. "We're setting up the next demonstration. I'll bet money your parents are proud."

I nodded once. I hoped they would be.

After a deep breath, I headed over. My father and my mum were waiting for me in the first bit of shade provided by the awning. They were all smiles, and before I even managed to say anything to them, my father pulled me into a giant hug.

I was afraid Deimos would react again, but nothing happened. He felt... distant. More distracted. His emotions less fierce.

"Amazing." My father patted my back with enough force to wind me. "You should've heard what they were sayin' about someone with your background. No one had a coin bet on your name."

They were *betting on us?* That fact intrigued me. I hadn't even thought of it. Who had they expected to win? There weren't many of us...

I patted my father on the shoulder. "I'm a fast learner."

"You always have been," Mum said. The moment my father released me from his grasp, my mum pulled me into a gentle embrace. "So smart. Too smart. I'm so happy it's serving you well."

As my parents whispered more praise, I took a step back and held my breath. I glanced between them, meeting their eyes. What could I say? "Thank you," was all that came out. "Sorry if I haven't been appreciative. Of everything."

It was difficult to articulate my thoughts sometimes. Especially when I had been childish for not thanking them before.

"You never mind that," my father said. "You're a fine young man. I'm a lucky man."

My mum nodded along with his words.

That made me feel a little better. I exhaled most of my anxieties away. It wasn't all celebrations, though. Ashlyn hadn't come to the stands with me. She didn't seek out her father, and it was clear from his stiff posture and slight frown he didn't want to see her, either.

The other noble arcanists whispered condescending statements to one another.

"I can't believe a typhoon dragon arcanist lost," one woman said.

Another replied, "Perhaps the Academy knows what it's doing after all if a lowborn boy could pick up fighting prowess like that in just a short time."

"Or perhaps the archduke's daughter is just weak. She was born sickly, you know. A real disappointment."

Then I noticed Professor Helmith sitting in the far back of the cushioned stands. She waved me over with a gentle motion of her hand.

I hugged my parents one last time. "I'm going to speak to some of my professors before the next competitions begin," I said.

"Good luck with the rest." My mum embraced me tighter than ever before.

Then I headed over to Helmith. She smiled as I approached, but then she glanced over. Kristof was next to her, but so were two people I didn't recognize. The mysteriously beautiful woman—her blonde hair so radiant and shining, it even eclipsed Ashlyn's—and the plain man I had seen earlier.

The woman didn't have an arcanist star, but something about her...

I knew she was an arcanist.

My mimic abilities allowed me to sense the threads of power that led from an arcanist to their eldrin, and she had one. Somehow. Even if I didn't know what kind of arcanist she was.

And the plain man was even stranger than the woman. He was tall— wiry and lean—with black hair slicked tight to his head. His arcanist mark was a star with *nine* points, and the creature woven throughout was some sort of blob. It shifted as I stared at it, like the image on the star was capable of taking any form.

Which meant...

"You're the Mother of Shapeshifters arcanist," I said aloud.

Twain leapt around my feet. "Really?" He searched the stands with his gaze, but his ears drooped after only a moment. "I don't see anything out of the ordinary."

"Gray," Helmith said, bringing my attention back to her. "I'd like you to meet my uncle and aunt. This is Ryker Blackwater, and his wife, Karna."

The beautiful woman had a face that was too perfect. She had no flaws, no hint out of place. When she smiled, her teeth were so white, I swear they had never known the stain of food. Her blue eyes, as brilliant as the sky, pierced into mine.

"Nice to meet you," I said to her. Then I peeled my eyes away to face Ryker. "Uh, I'm a mimic arcanist and—"

Ryker stood. I didn't see his eldrin, even though I was actively looking for it.

"Rylee told me all about you," he said. "Would you like to step into the Academy for a short chat? I'm sure we'll be back in time for the rest of the festivities."

"I'd love that," I said.

"Oh. Good. Glad to hear you're eager." He turned to his wife. "I'll be right back, my love."

"Don't scare the boy," Karna replied with a purr. Then she winked at me.

I didn't like that.

Her voice was too sultry. She had a way with allure and sensuality, and it almost felt like a trap. How had a plain man like Ryker Blackwater ended up with a woman as striking as Karna? I didn't ask—since that would be beyond rude—but I was curious.

"Where is the Mother of Shapeshifters?" Twain asked as we walked out of the stands. He hopped up and down, his energy at maximum. "Will we meet her soon?"

"Oh, she's here." Ryker gestured to the field, and then to the Academy. "She's all over the place. The headmaster said she could be here, just to speak with you, Gray, but she had to stay out of sight." He chuckled nervously, which was odd. "I think Adelgis didn't want any of the other arcanists to see I was allowed to keep my eldrin when they weren't."

She was all around?

I tried to spot any mystical creatures out on the field, or in the Academy, but didn't see anything.

Where was she?

Even when I tried to feel Ryker's thread of magic, something was wrong with it. Other arcanists had strings of power that were effortless to feel, but Ryker's was like... a frayed rope. Powerful, but scattered and unraveling.

I didn't know what that meant.

As we approached the Academy, I glanced over my shoulder. Several students watched me leave, including my brother and Ashlyn. I waved to them, hoping they would understand.

Once we reached the stone steps into Astra Academy, Ryker exhaled. "I, uh, I'm not very good with conversation." He shrugged. "I usually let my wife do all the talking, so you'll have to forgive me if I don't start any amazing conversations."

"I just want to learn everything I can about mimics," I said.

"Uh-huh. Well, MOS can help you with that."

"Who is *MOS*?"

Ryker nervously chuckled a second time. It was weird. "MOS is what I call my eldrin. It's, uh, shorter than her full title. And she doesn't have a name. Not, like, a real name. Just her title. Sorry—it seems to be a trait all unique creatures share."

I didn't know how to respond to that.

We entered the Academy, and I almost flinched.

A single brown bunny stood in the middle of the Academy hallway. It was small, like most bunnies, with a bright white tail and ears as long as pencils. It stared at me with red eyes, as though it had been waiting for a long while. When Twain spotted the bunny, he froze.

"Are you okay?" I asked my eldrin.

"*Mother*," Twain whispered. "You're here."

CHAPTER 42

THE MOST ANCIENT SHAPESHIFTER

The brown bunny twitched its tiny nose.

Then a *second* bunny hopped out from the hallway shadows, its eyes a glistening black. Was this MOS as well? Was this mystical creature actually *two* creatures? That would be rather powerful, if it were true. But maybe MOS just controlled normal animals, similar to the dierkes knoll dragon?

Before I could form more of a hypothesis, a *third* bunny hopped out from the darkness. And then a fourth. And a fifth.

And twenty more.

They hopped into the center of the hallway, heading for the rabbit with red eyes. As Twain and I watched in silence, all twenty-five rabbits piled together, their legs kicking and squirming, their tiny mouths open, as if to scream, but no sounds were made.

Instead, the bunnies slowly melted into each other.

Their fur, their flesh—their eyes, ears, and long legs—merged like melting ice into water. The only part of this freakish lump I could stare at were the red eyes. They stayed locked on me, never glancing away, even as a second rabbit face slid between the eyes, melting into place with all the grace of candle wax.

Then all the rabbits solidified into place. They froze, their mouths open, their eyes wide, their legs and ears jutting out in all directions. Some underneath the mass of flesh, some above. The many sets of whiskers twitched and twirled. Some of the noses sniffed the air.

I had never seen *anything* like it.

The *blob of rabbits* stood. Dozens of rabbit legs held up the mass of flesh, and it scuttled forward.

I held my position, my heart pounding.

"Interesting," I said—no, Deimos said—his amusement in my thoughts.

"Mother," Twain repeated, love in his voice. He ran forward to meet the hideous lump. With all the love a child could show a parent, Twain purred as he nuzzled the main face.

If there *was* a main face.

Eight rabbit arms twisted together to form a human-like arm, complete with five furry fingers. With that disturbing arm, MOS reached down and patted Twain on the head. I shuddered just imagining that creature touching me, but Twain purred.

"My child," MOS said, her voice echoing, as though the many rabbits were trying to speak as one.

"This is Gray Lexly," Ryker said.

I jumped when he spoke.

I had completely forgotten Ryker was here. I had been too busy focused on this abomination to remember a normal—and very plain—man was still in the hallway.

"He's the mimic arcanist Rylee was telling us about," Ryker concluded.

"Ah," MOS whispered. She returned her red eyes to mine. "The one who bonded with my lost mimic. I did not approve your bonding... with my precious and special child. All potential mimic arcanists must meet my standards—and you have not."

"I'm sorry?" I wasn't sure how to answer that.

"He's taken good care of me," Twain interjected. He puffed up his orange fur. "And you shouldn't talk to him like that."

Twain stood as tall as he could, but he didn't compare to the blob of bunnies. MOS was at least four feet of writhing, furred flesh. Twain was still small.

"Are you upset, my child?" MOS asked, kinder than before.

"You... Why did you leave me?" Twain's voice warbled when he spoke the last word. Was that why he had wanted to speak to her? "G-Gray was there for me. But... But you left me. I... I was alone for so long."

With her unnatural arm, MOS patted Twain a second time. Her red eyes dimmed with water. "I'm so sorry, flesh of my heart. When the last human came looking to bond with a mimic, I gave birth to two, rather than one. Since a human can only bond with one mystical creature, he couldn't take both. He bonded with your sibling, and you ran off."

"He ran off?" I asked.

Ryker held a finger to his lips, trying to silence me. I stared at him for a long moment, ready to argue, but I decided against it. This was Twain's moment to speak with his parent. Perhaps he had to face this himself.

"I don't remember that," Twain whispered. His long ears drooped. "Why didn't you come find me?"

"I'm so sorry, my child."

But MOS offered no other explanation.

Who was the last human to bond with a mimic? Besides me, of course. Was she talking about Zahn, Deimos's brother? *He* was a mimic arcanist. I had seen his mimic when we fought in the Academy basement.

Twain ran to my feet. He threw himself onto the top of my boots and just hugged me. "Gray came to find me. We've been a team ever since."

MOS said nothing. The rabbits squirmed and wiggled, their little contorted faces glancing around the massive hallway.

I just...

Couldn't look away.

I'd had hundreds of nightmares in the past, and nothing ever looked quite like this *Mother of Shapeshifters*. She was unique. No other mystical creature had her demeanor or otherworldly grasp on reality. She had assumed the rabbit blob form as though it were *more normal* than a simple rabbit. What kind of thought process led to that? Something alien.

MOS clearly didn't mind changing her shape.

Perhaps that was the key to achieving a true form with Twain?

"If this man has taken good care of you," MOS whispered, "then he has my approval. He can be a mimic arcanist."

I laughed to myself. "Was that even in question?" I turned to Ryker. "Was she planning on taking Twain from me?"

Ryker forced an awkward smile. "Uh, well, do you have anything else you wish to ask her?"

It bothered me that he didn't answer.

I turned away from him, suddenly aware that we were alone. Had MOS been planning to take Twain if she didn't like me? And this was an ambush? I shook away the thoughts. That was just paranoia fueling my doubts. No one was taking Twain from me. Not now, not ever.

I scooped Twain into my arms and held him close. "I do have a question. Two, actually."

MOS waited, her body jiggling.

"How can I help Twain achieve his true form?" I scratched under his left ear. "Does he require a virtue? Or a geas?"

I remembered our class on true form creatures. Either an arcanist had to embody a virtue—like how Helmith had embodied *hope* in order to achieve her ethereal whelk's true form—or an arcanist had to complete a *geas*. A geas was just a weird way of saying a *quest* or a task they had to perform to help their creature transform.

"Mimics require a geas," MOS said, much to my disappointment.

I sighed. This was fine. I'd do whatever it took. "Can you tell me what it is?"

"I can." MOS scuttled closer, her many rabbit feet scratching across the rug of the hallway. "Listen closely. A mimic arcanist must defeat the most ancient shapeshifter in order to achieve a true form with his eldrin."

I waited, hoping she would provide more details.

Silent seconds went by.

"Who is the most ancient shapeshifter?" I finally asked. I pointed at her disgusting, lumpy body. "Is it *you*?"

I could defeat her easily.

"No," MOS quickly replied.

"Then who is it?"

"The most ancient shapeshifter has been around since the beginning of time."

I rolled my hand. "And who is it? I'll defeat whoever I need to."

Twain frowned. "I've never heard of an ancient shapeshifter before..."

MOS rested on the ground, her little rabbit feet splayed to the sides of her round body. "That is all I have to tell you. If you cannot deduce the identity of the most ancient shapeshifter, then you will never achieve a true form with your mimic."

"You can't give me a hint?" I asked. "I mean, this is pretty vague. Anyone could be a shapeshifter if they were a doppelgänger arcanist, right? You wouldn't even know if you met one? Maybe I've already met the most ancient shapeshifter."

"You have," MOS cryptically replied.

My words caught in my mouth, stunned. "I... I have?"

"Yes. You have." MOS's red eyes glittered. "Everyone has. The most ancient shapeshifter knows everyone."

My thoughts swirled as I finally understood.

This was a riddle.

The most ancient shapeshifter... wasn't a literal person.

But if it wasn't an arcanist or a mystical creature, what was it?

While I thought about that, I decided to ask my second question. "Professor Helmith said I should ask you to enchant me with a rune, so that I can take part of your magic with me forever." I patted Twain. "Do you have an ability or skill that would help me?"

"I have... the ability to shift my flesh," MOS replied, her creepy arm flexing its freakish fingers. "A mimic arcanist with the ability to rearrange their body could become unrecognizable."

"Any part of my body?" My thoughts went to a million places, some hilarious, some inappropriate. I felt it was best not to voice my examples. "That sounds... interesting."

"Indeed."

Ryker forced a high-pitched chuckle. "I don't like it, personally. It feels bizarre. Perhaps you would want my wife's magic? She's a doppelgänger arcanist, and she has enchanted people before. Her rune allows people to shift their appearance. Change hair color, skin tone, all that."

"But MOS's is more versatile?" I asked.

Ryker nodded.

And more disturbing, obviously. But I understood now why Professor Helmith had suggested I ask the Mother of Shapeshifters to help me. She was powerful. More than other shapeshifters—just in a nightmarish way.

"If Gray had your ability, could he become *anything*?" Twain asked, his ears perked. "Like, a cat?"

MOS's many little rabbit mouths silently laughed. I cringed back, unsettled.

"His physical form... could do almost anything," MOS finally replied.

I tapped Ryker on the shoulder. "All right—can you enchant me?"

He half-shrugged. "Oh, yes. As soon as the headmaster agrees. We need tools to use the occult ore. And you'll need to pick a spot on your body. The larger the rune, the more occult dust we'll need. A-All that stuff. I don't know if you've learned it all in class, yet."

Damn. That meant I wouldn't be getting the rune right now. But soon. And I knew the perfect place for the rune on my body. I had given it plenty of thought. I didn't want it to be noticeable, so I would need to keep it from view.

A horn trumpeted, and the faint sound of cheering managed to waft in through the windows. The rest of the competitions were about to take place. I couldn't miss those.

I glanced down at Twain. "Do you want to stay here and talk to your mom for a bit? I need to get back to the field."

"I want to stay with you," Twain muttered. He dug his kitten claws into my shirt. "Let's go win."

"Okay."

I nodded to the lump of rabbit flesh. Then I did the same with Ryker. The tall man half-smiled and motioned to the door. "Go on without me."

That was odd. But then again, everything about this man was odd. I wasn't frightened by him, but I certainly wasn't enamored of him, either.

Determined to make it back in time, I exited the Academy and headed down the stone steps toward the training field. The marble stage was still there, but no one was on it. Instead, arcanists and their eldrin were racing around the track, flying like the wind.

I stood on the stone stairway, thankful I hadn't missed any event I wanted to take part in. Instead of worrying, I mulled over the riddle.

"What is the most ancient shapeshifter?" I asked aloud.

Twain shook his head. "I don't know..."

"Fear," Deimos stated, confidence in his tone.

His response stilled my thoughts. Was he right?

Deimos elaborated. "Fear can be anything. It can be physical. You can be afraid of spiders. Afraid of heights. But it can also be conceptual. You could be afraid of loneliness. Aging. Loss of memory. And your fears always change. What you fear as a child isn't what you fear as an adult. It is the ultimate shapeshifter—the only one that has been around since the beginning of time. The only shapeshifter *everyone* knows."

The more he spoke, the more I knew he was correct.

The most ancient shapeshifter *was* fear.

Which meant, in order for Twain to achieve his true form, I had to defeat fear itself?

"But that's not possible," I whispered. "No one can *defeat* fear. That's an impossible task."

Deimos didn't reply.

My eldrin, on the other hand, squirmed in my arms. "You can do it, Gray. I know you can." He gasped, startling me a bit. "W-Wait. I just realized something!"

"You know how to conquer all my fears?" I asked.

"No. I just realized... *I'm also a twin!*" Twain purred so loud in my arms, I practically shook. "Didn't you hear my mother? She said *two* mimics were born at the same time. Gray, I'm also a twin! It's fate that we're together. Definitely! We're special. Me and you." He stared up at me, smiling wide.

I patted his head. "Yeah, I guess that's true. I hadn't thought of that."

"Oh, and you can definitely defeat fear. Somehow." He waved his cat paw. "I'll be there to help."

More pain lanced through my chest. I groaned as I doubled over. Twain twisted in my arms as I fell to one knee.

"What's wrong?" he asked, panicked.

But I couldn't answer. Agony had stolen my voice.

What was happening? My vision tunneled, and it was difficult to even breathe...

CHAPTER 43

THE UNICORN RACE

I gasped for air, and the pain slowly subsided.

Twain continued to stare at me, his eyes wide. There wasn't much to say, though. My chest had hurt, and now it wasn't hurting anymore. Once I was able to exhale without any prickle of injury, I stood.

"Deimos?" I asked.

He didn't answer.

This was somehow his fault, I felt it in my bones. What was he doing?

The warming afternoon sun invigorated me. I forced myself to stand, and then I stroked Twain down his spine. He eventually purred and closed his eyes, as if he was ready for a cat nap.

I walked down the rest of the stone steps and stood at the side of the grass, watching the last half of the race. There weren't *that* many arcanists racing. Ten in total. I recognized Knovak straight away. His white unicorn glittered in the light, and Knovak himself had dressed in all white for the occasion, matching his eldrin.

"There's Knovak," I whispered.

Twain motioned with his paw. "There's Nini and Sorin. Aren't you rooting for them to win?"

"Eh. I think... I want Knovak to win more, actually."

"Not your brother?" Twain growled. "Betrayal!"

"I don't know. I just think Knovak needs the win. For his confidence."

For whatever reason, some arcanists at Astra Academy were obsessed with the tier of their eldrin. The lower-tiered mystical creatures weren't worth their time—only their scorn. And the higher-tiered creatures got all the praise.

Actually, it wasn't just the students at the Academy. All the nobles in the stands had said dragons were the most powerful, and *of course* they would be the ones to win the sparring matches. Everyone just preferred the higher-tiered creatures.

As I watched the race, I kept that in mind.

All the arcanists were racing *with* their eldrin, which was amusing. The nixie arcanists, Roy and Perana, the people who had bullied Knovak, were using their water and wind abilities to slide along the track on a personal pathway they evoked around their feet. They skated along, practically hydroplaning, going faster than if they just ran forward, their nixies also helping them to create paths.

Roy and Perana were beside a nimbus dragon arcanist. He must've been a second-year, probably someone studying to become a knight, because I had never seen that arcanist before. With the help of his small dragon, the man was flying. The clouds and wind kept him up, and he flew around the track, his boots barely touching the dirt.

Sorin and Nini were merged with their eldrin. Sorin occasionally stepped through the darkness, but since afternoon light bathed the whole training field in bright illumination, he didn't have much ability to go fast. Plus, it was obvious to me he wanted to stay close to Nini. She ran with her reaper on, and all the other racers avoided her as though she had leprosy.

If Nini could blood-step, she probably would've been much faster, but there was no blood anywhere near the training field.

Despite the other arcanists using their magic to the fullest of their abilities, it was Knovak who was out in front. He was basically running at full speed, but never growing tired. His unicorn magic gave him a larger stamina range than the average person. That was a huge advantage in a race, and Starling, his unicorn, kept pace, his mane glittering in the sunlight as he ran.

The nimbus dragon arcanist, along with Roy and Perana, were gaining, however. Unicorn endurance wasn't infinite.

The race was close, and I clapped as Knovak was the first to round the last bend.

"You can do it!" I shouted.

He probably couldn't hear me, but just in case, I wanted him to have that little bit of encouragement.

Then something bizarre happened. Roy and Perana surged forward with their water and wind. Then they tripped—straight into Knovak. All three tumbled into the dirt, face-first. They were a tangle of limbs as all three tried to stand, but it was too late. The nimbus dragon arcanist dashed past them and crossed the finish line first.

That dragon arcanist had won.

Captain Leon came over and lifted the arcanist's hand. "We have our fastest racer! Brisko Omri, the nimbus dragon arcanist!"

Knovak, Roy, and Perana all got to their feet, but not before two other arcanists flew by. Despite the fact Knovak had been first for most of the race, he came in *sixth*. That was terrible luck.

I jogged down to the track and headed over to the finish line. My brother and Nini crossed as seventh and eighth—hardly a fantastic time and score—but I headed to Knovak first. He had separated himself from everyone else, his head hung, his shoulders slumped. His once pristinely white clothes were now smeared with mud.

"Hey, Knovak," I said as I hurried over. "Wait up."

Knovak barely responded. He glanced over and then went back to glaring at the ground.

"No need to feel bad." I stopped by his side and crossed my arms. "Nothing was on the line. We're not even getting trophies for this. You're fine."

"It was intentional," Knovak snapped, though he kept his voice low. "The other arcanists *intentionally tripped me* so Brisko would win."

I held my breath for a long minute. Then I asked, "How do you know that?"

"Roy said Brisko was going to win. Right before the race. He just..." Knovak balled his hands into fists. "I don't have any way to prove it. But I know. They didn't want me to win. None of them. They were going to do whatever it took to stop me."

I tensed and then turned around on my heel. Sure enough, Roy and Perana had gone over to the winner. They were all celebrating, as though *they* had won. They even waved to the stands, pointing at the little nimbus dragon and smiling.

"Of course I would win," Brisko said, his nasally tone distinct. "It's only natural."

He was the type of man with hair so styled, it didn't move when the wind blew by. Every brown strand was as dead as wood and as polished as a table. His nimbus dragon landed on his arm, and the two of them laughed together.

It enraged me that their plan to harm Knovak would go unpunished. I walked over to Captain Leon, who stood to the side, speaking with Piper about the next event.

"We should set up the last of the obstacles," he said. "And just have the second race right away."

Piper nodded. "All right, but it'll take me a few minutes."

I tapped Leon on the shoulder, and he turned around, his face set in a stern expression, but the corners of his eyes were wrinkled in delight.

"Ah, there's the arcanist who won the first event," Leon said, patting me on the shoulder. "Can't wait to see how you do in the next event."

"Thanks." Then I gestured to that cheating gaggle of arcanists. "But you need to speak with *them*. They didn't accidentally trip—it was intentional. They're cheaters."

Leon glanced over, and then quickly returned his attention to me. "It looked accidental to me. Do you have any proof they were being malicious?"

"No. Except for their smug faces. Look at them. No one is that smug for losing. They're just bothering Knovak."

"Come, my lad." Captain Leon ushered me away from the side of the field. He lowered his voice as he said, "I can't act on an accusation without any sort of evidence. No one was hurt here. There's no prize for winning. Let them have their little celebration, and just toughen up for the next time."

That irritated me more than normal. Deimos's own emotions seemed to mix into mine, and his hatred of the situation felt just as real. Why was he upset?

I gritted my teeth and then nodded once. Captain Leon wasn't going to do anything, and unfortunately, punching everyone in their face wasn't an appropriate solution to this problem—even though it had been last time.

Those thugs were getting trickier. They couldn't openly punk Knovak, so now they were reverting to underhanded tactics. Too bad it was coming at the cost of Knovak's self-esteem. He had already seemed shaken after Deimos defeated him at Ashlyn's cotillion. Now he couldn't even win a race without other arcanists cheating to take it away from him.

"Maybe you should give Knovak some comforting words," I said to Leon. "He really wanted to win."

"I will, I will." He slammed a hand on my shoulder. "You're a good friend. I'll make sure Knovak knows he did a commendable job." Then Captain Leon walked off, his shining armor brilliant in the sunlight.

"My brother was often the target for cruel games when we were children," Deimos whispered.

I combed my hair back with my fingers. The anger I felt seeping into my thoughts made more sense now. "What did they do to your brother?" I asked.

"The children in the arena gutters would drag Zahn to the tophets to frighten him."

"What are *tophets*?"

"Burial grounds for infants and babes."

My heart practically fluttered in horror. Flashes of images appeared at the edge of my thoughts. Small tombstones and shallow graves. I had a memory—or perhaps it was Deimos's memory—of kids shoving a little boy into a hole. They shouted at him. Told him he belonged there.

Zahn...

He was crying.

"What did you do?" I whispered. I shook the images away as I headed back to the stands.

"I took one of the broken headstones and I bashed in the skull of the strongest child bothering my brother," Deimos replied, his words precise, his tone cold. "They never attempted to frighten Zahn again."

Wow. The more I heard about Deimos's life in ancient times, the more I realized how good I had it modernly. I couldn't imagine living in a city where I had to cave in the head of my enemies before the ripe old age of ten.

"Let's just hope Knovak doesn't need something similar to get out of his situation," I said.

I stood at the starting line for the obstacle course. Just like the eldrin race, there were only a total of ten participants. Since we were allowed to self-select which competitions we were competing in, it was clear the *races* were the least popular of the lot.

No one in my class had volunteered for this event.

I glanced up and down the line, hoping I'd see someone I recognized. The first person I noticed was Legott, the man with the winged snake. He waved to Phila in the stands.

"Watch," Legott called out. "I'll win this in your honor!"

Phila waved back by simply folding her fingers up and down. She had a perpetual smile, but something about it seemed strained this time.

The other two people I recognized were Roy and Brisko. They wanted to win another race, did they? I chuckled to myself. No matter what—they weren't going to win. Because I was.

"Listen up," Captain Leon bellowed, more to the crowd than to the arcanists waiting at the starting line. "This obstacle course is for the arcanists only. They are allowed to use their magic and skills, but they aren't allowed to interfere with one another. Anyone caught doing so will be disqualified."

I wished he would hurry with his explanation. The afternoon sun cooked everything it touched, and I was, unfortunately, one of the things it was touching.

"No teleporting, either," Leon said, pointing to us all. "You must *physically make your way along the race.* With your bodies visible. No invisibility. None of that."

There went my first strategy. I had planned on taking Piper's rizzel magic to 'port around the track until the end. I'd have to think of something else now.

"First, our arcanist students will have to run through a swamp of mud. Then they will have to climb over a wall, and swing across bars until they reach the path of thorned hurdles to jump over."

The obstacles were positioned all the way around the training field, giving everyone in both stands a clear view of the action. The mud pit was kept moist thanks to the efforts of the professors. Some of them kept it cool and hydrated, despite the best efforts of the sun to dry everything out.

The wall was at least fifteen feet tall. It had handholds, which was pleasant, but it was definitely a trek and a half to reach the top. The metal bars we had to swing between were far apart, but wide enough for multiple people to attempt the crossing at once. A pool of water was positioned beneath, so falling meant moving slower.

The final leg of the race—the hurdles—were clearly someone's sadistic fantasy brought to life. At first, they started low, with a few hurdles about ankle height, but each was covered by a thorny vine. The thorns were the size of my thumbs and as sharp as talons, each ending in a slight hook. They could slice through bricks, no doubt in my mind.

The hurdles just got taller and taller, until the final one at the end of the race, which was at least three feet above the ground. How bloody did they want us by the time we crossed the finish line? We could dye the stands crimson if even a single person tumbled hard over a hurdle.

"Remember to use your magic," Captain Leon said as he waggled a finger. "Are you all ready?"

"This reminds me of the First Hevron War," Deimos whispered to me.

"Are you okay?" I asked, keeping my voice low. "You stop talking to me from time to time. Gets me worried."

"During the war," Deimos continued, ignoring my commentary, "we dug trenches to hide in, and ambush the enemy. The mud... It clings to everything. And slows you down."

"Go!" Captain Leon shouted. A trumpet sounded at the same time.

I didn't have an opportunity to fully comprehend what Deimos was trying to tell me. Instead, I rushed forward along with the other arcanists. When we reached the pit of mud, which was at least twenty feet long and two feet deep, the first few arcanists splattered into the mud and basically became stuck.

They grunted and whined as they attempted to slosh their way through the grime.

A yeti arcanist, a young woman with spiky black hair, held out her hand and evoked ice over the mud pit. Once the ground was solid, she walked across the surface, never getting stuck. A few arcanists followed behind, but the evocation didn't last forever. As the ice thawed, several arcanists sank into the gooey depths.

I understood what Deimos was trying to say now. The ones with the mud were getting slowed—even after they managed to pull themselves out. The sticky grime clung to their clothes, weighing them down. Legott managed to blast wind from his palm and free himself, but he was still grimy as he hurried along.

I closed my eyes, tugged on the yeti's magical thread and stole their icy abilities for myself. My arcanist star burned, even as I held out my hand and evoked ice.

"Perfect," I muttered.

I dashed across, now in the middle of the pack. In theory, I could always take the magic of whoever solved the "puzzle" before me, but that wouldn't allow me to win. And I had to win. Which meant I needed to come up with my own solutions.

Once at the end of the mud pit, I stared at the daunting stone wall. Ice didn't help the yeti arcanist. She had to slowly climb up, using the handholds the whole way.

The handholds resembled hooks pointed skyward. It was easy to cup one's fingers over the top and lift yourself—if you had enough strength.

Legott was halfway up the wall, but the mud on his hands was causing him to slip. Roy and Brisko took a moment to clean themselves. Roy's nixie magic allowed him to evoke water everywhere.

Again, I tugged on a magical thread—this time the one leading to Raaza's kitsune.

I held my hands out and evoked his fox fire, the whole time picturing a long rope. That was what I needed right now. A tool to help me go faster.

Flames burst from my palms and then solidified into a silk rope. It was at least twenty feet long, and it spiraled out of my grasp and half fell to the ground.

"He's cheating!" someone shouted.

Captain Leon shook his head and crossed his arms in front of his chest. "Fox fire is allowed. Keep going."

With a smirk, I made a loop and then tossed the rope onto a handhold near the top of the wall. Once secure, I quickly made my way up, my feet planted on the stone wall as I dragged my weight upward with my arms.

At the halfway point, though, another lance of pain went shooting through my chest. I gasped, and then my hands on the rope slipped.

After a short fall, I hit the ground on my back, winded.

CHAPTER 44

THE FINAL COMPETITION

"Get up," Deimos said.

My blurry vision tunneled. I stared up at the blue sky, acutely aware I was still on my back. The other racers were almost to the top of the wall. I was so far behind, and my neck hurt.

"*Get up.*"

My reality, and Deimos's memory, swirled together. I was in some sort of gladiatorial arena, while at the same time, I was at Astra Academy. In one reality, people were cheering for me. In the other reality, they were booing, and hoping for my death. No matter the situation, I was angry at myself.

I couldn't lose.

I refused to lose.

"That's it," Deimos said through me. "Now, stop holding back. Win this."

Power flooded me. It was the abyssal dragon magic—it fueled me, giving me speed and strength the likes of which no normal person had.

With the willpower to fight, regardless of the circumstances, I stood. Then I leapt for the wall. The handholds were easy—I practically flung myself to the top of the wall, the power in my arms vast.

I met a few other arcanists at the top of the wall. They stared with wide eyes.

"Weren't you just on the ground?" one asked.

But I ignored them.

The metal bars we had to swing across were fifteen feet above the water, and spaced a few feet apart from one another. The other arcanists swung, one bar at a time, making sure their grip was perfect before swinging to the next.

I grabbed the first bar, and then swung myself two down. My fingers barely touched the next before I let go and hurled myself to the next. It was easy. I felt no fear of falling, or even like I would slip.

Brisko and Roy were near the end of the bars, ahead of everyone.

The anger I felt when seeing them wasn't entirely my own. Deimos hated them. He thought of them like the children who teased had Zahn. If it was left up to Deimos, he would murder them—I would bet money.

I swung past both arcanists and then leapt off the bars in a feat of pure athleticism. Once my feet hit the ground, I took off toward the thorned hurdles. Roy and Brisko leapt down a moment after me, and they sprinted to catch up.

So I went as fast as I could.

I jumped over the ankle-high hurdle, and then one that was knee-height. When the hurdles got taller, I leapt with precision, never going too high because then I would lose too much momentum.

I went faster and faster, running at a pace that I would never normally be capable of maintaining. The thorns came close to my thighs, but they never touched me. My heart raced, and for some reason, Deimos seemed to encourage me to win with a phantom hand of support.

When I crossed the finish line, I had to force myself to slow down by digging my heels into the dirt.

I turned around. The others weren't even halfway through the hurdles. Brisko had cut himself on one, and Roy's pants were caught on the thorns of another.

I had finished long, long before them. It was so shocking that even Captain Leon had to shake his head to seemingly remind himself he was supposed to announce my victory.

"Oh, uh, Gray Lexly has won!" Leon jogged over, grabbed my wrist, and held my hand aloft. "Congratulations to our resident mimic arcanist!"

Cheers came from the stands with the students, and Raaza even threw fox fire confetti into the sky. They yelled my name and shouted boos at Roy and Brisko.

My father and my mum made their presence known by standing and pointing. They bothered everyone sitting next to them, as if to point out I was their child, and they were proud.

The professors even clapped for my victory.

But not the majority of the noble arcanists. Some of them stood to get a better look at me, but most regarded me with suspicion. I didn't blame them, actually. How had I run so fast? They didn't know. And it seemed like they desperately wanted to know my secret more than they wanted to congratulate me on my success.

Captain Leon let me go, and I nodded to him.

The bizarre dream-like state I had been in was long over. I no longer saw the arena, or heard the calls for my death. The terror remained, though. I jogged over to the stands, thankful to see Sorin, Twain, Nini, Thurin, and Waste all waving for me to join them on a brick bench.

Ashlyn waved at me this time, and that also dispelled the last of the fear that lingered from the memory. Her dragon nodded once in appreciation, and it felt welcoming.

Deimos...

I just realized, as I climbed the brick steps to my seat, that Deimos and Zahn never had friends and family to return to. All they ever had was each other.

The archery competition was interesting.

They didn't have normal targets that stood in place, like the ones we had used in *Combat Arts* class. No. They were using *imp targets*. I had seen these before, during another class.

Imp targets were the size and shape of teacup saucers. They had smiley faces drawn on one side, and nothing on the other. The saucers also had little ornamental dragonfly wings that buzzed at an impressive rate. The imp targets darted around the sky, but never went too far, as though held to the stage through invisible string.

Everyone participating in the event stood on the marble stage. The imp targets swirled around, their smiling faces always pointed at the arcanists.

"Listen up," Captain Leon said. "This is a timed competition. The archer who shoots down the most targets wins. You may use your magic to help you, but you cannot break any targets with anything but your arrows, do you understand?"

The people on the stage nodded their acceptance.

"Then, if you're ready..."

Phila stood in the middle of the crowd, her black bow clearly visible, even from afar. She waved to us in the stands, and I waved back.

"You may begin!"

A flurry of arrows shot into the sky. The imp targets darted up and down, dodging the projectiles with surprising grace. The noble arcanists in the stands chuckled and laughed, most pointing at the spectacle. They must not have known what the imp targets were—mischievous devices meant to cause heartache.

"*You can do it, Phila,*" Nasbit cheered.

When the first few shots didn't land, the arcanists on the stage began using their evocations. Phila nocked an arrow and then evoked her wind with a shot. Her arrow sailed through the air at surprising speed, shattering one of the imp targets on impact. The poor little saucer couldn't get out of the way in time.

One of the archers turned his arrows invisible and then shot. For some reason, that worked—the imp targets didn't dodge like they had when the arrow was visible. It made me wonder...

"I should've participated in this event," Raaza muttered as he glared at the competitors. "So many of these fools are wasting their shots!"

He wasn't wrong. Arrows were flying everywhere. When a few sailed toward the stands, Maryanne, the Academy's housekeeper, used her telekinesis to block the projectiles. The arrows bounced off her invisible shields, and she gave everyone in the stands a playful wink afterward, as if to assure us that nothing would happen.

I was glad this competition was timed. A single minute felt like an eternity when everyone was missing so often.

When a trumpet sounded, the contestants lowered their bows. The archery competition had lasted a grand total of five minutes, and only ten imp targets had been shot down. At least fifty remained in the sky, darting around like mosquitoes.

"And the winner is... Phila Hon!" Captain Leon clapped as he stepped onto the marble stage and headed over to her.

Phila clapped for herself. Her coatl, Tenoch, even leapt onto the stage and flew over to her. The pair hugged triumphantly.

The nobles in the stands cheered for her victory, some pointing and cheering her name specifically. Was Phila's family here? I wondered, since I hadn't really seen a hint of them. Where were they?

But perhaps I would see them later at the fundraiser. And since so many of the nobles were impressed with the skills on display, perhaps they would donate more than ever before.

"This is the final competition of the day," Captain Leon shouted, his voice carrying over the training field. "Any students who didn't participate in the other competitions will be asked to participate here. I'll let our resident *Combat Arts* professor explain how it works."

Professor Jijo stepped onto the marble stage. Leon bowed his head and then leapt off the side, giving Jijo everyone's full attention.

Jijo was dressed in a tight-fitting white shirt with no sleeves. His black runes sparkled with power, and when he smiled, I knew it was one filled with confidence. He stood straight and then said, "This competition is between me and the students. The students will have all the skills and magic they have learned thus far, and their eldrin, whereas I will be limited to just my physical capabilities. They must knock me out of the sparring circle before I get them. The first to do so is the winner."

That meant, in theory, if someone had opted out of the previous competitions, and then waited long enough here—for someone else to defeat Jijo—they could avoid competing altogether. I glanced over at Nasbit, knowing the man probably wanted that outcome most of all.

Jijo's nimbus dragon flew around the stage, no wings, just wind and clouds. He snickered as he said, "Only one student at a time can fight! So, the first students can end this all early, but my arcanist will be at his full power."

Jijo went to the weapons rack and pulled out two of the practice swords. With one in each hand, he walked back to the sparring circle. He pointed to the stands with the students and waited.

The sun was on its downward trek, the sky a mix of blue and yellow. This prelude to dusk added a dramatic flair to the mood. The crowds were silent.

Who would go first?

I almost volunteered, but then I had a hilarious idea. With a smile, I glanced over at Phila, who sat on a bench just one below me. "Phila, wouldn't it be amazing if someone we knew beat Professor Jijo?"

She turned around to stare at me, her eyebrows squished slightly together, as if confused by my question. Or perhaps just confused as to why I was asking her.

"Oh, yes," Phila said. "If anyone actually bests Professor Jijo, it will be a spectacular feat."

Nasbit sat a little straighter, his expression grim.

But then—just like I was hoping—Legott stood from his seat. "I will go," he shouted. He hurried down the stands, his winged-snake eldrin, the amphiptere, following behind. Without a second's hesitation, he grabbed a practice sword and leapt onto the marble stage to face our professor.

Captain Leon nodded. "We have a challenger!"

Legott stepped into the circle, his eldrin close to his legs. Jijo bowed at the waist, which seemed to confuse Legott. After a moment of bumbling, he bowed in turn.

Then a bell chimed.

I thought Jijo would just throw this punk from the circle, but instead, he waited. When I gave it some thought, I understood why. The Academy wanted to showcase our skills. That wouldn't happen if Jijo just throat-punched this man into oblivion.

Legott rushed forward. He hunkered down into a swordsmanship stance, and then thrust his practice weapon as though this were a normal practice match. Jijo knocked away the blade, his smile fading slightly.

He was already bored, I could tell.

With perfectly rehearsed moves, Legott swung and thrust, but each time, Jijo parried. Then Legott's eldrin decided to get involved. The winged snake dove at Jijo's legs and wrapped him up tight. The *Combat Arts* professor sighed and then *whapped* the mystical creature in the side of the head.

The snake fell off and hissed.

Legott evoked wind—just like a coatl arcanist—but it seemed weaker, somehow.

Jijo wasn't pushed back. Instead, our professor decided it was time to end this match. He stepped forward, and then with a one-two swing of his practice swords, he struck Legott in the gut and then straight in the center of his sternum.

Completely winded, Legott wheezed as he doubled over. Jijo struck him in the side, and Legott tumbled out of the circle. His eldrin chased after him.

It was an embarrassing fight—for Legott. Somehow, Jijo made it also seem boring, like this was so rote and uninteresting, he was barely paying attention. The injured student made his way back to the stands, his head drooped.

"Our student gave it his all," Captain Leon shouted. "Is there anyone else who wants to try?"

Jijo turned to look at me.

Me.

Specifically.

Or more likely—Jijo really wanted to test his might and skill against Deimos. It was a point of pride, I suspected. Jijo didn't like losing. I saw it in his eyes.

"We should face this Ayless scum in battle," Deimos whispered.

I was about to stand up to accept the challenge, when someone else beat me to the punch.

"I'd like to try," Nasbit shouted from his place in the stands.

CHAPTER 45

THE FUNDRAISER DINNER

Everyone held their breath as Nasbit and Brak traveled down the stands. Together, the pair walked over to the weapons rack, picked up a practice hammer, and then headed for the marble stage.

"Doesn't Nasbit hate competing?" Raaza whispered to my brother. "What's he doing?"

Nasbit climbed onto the stage, and his stone golem rolled onto the platform a moment later, his boulder body crashing around the whole time.

Captain Leon's eyebrows shot for his hairline. "Well, it appears we have our second challenger."

After rubbing his hands together, Nasbit sucked in a deep breath and then stepped into the circle. Brak stepped in with him, "puffing out" his stone chest like a contender.

"You can do it!" Phila shouted. "Go, Naz!" She clapped, and then elbowed Exie.

With a sigh, Exie also clapped.

A bell chimed, and I almost wanted to look away. I didn't want to see Nasbit get pummeled into a pile of rubble. Thankfully, Jijo waited, just like he had with Legott.

For a long while—painfully long—Nasbit stood there. He held his hands in tight fists, one clenching his practice hammer. His golem stood next to him like a silent sentinel, never moving, but maintaining an air of intimidation.

A full minute went by. What was going on? Whispers and murmurs in the crowd began to grow. At this point, Jijo sighed and stepped forward, his two weapons at the ready. Nasbit didn't move, but his face did drain of all color.

Was he afraid? Was that why Nasbit wasn't moving?

"Don't give up!" Phila shouted. She clapped harder. She even stood from her seat. "You can do it!"

Bless her heart—Phila really wanted him to win.

Jijo advanced, despite the cheering. He swung with one of his wooden weapons, aiming for the side of Nasbit's neck.

And then, to my absolute shock, Nasbit took that hit like he was a stone statue. The wooden weapon hit his skin with a *clack*. Even Jijo seemed shocked, which was unfortunate for him, because Nasbit reached out and touched his arm. Then there was a sandstone ring around Jijo's wrist.

Nasbit had... evoked sandstone.

He had been standing around, slowly evoking pebbles of sandstone into his hands. That was one of the downsides of the stone golem—their evocation was so slow. But now that he had gotten it on Jijo, Nasbit could manipulate it. He waved his hand, and the small sandstone bracelet turned into a reverse-thorny nightmare. It jabbed into Jijo, drawing blood.

The red droplets stained the white marble stage.

The professors and noble arcanists gasped so loud, I heard them all as an echo.

Despite his injury, Jijo didn't seem concerned. He leapt away, his wrist bleeding. "You finally found a spine, Arcanist Dodger," he said with a chuckle.

Nasbit took a deep breath. "I..."

Then he grabbed Brak. After another deep breath, he *lifted* his eldrin. People in the stands stood, obviously shocked and losing the ability to blink.

"...will..."

Nasbit hefted his eldrin over his head, his arms shaking, his body trembling. Brak had to weigh at least a few hundred pounds. He was nothing but boulders. But stone golem arcanists could augment their strength and durability... Had Nasbit really practiced? Had he learned how to use his magic for combat?

All to impress Phila?

"...make myself..."

Nasbit spread his feet wide, his face red.

"...*better!*"

"What was that?" Jijo asked, clearly baffled.

Nasbit *threw* his stone golem. He just... threw it. Brak hurtled through the air like the rock he was. Jijo—and everyone else, for that matter—hadn't expected that. Our *Combat Arts* professor wasn't slow, though. On instinct, he dashed out of the way, wind and clouds rushing around him as his nimbus dragon magic came into play. He moved without resistance, faster than he had any right.

Brak sailed past him and crashed onto the marble stage, cracking the beautiful stone upon impact.

Everyone was silent.

Then Captain Leon stepped up onto the stage. "I... I'm sorry, Professor Jijo, but... You're disqualified. You weren't allowed to use your magic. Our winner is, uh, Nasbit Dodger, the stone golem arcanist."

All the students shot up from their seats and cheered. It was amazing. Nasbit hadn't really *won*, because Jijo was fine, even if bleeding a little bit, but he had proven his courage as far as I was concerned. I suspected everyone else felt the same.

"He did it!" Phila shouted, her voice drowned out by the clapping and cheering.

Captain Leon grabbed Nasbit's wrist and held it high.

The professors in the stands clapped, and so did some of the noble arcanists, but it was clear more of them were confused than anything else. Professor Jijo had lost after two students? I wondered if they attributed that to the *amazing* teaching methods of Astra Academy.

Perhaps the fundraiser would do better than anyone imagined.

With the sun setting, and the competitions over, all students were dismissed. Most headed for their dorms, but some—like me and Sorin—were headed to the fundraiser dinner. However, I still wanted to go back to my dorm for just a moment.

I wanted to have Vivigöl with me. It felt odd being away from it for so long, as though the cold touch on my skin, while hidden under my clothing, was somehow a reassurance.

Once Vivigöl was secured across my chest as a bizarre piece of jewelry, I headed into the hall and met up with Sorin. I wore my best white shirt, my crisp, black trousers, and my robes over everything else. A classic uniform, I would say.

For some reason, Nini stood with my brother out in the hall, and she was wearing... fewer clothes than normal.

Tonight, instead of thirty-seven jackets and a whole tent, Nini wore a single shirt, a skirt that went to her knees, and her school robes. Her glasses were polished to the point the glass was practically invisible, and her red hair had been tied back in a ponytail.

It really showed off her reaper arcanist mark.

Waste hovered nearby, his cloak fluttering and his chain rattling. He stayed a few feet away at all times, which was probably for the best.

Nini waved as Twain and I approached, her cheeks pink, her gaze half on the floor.

"Hello," I said with a hint of confusion in my tone.

"The headmaster said I had permission to bring Nini with me," Sorin said as he pushed his shoulders back. "I wanted her to officially meet Mum and Dad." His smile radiated all his feelings on the matter. "I can't wait."

With a shrug, I motioned to the hall. "Let's head over, then."

I picked up Twain and followed my brother down the hall, barely taking note of the surroundings. My chest kept hurting, and my thoughts were jumbled. All throughout the day, as though bombarded by blows from an unseen foe, I felt the strike of agony. Deimos never answered me about where it was coming from.

It kept me distracted. Not focused.

"I'm nervous," Nini whispered to my brother.

"I'll be with you." Sorin wrapped an arm around her. "If you get too anxious, just grab my hand. I'll make sure you get to a quiet place to calm down."

We traveled through a good portion of the Academy, away from the areas I was the most familiar with. Again, I barely took note of my new surroundings as my thoughts continually looped back to the mysterious pain flaring through my torso. It was as debilitating as before...

But it still worried me.

When we approached a large set of doors, I forced myself to pay more attention.

Sorin pushed one door open and held it for Nini and me.

The bright lights that dominated the vaulted ceiling rivaled an afternoon sun. Guests clad in resplendent silks and glittering jewelry milled about the large banquet room. Standing tables were positioned near the walls, for people to mingle, and long dining tables were set up near the back, for the official dinner portion of the evening.

The air was alive with the soft hum of energy and conversation. It all harmonized with the delicate strains of an unseen orchestra, blending into a sound that was both inviting and daunting. Where were we supposed to go? Who to talk to first?

The Academy's outstanding chefs had crafted exquisite bite-sized treats for everyone to nibble on before the main meal. Small quiches, tiny cupcakes, and palm-sized bread loaves were placed on every standing table.

In the middle of the room was some sort of decoration. Or perhaps a display? It was an ice sculpture of a dragon, but inside, delicate blooms of fire blossomed and twirled, held in a bubble that never melted the sculpture.

"Wow," Sorin said as he entered the banquet hall. "Thurin, are you seeing this?"

"I am, my arcanist," his shadow said from his feet.

Nini grabbed my brother's arm. Her eyes were so wide, they were practically larger than her glasses. "This is amazing."

Together, we meandered over to the first table. A group of men I had never seen in my life were all muttering to themselves. I saw they had arcanist marks on their foreheads, but their eldrin were nowhere to be seen.

That meant they were noble arcanists—the ones whose eldrin were far from here.

They all wore blue attire. It was so navy and tailored, it reminded me of military uniforms. Gold medals hung from their chests, and silvery epaulets adorned their shoulders.

"Arcanists these days are soft," one of the men said, his voice low, and almost unheard as I walked by.

"None of them would last one day in a real battle," another man said.

"Gone are the days of real warriors. Now they just pretend. Did you see those bouts? When I was their age, I was fighting pirates on the daily."

We left their table and continued on, but their words stayed with me. I wondered how many arcanists felt like we were "soft."

"Deimos," I whispered. "Do you think the arcanists in the Academy are weak?"

I half expected him not to answer, but then his thoughts drifted into mine, and he replied with my voice. "They're children of prosperous times. They never know how great their lives are, as they have nothing to compare. They aren't weak—they're just untested."

I chortled to myself. "Untested, huh?"

Gilded goblets caught the light cascading from the ceiling, and I glanced over to watch a few arcanists give a toast.

"Oh, I can't wait to see how these arcanists turn out," one lady arcanist said with a chuckle.

"Yes, quite."

I supposed those were the arcanists whose purses held the future of the Academy's finances. Hopefully they would donate enough to help the headmaster accomplish all his goals.

Sorin and Nini turned and pointed to a table with my father. He was so easy to spot—he was probably the portliest man in attendance.

"Gray, look," Sorin said. "C'mon, let's go see them."

"I'll catch up with you." I waved him away. "I, uh, need to find someone else."

My brother met my gaze for a long moment. He didn't argue with me, though, and for that, I was grateful. He took Nini and headed over to the table in the corner of the banquet hall to speak to our father.

First, I wanted to see Ashlyn and her father. Then I wanted to see Ryker and MOS again. Perhaps we could set up a time to get my rune.

Twain shifted in my grip, getting comfortable. "We should eat some fish."

"First, help me find Ashlyn."

"Oh, she's over there." Twain pointed with his nose, his whiskers twitching. "See? Her outfit is blue. Like her dragon."

I followed the tip of his nose to Ashlyn at the far end of the banquet hall. She wore a dress as blue as the ocean, and her blonde hair hung elegantly past her bare shoulders, fluttering behind her whenever she moved.

She stood next to her father, the archduke, who wore a long sapphire coat and a pair of white trousers that were as crisp and clean as the day they were made. In his outfit, he seemed muscular and commanding, but his expression was one of disappointment. His lips curled downward, his eyes narrowed.

I headed in their direction, intent on making my presence known.

Perhaps I should just tell Archduke Kross I cared for his daughter...

Maybe that would help the situation.

.

CHAPTER 46

CROWDS

As I crossed the banquet hall, I also kept an eye out for Ryker. He was so unassuming that it was difficult to pick him out in a crowd. No runes on his skin, no scars or flashy decorations. His wife, on the other hand—I spotted her immediately. She stole the show at her table, chatting with guests.

I made a mental note to go see them.

But as I was staring at them, I bumped into someone else. I stumbled, and muttered an apology, only to notice my professor, Piper, and her rizzel eldrin, Reevy, who sat perfectly perched on her shoulder.

"Gray?" Piper swished back her black hair, hitting Reevy with her locks in the process. "Congratulations on winning two competitions." Her eldrin wildly waved his arms around, clearing the hair away. Then he *popped* and teleported to her other shoulder, his ears down.

"I had been hoping to win three competitions, but Nasbit beat me to the last," I said.

"Well, we were *all* surprised by that... But I'm glad he had a victory." Piper smoothed her clothing and then glared at me. "How do I look? Perfect? Tell me nothing is out of place."

I hadn't even been paying attention to her clothing. When I did, I realized she had a black dress with white fur around the collar and sleeves. It was nice, I supposed.

"You look amazing."

Piper loosened her shoulders, lifted her head to accentuate her long neck, and then held a hand to her chin. "Better now, right?" Before I could reply, she waved a hand. "Oh, here he comes. Say something about how you only won because of my incredible teaching prowess."

Who?

I glanced over just as Professor Ren joined us. He wore his usual school robes—open enough to see most of his chest—and he carried two glasses of sparkling wine. He handed one to Piper and then gave me a confident smile.

"Ah, our star pupil. Congrats."

"Thanks." I half nodded to Piper. "I was just stopping by to thank Piper for all the advice she has given me since I joined Astra Academy. Her class has been the best."

Mostly because we did whatever we wanted for the most part, but I omitted that last bit.

Ren lifted an eyebrow. "Oh, really? I better improve my own pedagogical pursuits if I'm going to keep up."

Reevy immediately scrunched his eyes and silently mouthed the word *"Pedagogical?"*

I shrugged.

Then I stepped around the pair. "Well, have a wonderful evening."

Piper slipped her arm around Ren's and offered me one final smile before turning all her attention to Professor Ren. He *tinked* his glass against hers, and they chatted quietly as I wandered away.

I wondered if they would teach more classes together, since it was apparent they were becoming close.

"Did you see that there is a reaper arcanist here?" a lady arcanist whispered as I walked by.

Her companion, another lady arcanist, both in fine ivory gowns, replied, "How unsettling. I hope we aren't seated next to them."

Sometimes I forgot how others thought of certain eldrin. All today, the noble arcanists were obsessed with those who had bonded to dragons. Now they wouldn't even dare associate with Nini.

"Oh, look," someone else in the crowds said. "There's that talented mimic arcanist. The one who won multiple events."

"Where? Oh, there he is. He seems so *roguish*."

"He beat the archduke's daughter. How embarrassing. How much did the archduke spend on personal trainers? A fortune, I tell you."

Soft, stifled laughter followed the commentary.

That was all I needed to hear. I continued without acknowledging the statements, my goal clear.

Ashlyn and her father were set apart from the rest of the crowd, their conversation hushed, but loud enough that I caught some of it as I approached.

"I don't want to leave, *Father*," Ashlyn said, her words curt.

"Your failure was shameful." Her father shook his head, his strong jaw clenched. "At least your mother wasn't here to witness your loss, though no doubt word will reach her."

Ashlyn crossed her arms. She wanted to say a lot, but she kept it bottled, her self-control legendary.

Archduke Kross motioned to the room. "Do you not see their glances? Each snide remark is a judgment on our whole family. The fact you want to stay just tells me you don't understand the gravity of your actions. You never should've lost to *anyone* in your class. Pathetic."

When I reached them, I coughed loud enough for the next table over to know I had arrived.

They both turned, and Ashlyn widened her eyes. Her father regarded me with a sneer, but it softened in an instant. With all the etiquette and pomp a man of his standing could muster in a tense situation, Archduke Kross said, "Good evening, Gray Lexly."

"Hello." I set Twain down and then straightened my posture. "The decorations are delightful, aren't they?"

"They're exquisite." The archduke bowed his head. "And congratulations on your many victories. Truly, you must be talented, since you come from such unfortunate circumstances and rose to such prominence in less than a year."

Such unfortunate circumstances.

Something about his words stung, like he thought less of *my* family, even though his was a mire of bloated expectations, guilt, and passive-aggressive manipulation. He thought he was better than my family? *Him?*

But I kept that to myself. I felt a twinge of guilt myself, since I had thought less of my father for so long, even though he had just been trying his damnedest to keep us safe.

I ran a hand through my hair to cool my temper. "I just take my education seriously."

"I can see that." The archduke shot Ashlyn a sideways glance. "Aren't you going to congratulate Gray, my daughter? He bested you, after all."

I had never seen Ashlyn's spirit drain so fast. Her eyes were dull when she turned to me, her expression a simple smile, nothing more than a mask. "Congratulations, Gray."

Few things in life hurt as much as seeing her so... dejected. This wasn't Ashlyn. This was nothing like her.

"And aren't you going to thank him for all the people he helped during your disaster of a cotillion?" The archduke motioned for Ashlyn to speak again. "He deserves your thanks."

"Thank you, Gray," she dutifully repeated. "For using your mimic magic to help my guests. So many arcanists owe you a great debt."

Ashlyn had spoken every word with the vibrance and life of a corpse.

"I'm sure you were flooded with letters of gratitude," Archduke Kross said.

Which was odd, because not a single arcanist had written to thank me, not even Valo, whom I had personally saved. I hadn't even thought about the people I had rescued during the attack at Ashlyn's event, mainly because *I* was the reason there was an attack in the first place.

But I wasn't going to tell the archduke that.

"It was no trouble," I finally said. "I mean, I thought the other arcanists would help, since some of them had creatures who excel in the water, but since no one else stepped up to the challenge, I did what needed to be done."

This was a subtle slight to Ashlyn's fiancé, since he was a *leviathan arcanist,* and definitely should've helped, but he was too much of a chump to do anything other than cry.

"Yes, well, some of the guests had already had their fair share of drinks," the archduke said with a chuckle. He then sharply turned to face

Ashlyn. "And speaking of which—perhaps we should hurry home. We might be able to have dinner and drinks with your mother and brother if we're quick enough. I've already left the headmaster a sizeable donation. I doubt he'll miss us."

Ashlyn's woebegone gaze fell to the floor. "Of course, Father."

"Pack your things and meet me on the dock. I'll be there shortly."

Ashlyn didn't agree or disagree—she just left. Her blue gown flowed behind her as she did exactly as her father wanted. I watched as beautiful strands of her hair caught the light and shimmered.

"Archduke Kross," I said as I stared into his icy gaze. "Do you mind if I speak frankly?"

"Not at all. Say whatever is on your mind."

"I admire your daughter." I hoped it wasn't too forward, but I mostly wanted to end this conversation as quickly as possible. Ashlyn didn't look like she was in a good place, and I wanted nothing more than to speak with her.

But Archduke Kross didn't reply to my statement.

So I continued.

"Ashlyn is the most incredible person I've met."

"Ah." The archduke chortled. "I see. Well, let me stop you there. If you want to join the Kross family, and escape the doldrums of your island life, you should've said so. My niece, Priscilla, is a beauty like no other. She has been looking for an arcanist of your talents."

"That's nice, but she's not Ashlyn."

The archduke stopped himself for a long moment to mull over my comment. "What?" he finally asked.

"Your niece isn't Ashlyn. I said *Ashlyn* is the most incredible person I've met."

Twain sat on my boot and glared up at the archduke. While my eldrin said nothing, it was clear from his expression he felt the same as I did.

"*Ashlyn*," the archduke said, stressing the word, "is neither the most stunning, nor the most magically talented, as you proved in your little sparring match. She isn't the best of anything—a problem that, as her father, I shall work to rectify."

"Listen, Priscilla might be a beauty, but no one smiles like Ashlyn does when she's confident. No one has silent conversations with me in just a few simple glances like Ashlyn. And, probably her most impressive trait—no one puts up with a deluge of negativity and still strives to do better like Ashlyn."

"Yeah," Twain interjected. "And no one snorts lightning like her eldrin. He's also amazing."

I hadn't known Twain felt that way about Ecrib.

Archduke Kross allowed some of his forced charisma to fade. He scowled at me with an overly judgmental expression.

"I see," he said. "You wish to be with my daughter, despite the fact she is already betrothed."

I nodded once. "I think I exceed any standards *Valo* set. And if you ask Ashlyn, you'll find she wants something else in a man than what *he* brings to the table."

The archduke's frown deepened. "Disregarding the complete embarrassment it would be to cut off an engagement we already publicly announced, what would be the first thing you did, as my daughter's fiancé, if I allowed such a thing? What sort of public statement, or show of loyalty, would you make that would help the Kross family?"

I hated every word in his smarmy questions. And after everything he had said about Ashlyn, and my family, I wasn't feeling charitable. All I felt was anger.

"If Ashlyn was my fiancée, the first thing I'd do is tell you to *back off*," I said, my words heated. "Because no one talks to my future wife like she's trash and gets away with it."

CHAPTER 47

SOUL GRAFTING

S ilence.

The archduke's nostrils flared.

Obviously, he didn't appreciate what I had said.

The conversations around the banquet hall sounded louder than ever. In my brief moment of reflection, I partially regretted my words, if only because it had likely made the situation tenser.

I didn't regret the content of my words, though.

I had meant every single one of them.

"I didn't realize you were so smitten with my daughter," Archduke Kross eventually said, his words drawn out and emotionless. "But you realize I'd never allow someone into the family who openly disrespects me."

"Good thing I did it privately, then," I darkly quipped.

"I have never treated my children as anything less than exceptional." Archduke Kross ground out every word. "I hold them to high standards because I know they can meet them."

I held back a scoff. "You're pushing your daughter away when all you spew is criticism. Ashlyn is amazing. We both know it. You make your whole family look bad when you say she's anything but exceptional."

"The Kross family is *my* family, first and foremost. *I* have made it great, and I will *continue* to make it great in the best way I know how. So, if you truly wish to earn my daughter's hand in marriage, you will choose your next words wisely."

I wondered if Deimos's thoughts influenced me, because in that moment, I wanted to tell the archduke to find a tall cliff and throw himself from it. What was so great about *his* house? I didn't know what it took to become a noble, or to be given status, but it was probably an easier route than pleasing Archduke Kross. More satisfying and fulfilling, too.

What if Ashlyn and I just made our own noble family?

"Father?"

The archduke and I both whirled to face Ashlyn. She had returned, though I didn't know when. I had been too busy having a staring match with her father.

"The headmaster said he wanted to speak with you before you left," Ashlyn said, her monotone voice telling me she hadn't heard our earlier conversation. "So it appears we'll be having dinner here after all."

"Unfortunate." Archduke Kross placed a hand on her shoulder and turned her away. "But we can use this opportunity to mingle. We can speak with the Savan and Ren family representatives. It's important to have their support."

He spoke as though I wasn't even present.

"What about Gray?" Ashlyn said, glancing over her shoulder and meeting my gaze.

She was confused, and with a single look, she silently asked me why her father was so cold.

I shook my head once, telling her the conversation had been a rough one at best. Ashlyn returned her attention to her father, her face neutral.

"Gray needs to time to formulate his next few statements to me." The archduke headed into the center of the room. "While he thinks hard about his relationship with our family, perhaps you and I should speak about Valo. He was *useless* during the attack on your cotillion."

"Uh... Yes, Father."

"It was a shameful display. You deserve someone who will defend you. And someone who will... stand up for you, no matter who they must upset to do so."

Ashlyn didn't reply. Instead, she gave me one final glance before disappearing into the crowds with her father. She seemed hopeful, which I appreciated.

Despite that, I was disappointed Archduke Kross maintain control of the situation.

The melodic music didn't ease my anger. I just... stewed. I *wanted* to cause a scene, and force this to some sort of conclusion, but I knew that wouldn't do me any good. And Ashlyn didn't want that, either. She clearly wanted her family to be proud, or at least, accepting of her.

With a frustrated groan, I raked my fingers through my hair.

"Don't worry, we'll set him straight next time," Twain said.

I picked up my eldrin and patted his head. "We'll see."

"Ashlyn will still be attending the Academy, right? We'll have another chance to speak with her blowhard of a dad."

I chuckled at Twain's comments.

But that made me wonder how Deimos felt. Wasn't this the time for him to chime in and tell me the best course of action was to murder someone and wear their skin like a coat or something equally dramatic?

But Deimos said nothing.

"You don't have any advice for me, Death Lord?" I whispered.

Nothing.

A dull ache spread through my chest, and I rubbed my sternum. Something was wrong. Sweat dappled my skin, and after I took a deep breath, I realized I wanted fresh air. I turned and glanced around the banquet hall. Glass doors that led outside were all positioned on the eastern wall. I headed for them.

On the way, I almost ran into a tall table filled with a bunch of gaudy arcanists dressed in jewelry and magical trinkets. I barely paid attention to them, but one of them stepped in front of me.

Knovak with his unicorn.

"Gray? What're *you* doing here?"

"I was invited," I intoned. "Why are *you* here?"

"I'm part of the Gentz family, thank you very much." Knovak narrowed his eyes into a glare. "We're very wealthy, even if we haven't been granted the title of *noble*. My family donates to Astra Academy every year. And, since I bonded with my mystical creature in the Menagerie, they're donating *extra*."

"That's great."

I just wanted outside as quickly as possible. With careful movements, I stepped around Knovak, and then his unicorn, and headed for the glass doors.

Knovak followed. For some reason.

"Are you unwell?"

"Eh." I forced a shrug. "I've been better."

He kept close. "I'll join you outside."

"Fine."

The instant I stepped outside, and the chill air washed over me, I felt better. This was a second-story balcony that overlooked the Academy's main courtyard, and I stumbled my way to the railing.

"Gray?"

I flinched and whipped my attention to a woman hovering around in the darkest corner of the balcony.

Nini.

She stood with her reaper, her robes pulled tight over her body. "What're you doing here?"

I shook my head. "I needed some air." With Twain still in my arms, I leaned my side against the railing. "What about you?"

"I, uh..." Nini glanced at her feet. "I don't think I belong here. The other arcanists... They don't want me or Waste around."

"Most reaper arcanists don't attend events like this," Knovak said, interjecting himself into the conversation.

Starling, the little unicorn, nodded along with Knovak's words. "Reapers are harbingers of death. Not fun and whimsical mystical creatures."

Nini held the cloak of her eldrin, her hands shaking.

"Isn't my brother keeping you company?" I asked. I set Twain down, unable to hold him any longer. The pain grew at an alarming rate.

"Sorin went inside to get us drinks," Nini whispered.

"Ah."

I didn't want to bother anyone with my phantom agony, so I kept it to myself. What were they going to do about it, anyway? Hopefully it would subside, just like every other time.

Knovak swished his arm around in a dramatic flourish. "Well, we don't need that celebration inside. We can have our own celebration right here. On the balcony." He gestured to the courtyard. "We have a view. Good company. And the music is still audible. What more could we want?"

Nini nodded. "I suppose... That's a nice way of looking at it."

"May I join you?"

The gruff voice startled me. That was the second time since entering the balcony, and I wondered if I just wasn't paying much attention. I glanced over and noticed a giant tree branch attached to the very corner of the far end of the balcony. It was meant for mystical creatures, and the branch led all the way back to the treehouse.

Ecrib sat on the branch, his finned tail dangling over the edge as he relaxed on the smooth wood.

"What're you doing here?" Knovak asked.

"My arcanist told me we were leaving, but then she changed her mind. I've been sitting here ever since." Ecrib snorted. "I'm too big for the festivities inside."

"Of course you can join us for our own celebrations." Knovak pointed to a spot on the balcony.

The typhoon dragon lazily picked himself up and walked down the rest of the branch pathway. He leapt onto the balcony, shaking it a bit, and then headed over for us. Although Ecrib's normal demeanor was one of aggression, now he seemed melancholy.

The dragon gave me an odd glance, but I wasn't in the right state to speak with him.

My pain had gotten worse.

So much worse.

It was as if someone had stabbed me with a needle, and was slowly sinking it into my chest, one inch at a time. I leaned on the railing of the balcony, taking in deep breaths. That seemed to ease my agony, but only a small amount.

What was going on?

"Gray?" Nini asked.

"I'm fine," I preemptively stated. "Just fine."

"You don't look well."

I dismissively waved away the comment. "What? Me? I'm totally healthy." I spoke the last word with a grunt, a comical punctuation to a terrible lie.

The others all stared, and I attempted to maintain a straight face. Was Deimos breaking free of the dreamscape cage Professor Helmith had placed him in? Or was something worse happening? I knew the answer, because if Deimos was freeing himself, this would've gone differently.

No.

He was in trouble.

I knew. I felt his anger.

Knovak placed his hands on his hips. "Well, as long as you think you're okay... Maybe we should bring food out here."

Nini nodded. "Yeah. I like that."

"Remember to get fish," I said.

And then I vomited.

I didn't barf up food or anything in my stomach—I vomited salt water. It came out in a burst from my mouth, and splashed across the balcony, my lips trembling. It was so salty, I almost puked normally.

"G-Gray?" Twain said, his fur puffing out on end. "What is this?"

"I..." It took most of my willpower to swallow. "I don't know."

The water had the stench of death. I grabbed my shirt and twisted my fingers into the fabric. Vivigöl pulsed against my skin. The weapon... I was tempted to grab it and hold it at the ready. I was in danger.

The glass door to the balcony opened, and I glanced up, hoping to see my brother.

I needed Sorin.

But instead, it was Ashlyn. She had left her father's side and come to visit us. Or perhaps she was looking for a way to escape the fundraiser herself? Either way, here she was.

"Thank the good stars you're here," Knovak said. He pointed to me. "Gray is barfing up water."

"What?" Ashlyn asked.

Her eldrin moved to my side. "He's not well." Ecrib sniffed the water on the balcony. "This is water from the midnight depths." His eyes widened, and his pupils narrowed into slits. "Which means..."

I vomited a second time, more water than before. My insides burned, but Deimos's thoughts were coming in clearer now. He didn't speak to me, yet I somehow sensed the situation.

Death Lord Naiad...

She was attempting to graft Deimos's soul to her dragon. And since part of his soul was attached to mine, Naiad was trying to tear me from the realms of the living. She wanted Deimos's soul in the abyssal hells.

She was going to inadvertently kill me to do it. Or maybe something worse.

"You all should get away from me," I said between gasps for air. I coughed up more water, and it was difficult to speak.

Ashlyn rushed to my side. "Wait. Let me help." She placed her hand on my shoulder. Then, with some concentration, she pushed some of her typhoon dragon magic into me. Her augmentation flooded my lungs and eased the pain.

I could now... breathe underwater.

Or in this case, breathe with water in my lungs.

I felt better than before. Not normal, because the pain was mounting, but better. I glanced up at her. "Thank you."

"We should get you inside," Ashlyn said, her eyebrows knitted. "Come on." In an attempt to force levity, she said, "You'll be happy to hear my father is off with the headmaster. We can take you someplace private. Away from all this."

"No. *No.*" I shook my head. "You all need to get away from me. Something is happening in the abyssal hells. I think Death Lord Naiad is winning, and... Deimos is dying."

Nini's eyes widened. "Wait, I thought we had more time? I thought Deimos said Naiad wouldn't be getting the last remaining Death Lords?"

Knovak, Ashlyn, and Nini crowded closer to me—the exact opposite of what I wanted them to do. Didn't they understand? Something terrible was happening. I didn't want to put them in danger.

"She can't get you," Knovak said. "She's in the abyssal hells. You're here."

"The gate Zahn created..." I gripped my shirt tighter. "Deimos told me... It was linked to his soul. I don't know how that will affect Naiad's grafting. *Please.* Just leave me. Tell the professors. Anyone else. But get away. *Right now.*"

I didn't want them to get hurt.

Why wouldn't they leave?

"Oh, Gray," Nini whispered. "Your brother will be back soon. We'll help you."

"C'mon," Knovak said, placing a hand on my shoulder. "Let's just get inside. Someone will see. They'll rush over."

A terrible yank from inside my chest felt exactly like the tugging sensation I experienced with teleportation. The others grabbed me, pulled me, pushed me. The teleportation was painful and tortured—and somehow wet.

My feet left the balcony of the Academy and landed in ankle-deep water.

CHAPTER 48

SHOWDOWN IN THE ABYSS

No moment in my entire life had prepared me for this.

I stood in a mire of dark water, where every ripple and wave formed the face of tortured individuals. The black rocks beneath the surface were swirls and spirals, and the small white rocks between them were twisted faces with varying expressions. Some sad, some delighted, some pinched in disgust.

I took several steps backward, my boots splashing through the mire of misery.

The sky above was a swirl of red and charcoal gray. Motes of light danced through the air—fireflies?—and some formed into the shape of a crescent moon before darting away.

When I glanced around, my heart sank into the depths of my stomach. I was underground. In a cave? The sky was a haze—an illusion—and gargantuan roots the size of rivers cascaded into the murky waters, with tiny roots that resembled human hands jutting out at various places. The small root hands grabbed at the fireflies, attempting to snatch them from the air. Whenever they did, the victorious hand recoiled back into the root, taking the insect with it, and never returning.

The dark water ran from waterfalls that seemingly fell from the haze of the sky. I was surrounded on all sides by roots, streams of water, and clouds of haunting fireflies.

It was cold. Everything smelled of burnt incense and salt. Goosebumps prickled across my skin, and my breathing became ragged.

I was in the abyssal hells.

That wasn't possible.

"Gray!"

I whipped around, splashing the water. Soft moans and strangled gargles rang out from the splashes.

Not even in my worst nightmares had I seen such a desolate and haunting landscape.

I wasn't the only one here. Somehow—because the fates couldn't just thrust this burden on me alone—Ashlyn, Nini, and Knovak were splashing through the wicked waters. Their eldrin had come with us, drawn by the soul grafting that had dragged us all here.

It was because they had been touching me. If they had just let me go, and left me alone, they wouldn't have come with me.

Even Twain...

My mimic leapt from the waters, his eyes wide. I scooped him into my arms just in time to spot the monster that had brought us here. Twain clung to my shoulder and refused to let go.

"What is this?" a woman asked, her voice both feminine and severe.

She didn't need an introduction—her scars and battle armor said it all.

Death Lord Naiad.

Her scalp was free of all hair thanks to the deep scars that ran like knife injuries from her forehead down to the base of her neck. Her arcanist mark was the seven-pointed star with a dragon, but she had also gone out of her way to carve two swords into the side of the star, the bizarre scarring noticeable more than the dragon.

Naiad wore a small chest piece, and a skirt made of bone, skin, and twisted metal. Barely any armor. Naiad relied on agility in combat, that much I understood both from her appearance and Deimos's knowledge. She used fast strikes. Many slashes. Overwhelming force.

Blood-red paint marked her body. She had painted handprints to make it look as though people were grasping upward along her limbs.

Hand prints on her legs, torso, and arms made it look like she had crawled out of a pit of corpses.

Her eyes were dark and beyond intense, and her complexion a lush tan. Muscles rippled underneath her skin, as though she had spent hundreds of years just honing her body.

Two abyssal dragons were in this hellish swamp with us. One by Death Lord Naiad's side, and one lying in the water.

The one standing was everything I remembered. It walked on four legs, but its body was a rotting pile of sickly scales, skin, and muscles. Mucus covered the dragon, dripping off every portion of its body. The beast's wings were a cobweb of transparent faces...

They were grafted souls.

So many souls.

The mouths of the faces were open, their eyes nothing but circles. The faces in the transparent wings moaned in agony, some whispering their fears between cries.

A few of the souls sparkled—their magic still contained within.

They were the other Death Lords.

The second abyssal dragon, the one lying in the water, was similar, but the souls on its body were less numerous, and it was missing one of its front legs.

That was Deimos's eldrin.

And as soon as I thought that, I spotted Death Lord Deimos in the shallow mire waters near Naiad. His bone and metal armor had been shattered, and he was motionless on the side of one of the many gigantic roots, half his body submerged in water, half his body above it.

Tiny root hands grasped at Deimos, the little fingers raking across his exposed flesh. The hands didn't seem to be hurting him—just grasping and ineffectively clawing, as though they wanted him but were too weak to carry him away.

Deimos didn't move. His eyes weren't even open.

The chest piece of his armor had been torn asunder, and a terrible rent in his flesh told me Naiad had attempted to graft his soul from that very opening.

"Never in the many millennia I have lived," Naiad said, slow and soft, "has a soul summoned others when it was in danger."

"Where are we?" Knovak asked, his voice high-pitched with panic. His unicorn splashed the waters as he ran around Knovak's legs.

Ashlyn and her dragon stood their ground, but they were shaken. They wildly glanced around, taking in the situation just as I had.

Nini gulped down air. Her glasses had fallen off at some point, and her expression bordered on manic. When I thought she was about to take off and run, her reaper swaddled her in his cloak. They merged, and Waste's strength—and courage—obviously melded into her.

With Waste's scythe in hand, Nini turned to face me, her expression grim.

"We shouldn't be here," Nini and Waste whispered together.

Naiad stepped forward, and her dragon followed. Her eldrin was the size of a house, its large head gazing down on us all with its six eyes.

"Wait," Naiad whispered. "You weren't summoned for protection. The reason I can't fully take Deimos's soul is... one of you has a piece of him. What a clever ploy. One I never thought Deimos would stoop to."

Naiad reached over to her dragon. She placed her palm on the beast, and then her hand sank into the rotting flesh. It *plunged* deep into the monster, her arm disappearing to the elbow, and then she withdrew a golden halberd, a type of weapon that was best described as a sword attached to the end of a spear. It was entirely made of a dark gold material —sickly gold—that told me the halberd had been crafted from abyssal coral.

I grabbed at the collar of my shirt, and pulled it down, revealing Vivigöl.

Death Lord Naiad raised an eyebrow—one just as scarred and hideous as her scalp.

"Wh-What's going on?" Knovak asked.

I splashed forward as I ripped Vivigöl from my body. It *click-click-clicked* into the shape of a trident. "Stand back," I told him, trying to sound confident.

I wasn't, for the record, but I wasn't about to let this lunatic Death Lord hurt the others. No—they were all here because of *me*, and I wasn't going to let anyone get harmed. I didn't care what it took. I was going to handle this problem.

"Gray," Ashlyn whispered. "This is the abyssal hells."

"Just stay behind me." I held Vivigöl tightly as Naiad advanced. "Don't let her touch you."

That was how she did it. Naiad needed to pull someone's soul out of their body and carefully graft it to her dragon. Deimos's knowledge served me well in this regard.

"You wield Vivigöl?" Naiad asked, her expression shifting to anger. "Only Death Lords may touch such sacred weapons."

"I'm a discount Death Lord," I quipped. Then I remembered Deimos's words about maintaining distance in a fight. Vivigöl transformed again—this time into the chain whip I had used before. "I've trained in combat while I was in the realms of the living."

Death Lord Naiad stopped her advance.

Her dragon flared its disgusting scales, and slime oozed from within.

"You aren't with the living anymore," Naiad sweetly whispered.

With a wave of her hand, *things* stirred within the waters. A few seconds later, dozens of people rose from the shallow depths, forming from the slime and gunk of the mire itself.

They were... the shambling monsters I had seen emerge from gate fragments. They were the half-souled monstrosities that haunted my nightmares.

These were soldiers in Death Lord Naiad's army of the damned. Her ability to manipulate souls meant she could call them to fight for her.

And her manipulation was powerful. When my brother controlled the darkness, he did so with bits at a time. Maybe a room's worth of shadow? And when Jijo demonstrated his ability to manipulate the clouds, he had done so over the entire training field. He was a more powerful arcanist than my brother.

But neither of them compared to Naiad.

The souls in the whole accursed swamp sprang to answer her magic. Hundreds of bodies, each with claws and fangs befitting a monster, stumbled forward. They flexed their claws and headed for us; some even emerged near our feet.

"*What is this?*" Knovak shouted.

Starling stabbed one with his unicorn horn. "Back, foul monster!" The corpse staggered into the water, but it wasn't defeated.

Ecrib's scales flared, and lightning flashed across his body.

Nini hefted her scythe. "We're going to die here..."

"Don't talk like that," Ashlyn confidently said. She pressed her back against her dragon. "Focus. *Focus.*"

"Kill them," Naiad said, though I suspected the verbal command was unnecessary. Or perhaps... it had been intended for her dragon. "Tear them limb from limb. I only need Deimos and his *discount Death Lord.*"

She lunged for me, faster than I had anticipated. Naiad thrust with her halberd, puncturing my gut in one brutal go. The tip of her weapon was out my back, my blood splattering into the water all around us.

The abyssal coral of her blade...

Naiad could use her abyssal dragon magic through it. She was attempting to mess with my soul. It was worse than the physical injury itself.

"Gray!" Twain yelled from my shoulder.

Deimos wasn't really awake enough to give me his magic, so I had to take it for myself.

I didn't even need to close my eyes. I tugged on the thread of magic that led to one of the abyssal dragons, and Twain bubbled and shifted.

This clearly surprised Naiad. She leapt away, her attention on my eldrin.

Twain grew in size, his hulking form taking the shape of an impressive abyssal dragon. My arcanist mark burned, but I knew what I needed to do. I used the magic of the dragon to heal my injury—and to give me more strength. The damage the abyssal coral had done was more severe than anything else, but as an abyssal dragon arcanist, my soul was mended much faster.

With Vivigöl held tightly, I lashed out the chain whip and struck a startled Naiad across the arm. I drew blood, but she was barely disturbed. Her attention remained on Twain.

The undead monsters shambling through the swamp went for Ashlyn, Knovak, and Nini. I turned, fearful they would get hurt, but I was surprised by what I found.

Nini cleaved through any who dared to get close to her. Her scythe cut through their waterlogged bodies, and she swung over and over again, culling the damned with a gritted determination.

"Get away," Nini and Waste said together. "*No one get near me!*"

Ashlyn and Ecrib attacked with their magic, using the might of the typhoon dragon to rend their foes. When they got near, Ecrib bashed them away with his finned tail or crunched the heads of corpses who were too large to be toppled.

But Knovak and his unicorn...

They were frozen in terror.

I held out my hand. Abyssal dragon arcanists evoked *raw magic*, and did so like a solid beam of light that sliced through most objects. I used my new evocation and blasted the monsters before they could touch Knovak, saving him from an untimely death.

"*Get behind Nini,*" I commanded.

But then Naiad's dragon charged forward.

"*Twain,*" I shouted.

My eldrin rushed to meet the Death Lord's beast. The two dragons slammed into each other, quaking the area with their might. The water splashed, the roots trembled, and the fireflies danced around us, as though excited for the bloodshed.

The stone faces beneath the surface of the water shifted to expressions of concern.

I tried to ignore that.

Naiad shook off the distractions. She flew at me again, this time swinging her halberd at my neck. She wanted to decapitate me. I stepped back, my foot hitting one of the undead, but I didn't flinch. I ducked under her swing, whipped my weapon around, slashing the waterlogged corpse, and then jumped to stay close to Naiad.

Vivigöl *click-clicked* into a sword.

Clearly, my ability to change startled her. Her dark eyes met my gaze, and her hatred burned bright. From my magic to my weapon, I was malleable—not standard, but ever-shifting. She hated it. And before she could move, I thrust my sword forward, cutting straight into her collarbone. Naiad's blood mixed into the mire.

But she just smiled. Naiad stepped away, and her abyssal dragon magic stitched her body back together, a blue ooze forming over the injury.

"I barely felt your strike," she taunted. "I see the Death Lords in the realm of the living are *weak.*"

Normally, when arcanists were injured, they lost a bit of concentration and any ongoing magic ended. But that wasn't the case with Naiad. No amount of pain seemed to disturb her concentration. None of her monsters collapsed, none of her magic ceased. She was still strong, fast, and bloodthirsty.

I leapt farther away from her, painfully aware that Death Lords couldn't die like normal people.

Naiad could fight forever. And I couldn't.

The whole swamp shook as the abyssal dragons clashed. They dug into each other, Twain using his claws and fangs to tear off chunks of rotted flesh. The other beast breathed raw magic, destroying part of Twain's arm.

My heart beat hard against my chest.

Because Deimos's soul was trapped in mine, the power of the abyssal dragon didn't hurt like it had when I used it months ago. Now the abyssal dragon magic felt natural and smooth.

I couldn't stop thinking about the others, however. When I chanced a glance, they were still fighting for their lives. Nini culled dozens, her swings slowing. Ashlyn was barely able to fend them off.

Her lightning wasn't as effective against the undead as it was against living people.

Naiad slashed with her weapon again. I dodged, and then changed Vivigöl back into a chain whip. With a hard snap of my wrist, I lashed at Naiad, striking an exposed portion of her leg and drawing more blood.

She hadn't even moved. Her skin healed, and Vivigöl *click-clicked* back into a sword.

Naiad watched, her expression growing furious.

"What are you?" Naiad hissed. "*What kind of magic changes like this?* Your arcanist mark changes... Your weapon changes... Impossible."

Had she never seen a mimic arcanist before?

I suspected not.

"In the realms of the living, we made our own Death Lords," I said. "And I'm one of them."

Vivigöl clicked and shifted into a scythe. With all Deimos's skill, I lunged and slashed. Naiad spun her halberd around to block. Our metallic weapons clanged hard against one another, and the water rippled away from the force of our blow.

We weren't normal individuals with average levels of strength. We both had abyssal dragon magic filling our bodies with extreme power. When we clashed again, the clang was louder, and harsher, and the water splashed away from us.

The rock faces twisted in delight. The smaller root hands reached and grasped for us.

It was like the environment was hungry for our souls.

"I absorb magic," I said through gritted teeth, smiling. "Just being around me weakens you."

Nothing about that was true.

But Deimos had been right—I loved deception. And Death Lord Naiad had revealed her weakness. She knew nothing about me. Now I was going to fill her imagination with lies.

Her face contorted in rage. She bashed her halberd against the scythe, knocked me back a few feet, and then unleashed her evocation. A light of magic, so powerful it lit up the mire, blasted from her hand. I barely dodged aside and then unleashed my own evocation.

I tried—so hard—to evoke as much magic as I could, but my magical skill was nowhere near hers. Naiad's had been like the sun, and mine was a bonfire. Her beam of magic had destroyed one of the many nightmarish roots, and mine just ripped apart more corpses.

Despite that, I stood straighter and chuckled.

"I'm just getting warmed up," I said. "*Keep using your magic.* The more I gather, the more this fight turns in my favor."

A bluff only worked if the other person believed.

And for a small moment, in the heat of this abyssal showdown, I feared she saw right through me. But perhaps, since Naiad didn't interact with many people down here in the depths of these watery hells, she ate up my words.

Naiad yelled, and her dragon broke away from Twain. She leapt onto her eldrin, and the abyssal dragon spread its cobweb of souls it called wings. They took to the "sky," flying through the fireflies.

"You can't take my magic if I'm not close," Naiad said with a dark chortle.

And then her dragon blasted magic down from above. The glowing beam hit the water and splashed it in all directions. The dragon had missed, but that was only because it was in such a hurry to get away. It flapped its soul wings and went higher and higher, preparing for a bombardment, I was certain.

"Gray!" Twain said, his voice twisted and disgusting. He turned his dragon head to me, and his six eyes told me everything.

He was tired.

Twain would transform back into a kitten soon.

I was running out of time.

Determined to somehow fight off Naiad, I stormed through the water. I cut my way through the corpses until I was at Deimos's side. He didn't open his eyes, but I knew he was alive.

Why wasn't the fragment of his soul within me capable of speaking? Was it because he was so injured?

Deimos's armor was broken in so many places, and his flesh was mangled. I stood next to him, my hands shaking.

"Get up," I said.

He didn't move.

Naiad circled in the sky, manipulating more corpses to rise from the water and go for the others. They were growing tired. Her army was endless. We would surely lose at this rate.

"*Get up*," I yelled. "*Get up and fight*! Or are you so weak that you're going to just die, is that it?"

Throwing his words back at him was a small joy I took in the middle of this nightmare. If Deimos didn't stand—if he didn't get on his dragon and help us—I didn't think we would win.

CHAPTER 49

THE WRAITHBORNE ORCHARD

With hesitant movements, I reached down and placed my hand on Deimos's injuries. I didn't know how to manipulate souls, and I wasn't even going to try. But Death Lords couldn't die—not like this. He was fine, and maybe having his soul fragment close would be enough to help.

Death Lord Naiad unleashed her evocation. Both she and her eldrin evoked beams of glowing-hot raw magic. They rained straight down, like pillars of death, crashing into the water. And then when the dragon flew by, the two beams of power acted like blades, slicing through the corpses, the water, the roots, the fireflies—burning and destroying everything they touched.

Naiad flew our way. Her evocation tore through Deimos's dragon. His eldrin yelled out, the scream an echo in the hells.

But when the beams headed for Ashlyn and the others, I had to intervene. I was fast—empowered by the abyssal dragon magic—and I rushed through the water. Ashlyn, Ecrib, and Nini dove to get out of the way, but Knovak was shaken. He didn't move.

I slammed into him, saving him from Naiad's attack, but getting burned in the process. I yelled as I collapsed into the water, my heart pounding.

For a short moment, I lost my vision. Although I was panicked, I kept reminding myself I couldn't die. It would be fine. *I couldn't die. It would be fine.*

But it hurt so much.

And the instant Twain untransformed, I would succumb to any lingering injuries.

I tried not to think of that as I got to my feet. My sight slowly returned, and Knovak stared up at me in disbelief.

"Stay with Nini," I told him as I sloshed my way back to Deimos.

When I got close, Deimos groaned as he turned to his side. Was my presence helping? I didn't know, but I hoped so.

"*Get up,*" I yelled again.

That seemed to help.

Deimos pushed himself to his feet, blood weeping from the injuries. He fluttered his eyes open, and just barely managed to stand. He regarded me with a twisted look of confusion before glancing over at his injured eldrin.

I hadn't been paying attention to my surroundings.

Two bloated corpses lunged for me. One raked its claws down my back. My fancy dress clothes weren't competent armor. I clenched my jaw in agony as the claws tore through me. The second corpse attempted to bite my arm, but Vivigöl transformed into a sword and I slashed at the monster's face, cutting it down.

Deimos held out his hand and evoked enough magic to kill the other.

So many corpses...

"Do something," I said to Deimos. "*Stop this.*"

"I can't." Deimos wrapped an arm around his torso, stopping the blood flow. "Her magic is empowered by the Death Lords she's grafted. Her manipulation trumps mine."

"Then we have to bring her down!" I grabbed his shoulder and pointed. Naiad was coming back around, her abyssal dragon an abomination given flight. "You can graft her soul, can't you? If we hold her down?"

We didn't have time to discuss this. Twain was about to lose his transformation. It was now or never—and perhaps with *two* Death Lords, we could defeat her.

Deimos must've been able to sense my desperation. "When she gets close." He sloshed through the water and made it to his eldrin's side. With a confident hand, he healed the beast's injuries, and the dragon flared to life. The souls of its wings screamed, and they both turned their attention to the incoming Naiad.

"Twain!" I shouted.

My eldrin knew what to do.

While Ashlyn, Nini, and Ecrib continued their desperate fight against the corpses, their moves sluggish, their magic weaker than before, I prepared for one final attack.

Death Lord Naiad neared.

I evoked raw magic. It was a beam, weaker than my previous, but still strong enough to incinerate flesh. Deimos's evocation was a brutal blast of bright magic. So was his dragon's. Twain's final blast trapped Naiad in the sky—the four beams were too much to dodge.

Her dragon leaned to one side, caught some of the evocations on the wing, and then screamed. It turned again, and hit another, burning from the raw damage.

Would she fall? Would it be enough?

The souls of her dragon's wings rearranged themselves. Some were consumed as the injuries to her eldrin vanished. The abyssal dragon roared as it took higher to the sky. I should've known—the Death Lords wouldn't be taken down so easily.

But then Naiad pointed to the distance, beyond the roots and black waterfalls. Her dragon soared through some of the water, and a splash of mist wafted down onto the mire.

Was she leaving?

Naiad's dragon's wing flaps and breathing grew distant.

The corpses in the mire screeched and then collapsed into the salt water all around us. They broke apart and dissolved, their bodies nothing more than swamp grime. Ashlyn's dress was ripped in a hundred places, barely still on her body, and Ecrib bled from numerous injuries.

Knovak and his unicorn were dirty, but unharmed. I hadn't seen them fight.

Nini...

Multiple chains hung from her reaper, each link distinct, but nameless. They rattled as she staggered forward, her scythe held tightly in both hands.

"Gray," Nini and Waste both said, their voices shaky. "I feel... different..."

When a reaper arcanist gathered enough chain links, they achieved their true form. Nini's reaper was transforming... The chains themselves twisted into lanterns. Soul-like faces danced within them. The lanterns floated as effortlessly as the reaper floated, each as bright as the last.

Three lanterns sprouted from the chains, but Nini's mark didn't yet glow. She had near a hundred of this links, and her scythe glittered with gold, silver, and rubies embedded in the handle.

"Gray," Twain called out, drawing my attention to him.

Twain's giant dragon body bubbled. He transformed back into a kitten and then fell into the waters with a soft *splash*. I ran to him and scooped him up into my arms, his wet fur clinging to his small body. He looked like a little rat.

"Gray," he whispered, smiling. "We did it. Everyone is alive."

"You need to rest." I held him close. "Don't worry. I'll get us home."

"Okay..."

He closed his eyes, a soft purr on his breath.

I cradled him close, not sure how I was going to accomplish that. Where was *home*? We had basically been teleported here, and there was no way to exit the abyssal hells. We were trapped. Forever.

Despair ate at me.

Ashlyn pushed her fingers into her tangled blonde hair. She glanced around and then walked over to me. "Gray?"

"I'm thinking," I said.

Knovak stumbled over as well. "Gray..." His unicorn pressed himself against my legs.

"Don't worry." I patted my eldrin. "We're going to get out of this. Everything will be okay. Remember—Deimos once emerged at Astra Academy, right? That means we can get back there, too."

My words clearly calmed them all. Ashlyn exhaled. She placed a shaky hand on my shoulder. "Thank you."

Knovak definitely relaxed, his anxiety waning enough for him to think rationally. "You're going to get us out of here?"

I nodded once. "Of course."

Nini, still merged with her reaper, stepped closer. The lanterns glowed with a bright yellow, but powerful blue magic radiated from her cloak. It oozed out, and reminded me of the abyssal dragons.

"Gray," Nini and Waste said perfectly together. "We can't... we can't stay here long."

She didn't elaborate, but I understood why.

Ashlyn and Knovak were dying. Their death would be slow, as the abyssal hells clearly drained life from the living. Because of my connection to Death Lord Deimos, the hells weren't tearing at my soul, but the others weren't as fortunate.

Nini was in a similar situation. As a reaper arcanist, her soul wasn't under assault.

Death Lord Deimos half-collapsed on the side of his eldrin. He took in a deep breath and then stared at me with his intense gaze. "Come," he said with a pained exhale. "This way."

Everyone immediately turned to me. They wanted to know what to do. Could we trust Deimos? No one said a word. They waited with bated breath for my decision.

"We can't go," I said to Deimos. "We have to get home."

Wandering the many layers of the abyss would surely get us *all* killed, especially since Death Lord Naiad was still somewhere close.

Deimos growled some sort of curse under his breath. "Zahn has a way. That's why I came here... to the *Wraithborne Orchard...* It's so I can escape to the realm of the living."

The Wraithborne Orchard sounded familiar. Deimos's memories informed me about this place—where trapped souls were torn apart and then reincarnated as creatures of nature. The souls traveled through the giant roots, upward, beyond the waters.

I shook the thoughts away.

Somehow, this place was closer to the realm of the living. Was Zahn close? Were *we* close to escape?

"*Come with me,*" Deimos commanded, "and stop asking questions. Before Naiad returns... and realizes she still has the upper hand."

The waters around us rippled. Soft whispers emanated from our wakes. Ashlyn, Ecrib, Nini, Starling, and Knovak were tired.

"Is it far?" I asked.

Deimos chuckled. "What does it matter? Will you venture in a different direction if I say *yes*?"

"I just want to know."

Deimos's dragon turned its disgusting head and pointed with the tip of its reptilian nose. There were several dark waterfalls off in that direction.

"It isn't far," Deimos whispered. He took a shallow breath. "Zahn is waiting for me. We shouldn't dither."

Ashlyn tightened her grip on my shoulder. "Can we really trust him?"

I nodded once. "We can. It'll be okay. Zahn will get us out of here—I'm pretty sure."

It wasn't like we had many other choices. And I refused to let anyone here die. I'd do whatever I had to in order to protect them.

We just had to escape the abyssal hells, before it was too late.

THE END

BLOOPER SCENE

In the middle of the fundraiser, I stood in front of Archduke Kross. I had made my intentions clear—at least, I *thought* I had made myself clear.

"Ah." The archduke chortled. "I see. If you want to join the Kross family, and escape the doldrums of your island life, you should've said so. My niece, Priscilla, is a beauty like no other. She has been looking for an arcanist of your talents."

"That's nice, but she's not Ashlyn."

The archduke stopped himself for a long moment to mull over my comment. "What?" he finally asked.

"Your niece isn't Ashlyn. I said *Ashlyn* is the most incredible person I've met."

Twain sat on my boot and glared up at the archduke. While my eldrin said nothing, it was clear from his expression he felt the same as I did.

"*Ashlyn,*" the archduke said, stressing the word, "is neither the most stunning, nor the most magically talented, as you proved in your little sparring match. She isn't even—"

I held a finger up to his mouth. "Shh."

The man harrumphed and stepped away, his lip curled in disgust. He rubbed his whole face, as though I had diseased him with my mere presence, and now he needed to thoroughly clean himself.

"I've heard enough," I said. "Ashlyn and I are going to make our own family—*a bigger, better family*. With blackjack, and hookers!"

"Well, maybe not that last thing," Twain whispered. "Can you even say that in a young adult novel? It's a pretty specific and obscure joke..."

I ignored my eldrin's commentary. "The point is, we don't need you. You're holding us back from greatness, not gatekeeping some grand prize, like you think you are."

"How impetuous." The archduke sneered.

With a scoff, I turned away from the man. Then I held Twain close to my chest and whistled, gaining the attention of everyone around me, including Ashlyn. "C'mon," I said to her, motioning with a quick move of my chin. "We're getting out of here. Your father can drown in the abyssal hells for all I care."

Ashlyn hurried to my side. After smoothing her blonde hair, she smiled. "You're so manly, Gray. Leaving a grand party in dramatic fashion is all I've ever wanted in life."

"Is this, like, a dream?" Twain asked, genuinely confused. "Because I don't think she would ever say that."

"We're gonna go find those Death Lord worshipping cultists," I said. Ashlyn nodded.

"And then we're going to raid their operations, steal all their money, trinkets, and artifacts," I continued.

"I love where this is going," Ashlyn said as we reached the doors out of the banquet hall.

"Finally, we're going to build our own house, and it's going to be bigger and more badass than anything anyone has ever seen before."

"A flawless plan."

And then that was exactly what we did.

THANK YOU SO MUCH FOR READING!
Please consider leaving a review!

Gray's story continues in *Death Lord Arcanist*!

To find out more about Shami Stovall and Astra Academy, take a look at her website:

https://sastovallauthor.com/newsletter/

To help Shami Stovall (and see advanced chapters ahead of time) take a look at her Patreon:

https://www.patreon.com/shamistovall

Want more arcanist novels? Good news! The Frith Chronicles is where is all started! Join Volke and the Frith Guild as they travel the world.

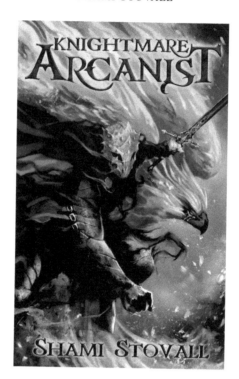

ABOUT THE AUTHOR

Shami Stovall is a multi-award-winning author of fantasy and science fiction. Before that, she taught history and criminal law at the college level and loved every second. When she's not reading fascinating articles and books about ancient China or the Byzantine Empire, Stovall can be found playing way too many video games, especially RPGs and tactics simulators.

Shami loves John, reading, video games, and writing about herself in the third person.

If you want to contact her, you can do so at the following locations:

Website: https://sastovallauthor.com
Email: s.adelle.s@gmail.com

facebook.com/SAStovall
twitter.com/GameOverStation

Printed in the USA
CPSIA information can be obtained
at www.ICGtesting.com
LVHW062206150923
758128LV00007B/17/J